HANNAH

PAUL-LOUP
SULITZER

*Translated from the French
by Christine Donougher*

POSEIDON PRESS

*New York London Toronto
Sydney Tokyo*

POSEIDON PRESS

Simon & Schuster Building
Rockefeller Center
1230 Avenue of the Americas
New York, New York 10020

POSEIDON PRESS is a registered trademark
of Simon & Schuster Inc.

POSEIDON PRESS colophon is a trademark
of Simon & Schuster Inc.

Designed by Pedro Quintana
Manufactured in the United States of America

1   3   5   7   9   10   8   6   4   2

Library of Congress Cataloging-in-Publication Data

Sulitzer, Paul-Loup, date.
Hannah.

I. Title.
PQ2679.U457H3613   1989   843'.914   88-28388
ISBN 0-671-69423-X

---◆---

PROLOGUE

Summer came early to the vast plain that stretches from the Vistula to the Ural Mountains, thousands of kilometres to the east. Gazing into this remote emptiness gave one a feeling of terrifying dizziness; her father, 'Reb' Nathan, had often spoken to her of this disquiet. He had that strange ability to wander in imagination among the stars, to dream big and tall, an ability that she would inherit from him. He often talked of these things in her presence: the magnitude of the universe, his doubts about how best to behave in this world; he confided in her even though she was a little girl, the youngest of his three children. There was between the two of them an extraordinary closeness that she would know with no other man. She would always remember her father's large hands seizing hold of her with gentleness and authority as they carried her up into the air, on to a level with his reddish-blond beard. He would laugh heartily and — in that voice of his, the one that imparted secrets she could not understand, secrets of vital importance — he would declare: 'Nothing in the world is more mysterious than a little girl.' They had the same enormous grey eyes, the same straight nose, the same high brow, unlike Yasha and Simon, who had their mother's black slit eyes. It was Reb Nathan who taught her to read from the Mishnah and the Gemara, in the Talmud, and indeed from the midrashim; she would remember how they read passages from the Pentateuch together, in Hebrew and Aramaic, before she had yet grown to meet his waist, as if he was racing to pass on to her the best in himself before the early death he knew would be his.

Having arrived even before Shabuoth, the summer was exceptionally hot and dry. At first it promised a rich harvest, but the ears of corn hardly swelled at all, the stalks stubbornly refused to fill out, and before long – lashed by a burning wind – the crops were flattened to the ground. The cattle seized this marvellous opportunity to be troublesome; most of the cows stopped giving milk, while some went so far as to lie motionless on their backs, their swollen stomachs and stiff legs pointing skywards. At the same time, a fungus attacked the trees, and after a vast flock of birds flying from the east had wreaked havoc on the seedlings, insects infected the fruit crops with disease. It was in all ways a summer of waiting, of time suspended. In both villages – one Jewish (the *shtetl*), the other Polish – villages which lay three kilometres apart and which for centuries had managed to ignore each other's existence – people had the same sense of latent menace.

In April, on the first of the eight days of Passover, Hannah had turned seven. She was still very much a little girl, despite all her father had managed to teach her. Her keen, sometimes cruel intelligence was still dormant within her; she had only just made the painful discovery that the Passover festivities had not been invented to celebrate her birthday. Yasha and Simon had laughed at her incredible naïvety, although they had also taken great pains to foster her delusions. She was as small as she was young, as thin as an owl on the eve of Shabbat. Furthermore, she had the big, wide, serious eyes of an owl, eyes that, as she seemed to know already, would be her only claim to beauty. She spoke very little, and rarely to the other girls of her age, or to Shiffrah, her own mother. She made an exception for her elder brother, Yasha, since his regular attendance at Talmudic school had made of him an adult. As for her father, she saw little of him as he was often away trading in cloth, once a year in Petersburg, often as far as the shores of the Black Sea, frequently to Gdansk, Lodz and Lublin.

Hannah's world was a tiny one: she had not so much as taken ten steps along the road to Lublin, going north-west; nor had she dared to venture into the pine forest that marked the boundary of the *shtetl* to the west, perhaps because Yasha had told her it was haunted by dybbuks and by Shibta, the she-devil who lured little children with her cakes kneaded with a magic lard and the fat of black dog. The only door that opened on the outside world for her was the orchard gate. She often ventured through it, at first stepping carefully in the footprints her mother had left behind in her daily excursion to collect the herbs and plants of which her ointments were made. Later she made deeper forays of her own into the orchard, in secret. Reb Nathan and Shiffrah's house was the southernmost one of the *shtetl*. A vegetable garden and three rows of apple trees extended the property further. Beyond the orchard was a path that skirted round a copse of silver birches, then followed the course of a stream (in Hannah's eyes, it was a river), and led, twisting and turning, to the Polish village, although no one ever followed it there. To the east lay the vast, ocean-like expanse of fields and of the plain. On her first few outings Hannah went just as far as the silver birches, where the path became a leafy bower, then slipped under the overhanging branches. Soon she ventured beyond the trees, however, until the day when all the sounds of the *shtetl* died away behind her and she was immersed in absolute silence, in solitude, but also in fragrance and a golden light. Probably she was unaware of the beauty of the silent plants around her, and yet with amazing prescience she straightaway felt at one with them, and steeped herself in them; all her life she would feel a bizarre, mysterious sense of complicity with plants and flowers.

At a certain spot the path went into a bend and climbed a mountain two metres high, forcing its way through a bramble thicket, a veritable forest of thistles that towered over Hannah's head. This was the last frontier; beyond it and the willow groves the horizons broadened, so that one could see as far as the Polish village, with its onion-shaped bell-tower. Hannah crossed this frontier the day she learned that the Passover festivities had not been arranged with her birthday in mind, a day when shame and distress made her want to isolate herself even more than usual.

The scorching and bloody summer of 1882 was but weeks away. Her meeting with Taddeuz was imminent.

1

THE HORSEMEN

She stood absolutely still on the edge of the bramble thicket through which she had just crept, clutching the two honey and almond pancakes in both hands. And just as he had been the last time Taddeuz stood fifteen metres away from her, intent on his work.

The first time he had been bending down in exactly the same way, the water up to his ankles, almost completely undressed, the pale gold blondness of his hair and the incredible whiteness of his back reflecting the harsh light, presenting her with the clean line of his shoulders running into the curls on the nape of his neck. When he straightened up to survey his work – a kind of stone dam across the stream – the sweat trickled down his cheeks like tears. He stripped completely and sat in the water, throwing back his uncannily beautiful face to the sun. Hannah had never seen a boy naked before, and failed even to connect this sight with her brothers; she actually thought she was seeing a dybbuk, one of those creatures that no one had ever provided a precise description of. It took her breath away. She should have fled but she stayed, crouching boyishly on the edge of the thicket. She spent at least an hour in her lair in the undergrowth, invisible behind her curtain of thistles, slowly breathing in the hot dusty air. She watched her dybbuk get dressed and only emerged from her hiding place long after he had gone. On that occasion, she did not dare approach the spot he had just left, but within the next few weeks, having witnessed the same scene often enough from her hiding place, she had ventured to inspect his work once he had gone.

In the meantime Hannah made enquiries about dybbuks, although she didn't tell anyone the reasons for her interest. Simon was absolutely categorical: a dybbuk could be big or small, fat or thin, black or white, old or young, man or woman – or both simultaneously (this left Hannah very confused); it could appear by day or by night, alone or in the company of others of its own kind. Details as precise as these did not entirely enlighten Hannah. Fortunately Yasha eventually proved more explicit; obviously there was a reason why everyone in the *shtetl* talked of him as the best student at yeshiva, and why his beard was beginning to grow. Among other infallible ways of identifying dybbuks there were two sure signs, he announced: a dybbuk was bound to have webbed feet, and a dybbuk left no footsteps, even when it walked on soft ground. At that point all became clear for Hannah. Her false dybbuk had perfect feet and invariably left footprints in the mud by the stream.

The next day Hannah made sure she got to the stream first and – in clear sight on the largest of the stones he had used to build his dam – set down one of the honey and almond pancakes she had been given for her breakfast. She then immediately hid in her thistle den, delighted to see the strange boy calmly accept her offering minutes later. Her generosity became a ritual. It was a month before they approached each other, and then it was on his initiative. He had a very gentle demeanour and a princely manner with Hannah, and he seemed not at all deterred in his friendship by the fact that she was a girl and a good three or four years younger. At their first meetings, he nonchalantly explained his dam and his reason for being to her: he had to do something during the holidays before he returned to Warsaw, and he was combating boredom since none of the children in the Polish village knew how to read. 'I do,' said Hannah suddenly, quite feverish at being so bold. To prove it, she traced one or two words with her index finger in the black silt. In Yiddish. Miraculously, he knew a little, and his blue eyes seemed to gaze at her with new surprise and interest. Here their friendship began, though it is likely that neither noticed.

In silence they ate their pancakes, Hannah quivering with a happiness such as she had never before experienced, not even when seated in the doorway at nightfall, listening to her father talking. Taddeuz was another thing altogether: she had found him herself, and he was all hers. For the first time she was fully conscious of the world, aware that – though it wasn't yet seven in the morning in the month of Elul – the heat was rising and the air seemed still. Along the path Hannah noticed the strange absence of squirrels and field mice, which she usually saw on her way. But she didn't dwell on this for long, having concentrated more on getting away from the house. This morning it had been easy: Reb Nathan had taken his two sons to some important meeting, and Shiffrah had gone out with her assortment of balms to visit a sick child, all the while lamenting the fact that she didn't have any sanicle seeds, which curb dysentery and the spitting of blood. Hannah needed only to bring home some sanicle to justify her absence.

Taddeuz finished eating the second pancake, not having thought of sharing them any more than he had on previous occasions. Hannah was not in the least put off; it was already so extraordinary that he should be willing to eat her breakfast. With his distinctive delicacy he brushed the crumbs off himself then stretched out, resting on his hands, and drank straight from the stream. Only after a minute did he seem to remember she was there: 'Are you thirsty?' She nodded shyly. He drew her very close and showed her how to perch on the rocks. To no avail. She couldn't touch the water with her lips, fearful of wetting her dress. That was when he did the most marvellous thing: cupping a little water in his joined palms, he offered her a drink from his very white, very slender hands.

'More?'

She shook her head, scarlet-faced; her tongue had come into fleeting contact with Taddeuz's skin. He laughed, studied her, laughed again. Until that day, which must have been the tenth or twelfth time they had met, he had never asked her a single question about herself. He scarcely knew her name. On the other hand, he had spoken a great deal about himself: he was the only son of a tenant farmer on the count's estate, he was here only in the holidays, generally he lived in Warsaw, about which he spoke constantly. At best, theirs was a monologue, and she was never quite sure he was speaking to her. He stopped laughing, no doubt touched by the adoration he could see in her huge grey eyes. Then he did a second marvellous thing: he dug his hand into his pocket and drew it out, balled into a fist:

'Here.'

He turned his wrist and revealed a small object. Hannah was seized with a sense of panic.

'Go on, take it,' he said. 'It's a present. A scarab.'

He had carved it himself, he told her with a little self-mocking smile. The object was made from dark, almost black wood; two red eyes glistened in the early morning light like carbuncles. It hardly bore much resemblance to a scarab, but what did that matter?

'For me?' she finally managed to say.

Trembling, she put her hands behind her back in her panic-stricken attempt to refuse this fabulous gift. Laughingly, he insisted she take it, bringing her arms forward from the shoulder and prying open her fingers. She was wide-eyed, on the verge of tears, while he laughed even more heartily. He stepped aside, puffed out his chest, and stretched out his arms, feeling extremely satisfied with himself; his completely spontaneous generosity delighted him and gave him the sense of being all-powerful. Somehow it left him with a great yearning for movement and space. He looked around: an embankment scarcely a metre high ran alongside the river, marking a boundary. Beyond were fields. The corn was a swelling sea, punctuated only by a barn far in the distance, like some island or boat. He was seized with the desire to make his way to it, and was already scrambling up the slope. Just as he was about to clear the top he called to her:

'Are you coming?'

In the middle of the glade below, Hannah looked tiny in her black velvet dress, her triangular face swallowed up by her copper-coloured tresses and those huge eyes of hers. She clutched the treasured carving tightly in her hands.

He gave her a winning smile. 'I'm your friend, aren't I?'

Exalted, Hannah clambered up the bank; when she had hauled herself up to where he stood, he took her by the hand. They descended the embankment together, and together entered the cornfield.

Neither of them paid any attention to the double alert that sounded out just then, either to the harsh, insistent tolling of the church bell to their left or to the anguished plaint on the temple's ram's horn to their right.

They covered seven or eight hundred metres. Taddeuz did all the talking: he was going to be eleven years old next Christmas and therefore – he had been promised – after the following spring he would be allowed to stay in Warsaw full-time, never again having to return to live among these stupid peasants. He planned to read every book there was to be read, and he was going to become a lawyer, or an explorer, unless of course he wrote books himself, in which case he was bound to become famous all over the world. As he uttered this last sentence, he burst out laughing, aware of the full dimensions of his plans. Hannah did not follow suit. To have mocked him would have been a sacrilege; she loved him, and was to love him infinitely more than he would ever love himself.

But neither of them knew such things as they waded together through the waves of corn. They walked in the sunlight, and though the sun hadn't yet quite cleared the horizon it was already stunningly hot. Soon they found themselves on a gentle downhill slope, so that when they reached the path they were in a hardly discernible depression; ahead was an undulating landscape that shut out what lay to the east and closed in their horizons. Hand in hand, they climbed the slight incline, now treading barley underfoot. The plaint on the ram's horn and the tinny church bells continued without pause, but they could not compete with Taddeuz's impassioned talk of Warsaw.

At the top of the slope they came upon the horsemen.

There were about fifty of them, maybe more, and behind them marched an entire troop of men. For Hannah and Taddeuz only the horsemen counted; they rode at a gentle trot, their strength seemingly implacable, the silence punctuated at intervals by the brief snorting of a horse. They carried red and black banners, some of them emblazoned with a white cross; their lances were decorated with pennants and oriflammes. The clouds of dust that they raised from the dry ground shrouded the rank and file, making them seem even less important. They appeared as if out of a legend, the orangey-red sun only exaggerating their stature. Taddeuz was transfixed, his fascination extended to Hannah by the tension with which he gripped her hand. In her free hand she clutched the scarab. The soldiers may have seen the two children's heads peering over the crest of the barley-sown rise, but they gave no sign. Instead they passed on by, changing course and starting to head north. As the column swung round several carts were revealed, all of them filled with men, some in frockcoats and wearing hats, others in smocks with caps on their heads, but all of them armed with scythes and pitchforks and sticks.

'Germans,' whispered Taddeuz.

He meant they were weavers, who had probably come from Lublin, where the mills had been established. He squatted low on the ground and pulled the little girl down beside him. It grew hotter with every minute that passed. A field mouse stopped to sniff the air quickly, then darted into the dry barley forest. Something was happening in the sky to the east. Level with the horizon was a single, large black cloud with a reddish hue near its base; it turned grey-black as it climbed towards the sun.

'The place is on fire,' said Taddeuz, who must have known exactly which village was on fire, as the huge estate belonging to the count and managed by his father was adjacent to it. But he went no further in his commentary, possibly because he did not understand the mission of the troops he and Hannah had just seen and which had begun to disappear into the forest of birch trees, because he had not registered that a pogrom was just about to be unleashed. If he did have any presentiment of danger at that point he at once dismissed it from his mind; Taddeuz was already adept at turning his concern away from anything that might prove unpleasant.

The sound of the marching column grew faint. Taddeuz caught one grasshopper, then another. And he immediately invented a game: a jumping competition. Taddeuz's grasshopper beat Hannah's eight times out of ten, even though he had magnanimously designated the larger of the two insects as the bearer of the little girl's colours. That Taddeuz's grasshopper should win consistently seemed to her in the natural order of things: she would have been appalled if she had won. Once this first game of theirs was over he thought up others. They plaited grass, an art which Taddeuz performed with incredible skill while Hannah remained handicapped by her obstinate refusal to let go of her scarab. They wandered over the surface of this limitless plain, drawing a huge semi-circle around the barn, against which were stacked a few sheaves of corn.

All the while they kept the birch forest and the *shtetl* behind them, so that they did not see the smoke starting to rise, or the horsemen heading back towards them.

Yasha found them lying flat on their stomachs, both of them with their faces pressed level with a burrow.

*

Until that day Hannah had known two Yashas. There was the Yasha of her earliest memories, of her years of infancy, the messy little boy who paid her hardly any attention at all and who, like all boys, was rough with her when he did. Then there was the Yasha transformed by the schoolhouse, the one who wore a kaftan and boots, side-curls and a black hat, who spoke softly to her, and sometimes even smiled at her from the lofty eminence of his thirteen years.

She raised her head when Yasha's shadow fell on the entrance to the burrow and didn't recognize either Yasha in him. This Yasha was paler than usual, his head bared, his curls plastered down with sweat. He was panting, and she assumed he had been running about looking for her. She also understood the terrible anger in his black eyes was his anger with her for having done that morning what she had done all the mornings before: she had gone to meet Taddeuz, a Gentile. She was opening her mouth to explain her friend to her brother when Yasha's hand seized her by the neck, gripping her with irresistible strength. His other hand covered her mouth. 'Be quiet,' he whispered in a hissing voice. He drew her to her feet, and pushed her on; only after they had gone several metres did she make any attempt to resist. Turning back, she saw Taddeuz, greatly astonished, watching them go. She wasn't able to see any more than this. Yasha's grip tightened, almost strangling her. They walked about thirty paces and stopped in their tracks. Yasha pinned her to the ground, behind a screen of barley stalks. Once again she tried to struggle, seized with her own rage.

What happened next calmed her at a stroke: Yasha suddenly ceased to exert his strength on her. Instead, he took her in his arms with infinite tenderness: 'For the love of God, Hannah!' Again, he spoke in a whisper. She stared at his face and at last saw it as it really was at that moment – pale not with anger but with grief. He had been weeping and was weeping still. His kaftan was torn in several places and through one of these rents she could clearly see a bleeding wound on his chest beneath his left shoulder; on his neck, or more precisely below his ear and jaw, was evidence of another blow. In that moment her love for her brother took precedence over everything else. Hannah began to cry, too. Yasha set off again, drawing her along with him, and though she still understood nothing she made no further attempt to resist. He made her walk hundreds of metres, forced her to bend down, sometimes even to remain absolutely still, to flatten herself on the ground, on the alert, watching out for something or someone she was unable to see. This trek across country could well have been a tremendous game, of the kind she had often played with Yasha. But this clearly was no game; she could see that Yasha was scared.

The barn suddenly appeared before them. Later Hannah realized that Yasha had been using the wooden building as a screen, trying to keep it between the horsemen and them. They went inside. It was dark, especially after the glare outside, but it smelled wonderful. Yasha was careful not to touch the door; they slipped through the gap. For a few seconds he stood there, straining to see if anyone was coming.

With his back still to her, he asked quietly: 'Who is he?'

She pretended not to understand. He explained that he was talking about the fair-haired boy.

'Taddeuz,' she said, as if his name alone would justify everything.

Yasha turned round and walked towards her; for the first time she noticed that he had been wounded, badly wounded, in the leg as well. There was dried blood on his left boot and on the hem of his *roubachka*. He took Hannah's face in his hands. Despite the six years' difference in their ages he was not much taller than she. He had always been small, his deep black eyes and the kind of greyish veil cast over his features by countless hours spent poring over sacred books belied any impression of boyishness in him. With his ink-stained fingers he caressed Hannah's cheeks.

He said in a very sad voice: 'They killed him, Hannah. They killed our father. He went out to meet them, to speak to them and appease them, and they killed him.'

'They?' Hannah was about to ask. But the door opened wide and Taddeuz's tall silhouette stood out against the dazzling rectangle of light. As though by chance, he stood in a ray of light that filtered through the skylight in the loft, in just the spot where a halo could form round his blond hair. He stared at brother and sister and smiled, a little embarrassed at having followed them but obviously content with himself too for having persisted.

'You'll attract the horsemen,' said Yasha in Polish.

'He's my friend,' Hannah said at once.

She was suddenly afraid she would have to make a choice. She repeated to herself the words Yasha had just spoken, about the death of their father, but their meaning escaped her. Suddenly they heard the sound of horses stamping, and voices, and laughter. All of it was in Russian, Hannah knew, but she did not understand what was going on. The noise drew closer. They were obviously coming to the barn. Yasha's hand fell from his sister's cheek to her shoulder. 'Climb up! Quickly!' he whispered, pointing to a ladder and helping her to mount the rungs. At the top of the ladder she found straw from the previous summer that was quite rotten. 'Right over there,' Yasha told her, directing her to crouch down two or three steps from the skylight. She drew up her knees and put her arms round them. The idea of her father's being dead was beginning to become real to her. She could scarcely have noticed that Taddeuz had also climbed up into the hayloft and now stood in front of the skylight, alternately looking out and then in the direction of his two companions with a perplexed but vaguely amused air. Yasha called to him in a low voice, telling him to stand away from the window where he was likely to be seen. For a few seconds the blue eyes challenged Yasha's dark gaze, but Taddeuz eventually complied. He moved to the side and leaned against the wall with his hands joined behind his back, looking bored with the whole situation.

'He's my friend . . .' Hannah persisted, aware of the tension between the two boys.

'Be quiet,' whispered Yasha.

His voice was really no more than a murmur. Yasha lay face down in the straw at the very moment the horsemen reached the door of the barn. The lengthening shadows of the three men on horseback crept across the ground below. They stopped. Silence. Then there was a quiet conversation in Russian, of which Hannah could understand a few words but not the general drift. She did however, see the effect it produced on Yasha; she saw his black eyes grow large and saw him begin silently to gasp for breath, his mouth wide open. When he spoke she read his lips rather than heard his words: 'They're going to set fire to the barn.' He slid over to her, put his arm around her narrow shoulder, drew her against him and kissed her forehead. 'Don't move. Don't be afraid.'

Then with his eyes fixed on Taddeuz's, he stood up. He descended the ladder, all the while holding the young Pole with his gaze.

Until he disappeared.

There were eight horsemen, three of whom had come to the door of the barn. One of these three was already preparing a firebrand. He stopped what he was doing when he caught sight of Yasha's frail little figure and began to laugh:

'Now look what we have here. The rats are coming out of their holes! Are you alone?' he asked.

'I don't know your language,' Yasha replied in Yiddish.

The horsemen began to speak among themselves in Russian. They were all in uniform, but there was no officer among them. Two of them seemed to recognize Yasha; they'd seen him in the village, struggling while the mill workers killed his father. They seemed unsure as to how to proceed. Several of them had evidently been drinking; probably they had found plenty of wine when the *shtetl* had been pillaged. Eventually in hesitant German they repeated:

'Are you alone?'

'Yes,' said Yasha.

'Hey, hey, Jewboy!' one of the soldiers shouted, laughing.

'I'm alone,' Yasha repeated. And he added: 'And the barn belongs to Poles. Not to a Jew.'

'Don't lie. You must be lying.'

A lance was extended, the point of it touched the wound on Yasha's chest.

'Come here.'

He stepped out of the barn, and walked between the horses. The heel of a boot connected violently with his face, knocking him to the ground. He deliberately rolled as far as possible and then got to his feet again. He began walking, distancing himself a little further from the barn with every step he took. In such a way he got past the first row of horsemen. Then he was pushed off balance by the breast of a horse rammed against him. Again he fell, and again he got to his feet. He was staggering; the wound in his leg had opened up and was bleeding heavily. Yasha made his way through the second row of horsemen and continued on without anyone trying to strike him again. At that moment he seemed very close to succeeding not only in saving his own life, but above all in preventing the barn from being burned. He continued on a few metres more and began to sense that the horsemen behind him were beginning to feel mollified, nonchalant, tired. They seemed on the verge of turning away and leaving him alone.

Then the cry rang out; Taddeuz came tearing out of the barn like a streak of lightning, screaming that he wasn't Jewish. The next moment Yasha was running hell for leather, doubtless with no other hope than to draw the horsemen as far away from the barn as possible, realizing that the discovery of his lie would change everything. The horsemen very quickly caught up with him; the shaft of a lance struck him in the small of his back. All the weight of the horse and its rider was behind the throw. He fell forward with his arms upraised, crying out with the pain, but only very briefly.

Hannah heard his cry. She had understood very little of the conversation, able only to identify her brother's voice. And she had misunderstood Taddeuz's sudden lunge to the bottom of the ladder; she had thought he was intervening to save Yasha. In turn she almost climbed down the ladder as well, but because Yasha had told her not to move she instead huddled up in the rotten hay. Yasha would come back. He and Taddeuz would get used to each other, and they would become friends.

She didn't know who had cried out; it had been so brief, and the voice so hoarse, that it could have been anybody. Then she heard another conversation, this time in Russian, and she began to think that Taddeuz had made peace. More out of curiosity than fear, she hoisted herself up to the skylight.

Yasha's body was the first thing she saw. He was thirty metres away, flat on his stomach, immobile. He was within five metres of a cornfield in which he could have hidden had he been able to reach it. To the left, the horsemen were departing. Where was Taddeuz? She finally saw him: one of the horsemen had hoisted him up on the saddle behind him. This much Hannah immediately understood: not only was Taddeuz leaving, he was doing so of his own free will, having slipped his arms round the soldier's torso, his cheek resting against the man's back. She was at once struck with a sense of desertion and betrayal, even while she hardly believed what she saw. As the band of men trotted away Hannah could only stare at the figure of her friend, who was now making lively conversation with the soldier.

A good two or three minutes more passed before the first flame rose from below, where the brand had been thrown. The blaze extended, unhurriedly, to the foot of the ladder. Soon the entire far wall of the barn was in flames.

'*Yashale!*'

He didn't move straightaway. She shouted again, several times without panicking, while a few metres away the ladder consumed by flames crumbled, and the fire breathed closer. Yasha didn't get up, but he began to crawl. Still on his stomach, he slowly made a 180-degree turn. Only then did he manage to detach his face from the ground; he raised his head like a lizard. Reaching out with his arms he sank his fingers into the dry earth. He pulled himself along and edged forward a few metres. 'Jump, Hannah!' he wanted to yell but only his lips articulated this command. Hannah continued to scream; the floor on which she was standing was now on fire. Again Yasha reached out, clung to the stubble with his nails, dragged himself along. He was only twenty metres from the barn.

'*Jump, Hannah!*'

He invested this cry with all his remaining strength and at last she heard it. She leaned out of the skylight and saw what he had been trying to tell her: there were haystacks directly below. She overbalanced rather than jumped – it was a drop of about four metres – and immediately crawled beside her brother.

Yasha's face had fallen to the ground again. She tried to turn him on to his back: he moaned like an animal maddened with pain. Then she tried to drag him away from the inferno. She realized that once the fire had consumed the barn it would spread to the haystacks and then to the stubble, finally to the corn that was still standing. And in that event, Yasha would be burned alive, he would burn if he could not move.

And that is exactly what happened. The hay burst into flames instantaneously, seconds before the building collapsed. The fire was spreading faster than she could drag Yasha away from it. He was still alive, despite his fractured spine, when the flames found his legs and then his hips. Hannah could read his lips as he cried out. 'Get away! Get away! Run!'

What happened then was very strange, especially given that Hannah was only seven years old, that her brother was in the process of being burned alive before her very eyes, and that, furthermore, for the first time in her life she had the bitter taste of betrayal in her throat.

She ran only a few metres away, just far enough to escape the reach of the flames. She did not plunge into the standing corn, but sought out areas where it had already been harvested, where the blaze would advance less quickly. And so it was that for a very long time she had a clear view of her brother's body battling with fire. She stood motionless, with an extraordinary self-possession, gazing first down at Yasha's dead body then into the distance at the small band of disappearing horsemen. Each time the fire grew nearer, she would calmly retreat a metre or more, until she reached the footpath, a natural firebreak.

*

Thirty-two years later Taddeuz Nenski would tell some of this story to Elisabeth 'Lizzie' MacKenna, concealing nothing of his 'betrayal'. As for the rest of it, the final minutes in particular, only Mendel Visoker would be able to provide an account.

Mendel the drayman happened to be about a kilometre away from the barn when it went up in smoke. He saw the horsemen when they first passed by, riding ahead of the mill workers, who travelled on foot or in wagons. He hid his own vehicle and his two horses in a willow grove beside the stream, not very far from the place where Taddeuz had built his dam. This was not his first experience of a pogrom; he had been beaten often enough to know the way these things worked. Quickly realizing that this pogrom's target would be the *shtetl*, he thought he could only take cover and wait. And so he did, in the sunlit grove. He saw the eight drunken soldiers ride past the barn the second time; he saw Yasha emerge from the barn and saw his attempt to escape; he saw him struck down by the lance and he saw him fall. He thought the boy was dead.

He saw no reason to risk anything – the horsemen were just two hundred metres away – until he set eyes upon the little figure in black standing in the skylight of the burning barn. Moving the horses out of the undergrowth would have taken too long, so he started running. It was while he was running that she jumped down on to the haystacks, crouched beside the boy, and began to elude the fire with uncanny composure. Occasionally he lost sight of her; at times the yellow flames seemed to engulf her, but she always reappeared, unharmed and unhurried, and each time Mendel would begin to race towards her again. Mendel, a man who believed in the devil with more conviction than he believed in God, began even to see Satan's hand in this little girl's slow dance around the fire.

Breathless, his legs trembling, he finally reached the footpath. He saw her crouching there, out of danger, her back to the fire. Before going to her, he glanced back at the boy's body. It was horrible; a black smoking object, appallingly contorted. He turned back to the little girl. She did not even turn around as he approached her. Her huge grey eyes were fixed upon the plain. She was motionless save for her hands, with which she fondled a black wooden object marked with two red dots.

2

MENDEL VISOKER

Mendel Visoker was twenty-four. He had indeed been beaten with cudgels, but on each occasion his assailants had taken the precaution of attacking him in a group of thirty or forty. Not only could he defend himself, but he was capable of hitting out (with a smile, what's more) *before* being attacked himself, whether his adversaries were Jews or Gentiles. That was what had happened in Lublin, in any event, where he had beaten six men who had not even laid a finger on him. He broke their bones because they had slashed the hocks of one of his horses on the grounds that he was giving their own carrier business too much competition – and, of course, because he was a Jew.

He was born in the far north, in the region of the Mazury lakes, but he had left his native *shtetl* at the age of fifteen. At that time he cast aside the phylacteries that, according to custom, he was supposed to bind to his forehead and his left arm when he prayed; later he cut off his sidelocks and shaved his beard. After working for a time in Warsaw – as a procurer for a brothel in Krochmalna Street, it was reported – he had saved enough money to buy his first horse and his first cart, and with these he began to travel the length and breadth of Poland, whether it lay within Russian, Austrian, or Prussian territory. Having broken all ties with his community, he might have contented himself with being a renegade. But he was a born agitator who behaved like a Jew among Christians and like a Christian among Jews, and who made a show of it. (If he went into a synagogue, he would do so dressed as a Pole, in cap and jacket, and he would deliberately take a seat in the part of the house of prayer reserved for women, singing the psalms in a stentorian voice. On the other hand, in Christian quarters he would wear a kaftan, even don a wig with sidelocks, and sport phylacteries. This was how he behaved in Kiev, the most ferociously anti-Semitic of Russian towns.)

The Lublin affair happened in 1878 and it provoked a great to-do, coming at the end of a long series of similar incidents. At that time, however, Tsar Alexander II of Russia had not yet been assassinated, and Procurator Pobiedonostzev had not yet been able to implement his plan for exterminating the Jews. In the end Mendel was not arrested, his six victims did not lodge any complaint against him, and the tsar's police kindly took the view that he was perhaps not entirely to blame. Such leniency on the part of the administration outraged the president of the Lublin Community, and with the support of the Elders he obtained a condemnation of the troublemaker: a maniac like him put everyone in danger and could bring down the wrath of the authorities on them all. In the end the drayman received a three-year prison sentence. Thirty-six months of jail failed, however, to tame him. As soon as he was freed, in the spring of 1881, the first thing he did was to take up a stand outside the home of Reb Baruch Fichelson, the community president, and grind out a song on his hurdy-gurdy all night long, a song that was all the more exasperating as it was full of praise for the generosity and intelligence of the wealthy Reb Baruch. The president tried to send a dozen workers from his mill to deal with the insolent fellow, but he was unable to find anyone willing to take part in the expeditionary force at any price. Mendel Visoker was not a colossus – he was hardly any taller than the average man – but he had a chest the width of a pair of Cossack twins, his fists were like tree-trunks, and he carried himself as if capable of decapitating a man with a single blow from the back of his hand.

Mendel Visoker leaned over the little girl, then reached out a hand when he recognized the grey eyes:

'I know who you are, you have your father's eyes,' he said. 'You're Hannah.'

The fire spread slowly westwards. It took its time, advancing with confidence in the absence of any wind. A very quiet crackling issued from the blaze. To a greyish-coloured background, a flame now and again added touches of bright orange, accentuated with fulgurant purple highlights. The horsemen were nowhere in sight on the shrunken horizon; the sudden emptiness where the hayloft had stood seemed strange. 'Don't go away, I'm coming back,' Mendel told Hannah, and he went to fetch his cart and his two horses, not very sure that she had heard him. When he returned he found her exactly as he had left her, still holding her bit of wood in both hands and clutching it so tightly that her knuckles showed white. Mendel was already seized with a feeling of disquiet: the little girl's reactions didn't seem at all normal to him. He thought she must be mad, driven out of her wits by the violence she had witnessed.

'You can't stay here.'

No reply. And the way she had her back to the fire, even though she was only twenty metres away from it . . .

'I'm Mendel Visoker, the drayman, from Mazury. I know your father.'

'My father's dead,' she said very calmly.

Mendel stared at her for several moments, feeling increasingly ill at ease. He turned his eyes to the north, in the direction of the line of birch trees behind which, nearly two hours before, he had seen the column disappear. A first detachment had already returned; the main body of the troop could reappear at any moment.

'When did he die?'

'This morning.'

'In the pogrom?'

'I don't know what a pogrom is.'

'It means "destruction" in Russian,' explained Mendel, still watching over the birch trees. 'Did your father die of an illness?'

'No.'

'So he was killed . . .'

'That's what Yasha said,' came her answer, although she did not budge.

'Yasha?'

'My elder brother.'

'The boy the Cossacks brought down with a lance, the one who was burned?'

'Yes.'

What an extraordinary child! thought Mendel, really worried. One of two things is possible: either . . .

But his thoughts on the matter went no further. At that moment he detected something moving behind the trees.

He said: 'Come along. I'm going to take you back to your *shtetl*.'

He knew already that she wasn't going to stir. Nor did she. He took her in his hands, very gently as though she were made of china, picked her up and sat her on the seat in his *brouski*. Then he climbed up, clicked his tongue and the two horses set off.

'I knew your father,' said Mendel, urging the horses to a trot. 'I met him six years ago in Danzig, where I live. When I live anywhere, that is. We often did business together, he used to give me goods to deliver. I even came to your house, but you won't remember, you were too young. And last spring, when I came out of prison, he was one of the very few people who showed me any kindness. I know that in '78 he even went all the way to Lublin just to tell Reb Baruch Fichelson that he was the biggest fool in the world. Do you know Reb Baruch Fichelson?'

Naturally she did not reply. Did she even hear him? Beyond the pointed ears of the *brouski*'s two horses, the birch trees drew nearer. And so too did the rabble that had undertaken the pogrom. It would pass them by on their right, and the trees would act as a screen, as Mendel had foreseen. He glanced again at the little girl next to him. If only she could cry! He would prefer it even if she screamed, her calm was entirely unnerving.

A hundred paces more and the team of horses reached cover. Mendel stopped them with a light pull on the reins, his professional eye noting with annoyance that one of the reinstraps on the horse on the left was about to break. The back-bands, the hames on their collars, and indeed the loin straps were hardly in any better condition. 'I'm going to have to get some new harnesses, and that's the truth of it,' he said out loud. He dismounted and stood facing both the *brouski* and the column marching past the flecked trees a hundred metres away. A feeling of anger surged up within him, an anger he was powerless to control:

'Look at them, Hannah. If your father really is dead, it was they who killed him. Look at them. Life and death should be faced head on, there's no other way around it.'

He couldn't help smiling, the way he always did in such situations. He hooked the reins on to the pommel of the saddle and removed from the wagonload one of the three new beams he was carrying, along with his bundles of cloth and his books. It was a long piece of oak that must have weighed about sixty or seventy pounds, but which he was able to brandish easily in one hand. And his anger continued to mount:

'If you want to live truthfully, Hannah . . .'

He was deliberately speaking very loudly, in a clear voice, in Yiddish. As he had hoped, the men in the column heard him. Their eyes fell on the stationary cart in the middle of the clearing, on the man wearing a peaked cap and the little girl beside him. Mendel's smile broadened, and he even gave them a wave of his free arm.

'Do you want me to kill five or six of them, Hannah? It's up to you. Tell me to kill them and I'll kill them. Maybe I'll kill more than that. Perhaps eight. Or ten.'

She finally turned and stared at him with her big inscrutable eyes.

'You see, I'm very angry, Hannah. And of course I'm full of sorrow too. Like you. That's what I want you to understand: I know what's going on inside your head.'

At least I hope I do, he thought to himself. He smiled at her, a very different smile this time, his teeth showing very white beneath his black moustache; it was a smile of incredible kindness. Out of the corner of his eye he could see that the column had suddenly changed course, having now skirted the birch grove. It was heading south and would pass at a distance of thirty metres from where the cart stood.

'Hannah? *Look at them!'*

He was suddenly taken aback by what appeared in those grey eyes, even though it was what he had anticipated and indeed hoped for: an alarming, icy-cold expression of hatred and sorrow.

She asked in a distant voice: 'Could you really kill eight or ten of them?'

'Six or eight, certainly. I'm very strong. Ten perhaps. I can always try.'

Silence. The grey eyes finally strayed to the side. She swivelled round on her seat, slightly. She surveyed the column.

Then very calmly she remarked: 'There are a good deal more than ten of them.'

'That's true,' acknowledged Mendel with a wild laugh. 'I'd say there were at least fifty, not counting the Cossacks.'

With her back to Mendel, she said: 'And when you've killed ten of them, what will happen?'

'They'll probably flatten me,' replied Mendel, laughing even more wildly. 'It annoys them, being killed. Massacres are supposed to be one-sided affairs. Can you see their faces now, Hannah? They're empty. They've killed, stolen, and raped, and now they're empty and sullen. One of two things will happen when I start attacking them: either they'll hit back straightaway or else they'll hardly defend themselves, they'll be so stupefied.'

'And you'll kill them all.'

'No, I don't think so. Because of the Cossacks. The Cossacks are very alert. They've done little all morning.'

He took off the jacket and Polish cap he was wearing and threw them on to the seat in the *brouski*. He rolled up the sleeves on his collarless Christian shirt, revealing his suntanned and monstrously powerful arms. With one hand he lifted the oak beam and carried it about fifteen metres into the clearing, near the spot where the column of men would have to pass.

Minutes went by; the column drew near.

'No,' said Hannah. '*No.*'

'No what?'

'I don't want you to die.'

The column came into the clearing. At the head of it rode an officer and six Cossacks. The officer could have been sixteen or seventeen, at the very most. He was blond with a ridiculous, embryonic moustache. He looked hard at the man standing before him, as broad as he was tall, with the most enormous arms he had ever seen, holding a beam of wood three metres long. Halting the column quietly, he walked his horse forward a few metres.

Mendel turned his broadest smile on him.

'What are you doing there?' asked the officer.

'I'm going to plant this and see if it takes root,' explained Mendel, pointing to the beam.

'You're Jewish?'

'That depends on what day it is,' replied Mendel in Russian. 'Not at the moment. Not since I was asked not to be, which wasn't very long ago.'

He thought he should probably start with this one. He could already visualize very clearly the blond tsarist head flattened by the beam. But the Cossacks would immediately come running and he knew he couldn't kill more than three or four of them, at best.

'I've a good mind to have you horsewhipped,' said the officer. 'Perhaps even to have you hanged.'

Mendel contented himself with a smile, at the same time thinking: 'Shut your big trap, Mendel. Keep mum. The little one asked you not to get yourself killed. This officer is a boy, a *schlemiel*. Let him have the last word and he'll go away.'

After a few minutes, the officer turned his horse round and did exactly that. The column did likewise. Mendel Visoker found it a little difficult to get himself moving again, so violently was he trembling with rage.

'You didn't kill them,' said the little girl behind him.

'It was you who didn't want me to, don't try and blame me for it.'

He came back towards the *brouski* dragging his gigantic club behind him. But he could feel her grey eyes burning into him, and, unbelievably, he couldn't bring himself to look up at her. He loaded the beam back on to the cart with excessive meticulousness, and busied himself securing the bundles, though there was no need for it. He checked the harness and examined the horses, which had never been fitter.

'I'm going to take you back to your wretched *shtetl*,' he said with angry determination. 'We'll see if your father's dead. And if he is, I'll have to sell his goods to someone else. One customer lost, ten more gained.'

But he still could not look the little girl in the eye. He checked the horses' reinstraps one last time. They would hold as far as Tarnopol, which was where he was headed. (There was a woman there, as there was in ten or twelve places between Danzig and Kiev, to whom he would pay his respects.) Having returned to his seat in the *brouski*, he played for a little more time by searching for the column in the distance: it was fast disappearing, and the fire in the fields was also diminishing. Mendel's remaining anger with himself died away; all that remained was the familiar rebelliousness that had possessed him for fifteen years, and which generally translated into loneliness, egoism, sarcasm. In other words, everything was returning to normal. That boy who had burned to death, the corpses that littered the *shtetl*, the women who must have been raped, the houses and crops that had been set on fire, all these things would be accepted, as usual, as gains and losses. 'They're going to resign themselves to it yet again – that damned resignation of theirs – and immerse themselves in their damned rituals, start reading their damned sacred books, and argue endlessly over what some damned so-called sage said or did not say two thousand years ago.' Mendel the drayman was himself once more: he had recovered his soundest weapon, his cynicism. It was either that or go completely mad. He felt astonished at having allowed himself to get carried away as he had moments before; he never got involved with anything that didn't concern him. Had he really staked his life on the say-so of a snotty-nosed child of six or seven?

He would have to stop this. He took up the reins. What he saw next astounded him. The little girl had leaned forward so that her chin was resting on her knees; she was wide-eyed and her mouth gaped open, so that she looked like someone trying to vomit but unable to, like someone who'd seen death very close up. And yet she did not make a single sound. This was not the distress of a child but the extreme distress of an adult: utter, unspeakable heartbreak.

Equally astonishing was what Mendel did next: he pulled Hannah close to him, drawing her with one hand to his immense chest, the way he might pick up a kitten.

And then it was he who started to cry.

The birch grove now fell away to their left.

'What is it that you're holding in your hands?'

'A scarab.'

'That doesn't look much like a scarab.'

'I know. But it doesn't matter,' she said.

Her face and her body were calm again as she sat docile and straight-backed beside him. Mendel walked the horses, making them skirt round the trees, deliberately getting them to follow in the wake of the column. There were clear signs of the Russians' passage: the pogrom had left a trail of destruction in its wake in the form of a cauldron, a bloodied dress, a mezuzah ripped from a doorpost. Mendel even saw a book with torn pages but didn't stop to retrieve it. Ahead of them, great clouds of smoke hung over the *shtetl*.

'Someone gave it to you as a present?'

He was talking about the scarab.

'Yes.'

'It was the fair-haired boy, wasn't it?'

Their eyes met and Mendel suddenly had a very strong, very unexpected feeling of familiarity, if not friendship, with the child. She nodded. Now Mendel had a clear understanding of the whole scene that he had witnessed from a distance: if the fair-haired boy hadn't come running out of the barn the Cossacks would have probably left the other boy, the Jewish one, alone. He searched her grey eyes: She obviously knew this already. Her Polish friend well and truly abandoned her and her brother, he almost got them both killed. And she obviously didn't hold it against him. Mendel wanted to be sure this was how she saw things and finally asked her. The question was greeted with silence. But for the first time since they met she opened her palm and gazed at the wooden object.

'It's true,' she said finally. 'He was scared. He's only ten and a half.'

'But you aren't angry with him?'

'No.' She said this without the slightest hesitation

'If it weren't for him, your brother Yasha would still be alive.'

This time she didn't reply. They reached the *shtetl*.

'He's my friend,' said Hannah in a dull voice. 'My friend.'

The *shtetl* was made up of three or four hundred dwellings, a synagogue with the rabbi's house adjoining it, the terraced ritual baths, and the schoolhouse. There was also an inn that stood a little apart, on the road to Lublin, not far from the crossroads where the government had positioned a statue of the Virgin. Christian travellers stayed there. It was an ordinary *shtetl*, exactly like hundreds, indeed thousands, of others. There were one thousand, maybe twelve hundred inhabitants in all, at least there had been until the May legislation, when the tzar's new laws drove hundreds of thousands of Jews out of their businesses in the East, and when Hannah's *shtetl* had welcomed its share of the subsequent exodus.

The pogrom had struck an overcrowded village.

When Hannah and Mendel Visoker entered the village the fire had just been brought under control. As the *brouski* jolted down the main street, people ran in all directions, through the smoke and the dust, chanting prayers and incantations. Water, almost turning to mud, spilled from buckets passed from hand to hand by a chain of survivors. And in the midst of all this, the *brouski* drove along in strange isolation, as though it were invisible, its two passengers sitting equally upright and impassive. Mendel counted sixty, perhaps eighty, houses or barns burned to the ground. At the market square, he saw a dozen bodies laid out, mostly those of men, who must have been dragged out of blazing houses before the buildings collapsed. He urged his horses in their direction. 'Why do I feel a stranger to this tragedy?' he wondered. He knew he ought to feel rage and overwhelming grief at the sight of this devastation. But he felt nothing, apart from a fascination with the complete calm of the little girl sitting beside him.

The cart came to within three paces of the bodies and stopped.

'Is your father one of these?'

'No.'

Mendel urged the horses to walk on, passing down the length of the street a second time, passing through the crowd again with the same bizarre sense of not being seen by anyone.

'Turn right,' commanded Hannah.

'I've been here before.'

He recognized the road. Silence overtook the frantic lamentations of the *shtetl*, the wailing and the running about, plunging the two of them into another world. Mendel Visoker had met Reb Nathan only five times, and yet he had the clearest memory of each of these meetings – one doesn't forget such men as Hannah's father. There were perhaps ten or twelve years between them but what they had in common was the sense of belonging to a world that was doomed, a lucid despair, the certainty that something else must exist, something they would have to find, that had not yet been discovered. 'I knew your father,' Visoker had told Hannah, and this was true, infinitely more so than those poor words could express.

'His horse,' said Hannah suddenly. 'My father's horse.'

She leaned forward, looking completely petrified. The *brouski* was no more than ten turns of the wheels away from the house, a little stone building with two chimneys and real glass in the windows instead of the bulls' bladder used in most of the other houses in the *shtetl*.

'And there's blood on the saddle.'

'He may just be hurt,' said Mendel.

He jumped down and picked up the little girl, intending to carry her inside the house. But with a gentleness he could not resist she struggled free. They went inside. He then remembered that in Danzig, the time before they'd last met (just after Mendel had come out of prison), he and Nathan had spent the whole night talking. They had discussed the New World, America, and Australia, they had compared their lives. And Nathan had talked a great deal about Hannah. 'I've an exceptional little girl, Mendel. For her, reading is like drinking water, and she understands what she reads. She comes very close to frightening me with her precociousness. And what you see in her eyes, Mendel . . . She isn't yet seven years old, Mendel,' Nathan had said. 'She'll turn seven before Passover, but . . . how can I put it? She's already the heart and brains of my house, the brains especially . . .'

The house had five rooms, as well as some outbuildings. It contained a staggering number of books. There was a man in the first room; he was elderly, tall, awkward-looking – Mendel would later learn that this was Berish Korzer, who was to become Hannah's stepfather by marrying Shiffrah. When Hannah came into the room, he made a clumsy gesture with his hands, but he was nailed to the spot by the look in the little girl's eyes and by her quick toss of the head. In the next room, Mendel Visoker came upon eight or ten people gathered round a bed, and among them an unimposing face: that of Shiffrah, Nathan's wife, Hannah's mother.

What happened next was to remain for ever engraved in Mendel's memory. The weeping ceased as everyone fell silent and made way for Hannah as though together acknowledging the exceptional nature of the relationship between the dead father and his daughter, the extraordinary personality – no one doubted it – of this tiny little girl.

There was silence as Hannah reached her father's bedside. The bed was raised very high, in the German fashion, so that the body was at about the same level as her eyes. After a lengthy stillness that transfixed everyone, even Mendel Visoker, she let one of her hands move over all his wounds, one after the other, finally stroking the dead man's hideously distorted face.

She did not weep. She pressed her lips for a moment to her father's lifeless hand, and she straightened up.

'That's not all: they've also killed Yasha. He was burned, along with the Temerl barn and the crops. I watched Yasha being burned alive.'

Even as she said this, she looked only at her father. In the commotion caused by her announcement she stepped back from the bed, turned away, and moved towards her mother. She buried her face in the folds of the thick black skirt, encircling her mother's waist with her arms, a gesture that seemed to everyone – everyone but Mendel Visoker that is – natural and understandable.

Mendel saw Hannah's clinging to her mother as a fraudulent concession to conventional behaviour. He did not question the reality of the dreadful grief she felt that day, quite the opposite. For a long time he would remain shattered by the intensity of her grief, and by her stubborn determination to endure her despair alone. But as the mother and daughter wept in each other's arms, Mendel alone wondered which of them was consoling the other.

He would be less unsure about the events of the weeks, the months and the years that were to follow the deaths of Reb Nathan and Yasha. In his view, there could be no doubt: it was Hannah's decision that they should stay in the *shtetl* instead of going to Lublin to stay with one of Shiffrah's sisters. It was Hannah who persuaded her mother that the three of them could survive alone with the money left by Reb Nathan and by selling the salves and balms Shiffrah had always concocted, even though this meant selling the house, even though it meant urging Shiffrah to marry old Berish Korzer.

And all these ploys had but one object: to allow Hannah to await Taddeuz's return.

Mendel lingered in the *shtetl* for a few days more, at first with good reason: he attended the funeral of Reb Nathan and his son, in a village where almost fifty other people, also victims of the pogrom, were buried. He accompanied his friend's body to the cemetery; he was there when, in accordance with customary practice, pieces of glass were laid on the corpse's eyelids, and a small pike placed in its fingers – these rites symbolic of the hope that on the day of the Messiah's Coming, the dead will be able to dig a tunnel to Palestine. He cast earth on the graves, and he, who hadn't prayed for fifteen years, allowed his voice to join with those of the others.

If he stayed on after the obsequies, it was for no obvious reason. Riding bareback on one of his horses, he would wander about the *shtetl*, where the scars of devastation were gradually being erased. He returned to the Temerl barn, to the spot where Yasha was burned alive. He looked for and found the exact spot where the puny body had met its end. Already the grass was growing again and at the sight of this indifference Visoker was possessed with a fleeting anger: where was meaning in this damned world where a child's agony could be destroyed in a few short days?

He walked his horse over the ashes of barley, corn and buckwheat. The vast plain around him was empty; there was no other horseman in sight. You could easily believe that nothing had happened, that the horsemen had never appeared on the boundless horizon and never would again. But of course they would come back, sooner or later; they always did. The sun was blazing hot. Mendel remembered the nearby stream. He went back over the same ground he had covered running to the rescue of a little girl who, all things considered, hadn't much need of him now. He reached the shelter of the willows and rowans where he had hidden his *brouski* and his horses, and from which he had observed the approach of the men who had conducted the pogrom as well as the happy cavorting of the small couple.

He urged his horse into the undergrowth, alongside the stream. He had spent a week now in the *shtetl* and when at last he emerged into the little clearing below the embankment, he discovered why, in fact, he had delayed his departure so long. There she sat, by the stone and branch dam. Her impenetrable gaze was fixed on Mendel Visoker.

'Are you alone?'

She nodded. Beside her lay a sack filled with freshly picked plants.

'I could have been anyone,' said Mendel. 'Someone who might have hurt you.'

'I saw you coming. From a long way off.'

She didn't move at all, but continued to stare up at him. Much to his regret, Mendel felt embarrassed. He finally looked away, his eyes settling on the dam.

'Did you build that?'

'Of course not.'

'Why "of course"?'

'Only boys play games like that,' she said indulgently.

'Your Polish friend?'

'Taddeuz, yes.'

'Is he the person you're waiting for?'

Mendel made an effort to look directly at his young interlocutor again. He saw her shake her head as she said, 'He won't come.'

And she continued as if, with that astounding maturity of hers, she had already guessed what Mendel's next question would be. She started to explain why Taddeuz wouldn't come that day, or on any day yet to follow, of the summer of 1882: he would be ashamed of his cowardice in the barn. He would avoid her, she knew, for as long as he remained in the neighbourhood, until he returned to Warsaw, where he went to school.

'He wants to be a writer or an explorer,' she said, a tender gleam in her eyes. 'I don't think he will ever be an explorer. He's too delicate. But a writer, maybe . . .'

Mendel looked at her, astounded, and thought: She talks of that little Polish boy, who after all must be three or four years older than she is, the way a mother would talk about her son. Or the way a woman in love would talk about her lover. Suddenly Mendel, usually so talkative, was at a complete loss for words.

In the end he asked her: 'And are you going to wait for him all the same?'

'Mmmmm,' she said, very calmly.

'And what if twenty years go by and he doesn't come?'

With an indulgent smile at Mendel's innocence she said: 'Oh, he'll be back!'

Mendel said nothing. He felt slight annoyance in the face of her seven-year-old arrogance, as well as anxiety and an affection that truly amazed him, since he had carefully avoided all emotional ties since adolescence. With a jerk of his head, he turned his mount around and rode off a few metres. He would go back to the *shtetl*, hitch up his *brouski* and take the road south to Tarnopol immediately. He had been here far too long already.

'Mendel Visoker . . .'

She called after him in her little quiet voice. He turned round, pulling gently on the reins.

'Yes?'

Silence. Then: 'I'm not beautiful, am I?'

It almost brought tears to his eyes, all of a sudden. She had straightened up, but this hardly made her seem any taller, and she stood there looking very frail in her ill-fitting black velvet dress. The rays of sunlight that penetrated the foliage framed her narrow, triangular-shaped face, with its high cheekbones and well-defined planes, without drawing it out of the shadows. Her mouth was a little too thin, and betrayed far too much determination; her copper-red hair promised to grow thick and heavy. The contrast with those big grey eyes – which at that moment were fixed on Mendel with painful intensity, as they awaited his reply – the contrast was striking.

An owl.

'That depends on how one looks at you, and who it is that's looking,' Mendel said at last, having hesitated for rather a long time, trying in vain to find a better answer.

Silence.

'I should have lied,' thought Mendel. 'Why didn't I lie?' And
when he saw a kind of sad half-smile appear on the little girl's lips,
his regret grew all the more keen.

He passed through the *shtetl* again some months later, on the eve
of the Sabbath before Hanukkah. It was a very cold day, even
though the sun was shining, and there was snow in the air. Mendel
Visoker had indeed been south, to Tarnopol; he had stayed two
weeks and almost settled there longer, so deeply cunning had his
woman there proved to be. He had then fled further south, through
the Ukraine and to Odessa. He was now on his way back, headed
for Danzig with a fortune of nearly four hundred and fifty roubles.

On reaching the *shtetl* he made straight for Reb Nathan's house,
but began to waver on the doorstep: what the devil was he doing
here, other than succumbing a little to the fascination that seven-
year-old mite exerted over him. He had been unable to put the
child out of his mind.

He found mother and daughter busy sorting dried plants on the
ground. Shiffrah offered him some chicory coffee, which he
refused. Hannah gave him only a quick glance. He explained, fairly
banally, that he happened to be passing and had dropped by to
make sure that the widow and children of his late friend were well;
he asked if there was anything he could do for them. With an
indifference to match his own, Shiffrah thanked him for his
concern. Hannah did not stir or open her mouth during his visit,
but appeared at his side just as he was preparing to remount his
brouski.

'You've got new horses,' she said.

Shiffrah remained inside the house, out of sight.

'Don't you have another brother?'

'Simon. He's at school. He's boring.'

'And you?'

'I'm a girl. And I can already read and write. I have no need to
go to school. Really none at all.'

'You can read as well as all that?'

She nodded. He had some books on the *brouski*, both for his
personal use and because he sometimes offered them as gifts to
buyers with whom he was trying to do business – there was
nothing like a little present for a merchant's wife or daughter to
help conclude a deal. He lifted up the canvas sheet at the back of

the *brouski* to reveal ten or twelve prayerbooks for women and several other religious works, as well as some of the classics of the period.

'I've already read those,' said Hannah scornfully, after a quick glance at the shelf. But before he could stop her, the impudent little devil had hoisted herself up on to the flat of the *brouski* and was eagerly bending over his books. She started to search through the piles, then straightened up in disappointment: 'I've read them all, the pedlars always have the same ones.' Then with a gleam of triumph in her eyes she unearthed the volumes Mendel Visoker kept for himself, the ones he would read while his horses slowly advanced on their endless journeys across the wide Russian plains. He said at once:

'Not those. They're mine. Besides, you're far too young . . .'

He might just as well have been explaining Maimonides to his horses for all the effect his words had on the child. She practically laughed in his face. As precise and quick in her raid as a falcon swooping down on a heron, she had of course picked out the three books to which Mendel was most attached.

She asked: 'And what are these?'

'Poems. You wouldn't understand.'

She gave him a sardonic smile and immediately began to leaf through the volumes. What she held in her hands was *Yod's Downstroke* by J. L. Gordon, a Russian Jew and a poet-fabulist-storyteller, who wrote with highly satiric verve, often making rabbis the butt of his wit. Mendel revelled in the stuff. But giving it to the child was an entirely different matter . . .

The second volume *In the Depths of the Sea* was by the same author and this time the target was God Himself, whom the author found thoroughly indifferent to the dreadful misfortunes of a young Spanish Jew. In a word, it smacked of heresy.

The third volume was *The Mysteries of Paris* by Eugène Sue, in the German translation by Schulmann.

'You don't even know German,' said Mendel, appalled by the prospect of the trouncing he anticipated.

'This way, I'll learn,' replied Hannah.

She really seemed to believe that the conversation was over. And to prove it she jumped down from the cart, clutching the three books to her flat chest with both hands.

'It's completely out of the question . . .' Mendel began.

Hannah opened her eyes wide, bowed her head sweetly, and smiled at him: 'You're going to lend them to me, aren't you,

Mendel Visoker?' And her humour, compared with her usual
gravity, was so sudden and so spectacular that Mendel was overcome by it. Here no doubt he recalled two other moments with
her: when she had clung to his chest like a little stray cat months
before and when she had asked him six days later, in the glade
beside the stream: 'I'm not beautiful, am I?'

'At least read them in secret,' he conceded.

'I promise. And I'll give them back to you next time.'

'If I ever come back to your *shtetl*.'

'You'll come back,' she said confidently, looking him in the eye.

As he watched her walk away Mendel was seized with a strange
melancholy. Usually when he departed from a place where he had
stopped over, leaving behind one of his countless women, he was
very cheerful, whatever he might say to the woman he was
deserting, and despite any promise he might make of a speedy
return. But that day, as the snows began to fall, he felt terribly
lonely. Mendel, you're mad! he thought. She's only seven, what's
got into you? It had just dawned on him that he was placing the
child in the same category as his fifteen or twenty mistresses. The
rabbi in Mazury who had taught him to read had been right:
Mendel Visoker was the maddest Jew in Poland.

He climbed back on to his *brouski*. When he was all set to leave
he half-turned his head, not entirely sure he wanted to submit to
those grey eyes, and called out:

'Has he come back?'

He could not remember the fair-haired boy's name, but she
understood his question at once.

'Not yet.'

Mendel made a habit of visiting the *shtetl*. He was a man who was
always on the road, who obeyed an imperative need to be on the
move – except when winter was at its most severe, and then he
would linger in Danzig with two Lithuanian sisters, blonde and
plump enough to keep you warm during the cold weather,
especially when you had one on either side of you in bed.

In 1883, he paid two visits, one in spring, the other in the
autumn. Both times he saw Hannah – since it was only for her that
he came. And both times he got the same answer: *Not yet*. But he
never again had to ask the question; she would tell him before
he'd even mentioned the subject.

Two visits in 1884; three in 1885, the year he went as far as Vienna, only in search of adventure; three more in 1886.

That year Shiffrah remarried, taking Berish Korzer, the 72-year-old tailor, for her second husband. It was clear to Mendel that Hannah had not objected to her mother's remarriage; otherwise it would certainly not have taken place. Yet Hannah did not think particularly highly of her stepfather. She told Mendel that she thought him a fool: 'He's so stupid that once when he was making a pair of trousers he sewed the pockets into the fly.' As the years passed, she often showed increasing evidence of the quiet, very acidic humour that so delighted Mendel. She was alarmingly precocious, her advance on her age becoming more marked as she grew older. Naturally, she learned German, from Eugène Sue or elsewhere, and taught herself Russian as well. Even her French was quite good: Mendel had managed to procure some volumes of French literature for her, as it was very much in fashion in Warsaw. With the sly hope of putting the little devil in her place, he selected Jean-Jacques Rousseau's *Emile* and his *Essay on the Origin of Languages* to start with; he had already tried to read through them himself and had found them hypnotically somnolent. His sabotage was a waste of time, however; she devoured the Rousseau as easily as he did his evening meal.

Still there was no sign of Taddeuz, however, and the sight of her waiting patiently for the boy would on each occasion drive Mendel Visoker to exasperation. He considered collaring the wretched child in Warsaw and dragging him off to the *shtetl* for a visit, if only so that she might see that her marvellously perfect Taddeuz surely wasn't worth her trouble. Ultimately he gave up the idea, because he could see very well that Hannah would reject his or anyone else's intervention.

There were two visits in 1887, when he was returning from Hamburg and Rotterdam, and another two in 1888. By then she was thirteen, and he was thirty. It was at this time that he began to think seriously of emigrating. In the end he was deterred from his plan by the very scale of the emigration phenomenon: if he had set sail as well, he would have felt he was following the crowd, like a sheep, when it had always seemed to him his way to go against the tide. But the population was very much on the move, not all of it Jewish: a considerable number of Christians had also left their homes, pouring westwards, most of them heading for the Americas. And in Danzig Mendel saw overcrowded ships weighing anchor,

and hordes of candidates for the long journey turned up day after
day at Russia's frontier posts with Prussia and Austria. Meanwhile
the pogroms and persecution of 1881–2, the May decrees ordering
expulsions and stipulating where people should live led to overpopulation in the Polish part of the Russian empire. Mendel had
seen the town of Brody, in Galicia, swell with the influx of ten
thousand refugees from the East.

The idea of escaping it all and never coming back was very much
on Visoker's mind.

His first visit in 1889 came a little before Passover. He found
Hannah the same as ever. Of course, she had grown – though she
would never be tall, taking as she did after the late Reb Nathan,
who was no more than 1 metre 60 – but she was otherwise
unchanged: flat-chested and narrow-hipped, slight if not slender,
pale-skinned, with a thick head of hair and those same extraordinary eyes. Gravity was the predominant trait in her character,
although she was also capable of sudden bursts of brusque, sometimes fierce humour, when her lightning intelligence flashed out.
At that time she was reading Hugo, Turgenev, and Goethe, in no
particular order, as well as several novels by Zola that Mendel had
read and for a long time had hesitated to give her. It was pure
pornography, after all, but after she insisted he finally brought her
the books, telling himself that he was a depraved madman encouraging a Jewish child of her age, living in a far-flung *shtetl* like this,
to read such things. She fascinated him more and more, especially
as he grew aware of how utterly, heartrendingly lonely her life
must be.

That spring she told him that her brother Simon, who was
sixteen, had gone to Warsaw to continue his studies with a
renowned rabbi – 'although he has less knowledge of books than I
have. But he's a boy and I'm a girl, even though I'm as flat as a
board.' As for her stepfather the tailor, who was not only outclassed
but downright terrorized by his stepdaughter, he was all puffed up
with pride at having succeeded in fathering two children by
Shiffrah after the age of seventy. These two pregnancies had made
his wife thicken out considerably; if there had ever been a time
when Visoker had thought of adding Shiffrah to his harem of
accommodating widows he abandoned the idea now. Shiffrah was
not ugly; she had a pretty face and a latent sensuality, which
Mendel the drayman was very quick to observe, and which he had

sometimes thought he might like to awaken. But what was most noticeable about her was her extreme insignificance and her predisposition to submissiveness: she had lived under Nathan's authority and after his death had passed smoothly under Hannah's rule, allowing herself to be persuaded to remain in the *shtetl* and to marry Korzer as well. As far as Mendel was concerned, Hannah had encouraged her mother to remarry just as she had managed to have her brother sent off to Warsaw. That little monster certainly manipulates us all, in the end, getting me to snaffle up all the books in Poland!

But it was not until his early autumn visit of 1889 that Mendel Visoker would truly experience the power of this extraordinary 14-year-old.

'I went to the village first,' said Mendel, 'but no one seemed to know where you could be.'

'You've found me.'

She had her back turned to him and was busy doing something, though he couldn't immediately say what. Then he saw her bare feet and legs, the rings of dampness that were starting to appear on the fabric of her grey dress, finally the drops of water in her loosened hair. He slowly realized he had very nearly come upon her while she was swimming naked in the stream. She was now simply, unhurriedly, getting dressed. Mendel's gaze rested on her waist, where the wet dress began to cling to her, and his heart suddenly started beating faster; it struck him that there was a curve here that he had not seen before.

'In any case,' she continued, 'no one in the *shtetl* ever cares to know where I am, or what I'm doing. I'm of no interest to most people.'

With that, she turned round. At that moment Mendel received one of the greatest shocks of his life: the Hannah confronting him was transformed; were it not for her eyes, he would not have recognized her. She's a woman, he thought, with incomprehensible pride. Within a single summer she had blossomed and he, who had probably collected one hundred and fifty mistresses over the course of fifteen years, who considered himself capable of appraising an entire female body from a mere glimpse of an ankle or a wrist or a shoulder, was astounded. Of course, she was still quite small, even though she must have grown four or five centimetres since the spring, but her body now had a fullness – or a promise of fullness – it had not had before. 'And it's more than promise, Mendel; she's going to have — she has already — one of the loveliest womanly bodies you've ever dreamed of!' He shook his head disbelievingly, and with some embarrassment; it did not take his encyclopaedic experience to imagine the young breasts under that everlasting dress, which was now sticking a bit too closely to her erect nipples for Mendel's comfort. He felt a warmth in his loïns and he was seized with the greatest rage he had ever known. Against himself.

Dismounting, he pressed himself against his saddle to find her staring at him, her arms upraised to rebraid her loosened hair, a hairgrip between her teeth. She seemed to have guessed what was going on inside him and to be mildly amused by it.

'Have I changed, Mendel Visoker?'

He gulped.

'Quite a bit, yes.'

He felt exceptionally stupid and began to shift his one hundred-odd kilos from one foot to the other, vaguely planning to do something out of the ordinary as a way of calming himself down a bit. Could he lift his horse on to his shoulders? As it was, he did not move at all. Nor did she, save to finish plaiting her two heavy braids and pin them together, in a sort of a chignon he had seen on no other woman. The number one Russo-Polish-Jewish expert on all questions relating to the fairer sex found himself again astonished.

'I . . .' he said at last in a hoarse voice, 'I'm very impressed.'

She removed her hairgrip from between her teeth and smiled at him.

'Thank you, Mendel Visoker. So, I've changed a great deal, it seems?'

He was far too busy trying to control his anger against himself and against the girl to notice the look of triumph in her eyes.

'I've brought your wretched books,' he said.

Regaining his composure, he added as sarcastically as possible: 'Only they're in Russian, from beginning to end.'

'That doesn't matter,' she replied, unperturbed.

'Fyodor Mikhailovitch Dostoyevsky, just as you asked for. I've read three or four of them: *Memoirs from the House of the Dead, Notes from Underground, Crime and Punishment* and something called *The Idiot*. This author's a real scream. You're going to die laughing.'

'Fine.'

Something about the way she said 'Fine' was what alerted him. Raising his head, he studied her carefully, as he would have the old Hannah, looking her straight in the eye. What a surprise! Gone was the sarcasm; now she was wide-eyed, the way she had been when they first met, just after Yasha's death and, worse still, when they had learned for certain that Reb Nathan was also dead.

This time Mendel understood. It may have helped somewhat that today they were in the clearing, decorated in autumn colours, where the remains of a seven-year-old dam still survived.

'He's come back? You've seen him again, is that it?'

She took one slow step forward, then walked deliberately up to him, resting her cheek against his huge chest. After a final hesitation, Mendel Visoker closed his arms around her. Despite all his anger – 'that child of a Polish bastard made her wait seven years!' – despite the burst of jealousy, what he really felt, much to his own surprise, was a wave of tenderness wash over him.

She told him that a seventeen-year-old Taddeuz, 'taller than you' and more handsome than even she had remembered, had re-appeared in mid-July (she used the Christian calendar). He was still gentle, delicate, light-hearted, so considerate and intelligent. For the first few minutes she had hardly dared open her mouth, but of course he had understood her shyness and began to speak about himself to put her at her ease. ('Son of a whore!' thought Mendel. 'Is he capable of talking about anything else but himself?') Evidently he was doing brilliantly in his studies.

'Taddeuz is two years ahead of everyone else and he's starting at university this year. He is going to be a lawyer, the greatest lawyer in Warsaw, in Poland, in Europe . . .'

'Oh, at least,' said Mendel.

Hannah broke away from him and paced about the clearing. She said that her first reunion with Taddeuz had been marvellously natural, and that 'No, Mendel Visoker, the past was not mentioned; why hark back to that moment of weakness?' Other meetings had followed. They must have seen each other seven or eight times in all, throughout the summer that had just ended.

'And where is he now?' asked Mendel.

'In Warsaw.' He had gone back two weeks earlier, she said. Someone as brilliant as Taddeuz, and as refined (here she used the French word *raffiné* in the middle of the Yiddish she was speaking) couldn't stay dawdling in a village in the middle of nowhere, with no one to talk to after all.

'Of course not,' said Mendel with bitter resentment. 'What could a genius like that do among peasants? I wonder why he isn't in Prague already, or Vienna, or better still in Paris? Everyone there must be feverishly waiting for him to enlighten them . . .'

He thought his irony would have little effect on her, and he was right. Hannah threw him only a quick scornful glance. But he couldn't help it. He was again in a rage; he simply could not accept Hannah's disproportionate feelings for Taddeuz. She had waited seven years for this little Polish rat who had got her brother killed and almost got her killed as well, and she now thought it marvellous that when they met again he should talk about himself. Of all the people who would ever love or hate Hannah (those who felt anything in between were rare), Mendel Visoker was without question the first to discern her extraordinary stubbornness and strength of character: his reaction was not simply a matter of jealousy, even if the jealousy was real. He knew that she was in danger of making a mess of her life because she held so firmly to 'that little rat'.

Hannah continued to pace and expound her subject with the wordiness of someone who has held their silence for an impossibly long time. She said that Taddeuz, despite his three year advantage over her and despite his studies, had read fewer books than she had; in any case he had not read the right ones. She had lent him, among others, Hugo and Taine and Renan and Barbey and Banville, for he could read French very easily, as well as Russian and German. She marvelled that he should know four languages, though they both knew she could read six.

Mendel cut in with a question: 'Who else have you spoken to about him, apart from me?'

She shook her head.

'Not even your mother?'

Her thin lips drew back in a smile. Obviously the idea of confiding in Shiffrah about anything at all had never occurred to her, and it greatly amused her.

He finally plucked up the courage to ask her the question that had been haunting him from the start.

'Did he . . . touch you?'

Silence.

'No,' she said. 'Not really.'

'What does that mean – *not really*?'

Her eyes remained fixed on him for a long time and he saw a fierce anger in her gaze. She lowered her head, and suddenly looked like a little girl in a grey dress again. In all the forty-odd years he was to know her, this was the only time Mendel Visoker would see her embarrassed.

'He kissed me,' she replied.

And then more precisely: 'Here.' She pointed to her lips with her index finger. 'Nothing else.'

A pause. Mendel turned away, again feeling a great desire to break something.

'Was that because you wouldn't, or because he didn't have the nerve to?'

'A bit of both.'

And she laughed, the fiendish little bitch! He heard her laughing behind him.

'He's still a bit slow on the uptake,' she said maliciously.

I wonder if I am any quicker? thought Mendel. He walked to the edge of the stream, took off his Cossack boots and dipped his bare feet into the water. His mood suddenly took a turn for the better and he was content to see the willow trees' yellowing leaves above his head: winter was coming, and he would spend it in Danzig with his two Lithuanians, blonder and plumper than ever, though he was beginning to tire of them a little; perhaps after all he would trade them in for that German woman with the green eyes, a widow, thank God, whose chest was as accommodating as her buttocks. At that moment, however, just as he was beginning to feel at peace with himself and with the world again Hannah moved in for the attack. Doubtless she had been waiting for just this moment: for all his one hundred kilos, his strength, and his experience of women, she was able, he knew, to manipulate him as easily as she could toss a buckwheat pancake.

From behind him she asked: 'Where have you come from?'

'Kiev.'

He had roamed about as usual, traversing the Ukraine and moving as far as Moscow at one point, on a whim. Business had been excellent for him that year. Though he still drove his old *brouski* he also had the means to buy one or two more vehicles and to hire the employees to go with them. He chose to do nothing of the kind, however, eager to remain on his own, even if it meant bypassing his chance of a fortune.

'And where are you going?'

'Danzig.'

'Via Warsaw?'

He froze as he realized what she was asking. He took his feet out of the water.

'Nothing doing,' he said. 'No, no and no again.'

'You don't even know what I'm going to ask you.'

He sensed that she was standing very close to him.

'It's one of two things,' he said. 'Either you want me to go and see your Taddeuz and take him a message or, worse still, you want me to take you to him.'

For a long time there was no reply. She stood just behind him. Then suddenly she said in a very small voice:

'I want you to make love to me, Mendel Visoker . . .'

It took him one very long moment to find the courage to turn around.

'You want me to do *what*?'

'You heard me well enough.'

'I heard nothing at all. I don't wish to have heard anything. You're mad.'

She bent down and clumsily pressed her lips to his. He leapt to his feet and bolted to the far side of the clearing.

'There's no denying it,' she said with quiet sharpness, 'I really have an effect on men.'

'Hannah, that's enough. *Don't come any closer*!'

'All right.'

She sat down and with great placidity began to smooth out the creases in her dress. In a very detached tone of voice, as though she were talking about a piece of sewing or the day's weather, she said:

'I'm not going to tell you that I love you. You wouldn't believe me. And it's not that I'm in a great hurry to lose my virginity.'

'You stay right where you are,' said Mendel, who was probably talking as much to himself as to her.

'And it isn't because I'm depraved. But I've been thinking: sooner or later, I'm going to sleep . . . well, sleep . . . I'm going to make love with Taddeuz. He has no idea what to do and neither do I. And one of us has to know.'

'By the horns of Beelzebub!' said Mendel.

'. . . Now, you're experienced.'

Silence. She bowed her head.

'You really feel like giving me a good hiding, don't you?'

'I couldn't have put it better myself.'

She sighed deeply.

'So the answer's no?'

'Positively not. Hannah?'

'Yes?'

'Please, don't ask me whether or not I'd like to.'

He looked at her in bewilderment and wondered how he could have been such an imbecile as never to have thought her pretty until that moment. She was suddenly radiant; she smiled as she'd never smiled before.

'So you'd like to. I'm happy to know that.'

'Go to hell.'

'I don't love you but I'm fond of you. Extremely fond of you, even. Good. Let's not say any more about it. Let's talk of the two things you mentioned just now. You're right and wrong. It's true that I want to go to Warsaw, partly because Taddeuz is there, but that's not the only reason . . .'

Now it was her turn to dip her feet into the water. Mendel saw her in profile as she sat down beside him and felt he really was seeing her for the first time. She was not and would never be beautiful in the ordinary sense of the word. But that little triangular face with the pale skin and high cheekbones, all dominated by those grey eyes, produced a bewitching effect; she seemed at once enormously purposeful and yet altogether fragile.

'Not the only reason and not even the main reason,' she went on. 'I want to leave the *shtetl*, Mendel Visoker. I want to get away . . .'

She did not ask Mendel Visoker to take any messages to Warsaw. Not this time. But next spring, if he agreed, he must take her. The next time he came by, if there was to be a next time. It was his decision: all he had to do was steer clear of the *shtetl* and never drive the wheels of his *brouski* through it again should he decide not to concern himself with her any more. In the meantime, whatever he might decide, she would be preparing for her departure. She had already thought of how she would win her mother over, and her stepfather, and even the rabbi; he too would have to have his say, but he was a decent fellow. She turned her head to fix her gaze on the drayman:

'I've thought of everything. Absolutely everything. Do you doubt it, Mendel Visoker?'

'Good heavens, no!' replied Mendel.

He was quite sincere. Deeply worried, but sincere. He didn't doubt for a second that she had indeed meticulously worked out every last detail of her departure. He would have the whole of that winter of 1889–90 to consider the matter, and he knew she thought him more sympathetic than anyone to her need to leave: Hannah only wanted Visoker to do for her as he had done for himself, to set her free.

But there were two crucial differences. First of all, Hannah would be leaving for a single destination, whereas he had simply wanted to get away; she was on the trail of a specific destiny. He would say later that he had known straightaway that her world would be infinitely larger than his had been.

The second difference was very simple: Hannah was a woman. And who had ever heard of a woman – much less a Jewish one – setting out on her own in search of her fortune?

All the same Mendel Visoker knew, even in the autumn of 1889, that he would come to fetch Hannah the following spring, when she would be fifteen years old. He didn't doubt for a second that she would be ready to leave then, though he hadn't the slightest idea how she was going to set about it.

3

TWO ROUBLES TO WARSAW

'I'm fifteen years old,' Hannah told the rabbi. 'And in case you hadn't noticed, I'm a member of the female sex.'

The rabbi closed his eyes, scratched his beard, and sighed in exasperation. He was not the most learned rabbi in Poland; though he had spent fifteen years in a renowned yeshivah in Lithuania, he was more than seventy and his studies were long behind him. He retained only a marked taste for dialectic, which he had had very few opportunities to indulge since the day more than forty years before when he had taken up his post in this remote *shtetl* to the south-east of Lublin.

Naturally, he knew Hannah; he had been present at her birth.

'If your father – may he rest in peace! – were still alive . . .'

'Which is not the case.'

'I'd appreciate it if you would let me finish a sentence from time to time. I am after all the rabbi, not you.'

'I'd be very surprised if I was ever to become a rabbi,' she replied suavely. 'For all sorts of reasons.'

Silence, followed by another rabbinical sigh. The rabbi couldn't remember terribly well how this had started. Though he remembered the circumstances well enough he couldn't recall any reasons that would have led him, a respectable rabbi, to establish a rapport of this kind with a child, and a girl at that!

It had all begun about five years before when he had learned that she wasn't attending school any longer, and he had gone to have a word about it with Shiffrah, who had not yet remarried. He did not set off with any great hopes: like everyone else in the *shtetl*, he knew that the daughter of the late Reb Nathan had always done only as she pleased since she had learned to talk – 'And since then, God guard her from the evil eye, she's never stopped!' His interview with Shiffrah had produced no results at all. Shiffrah suffered from a weakness of character that meant she opened her mouth only to say yes, never to enter into any dispute. The rabbi was left to tackle the child, who was nearly ten, himself.

Did she realize that by refusing to go to school any more she was in danger of remaining ignorant? She sniggered. She had been able to read and write for ages, she said: in Yiddish, Hebrew and Aramaic (admittedly not very well in Aramaic), as well as in Polish, and not too badly in German. The rabbi had then produced his copy of the Pentateuch to argue his point; she counterattacked with sustained fire, drawing on Midrash Rabba, on Sifra, on Mischan and Guemara. She knew as much, if not more, than a very good student almost twice her age.

That's how their *pilpoul* sessions had started, much to the rabbi's consternation. An invention of the Jews of Poland, who knew how to read and write in a country three-quarters of which remained illiterate, the *pilpoul* was a mental duel in which – assuming that the two adversaries have a knowledge of the Talmud that is in principle perfect, but at least equal – the superiority of one speaker over the other is established by the drawing of analogies between texts that appear to bear little relation to each other. It was a distillation of mental training beside which the discussions about the sex of angels among Byzantine priests paled. For the first three years, the rabbi inevitably carried the day, greatly enjoying himself; but after Hannah turned thirteen, these weekly contests had occasionally proved to be evenly balanced: for Hannah displayed a stunning intellectual agility. 'If only she were a boy!' the rabbi had often thought, admiring her ease in constructing vigorous syllogisms.

And again the stubborn girl was trouncing him.

'And your brother Simon?' he asked.

'Here goes,' thought Hannah. She replied:

'Still in Warsaw. He's eighteen and getting on fine. And his studies are going well. He's no more stupid than before. But no less, either. He wrote to us at Passover.'

Passover had been celebrated two weeks before. The rabbi scratched his beard again. He was clearly perplexed.

'Let's go back to the beginning,' he said.

'Good idea,' said Hannah.

'Be quiet.'

'I won't say another word,' she replied.

'You come here and tell me that your stepfather, Berish Korzer, who is seventy-five years old . . .'

'. . . But who's managed to give my mother two children, all the same . . .'

'Be quiet.'

'All right, I will.'

'. . . That your stepfather Berish Korzer, who is seventy-five years old, looks on you with desire . . .'

'That's putting it mildly,' said Hannah. 'If he did no more than look, it wouldn't be so bad.' Here she smiled sweetly at the rabbi. 'All right. I'll keep quiet.'

'. . . looks on you with desire and even tries to . . . fondle you during your mother's absence.'

The rabbi paused, expecting some further comment but this time, miraculously, she remained silent. So he went on:

'And this has been going on for months, since last year, and even before that – ever since you started going to take the ritual bath after menstruation, if what you say is to be believed. And furthermore, you claim you haven't dared speak of this to your mother, even after Berish Korzer offered to marry you once he'd divorced your mother. He has supposedly considered settling in Lodz, where he has some family living, and where you might join him. And in exchange for all these vehement promises, he has hoped to obtain from you . . .'

The rabbi searched for the right word.

'A foretaste,' suggested Hannah impassively.

'Your first favours,' said the rabbi. 'And this wretch, however decrepit he might seem, has not stopped forcing himself on you, day after day. So much so that the situation has become intolerable and, with the sole aim of preserving your mother's happiness and that of your half-brother and -sister born of this second marriage, you have no alternative but to leave the *shtetl* as quickly as possible in the cart of that miscreant Mendel Visoker, who was a friend of your late father – God rest his soul. And you will go to Warsaw, where your brother lives and where, by a strange coincidence, I myself have a younger sister with whom you might stay and who could find you work . . .

The rabbi stopped talking and a silence fell. He felt tired and very old, weighed down by bitter memories of his own arrival in the *shtetl* so many years before, when he had discovered that he was going to be buried alive in this remote village in the middle of an endless plain. In nearly half a century he had found only one man in this place with whom he could talk, really talk. And his daughter, who took after him in all things, in whom that intelligence was even more pronounced, sat now here in front of him. Not without weariness, the rabbi said:

'Hannah, I think that you think that I think that this whole story is pure fabrication. I know that you know that I know it is. By rights, I should go and see your parents and tell them what you've been telling me. I don't much doubt they will be appalled. That poor man Berish Korzer, whom I have some difficulty imagining as a satyr, would never get over it: he would choke with indignation and shame, it would kill him. So I'm going to remain silent about this whole affair. What annoys me most is that you always knew I would; that you reckoned on it.'

She held his gaze for a moment and actually lowered her eyes in the end.

'You're very intelligent, Hannah. Most certainly too intelligent for your own good. Is there anything between this Visoker and you . . .'

'No,' she said sharply. 'It's not that at all.'

'You want to go to Warsaw.'

'I want to go anywhere at all outside this *shtetl*. The time has come.'

He searched her face, convinced now that she was telling the truth. He could anticipate what she would do if he risked trying to suppress this story of attempted rape: she would be prepared to spread the lie round the whole *shtetl*. And in any event she would achieve her aim, she would get away. The rabbi did not hold this rather cynical blackmailing of hers too much against her; he had had all the time in the world to take the measure of her strength of character. And above all he knew – as well as anyone at that point – that there was no place for her and her cold, ambitious calculation here in the *shtetl*, even in Lublin. But the rabbi hoped too that there was another Hannah, compatible with and complementary to this one, capable of tenderness and warmth. And he hoped that if the ambitions of this Hannah could be satisfied, or helped along, the other Hannah might out.

'And what will you do in Warsaw?'

'I don't know yet.'

Silence. 'If anything were to happen to her,' thought the rabbi, 'I would remember for the rest of my life that she had gone with my help. Although, in actual fact, she would have gone with or without my help.'

'When do you want to leave?'

'Today. I'm ready.'

'You haven't left me much time to announce the news to your mother and to obtain her consent.'

'My mother can very well get along without me,' said Hannah. 'She's never needed me. She will even find it a relief not to have me around.'

'I don't know Warsaw very well any more,' the rabbi said to Mendel Visoker. 'In forty years and more things must have changed. But I think it's in Goyna Street.'

'We'll find it,' said Mendel.

He took the letter the rabbi held out to him, which was an introduction to his sister. The two men exchanged glances.

'I know,' said Mendel in a low voice. 'I'll look after her as I would my own sister. If I had one.'

He couldn't help putting a little irony into these last words and he reproached himself for it: for a rabbi, this man wasn't too bad. And he seemed visibly worried about the girl. 'If I were him, it's Warsaw I'd be worried about. The people there don't know what's coming to them . . .'

He took a final look at the little group, with Shiffrah standing to the fore, weeping. Mendel hoisted himself up on to the *brouski* where Hannah was already seated, very erect, her hands in her lap, looking straight ahead of her. He tried in vain to find something memorable to say on the occasion of this departure. He could think of nothing, apart from a very banal: 'We're off.'

The horse-drawn cart crossed the market square and set out along the road for Lublin.

'You ought to have turned around to say goodbye to your mother,' Mendel reproached her gently, feeling himself a little chilled by the lack of emotion in the separation.

She made no response, and for at least an hour they drove along

a road that seemed to run directly towards the boundless horizon
of this oppressively flat landscape without exchanging a single
word.

Finally Mendel spoke:

'I wonder what on earth you could have told them to make
them let you go so easily . . .'

'All kinds of nonsense,' replied Hannah, in what sounded an
awfully odd voice to Mendel. So much so that he leaned over and
examined the girl closely, only to discover that her little face was
contorted, her eyes open wide and her lips trembling.

Eleven days later, after a stay in Lublin where Visoker loaded the
cart with a consignment of hand-embroidered scarves and other
textiles, they reached Warsaw.

Hannah could see boats.

'The Vistula,' explained Visoker. 'And we're on the Praga Bridge.'

'I know.'

Her eyes followed a slow-moving white ship that had at least a
hundred people on board, including some musicians. Mendel began
to laugh.

'I was forgetting: you know everything.'

'No, but you brought me an atlas two years ago.'

Though she tried hard, she couldn't quite control herself: her
hands clenched together, she leaned forward chewing her lower
lip. Lublin had already impressed her, but Warsaw! Along the
thoroughfare was an incredible throng of people, enough to make
you think that the town's one hundred thousand or so inhabitants
had all come out on to the streets at once. In this sea of humanity
Hannah could make out women of extraordinary elegance, women
with huge hats, coloured dresses, diaphanous butterfly-wing para-
sols, and shoes of astonishing delicacy. Most of all it was their
enormous, nearly regal self-confidence that impressed her; the
men accompanying these women seemed to believe them infinitely
fragile and precious. She felt as if she had discovered another race,
a whole new world that she would now have to conquer.

Nothing else was of any importance after Hannah had seen this
walking display of luxury, not even the shops with their inviting
windows. Some of these windows held what she at first took to be
living beings in oddly fixed poses; later she realized that they were
a kind of statue, made of wax, displaying clothes for sale. She was
no more impressed by the stunning rows of tall buildings with their

balconies and their majestic entrances and monumental doorways; by the great number of carriages, some of them with four or six horses in harness, all in the service of only one man or woman; by the general air of opulence, or the bustle, or the vastness.

She was even less impressed by Mendel's litany as he pointed out the various sights one after the other: Sigismond's Column, the Saxe Palace, the Bruhl or Potocki Palace, the Visitandines Church, the Carmelite Church or the Church of St Anne, the gardens and parks, and all those fountains. In fact she barely listened to what the drayman was saying. These marvels left her indifferent. They were nothing but the decor of the new world she had just discovered and where she knew she belonged. She would take her place in it as soon as she could, because, of course, Taddeuz must be at home in it – but that was only a secondary reason; she felt a genuine excitement at her prospects – and a huge disappointment when the *brouski* finally emerged in the Jewish quarter.

'We've arrived,' announced Mendel. Of course, this wasn't a return to the *shtetl*; as in the rest of Warsaw, there were paved roads with large buildings on either side, and lamp-posts, and shops, workshops, and warehouses, and the same bustling throng. But the differences were still altogether obvious: the faces, and doubtless what went on inside people's heads, were the same as in the *shtetl*. 'I'm not going anywhere by coming to live here,' she thought, and aloud she said:

'I'm not staying here, Mendel Visoker.'

He gave her a sidelong glance, assuming that she was referring to Warsaw in general, and directed the *brouski* into a street on the right, where they came to a final halt. He hung up the reins. 'Here we are.' He pointed to a shop that had some faded notices in the window suggesting that milk, cheese and eggs might be purchased within.

'You're not staying where?'

'In this district. And with all the more reason, among these people.'

'But you will stay in Warsaw?'

'In Warsaw, I might.'

At that point a passer-by recognized Mendel and called out to him, and the two men began talking. Hannah, who until then had been examining the shop and had decided that it looked quite dreadful, turned her interest to the newcomer. She had unconsciously noted an intriguing hostility in Mendel's response to him.

He was a man of about thirty, dressed in straw-coloured trousers, a silver-sequined jacket and a red shirt. His flat black eyes stared at Hannah with imperturbable shamelessness. He asked Mendel who she was.

'She's a kind of niece of mine,' explained Mendel.

'I don't know whether I'm his niece,' said Hannah, 'but he's certainly not my uncle.'

She boldly returned the black-eyed gaze; the man was very handsome in a way.

'And who are you?'

'Pelte Mazur.'

The black eyes were laughing. 'Visoker, does your so-called niece always have such a ready tongue?'

As he asked the question, he let his eyes wander over Hannah's body, from top to bottom, even leaning forward to get a better look. He evidently appreciated what he saw.

'Hannah,' said Visoker then, in a reckless voice, 'this punk standing before you is called Pelte the Wolf. Stay away from him.'

'How old is she?' asked Pelte.

'Thirty-five,' said Hannah before Mendel had time to open his mouth.

Pelte the Wolf burst out laughing just as his feet left the earth's surface and he found himself dangling in the air thirty or forty centimetres above the pavement. Mendel's great paw held Pelte by the collar.

'Now just you listen to me, Pelte,' said Mendel very softly, 'and listen carefully: you touch the girl, you even speak to her, and I'll break both your arms, I'll even kill you. Did you get that, Pelte?'

'I think so, yes,' said the dangling Pelte, who was beginning to find it a little hard to breathe.

A crowd had begun to gather. Mendel smiled and asked:

'What do you say, Pelte, am I joking? Do you think I'm capable of breaking your arms and killing you?'

The Wolf uttered something fairly inaudible.

'You'll have to speak more clearly,' said Mendel, still smiling.

'I . . . I think you're quite capable of it.'

'Very well,' said Mendel, who completely relaxed his hold. 'Now, beat it, Pelte.'

For a moment his eyes followed the man in the yellow trousers as he went off in the direction of Krochmalna Street; he smiled again, his eyes as cold as death, when Pelte, just as he was about to disappear from view, turned round and gestured obscenely at him.

'Now, to get back to where we were,' said Mendel. 'What's all this about your not wanting to stay with the rabbi's sister?'

'I shan't stay here, that's all there is to it.'

The crowd dispersed and Hannah saw the disappointment in people's faces that no fight had broken out. Mendel Visoker sighed – he and Hannah were still seated side by side in the *brouski*.

'Now just you listen to me, Hannah,' he said, using not only the same words but the same tone he had used with Pelte. 'I brought you to Warsaw, just as you wanted, because it was better that it should be me rather than anyone else, because your mother and the rabbi agreed. And to bring you here, I had to go out of my way, it's cost me time I could have spent working; I'm prepared to waste a bit more time, but not very much. So, one of two things is possible . . .'

'I didn't leave my *shtetl* to come and live in another *shtetl* that's slightly bigger with streetlights.'

'One of two things is possible: either you stay quietly with the rabbi's sister, if she's prepared to have you, so that I find you here when I next come by, or else I shall tie your hands and feet together and gag you and I shall take you back to your *shtetl*. I am responsible for you.'

'No one's responsible for anyone else. And especially not for me.'

'I just happen to have an empty bag in the back. Now isn't that a fortunate coincidence?'

Hannah scanned his face. Mendel's performance with Pelte had delighted her. Of course, she ought not to have contradicted him when he claimed that she was his niece, but on the other hand, if she hadn't done so, he would not have had reason to grab the moron by the scruff of the neck and lift him off the ground. It would have been a pity to miss that. She studied Mendel Visoker and for a brief moment dreamed of what might have happened by the stream if he had agreed to make love to her, though she had never for a minute thought he would. That too would have been interesting. She was extremely fond of Visoker, but she also happened to be convinced that she could get him to do practically anything. Well, nearly. She gave him a very broad smile.

'On reflection, I think I'll stay with the rabbi's sister. If she's willing to have me.'

'She doesn't know you, and she has no idea what you're capable of. So there's a good chance she'll agree.'

Silence. They smiled at each other, accomplices again.

'Have you got some money at least?' he asked.

'Yes, two roubles.'

'That won't take you far.'

'It's a start. There are always plenty of solutions to a problem. *No.*'

'No what?'

'I don't want any of your money.'

Another silence. He cleared his throat, the way people do when they're embarrassed by what they're about to say.

'Hannah, now remember what I tell you. First of all, you must stay where I leave you. Will you promise?'

'Promise.'

'Next, as regards Pelte Mazur, as regards *all* Pelte Mazurs in Warsaw . . . I saw how you looked at him. That's no way to look at men. And besides, Mazur . . .'

He broke off, because she was sniggering and also because he was searching for the right way to phrase his statement. Charitably, she came to his rescue.

'I know very well what Pelte Mazur is, Mendel Visoker.'

'You know nothing at all about him.'

'He's a procurer, a pimp,' she said very calmly. 'Just as you were, according to the rabbi in my *shtetl*. If I let him, Pelte "the Wolf" Mazur will seduce me. That's the first thing. Then he'll sleep with me. That's the second. And then he'll teach me how to give pleasure to men – which I have no idea how to do, as it happens. That's the third thing. Then he'll put me in a brothel and he'll get the money that other men will pay to sleep with me. I think I've understood very well. Is that what you wanted to tell me?'

'By the horns of Beelzebub . . .' said Mendel Visoker soberly.

She flashed him a second, radiant smile. And she prepared to jump down from the *brouski* when she remembered she was in Warsaw, where she was going to become a lady. Probably ladies didn't jump down from *brouskis*; she held out her arms to Mendel.

'Would you help me get down?'

With a look of confusion that further awakened, had there been any need, the tenderness she felt for him, he did so. She took advantage of those few seconds when he took her by the waist to kiss him on the cheek and whisper:

'No man will ever seduce me if I don't wish to be seduced, Mendel Visoker. No man will sleep beside me if I don't want him to.'

Flabbergasted, he deposited her on the pavement and picked up her bundle, which contained one change of dress, a chemise, and three undergarments. She checked her bodice to make sure she was still in possession of her two rouble fortune, and the two of them went into the shop.

The rabbi's sister looked so much like a hayrick it would have been difficult to tell them apart. In fact she looked like an old and very fat hayrick that had seen a good deal of sun and of rain, which is to say misshapen, falling apart, and brown. She wore a limp brown bonnet from which, contrary to normal practice among married Jewish women, a few locks of brown hair escaped; it did nothing to flatter her broad, leathery face with her prominent, potato-like nose. She had no neck, so that her head seemed continuous with the rest of her copious body, which disappeared beneath a considerable number of skirts worn one on top of the other, all in shades of blackish-brown. For Hannah she was a hayrick who moved about on legs swollen by half a century spent standing for sixteen hours a day in the shop.

Her name was Dobbe Klotz.

She had a husband, whose name was Pinchos Klotz. He of course was as slight as she was immense; one could practically have reduced his volume by half if one had cut off his earlocks and beard and removed his hat. In the Klotz household he carried no weight at all. His only responsibility was to get up at two o'clock in the morning to fetch the fresh milk and eggs, the cream and cheese from a farm on the outskirts of Warsaw, and to return to Goyna Street with the goods at about five-thirty, in time to open the shop at six. Then he would set off on another expedition which would keep him out of the way until early afternoon, when he would make a second delivery or help stock the shelves; after this he theoretically went to the synagogue. He would reappear at the end of the day but immediately bury himself in the cellar under the pretext of stocktaking, and he would not re-emerge until the following day. He was a mere shadow of a man, only a suggestion of a husband.

The couple were nearly sixty and had never had any children. In fact, they had not spoken to each other for some thirty-odd years, united in one of those silent bonds of well-maintained hatred that only a perfect marriage can achieve.

Dobbe Klotz read the letter from her brother, the rabbi. Then she reread it. She was truly colossal, as tall as Mendel, and the look she shot him would have terrified a lesser man. Her small, keen eyes were tucked away beneath heavy eyelids that fell, like the rest of her face, in folds. If Hannah thought Dobbe a hayrick, Mendel thought her a rhinoceros, and he came very close indeed to calling Hannah back and helping her to find a kindlier refuge elsewhere in Warsaw with one of the many women who always offered him a favourable reception.

What happened next genuinely surprised him.

'And I'm supposed to take care of *this*, am I?' asked Dobbe Klotz, with but a glance at the adolescent child.

'And just who do you mean by *this*?' replied Hannah tartly.

The pachyderm turned its head round and looked her up and down. Thinking she was about to squash her like an insect Mendel took a step forward. He hardly needed to.

'You fat whale,' Hannah continued, 'I'm not *this*, I'm a young girl.'

Silence.

'A whale, eh?' repeated Dobbe, scratching her nose with her index finger.

'A whale. And what's more,' sniggered Hannah, 'that's being unkind to whales.'

Mendel took another step forward.

'Now,' said Hannah, 'one of two things is possible, as someone I know would say: either you let me stay or you don't let me stay. If you say no, Mendel Visoker and I will leave. There's no shortage of places to stay in Warsaw.'

The expression in the gimlet eyes became odder and odder. Dobbe asked Mendel:

'Is the little brat always like this or only today?'

'To be frank . . .' Mendel began.

'*Little brat*?' said Hannah.

'Hannah, please . . .' said Mendel, attempting to speak again.

But neither Hannah nor Dobbe Klotz were listening; they stood face to face, in as much as that was possible given the difference in their sizes.

'Can you read?' asked Dobbe.

'Undoubtedly better than you can.'

'And count?'

'Like a usurer. And the answer to your next question is yes.'

'I haven't asked you the next question yet.'

'You're going to ask me if I could look after your shop, which is as filthy as a pigsty. The answer's yes. I can do it – since you do it, it can't be very difficult.'

'That's what you think, is it?'

'Mmmmmm,' said Hannah.

Mendel looked at the two of them in disbelief.

'Assuming I let you stay,' said Dobbe, 'and I did say assuming that . . .'

'And assuming that I want to stay with you.'

'Assuming that too,' conceded Dobbe.

'Assuming all that,' agreed Hannah magnanimously.

'I'll feed you and give you a place to sleep . . .'

'Clean. Not like this. With a window and a light for when it's dark.'

'And why not silk sheets and a new wardrobe as well?' Dobbe snorted. 'Can you cook?'

'Completely hopeless,' admitted Hannah. 'And I'm not much good at sewing either.'

'Bed and board, nothing else. Not a rouble, not a kopek.'

'That doesn't matter,' replied Hannah calmly, 'all I have to do is steal from the till.'

Mendel closed his eyes, already imagining himself knocking on all the doors of Warsaw in the impossible hope of finding lodgings for the wretched brat whose tongue was too sharp for her own good. He waited for Dobbe Klotz to explode. She did indeed explode, but not exactly as he had anticipated: a first quiver ran across the uniformly brown surface of this heap of fat and shifts and skirts; the planes and creases of the face itself trembled; then a cavernous rumble rose from the entrails, like a volcano signalling its imminent eruption, until finally the laughter burst forth, shaking Dobbe Klotz's entire bulk. It was a laugh that measured up to the woman; the whole of Goyna Street all but shuddered with it. To this laughter Hannah added her own, so that before Mendel's astonished eyes the two women collapsed into a fit of genuine mirth.

A few moments later Hannah recovered enough to say:

'It's all sorted out now, Mendel Visoker. I'm going to stay here a while.'

Oddly, Visoker did not retain any memory of the humour in this scene. With the passage of time, he would say that his initial relief that this confrontation had turned out well – and that he was to be rid of the brat at last – gave way to an unpleasant sense of foreboding. He found two things unsettling: Hannah's rather too conscious cunning, her absolute certainty that she could manipulate anyone, man or woman, and the genuine madness of Dobbe Klotz.

Hannah was given a garret room on the fourth and top floor of the building in Goyna Street, all of which belonged to the Klotzes. She had felt anxious at first – having grown up among ladders she had never seen a staircase – but in the end she was delighted with her rooftop quarters.

It was there, in that unheated room measuring two by three metres, that she would reach the end of her adolescence; here she would live through the first of her dramas with Taddeuz Nenski as well as, of course, the Pelte Mazur affair.

As she had insisted, the room had a window, or rather a skylight. When the sun shone, which was rarely, it lit the room. If she climbed up on a chair, she could see past the rooftops of Warsaw to the Vistula, as far as the Praga forest. In between lay the palaces and churches and the monuments of the city.

And that was where Taddeuz was bound to be.

4

DOBBE KLOTZ

Dobbe finished checking the accounts and with her index finger scratched the potato-like appendage that served as her nose.

'What's this fourteen roubles, seventy-one kopeks, one penny?'

'Cheese for Reb Isaiah Koppel.'

'Reb Isaiah wanted such a huge quantity of cheese?'

'When I told him it was a perfectly unique cheese that came directly from the Carpathians, that his sole possession of it would make all his neighbours jealous, that it was a bargain not to be missed, in other words, yes. Reb Isaiah took the whole thing. If there'd been any more, that would have gone too.'

Hannah smiled at Dobbe. For more than two months now she had been working in the shop and her understanding with the Hayrick improved daily. She explained that the cheese did actually come from the Carpathians, from the Tatry Mountains in fact, and she had learned this from Pinchos. It had occurred to her that it didn't make sense to sell a cheese that had travelled so far for the same price as an ordinary cheese made in the farms around Warsaw. She thought she had done well to triple the selling price of the Carpathian cheese, even though its cost was the same.

'So Pinchos shares secrets with you, does he?'

That anyone should talk to Pinchos, on any subject, clearly came as a surprise to Dobbe. She had another question.

'And why this extraordinary price? Never mind the fourteen roubles, seventy-one kopeks, but what about the *one* penny?'

Without a word, Hannah turned back a page in the accounts book. On the reverse side was another column, which she had begun two weeks after she started work in the shop. She had not asked Dobbe to pay her any wages for her fourteen or fifteen hours' work every day, but she had made one suggestion: since the accounts had been so well kept for years and years, clearly it was possible to work out the shop's average income over the past thirty years in elaborate detail. And what she had proposed was that she should receive forty per cent of everything sold over and above the average after the day she started working there.

Dobbe's sharp little eyes had glinted; if there was one thing in the world that she knew how to do it was to keep accounts. And she had gone over them again and again, all night long or very nearly, before giving her answer. In the morning Dobbe had launched a counterattack:

'So you expect that because you're in the shop my turnover will increase?'

'Yes,' said Hannah, although she was only guessing at what the word 'turnover' might mean. Everything she knew of business at the time she had picked up during one of her readings of Zola's *Au Bonheur des Dames*.

'And by how much, do you think?'

'You can't expect me to tell you that,' said Hannah, imperturbably.

Dobbe had begun by saying: 'I'll give you ten per cent and that's only on con . . .'

'Twenty-five.'

'Fifteen. And no more.'

'Twenty. You're not risking anything, Dobbe. You've got a profit margin of sixty per cent, at worst, and you'll only be paying me if your earnings are higher than usual.'

Dobbe had finally agreed to twenty per cent, on the express condition – she must have considered herself a real devil to have gone so far – that if the turnover were to fall below the average figures, the loss would be debited to Hannah. This led to further discussion, all of which took place in hushed voices, since the two conducted most of their negotiations in the women's gallery of the synagogue, prayerbooks in hand. Hannah agreed, subject to one qualification: she would not be held responsible for more than twenty per cent of any losses. On only two days had her account been debited, and that was during the week immediately after they had made their deal. From then on, due to her presence in the shop and her cheerfulness with the clientele, the turnover had begun to rise with inexorable consistency . . .

'Let me explain,' said Hannah. 'Before Reb Isaiah came in – and I thought he would be our last customer that day – I had made a profit of roughly twenty-seven roubles, six kopeks. To be precise, it was twenty-seven roubles, five kopeks, and one penny . . .'

'. . . We reached the average turnover figure at the beginning of the afternoon. Everything we sold after that was subject to my commission, including Reb Isaiah's purchases. By selling him his cheese for fourteen roubles, seventy kopeks, I made twenty per cent of that, which came to two roubles, ninety-four kopeks . . .'

'That's correct,' Dobbe agreed impassively, going over the calculations in her head.

'Which gave me a total of twenty-nine roubles, ninety-nine kopeks, and one penny.'

'In other words, you put an extra penny on Reb Isaiah's bill to round up the figure.'

'Exactly. You owe me thirty roubles.'

That morning, during their free moments, the two discussed the question of how the extra penny should be accounted for. Dobbe Klotz maintained that the penny should be included in the day's total receipts and that therefore only twenty per cent of it was due Hannah, while Hannah argued that the penny had only been entered in the books in the first place thanks to her unrelenting honesty. In the end, it was the mathematical argument that won the day: it was after all impossible to divide one penny, the smallest unit of currency known to man.

That was the sunny spell in relations between Hannah and Dobbe Klotz; the time when the fat old woman with the difficult character, used to decades of living turned in on herself, was filled with wonder at the adolescent girl in her life, and began to feel a sullen tenderness – the only kind of which she was capable – towards her. This rapport would last for months and months, as Hannah became more and more important to Dobbe, and as tenderness, then friendship, developed into genuine love. It was however a crazily exclusive love, perverse even, and all the more dangerous because it brewed in the heart of a woman extreme in her sentiments.

After the sale to Reb Isaiah Koppel Hannah was given her thirty roubles and half a day's holiday. For the first time she ventured out in Warsaw on her own.

Krolevska Street was the address Taddeuz had given her when they had last met by the stream, at the end of the previous summer. Hannah had to ask the way three times but finally emerged into an impressive thoroughfare with palaces and luxurious dwellings on either side, where the wooden pavements found almost every-where else in Warsaw had been replaced by pavements made of stone. Hannah was not surprised by this: her image of Taddeuz, and of the splendour in which he must surely live in Warsaw, was only reinforced by it. She nonetheless wavered on arriving in front of a building that looked very much like a private mansion, separated from ordinary life by an elegant gate, a superb garden, and a flight of marble steps. At the top of these was an intricately-carved door embellished with locks, double handles, and a knocker made of a metal that seemed to Hannah to be gold. She hesitated before the door not so much from timidity, which was hardly in her character, as from a need to prepare herself a little more for their reunion.

Throughout her walk to Krolevska Street she had imagined this meeting over and over, rehearsed it in advance; she would knock gently, with elegance and distinction and Taddeuz would be there, on the other side of the door and . . . no, on second thoughts, she would probably find herself face to face with a servant; there would certainly be a servant to show her in, to lead her to Taddeuz, and Taddeuz would be amazed to see her in Warsaw. She and Taddeuz would sit in a drawing room, they would be served coffee, if not tea, perhaps even chocolate, and cakes, and they would talk of literature. She would tell him that thanks to a friend who was a librarian (how could she possibly explain who Pinchos Klotz was?) she had been able to read that man Schopenhauer he had spoken to her about the summer before . . .

She decided that another minute or so would not make any difference. She had already been waiting so long, and during her two months on Goyna Street she had seen absolutely nothing of the town. She began to walk along the pavement opposite. On her left was a garden such as she had never seen before with a towering gate. (Later she would discover these were the Saxe Gardens.) Through the railings Hannah could see children playing, driving hoops along with a dexterity that delighted her, or building castles out of sand with the help of tiny buckets and spades; these miniature implements seemed to Hannah the quintessence of wealth. Some children were pulling toys on the end of little pieces of coloured string, others were riding ponies; one child was even perched on an astounding machine that consisted of two different sized wheels, the larger of which was taller than Hannah, and somehow, miraculously, he was keeping his balance on it. Nearly all the boys wore sailor suits that reminded her of the Jules Verne books that Visoker had brought her; the little girls wore perfectly-fitted dresses. There were adults in the park as well but Hannah's impeccable eye told her to pay them little attention: they were only servants, *'gouvernantes'* as they were called in French.

Along the footpaths she saw women like those she had noticed two months earlier when riding through town in Visoker's *brouski*. A few strolled beneath fabulous umbrellas with that air of extraordinary self-confidence that had already amazed Hannah. But most of them were seated in the shade of a flowered arbour, at the tables of what must have been a *café*, if Hannah was correctly applying the vocabulary she had learned in books.

She knew it was time to go now; it might turn out that Taddeuz would bring her to one of these tables later. Why, after all, should they drink their chocolate in a drawing room when the weather was so fine? She crossed Krolevska Street again, avoiding with great virtuosity the noisy procession of droshkies, barouches and other landaus. She pushed open the gate, climbed the steps and reached the door, only then realizing that the door knocker was mounted beyond her reach. How exasperating! As though all the inhabitants of the chic neighbourhoods of Warsaw were two metres tall! She wanted to give the left door-panel a good kick, but then noticed a chain with a handle, made of the same gold metal as the knocker, to her right. She pulled on it, and heard it ring, and listened as footsteps sounded inside. The right-hand door panel opened. A grey-haired woman appeared, dressed all in black apart from a white lace apron; she looked at Hannah sternly.

'I should like to see Mr Taddeuz Nenski,' said Hannah in her best Polish.

'Who?'

'Mr Taddeuz Nenski. He's a friend of mine. He's from my *shtetl*. At least, not really from my *shtetl*, he's the son of the tenant farmer who works the fields beyond the Temerl barn.'

'I'm not doing very well here,' thought Hannah, quite accurately.

'Why did I say anything about the *shtetl* and the Temerl barn? I made it sound as though Taddeuz is Jewish, which he isn't. And after what happened at the barn, after his little moment of weakness, it wasn't very clever to mention it.'

The grey-haired woman stared at her in surprise. The word *shtetl* must have meant something to her, for she gave a friendly smile and said in Yiddish:

'You must have been given the wrong address, little one. There's no Taddeuz . . .'

'Nenski.'

'. . . no Taddeuz Nenski here, and never has been.'

And with that, the door panel closed in Hannah's face. For a good long moment she stood with her back against the door, wanting again to give it a good kick. 'Poor fool!' she said aloud, addressing the woman in the apron, Warsaw, and the world in general, along with herself. She was angry.

Disappointment came later, and dejection. She began to walk again, this time aimlessly. It was the beginning of August, and the bushes in bloom in the Saxe Gardens looked magnificent. Their perfume scented the air, though it competed with the smell of horse dung, with the reek of carriage oil heated by the sun, and with the stench from the gutter drains. By walking in a straight line, Hannah eventually came within sight of the Vistula. There were still boats on it. She crouched down, adopting the posture of her earliest youth, and closed her eyes. She began to envisage a return to the *shtetl* when a woman came up to her, troubled to see her on the verge of tears so close to the edge of the riverbank. The woman asked in Polish if there was anything she could do.

Hannah responded with a near-ferocious '*Nothing.*' She could manage very well by herself. Forced to fall back on her own resources she set off again, regaining her clear-headedness as she walked. All right, so Taddeuz had lied to her; he had never lived in that palatial building, nor, it was likely, in any other building in the better neighbourhood of Warsaw. Only someone as stupid as you, Hannah, would believe lies like that. The truth was that Taddeuz dreamed that he lived in a house of that kind, and Taddeuz had a tendency to believe what he dreamed.

It was all so obvious.

She found herself back in the city centre, in an unfamiliar street lined with elegant shops. She stood in front of a window that helpfully reflected back her image: 'Look at yourself, Hannah, just look at you! Frightful. Worse still: laughable.'

The girl in the window levelled eloquent eyes at her that blazed with cold fury; she was dressed like a scarecrow, in a grey frock that fitted her badly, and which had obviously once belonged to her mother.

'You're not pretty but at least you have a good body, you've got a bosom and hips; you need only remember the lecherous glances of Visoker and Mazur the Wolf to convince yourself of that. Not a bad body at all . . . but who can see it?'

As for her shoes, they were, she suddenly realized, hideous: shapeless old cracked-leather boots that had been Yasha's before they had been hers.

Again, she succumbed to momentary despair. But this second crisis lasted no longer than the first: shedding tears was dehydrating and benefited no one, and every problem had, after all, at least two or three solutions. Without a moment's more reflection she went into the shop and was instantly overwhelmed by the sumptuousness of it, by the admirably waxed parquet floor, by the wealth of curtains and wallcoverings and furniture. She betrayed nothing of her alarm. A young woman approached her of overpowering distinction, in a dress with a batiste collar.

'Yes?'

'I'd like to buy a dress,' said Hannah calmly.

The saleswoman stared at the grey hand-me-down, allowing her gaze to travel down to Hannah's boots, then up again.

'What sort of dress?'

'One that fits me,' said Hannah, as her eyes wandered along the rows of mannequins, to the oak counters and the armchairs with dresses draped over them. What happened next was to affect her life for years to come. (Later, when recounting the scene to Lizzie MacKenna, she would call it a show of chance.) She walked straight up to a turkey-red and black dress, one which was not even on display but had been thrown carelessly across the back of a couch.

'This one. How much is it?'

'One hundred and thirty-two roubles.'

The saleswoman made no effort to disguise the scorn in her voice.

'I want to see it,' said Hannah, hoping that was what one said at this point in the transaction.

A second clerk, wearing a similar collar but with delicate lace cuffs as well, appeared. She and the first saleswoman had a whispered exchange.

'May I see it?' Hannah insisted.

The whispering continued.

She was shown the dress. She didn't touch it, but simply asked: 'And will it fit me?'

Several more women materialized. It was nearly three o'clock in the afternoon, and this very odd child who spoke with such authority was the only customer in the shop. She settled her gaze on the face of each woman in turn; in the end it was because of those eyes of hers that she was shown the dress. It was held up against her body, level with her shoulders.

'It's slightly too long.'

She asked what was normally done in such cases, and was told that it would be possible to take up the dress a few centimetres. The shop would undertake this kind of work – once the dress had been bought. And paid for. The entire staff now stood watching raptly.

'I'm going to leave you thirty roubles,' said Hannah in a very clear, very calm voice. 'Will that be enough for you not to sell the dress to anyone else and to keep it for a short time? Will that ensure that my dress won't be sold until I come back with the rest of the money?'

On the condition that she would return before too long the deal was struck. Hannah placed one ten-rouble note, three five-rouble notes, four one-rouble coins, one fifty-kopek piece, four ten-kopek coins, nine one-kopek coins and two pennies on the polished oak counter.

'That's thirty roubles. I'd like a receipt, please.'

One was written out for her in extraordinary silence. She folded the piece of paper in two and slipped it inside her dress, between her breasts; with a curt 'Thank you,' she left the shop. Once outside, she was careful not to look back, knowing very well that several of the saleswomen had come to the threshold to watch after her. It was only when she thought she was entirely out of sight that she stopped and finally succumbed to the trembling of her body.

The entrance halls, the long corridors and the courtyards of the university were practically deserted. She saw only a few workmen in overalls making a considerable effort to look industrious. Eventually she found the caretaker, however, who told her that all the students were on holiday.

'I know,' replied Hannah (to whom this in fact came as news), 'but it's absolutely imperative that I find my cousin Taddeuz Nenski, to tell him that his uncle and aunt, that is to say my father and mother, have just died.'

Deeply moved by the touching dignity this tiny girl showed in her bereavement, the caretaker did all he could for her: he sent off one of his sons to the home of a secretary in the law faculty, who an hour later arrived on the scene himself. He also felt exceedingly sorry for her, and enquired about the circumstances of her tragedy as he rifled through his registers. Hannah willingly supplied him with further details: her parents had died when their house burnt down in a fire started by some drunken Cossacks; her own survival was a sheer miracle. She had managed to jump out of the window in her nightdress, and afterwards all she had been able to find to wear were these poor rags she had on. Like all good Poles, the two men had a considerable hatred of Cossacks, and her story brought tears to their eyes. They even offered to lend Hannah a little money, an offer that she refused with dignity: she still had two roubles left, she said, which a compassionate neighbour had given her. (These were the two roubles she had when she arrived in Warsaw with Mendel Visoker.)

She asked how Taddeuz was progressing with his studies. The secretary replied that he was doing marvellously: Nenski was a brilliant student two years ahead of others his age, and it would not be long before he became a lawyer.

'Well, at least that's one thing he didn't dream up,' thought Hannah.

She was given Taddeuz's address in an apartment building in a street in the Praga quarter, on the other side of the Vistula.

She arrived there at about five o'clock, having walked the length of the Praga Bridge.

This building was a far cry from those of Krolevska Street. It was an ordinary one-storey house on the edge of the unpaved road, down the middle of which ran sewage and rain water in a central gutter.

'I'm his sister,' explained Hannah to the fat Polish landlady. 'Not exactly his sister; his half-sister really. We have the same father, but not the same mother.'

And she went on to provide details of their father's broken marriage vows and his adultery.

The fat red-faced woman sniffed. Hannah's story did not surprise her at all; she had always known that men were contemptible, irresponsible pigs.

'You're talking about my father,' Hannah said sadly.

The woman granted her that as her eyes filled with pity: 'You poor little thing. How old are you?'

Hannah told her she was seventeen, that she had just arrived in Warsaw to claim an inheritance, and that she had hoped to be able to embrace her half-brother while she was there. She also hoped that he might protect her against all those lecherous men.

On the wickedness of men, the Polish landlady was more than ready to concur wholeheartedly; but she was also ready to concede that, for a man, Hannah's half-brother Taddeuz was very decent: he was quiet, polite, very mild-mannered and paid his rent yearly . . .

'But he's not at home,' interrupted Hannah.

No, he wasn't. He had left as soon as university classes ended, and had gone to Prague. He would not return until the end of August, at the earliest.

'Could I at least see his room?'

It surprised her, even though Hannah had been convinced beforehand that Taddeuz, with all his delicacy of nature, would not be able to live just anywhere. The room was lovely, with a little bathroom adjoining. The most striking thing about it was the terrace, on to which its two windows opened; it was adorned with flowers and offered a marvellous view of the centre of Warsaw, of the green bell-towers of its baroque churches, the superb architecture of the Stare Miasto, the Old Town, the ancient ochre-coloured ramparts. If you leaned over the balustrade you could see the Vistula flowing below.

'It's very beautiful,' said Hannah quietly.

She had to close her eyes for a moment, for she could imagine herself in this room and on this terrace with Taddeuz, watching the sun set – or standing here at dawn, which implied a great deal more.

'It's my best room,' the Polish woman was saying. 'And it's the best room in Praga, maybe even in Warsaw. Your brother was determined to have it at any price; he even pays for it in the summer, to be sure of holding on to it.'

Hannah walked up to the edge of the terrace: the flowerpots formed a kind of hanging garden. She went back inside: the room was remarkably clean, the numerous books arranged impeccably on the shelves. The bed was a four-poster of a dark fretted wood; here again Hannah's heart started to beat wildly, as she knew – or hoped, which was for her the same thing – that sooner or later she would lie naked in this bed. She walked away from the bed and read the titles of several books, some of which were law books but many of which were books of poetry: Slowacki, Musset, Byron, Shelley, Leopardi, as well as Towianski and Torwid, of whom she knew nothing. 'I shall have to read them,' she thought.

She finished her inspection by examining the desk where Taddeuz worked. A dozen sheets of paper lay on it, a red stone paperweight holding them in place. It was of exactly the same colour as the eyes of the scarab he had carved for her, and of the same material as her talisman was made.

'The furniture's his,' said the Polish landlady. 'And the flowers. You ought to go now. He doesn't like people coming in here. I'm not even allowed in to clean the place, he takes care of that himself. If you weren't his sister . . .'

'Only his half-sister. And as a matter of fact I should be . . .'

She lowered her head with just the right suggestion of shame and distress.

'I should be grateful if you didn't tell him that I came, nor even that I'm in Warsaw. Actually, I'm not staying, as I'm leaving tomorrow for Italy, with the legacy my grandfather left me. Taddeuz would be so sad and anyway . . .'

In a dull voice she told the landlady how Taddeuz's best friend had tried to rape her and was waiting patiently for a chance to try again. He was a lecherous madman, but how could she possibly tell Taddeuz? Would he believe her? What if he were to kill his best friend? Unless, both being men . . .

'They're thick as thieves,' said the Polish landlady with the fiercest conviction. 'Even the best of them, believe me, little one . . .'

'I'm afraid that's so true,' said Hannah as she left.

Dobbe Klotz looked at her in shock and horror.

'You want me to lend you how much?'

'One hundred and seventy-five roubles.'

'Why not two hundred?' sneered the Hayrick.

'Only if you insist,' said Hannah, unruffled.

Once again they were in the women's gallery in the synagogue, prayerbooks in hand. And once again they were whispering, despite the black looks that came their way from the rabbi's wife, whose job it was to keep order. Four days had gone by since Hannah had been to Krolevska Street, and since she had left a deposit of thirty roubles for a dress that cost one hundred and thirty-two.

'Of course the answer's no,' whispered Dobbe. 'No, no, and no again.'

'You should think about it a bit more.'

The sweet smell of the memorial candles burning beneath the menorah, next to the oil lamps and the sacred ark, rose up to the gallery.

'Let's pray,' said Dobbe.

'Why not?' said Hannah.

The voice of a visiting preacher droned on in the background; he happened to be talking about women, all of whom he considered likely candidates for hell, where their breasts would be ripped off with red-hot irons before they were stretched out on a bed of coals. Indifferent to these appalling prospects, Hannah remained silent and waited, sensing Dobbe's eyes upon her. As she had anticipated, Dobbe began whispering again at once. She asked the obvious question, not what the money was for, or how was she going to be repaid, but what would happen if she refused.

'I'll go away,' said Hannah. 'I'll leave you and Pinchos. I'd have no choice.'

She could not help but sense the blow she had just dealt the huge woman. She saw Dobbe's fat hands start to tremble, and to tremble so violently that – in a gesture of tenderness rare to her – she covered Dobbe's huge left hand with her delicate right one.

Dobbe Klotz was later to appear one of Hannah's greatest causes for regret. When she was much older and when she was to recount this scene to Lizzie MacKenna, she would confess the shame she had felt in resorting to blackmail.

Lizzie, I was just a dreadful child then, incredibly selfish and convinced there wasn't anybody I couldn't manipulate. That's my only excuse. Especially as I wasn't being all that clever, as it turned out; I never

foresaw what Dobbe would do later. All the same, I didn't doubt for a
moment that she would give me the money. It's terrible to have that much
power over somebody and to be so aware of it . . .

When Lizzie MacKenna heard the story of Dobbe Klotz she
immediately recalled that someone held a power very much like
this over Hannah all her adult life. She would be careful not to
mention the similarity, but Hannah would see straight through
her, toss her head and say: 'No, it was nothing like what's between
Taddeuz and me . . .'

Dobbe Klotz lent her the money in the end, though not without
fighting the loan for three or four days. Naturally, she ultimately
asked the second question: what did Hannah intend to do with so
much cash?

Hannah told her the truth, abandoning the idea of inventing
some outrageous explanation for the occasion.

A dress that cost one hundred and thirty-two roubles? The
Hayrick could not believe it, having spent only half that amount in
forty years on the nine or ten skirts she wore one on top of the
other.

'But that's not all,' said Hannah. 'I need some shoes as well. And
a bag, a hat, and some gloves. And a petticoat. Probably two
petticoats . . . Then another, simpler dress for every day. And shoes
to go with it.'

There was, not far away, in Goyna Street a shop that sold
women's clothes. Hannah was prepared to go and buy her second
dress there. She paid six roubles, twenty-three kopeks for it, after
bargaining for three days. When Dobbe said she failed to understand how Hannah could haggle over the price so bitterly and at
the same time pay one hundred and thirty-two roubles for another
dress that couldn't be very much different, Hannah replied that the
other dress was a dream and that one did not bargain over a dream.

Her answer did not prevent Dobbe from asking the third question: how was she to be repaid, with reasonable interest, the
money she was lending?

'I have plans,' said Hannah, 'which will earn you a lot of money,
on top of all the profits I've already brought you.'

Towards the middle of August, she returned to the elegant shop
on Cracow Avenue, armed with her receipt. She tried on the
turkey-red and black dress, which to the astonishment of the

saleswomen fitted her as if – except for the length – it had been made for her. Suddenly the slimness of her waist, the curve of her hips, the fullness of her breasts were revealed. Better still: the red she had chosen set off her grey eyes and her coppery tresses perfectly, as she could tell from the instant silence that greeted her when she emerged from the fitting room.

She herself remained impassive, even while she studied her full-length reflection in the large Venetian looking-glass. If there was ever a moment when her hopes of being just a little beautiful since she would never be pretty were confirmed, it was then before that oval mirror. She noticed how striking her bearing was, and how, when dressed properly, she seemed at once taller and older, with an air of lofty mysteriousness. Her vitality made her radiant, despite the natural pallor of her narrow face.

She registered all this with a cool lucidity, like a card-player counting the number of tricks in his hand. And when she was told that the alterations would take several days, it being August and the staff somewhat diminished, she replied that she could easily wait, but that she naturally expected a discount because of the delay.

In the end she paid only one hundred and twenty-five roubles for the red-and-black dress. There might be no bargaining over dreams, but Hannah's idealism had its limits.

Mendel Visoker passed through Warsaw again at the end of autumn 1890, and in the spring of 1891. On both occasions, of course, he went to Goyna Street. On his second visit he had trouble believing his eyes: the shop had expanded, taking over the one next door, and it sported a new sign. Where before there had been a sort of dark cave that smelt of sour milk, in which Dobbe Klotz lurked like a hibernating bear, Mendel found a bright and clean and remarkably organized room crowded with customers. The drayman also found Hannah in charge of two young salesgirls – one of whom he thought of particular interest – both of them dressed, as was Hannah, in white overalls.

'What the devil have you done with Mrs Klotz?' asked Mendel in amazement. He was surprised not only by these concrete transformations: but by Hannah, whom he found talkative and cheerful, constantly breaking off their conversation to call out to some customer or other. She had grown up a little and now displayed an almost wild kind of energy.

Dobbe Klotz, she reported, had gone out for an hour or two. Then looking Mendel straight in the eye she said:

'I must speak to you. This evening, after we close?'

It was two in the afternoon. Mendel had several business appointments, after which he planned to visit either the good Kryztina in Mirowski Street, or a very accommodating maid who worked for a rich Hasidic merchant from Leizer Przepiorko. He had not yet decided when he agreed to meet Hannah at the café-cum-grocery-store on Krochmalna Street instead.

He waited for her until after nine, when she still had not appeared. Had she been delayed in the shop? He went back to Goyna Street and found the door locked. He assumed she had forgotten him and that he would see her the next day. Then, because of the hour, he finally opted for Kryztina, who gave him an enthusiastic reception.

He was in bed with her – on top of her to be precise – when Hannah turned up.

She sat on the edge of the bed. Mendel cried out in a strangled voice: 'Get out of this room at once!' hastily covering his own and Kryztina's naked bodies. But Hannah simply made herself more comfortable, tidying the pleats in her dress as she explained that she was late because she had been delayed at a meeting with someone else. She had tracked down Mendel's *brouski*, which explained how she had managed to find him so easily. Her grey eyes seemed finally to notice Kryztina, who had sunk so far under the sheet only her blond hair and panic-stricken blue eyes were visible.

'How do you do, madam,' said Hannah in Polish. 'Don't let me disturb you. Do go on, please.'

'Get out!' growled Mendel, who was actually close to laughter.

'Does she understand Yiddish?' said Hannah, referring to Kryztina.

'Not a single word.'

'That means we can talk, Mendel Visoker. First of all: business. Things are going very well. You've seen the shop. Our takings have tripled, on average. On some days we make five times as much as before and business is increasing, especially since I persuaded Pinchos to take on someone to help him with his deliveries. The most difficult thing was getting him to buy two more carts and the horses to pull them. As for the second shop . . .'

'Heavens alive!' exclaimed Mendel. 'Couldn't all this have waited

until tomorrow?' All the same his amazement caught up with him:
'*What second shop?*'

'The one I've talked Dobbe into opening, near the Arsenal.'

'That's miles away. And it's not in the Jewish quarter.'

'Precisely. After all, we need a different clientele.'

Mendel sat bolt upright in bed, almost forgetting that he was
naked and that his covering had just changed dramatically.

'Is it really open, this second shop?'

'It is. And it's doing well.' She smiled. 'Nothing could be simpler,
Mendel Visoker. When people buy something they really need . . .'

'*Cheese?*' he asked, bemused.

'For instance. When they buy things they really need they're
ready to fight and argue over the last penny. On the other hand,
when they buy something they very well could do without for a
hundred years, then they're ready to pay any price for it.'

He burst out laughing.

'And what do you sell in this second shop?'

'Anything at all,' she said. 'Anything at all, provided it is
expensive and cannot be bought elsewhere.' They had begun with
groceries but she was beginning to tire of cheeses. She explained
that what was selling best at the moment were chocolates, cakes,
coffee, tea and liqueurs. As a matter of fact she was thinking of
opening a tea-room . . .

At this point in the conversation the Polish woman protested
that she was lying in her own bed, in her own room, and she
couldn't even follow their conversation. Mendel gave her a kindly
if distracted pat on the bottom and suggested she go to sleep for a
little while. Then he asked Hannah:

'And what money did you use to do all this? You had only three
or four roubles when you arrived.'

'Two roubles,' she corrected him.

She went on to describe how she had reached an agreement
with Dobbe Klotz which allowed her twenty per cent of any
additional profit made on sales over and above the average turnover. That was at the beginning. After that she had persuaded the
Hayrick to invest a little more. With all the rents she was collecting,
Dobbe had money, even more than she herself realized. She was
hoarding it, and that was of no help to anybody.

'Especially not you,' said Mendel, in a tone that indicated that
his initial delight was over, that he was beginning to feel a strange
uneasiness. Those grey inscrutable eyes held his gaze unflinchingly.

'Especially not me,' she concurred. 'So I persuaded her to invest it. First of all in renovations, extensions, additional staff, including Rebecca – you noticed her, I could tell, she's the very pretty one . . . Is this silly fool asleep now?'

It took Mendel a long moment to realize that she was referring to Kryztina. He carefully raised the sheet: the Polish woman had indeed fallen asleep. She was even snoring a little, very quietly. He nodded towards Hannah as he let the sheet drop.

'Then,' she continued, 'the idea of a second shop occurred to me. I had three hundred and fifteen roubles of my own, which wasn't enough. Anyway, I couldn't start up another business without Dobbe, it wouldn't have been right. So I suggested she invest money in it. She didn't have enough, which meant we had to borrow some.'

Mendel suddenly felt cold. He reached out for his shirt, which hung on a nearby chair, and put it on, taking great care to protect his modesty.

Unflappable, she continued. 'I must have been to fifteen or twenty moneylenders before I finally found one who was all right. At first, he only wanted to lend us the money with the building that the Klotzes own as security, and with interest payable on the loan. In the end he settled for a thirty per cent share of the business . . .'

'He did lend you the money then?'

'Of course.'

'Who is he?'

'Leib Deitch.'

Visoker recognized the name and began to feel even colder.

'You ought to have talked to me about it, Hannah.'

'You weren't here.'

'I'm sure you could have got hold of me if you'd really wanted to.'

'That's true,' she admitted. She lowered her eyes and fiddled with some nonexistent crease in her dress. Then, for the first time since she had burst into the room, Mendel noticed what she was wearing – an unusual black-and-red dress that went wonderfully well with her pale complexion and with those steely eyes. Visoker's eye for these things was just as keen as ever, even if he had been long on this particular occasion in noticing Hannah's attire. That little body of hers could drive a sainted man to damnation. His unease persisted.

'And what does Mrs Klotz have to say about all the risks you're encouraging her to take?'

'She does what I want her to,' replied Hannah. 'Always . . . it's just a matter of time.'

With these last words she looked up at Mendel with such triumph, defiance and confidence that he immediately understood the situation for what it was. What an extraordinary influence the wretched child must have over the old woman . . .

Mendel Visoker had no presentiment of the drama to follow; for the time being he felt only anxious, and at the same time proud. After all, it was thanks to him that Hannah had got to Warsaw. He was the one she confided in, and after her father he had been the first person to see that there was something exceptional about her.

'One of two things is possible,' he told himself. 'You can gloat and pride yourself on what the kid's already done and will go on to do; she's only sixteen, after all, though she looks five or six years older in that hat and that dress and with that manner of hers, damn it; you can say to yourself that she's got genius, and that it's a pity she's only a woman, otherwise, she might become extraordinarily rich and powerful one day; or you can let her scare you. Not only because of what she's done and the risks she's taken, but you can be afraid *for* her: because of the way she uses everybody, because she is able to read minds and win over anyone from you to poor Mrs Klotz. That woman is completely spellbound, and in danger of one day waking up to it. With all that savagery in her that could be terrible, traumatic even.'

What he said was: 'Turn around.'

'Why?'

'Because I want to get out of bed, that's why.'

She smiled mockingly, but she nevertheless consented to look away so that he was able to renew his acquaintance with that severe profile of hers; he saw her smile gradually fade, to be replaced by an expression of much gravity.

He put on his jacket and Polish cap and threw a final glance at the bed: Kryztina was sleeping the sleep of the blessed. Just the kind of woman he liked: he could turn up and leave without warning and he barely heard a word of complaint.

'Let's go.'

'And where are we going?' asked Hannah.

'To that obliging friend of yours, Leib Deitch,' he answered, as he chased her down the staircase.

They found Deitch swilling down German wine in the company of three or four other moneylenders. He was a corpulent man, as heavily bearded as two rabbis; if his fingernails could be used as evidence he was probably seen very seldom at the baths. He had no objection to showing Mendel all the documents relating to Hannah's loan and his shareholding in the shop near the Arsenal. He simply remarked:

'I didn't know she was your niece.'

'No one chooses his family,' snapped Mendel.

He read and reread the papers; everything seemed to him to be in order. He asked Leib Deitch if he really believed the second shop to be a viable proposition, and was assured by the moneylender that the initial results indicated it very much was.

'I didn't have any faith in it at first, but your niece's powers of persuasion are pretty unusual . . .'

'I know,' Mendel acknowledged. 'She even managed to convince me that I'm her uncle. But I wanted to ask you a favour, Reb Leib: you're a man of experience, and your good name is not something you have to worry about establishing any more; your prudence in investing money is legendary and as for your honesty, people speak of it even as far away as the Black Sea . . .'

Deitch's eyes flickered just a little.

'Yes, yes, I tell you, people speak of it,' Mendel went on. 'And bearing that in mind, I wanted to ask you to keep an eye on my niece. If anything were to happen to her . . .'

As he spoke Mendel Visoker puffed out his chest; suddenly the room seemed to shrink to half its size:

'. . . I'd tear the head off the person responsible. And I'm not the kind of man to worry about trifling things like bits of paper, with or without signatures.'

The café-grocery store in Krochmalna Street had just closed its doors; in the square nearby, two or three brothels opened theirs. Mendel thought suddenly of Pelte 'the Wolf' Mazur and was about to ask Hannah whether the pimp had tried to see her again, but at that very moment Hannah, who was walking beside him, started to speak after a rather uncharacteristic silence. Had he asked his question a great many things would have been different.

Hannah wanted to know if Mendel's longstanding plan to leave Poland for good and make his way to Great Britain, France, or America, was still on the cards.

'Or Australia?' she asked. 'You talked to me about Australia years ago, and about your friend Schloimele, who made his fortune in Sydney and who's forever writing to ask you to join him there . . .'

Her memory always surprised him. If he started to tell her some anecdote about a certain Priluki in Odessa, she would immediately correct him: he must be mistaken, or else there were two Prilukis, because eighteen months ago he told her about a Priluki in Kiev, who had four daughters, one of whom was christened Anastasia, and she had a beauty spot above her left breast. The worst of it was that she was always right. If he decided one day to write his memoirs, he would simply call on her; she would probably be able to reel off all the names, addresses and intimate physical characteristics of every one of the women he knew from the Black Sea to the Baltic!

'Any more news of your friend Schloimele?'

'No news. He wrote to me only two or three times, that's all.'

'More like five,' she corrected him. 'And that's not counting the other letter he's probably written that will be waiting for you at the Lithuanians' in Danzig.'

Oh, for God's sake, what the devil did Schloimele Finkl and Australia and Sydney – or was it Melbourne, he always mixed them up – have to do with him, or with either of them? What was she getting at? Was she trying to pack him off to Australia? Unless she wanted to emigrate there herself? She didn't even know where Australia was!

'I know perfectly well where it is,' she said calmly. 'You go down the coast of Africa – unless you're going through the new canal – and right at the bottom you turn left; then it's straight ahead, I've seen it in my atlas. Mendel Visoker?'

Until then they had been walking side by side along Krochmalna Street, on which the stillness of night was beginning to settle. But Hannah suddenly ran ahead and called out Mendel's name. He saw her standing at the corner motionless, with that introspective gaze she sometimes had. She said in a slightly dull voice:

'I saw him again, Mendel Visoker. I mean Taddeuz Nenski.'

'I know who you meant,' he replied, feeling a sharp pang inside. 'And?'

Next to her, on the pavement, stood a handcart. She leaned against it, gently, very upright, her arms crossed behind her, her movements very much those of a grown woman, not an adolescent girl. And there in the soft night, scented lightly by the pines of the forests of Praga, she began to tell him about her very odd reunion with Taddeuz.

5

THE ROOM IN PRAGA

In September of 1890, Taddeuz returned from Prague, just as his landlady had said he would. But a year of studies remained before his qualifying exams.

Hannah was at once alerted to his arrival by the espionage network she had set up, the first link in which was Taddeuz's landlady.

'Her name's Marta Glovacki, Mendel Visoker. She believes everything I tell her, as long as my lies conform to what she wants to hear. She's very much like a barrel of salt water, except that she smells stronger. She hasn't any teeth left, and almost no hair, but thinks that all men are after her. Well, once I understood how her mind worked, it was easy. I told her one lie to start with: that Taddeuz was my half-brother. She believed me. Very quickly I realized that wasn't going to be enough, so I invented something else: that I wasn't his sister at all; far from it. I loved him, and he loved me; but while I knew that he loved me he was completely unaware of it. I told her that back in our village, in the hay in a barn, he and I had . . . Anyway, to make a long story short, she believed me again. I even think she preferred the second version, and the intrigue; she's a barrel of salt water of a very sentimental disposition.'

Visoker again felt chilled by her placid cynicism. He himself had never suffered a great deal of remorse for the tall stories he had told to persuade people to buy the goods on his *brouski*. But

Hannah's cynicism was accompanied by a patient determination, and that seemed very dangerous indeed.

'. . . When I explained to the Glovacki woman that I was prepared to sacrifice myself for Taddeuz she believed me more than ever. She cried over it in fact. She can't read, and she certainly can't read French, otherwise I would have lent her *The Two Orphans* and *The Baker's Assistant*, which she would really have enjoyed. I told her that I wanted to wait until Taddeuz finally realized that he loved me, and until he had completed his studies, even if it meant losing him forever by taking the risk that he might marry some girl from Warsaw with a large dowry. That too made her cry, the poor woman, but it worked. Now she keeps me informed and tells me of all of Taddeuz's comings and goings. If one day he were to entertain some creature, as Marta Glovacki puts it, I should know about it within two hours . . .'

One of Hannah's problems, as far as Taddeuz was concerned, was that during the autumn of 1890 and the following winter she was working sixteen or seventeen hours a day. To take time off to cross the Vistula and go to Praga, would cost her several hours, and would mean relaxing her hold on Dobbe Klotz. (She never said this in so many words but it was certainly what she thought.) On some days the risk did not seem so great: as she went over the accounts again and again she saw that the figures were higher across the board. Every innovation had borne fruit, including taking on the two salesgirls in Goyna Street. One of them was named Hindele; she was eighteen, and had the figure and the gentle character of a cow. Dobbe terrified her but she nevertheless managed to sleep while working, keeping her eyes open to give customers their change, sometimes even keeping her arm outstretched, with the ladle for measuring the curds in her hand. That said, she was capable of working without complaint for eighteen hours a day, seven days a week.

Rebecca Anielowicz was quite a different kind of girl. (She was to reappear in Hannah's life as Becky Singer.) She was stunningly beautiful, cheerful and vivacious; like Hannah, she was sixteen. The daughter of a watchmaker in Twarda Street, she was a native of Warsaw. From her very first days in the shop, she and Hannah had been friends, as they would remain – despite several storms that blew their way – for more than half a century.

In the autumn of 1890 Rebecca seemed to Hannah the easiest solution to the problem of keeping an eye on Taddeuz.

'She's the only person, apart from you, Mendel Visoker, who knows everything about Taddeuz and me. I introduced her to Marta Glovacki as my cousin; she now acts as my go-between and uses her brothers and sisters – she has fourteen of them – as spies. If I leave the shop I can rely on her for many things . . .'

'For instance, to warn you of any bid for independence on the part of Mrs Klotz.'

'That's one way of putting it.'

'Hannah, oh Hannah!' Mendel couldn't help exclaiming.

'I've never cheated Dobbe of so much as a single penny, Mendel. She was horribly lonely before you took me to stay with her and she'll be lonely when I leave her, which is bound to happen. But in the meantime I shall have made her rich and provided her with affection, in my own way . . .'

Nearly three months passed between Taddeuz's return and Hannah's decision to contact him for the first time. The reports filed by Rebecca's brothers and sisters, who kept a tail on him day after day, were worthy of the Cheka, the Tsar's secret police. She knew all of his habits; he never, for example, missed a class. 'He isn't only studying law, he's also a student of literature. I told you, I think he'll be a writer one day, even if he doesn't know it yet. He writes poetry and also *des morceaux de livres* . . . Can you say that: bits of books?'

Mendel shook his head. How the devil should he know? His French wasn't particularly good, and he didn't know any writers . . .

'I've also made inquiries at the university, which confirmed what I'd already been told: Taddeuz is extremely clever. I'm not surprised of course: I always knew how intelligent he was. And then at the end of November I saw him again.'

At the end of November, Hannah took her second afternoon off. She went to the university and met her spy for the day, a friend of one of Rebecca's brothers. The young informant briefed the head of the network: the subject was currently attending a lecture on Russian writers. As the informant was fourteen and did not know any Russian he was unable to provide any further details. Hannah thanked him and told him he would be off duty for a few hours. Then she went to . . .

'Not so fast,' Mendel cut in. 'You really mean to say that you had that boy watched?'

'Day after day, week after week, month after month.'

'By *kids*?'

'By kids. At first just by Rebecca's brothers and sisters. But very soon, that wasn't enough. We had to take on more to cover the hours. I paid them in cheese. Not the best cheese, naturally.'

'How many altogether?'

'About thirty. Some I paid in sweets. Sometimes I even gave them a penny or two as a bonus. It worked very well.'

'God Almighty!' exclaimed Mendel, swearing like a Catholic.

It was just after midnight, and Krochmalna Street was beginning to empty. Only a few figures remained in the brothel doorways.

'Go on,' said Mendel.

At the university Hannah had gone directly to the lecture room where Taddeuz was attending a talk on Russian writers. Through the door she could hear a discussion of Lermontov – 'I haven't read him, but I'm going to' – and Gogol – 'I've read his *Stories of St Petersburg* and *Dead Souls*'; when a hubbub of noise announced that the lecture was over she hid in a corner of the foyer. She saw Taddeuz emerge in the company of some fellow students.

'He's more handsome than ever, Mendel Visoker. He's grown incredibly tall, he's much taller than you, and taller than all the others; he's a real prince. He wears a blue suit, which is cut well enough even if it is old and worn, like his shirt and his shoes, which need resoling . . .'

'Perhaps you could arrange to lend him some money?' suggested Mendel facetiously. 'After all you're now rich.'

'Perhaps I will, when the time's right,' continued Hannah, making a concession to Mendel's sarcasm. 'It's true, I do know how to make money. And if he's a writer, before he becomes famous . . . we'll see. Well, that day I followed him. He attended a second lecture, a law lecture. That went on for two hours. Afterwards he left the university and wandered along Cracow Avenue for a while with two friends. I couldn't hear what they said, I was too far away, but it was easy to figure it out: his friends suggested having a drink in a café, and he said no, even though you could see he wanted to. It was clear he didn't have enough money. He continued on his own . . .'

'And you came out of hiding?'

'No.'

'I don't understand,' said Mendel.

'I wasn't yet ready for that. I thought he was going to head back to the university, but instead he sat down in the garden behind it and started to read a book. He also wrote something. After an hour or so he set off again, crossed halfway over the Praga Bridge and for a long while just stood there watching the river . . .'

'And he didn't once catch sight of you?' asked Mendel, with a sudden lump in his throat.

'No. I was very careful. When he went back to Marta Glovacki's house I waited in case he came out again. He didn't. It got dark and he lit his lamp. He must have been working . . .'

She levelled her shining, now tender gaze on Mendel:

'I'm not mad, Mendel Visoker. And I love Taddeuz, I love him with a woman's love, not a child's.'

'Perhaps you've never been a child.'

'Perhaps,' she said. 'But that doesn't mean I haven't suffered. Quite the contrary.'

'Forgive me,' said Mendel, who thought that at that moment he probably loved Hannah as he never had before, with passion, tenderness and friendship.

During the winter, armed with the information supplied by her thirty spies whose services were paid in barley sugar and slightly overripe cheeses, Hannah was able to observe Taddeuz on four subsequent occasions. She had not, however, revealed herself to him. She simply wasn't yet ready . . .

Visoker's watch read twelve thirty. In Krochmalna Street a few petrol lamps and candles still lit up the façades of buildings; the Jewish quarter was sleeping. The air grew colder and colder; it was spring, but the nights in Warsaw were freezing. Apparently insensitive to the cold, Hannah made no move to go, still resting against one of the arms of the handcart. 'There's a kind of madness in her,' thought Mendel. 'But I would just as soon get myself killed for her sake.' Nonetheless he gave way a little to his jealousy and to the cold and asked:

'So doesn't this Taddeuz of yours ever see a woman? With all your spies you must know everything about his love life, the names of the girls, the number of times he's had them . . .'

If he had entertained the slightest hope of making her lose her calm he was wasting his time. She gave him an indulgent smile that implied that she was, if anything, proud of Taddeuz's feminine conquests. She did know a fair bit about Taddeuz's love affairs, and no, she wasn't jealous. It seemed quite normal to her that a man should become experienced before settling down. In her opinion men were different from women: 'And I'm not telling you anything you don't know, since you've had a good three hundred mistresses. A woman who behaved like you would be the greatest whore in Poland . . .'

She evidently was not jealous.

'Once I even saw him with a girl. They went into her house, near the Old Market Square. She was quite a pretty girl, though she had heavy legs. I know that Taddeuz doesn't like heavy legs. I even met the girl later, passing myself off as Polish. She's a little stupid and hasn't any money. Besides, Taddeuz soon got rid of her; she bored him, as I knew she would. It's true that I don't know of all the women he's had. He certainly must have had a great many, being as handsome as he is. But that doesn't matter. I'm more disturbed about someone called Emilia. She's the daughter of an eminent lawyer, and she's very rich. Not very, very pretty, but very rich. And she too finds Taddeuz handsome. It's a bit unnerving. Taddeuz only has his mother now, and she hasn't much money – his father died last winter. He's letting this Emilia get around him, and going along with what's easiest, as usual.'

'But you'll stop that from happening.'

'Indeed I will. Until he completes his studies, I won't worry; Emilia's father won't hear of a son-in-law who isn't qualified. But after that I'll need some money myself, and not just because of Taddeuz. That's why I opened the second shop near the Arsenal, and that's why I'm going to do a number of other things.'

'You're going to become very rich.'

'Yes.'

She spoke in a flat tone of voice: she was simply stating a fact.

'She's been in Warsaw for nearly a year,' Visoker thought, 'and in all that time I'm sure she's never written to her mother, or tried to see her brother Simon – or if she's seen him, it couldn't have counted for much, especially as she's been pursuing this Pole from a distance for more than ten months . . .'

'And what about the death of your brother Yasha?'

'That's all in the past.'

'Perhaps not for your Taddeuz. It's quite possible that he may still feel ashamed, even this many years later.'

'I shall cure him of his shame.'

'But you've never even spoken to him.'

'I wasn't ready to.'

'You haven't spoken to him because you're ashamed of Dobbe?'

'A little, yes. Of Dobbe and Pinchos Klotz, of Goyna Street, of the cheeses, of the Jewish quarter, of myself. And even of you. But that's over now. I'm not ashamed of anything any more.'

She smiled and, lowering her head, seemed to study her black-and-red dress and its trappings with an air of great satisfaction.

'You were waiting for a new dress and new shoes,' said Mendel with a scorn he immediately regretted. 'You had to have the dress and shoes of a Polish lady.'

She glared at him.

'You really don't understand very much, Mendel Visoker. I had to feel ready inside myself.'

'And when will that be?'

Again she lowered her head for a brief moment, then raised it:

'I'm ready now.'

Pinchos Klotz brought the cart round to the west gate of the Saxe Gardens, at the far end of the long avenue that led away from the Potocki Palace. In the months since Hannah's arrival at the Klotzes', Pinchos had said very little, even during the many times that Hannah had accompanied him on his rounds, and when she offered new ideas about the quality of the farm produce he was buying. In her opinion, the Klotzes' produce should be different from what people could find at the Yanash Market or anywhere else in Warsaw – different and of infinitely better quality. He continued to remain silent when he was directed by Dobbe to stock the shop not only with large supplies of dairy products but also with delicatessen. He likewise complied when he was told he was to have two helpers, and that he was to supply a second shop with produce from Germany, Switzerland and France.

All the same there had been recently a strange, wordless under-standing between Hannah and Pinchos, which had lately made him begin to emerge from more than thirty years' silence. She had found the chink in his armour and had begun to read aloud to him a poem that she liked: she was certain that he appreciated poetry, and indeed wrote some himself. She even took the liberty of telling him she would like to read some of it. One day, with horrible shyness, he handed her a few sheets of his scribblings: every square millimetre of paper was covered with ink. She knew exactly what to say about the poems while they drove along together in the cart, travelling from one farm to the next, and it hardly took all of her insight to see that he derived what was doubtless the greatest happiness in his life from her compliments.

Pinchos stopped the cart at the gate and sat absolutely still, holding the reins in his tiny, neat hands. He followed her with his big black eyes when she jumped to the ground.

'Thank you,' she said.

He nodded.

She smiled up at him; for the first time on that memorable day she let her nervousness show a little.

'Till six thirty, then?' she asked, though she hardly needed to. He signalled yes.

Silence.

Then: 'Pinchos? I'm a bit afraid after all . . .'

The little man's eyes lit up with a friendly gleam; he inclined his head a little.

'I understand,' said Hannah. 'You're sure that everything will be all right.'

He nodded again as he watched her walk away.

Before passing through the gate and into the Saxe Gardens she turned around to wave.

'Everything will be all right,' his eyes reassured her, as he lowered his head with a shy half-smile.

The head of her surveillance team was posted at the main entrance to the university. He was a thirteen-year-old named Maryan Kaden, who was Jewish on his mother's side. He told Hannah that Taddeuz was in a lecture room, that he had arranged to have at least one member of the team at each of the exits to the university buildings; and that he had set up a network of couriers: 'I shall be informed instantly of his exit, no matter which route he takes, and I will let you know.' Maryan Kaden was already within a few inches of being as tall as he would ever be. He was stocky, with a thick short neck, a serious look about him, and an extremely methodical mind. His father was dead and he had got himself work unloading goods on the Vistula docks. The week before, Hannah had promised him a better job as a driver and delivery man for the shop in the Arsenal.

'Where will you be?' he asked her.

Hannah pointed to the other side of the road, opposite the Staszic Palace, and said: 'Come and see me the day after tomorrow, at the end of the day, and the job's yours. A promise is a promise.'

She crossed Cracow Avenue. When the bells of the Carmelite Church began to toll five o'clock the chimes were followed after a few seconds by the bells of St Anne's and the more distant chimes of St John's Cathedral.

Five or six minutes later Maryan crossed the road; Taddeuz was about to leave the university. All the signs indicated that he would be stopping off, as he very frequently did, at the bookshop on Holy Cross Street.

And that he would be alone.

'I'd like a copy of *A Hero of Our Time* by Mikhail Lermontov,' said Hannah, her voice just a bit too loud.

Taddeuz stood two metres behind her. When he had come into the bookshop she was already there – if a little out of breath – and he had passed very close by, though he had not noticed her.

'In Polish, please,' continued Hannah. 'Not in Russian.'

She felt her pulse starting to race and almost began to tremble: Taddeuz was only one of a dozen or so people in the shop.

The bookseller had the Lermontov only in the Russian edition.

'I'll take it anyway,' said Hannah, fighting the urge to turn around. 'And I'd also like *Happiness* by Sully-Prudhomme, *The Sea* by Jean Richepin, Charles Baudelaire's *Short Prose Poems* – those titles in French, please. And could you give me, in German, Ludwig Uhland's *Ballads*, and also . . .'

From her red-and-black purse she drew out a sheet of paper and read out in a hesitant voice:

'. . . And also, by someone called Friedrich Nietzsche, a book entitled *Thus Spake Zara* . . .'

She stopped and smiled at the bookseller with a slight air of embarrassment: 'I can't read what I've written . . .'

'Zarathustra,' said Taddeuz's voice behind her. '*Thus Spake Zarathustra.*'

'Thank you,' said Hannah mechanically, still not turning around. 'That's it. Of course,' she went on, addressing the bookseller, 'if you don't have all those books, I can easily wait for them. Would you have them delivered to . . .'

Only then, as though struck by a sudden realization, did she slowly turn around, with exactly the right degree of surprise:

'Taddeuz?'

He was so tall; at least thirty centimetres taller than she was! He stared in disbelief, and what she saw in his eyes rewarded her beyond all her wildest dreams for the long wait and for the preparations she had been making for over a year. He was genuinely incredulous, unable to stop staring at her, at her dress and her hat. She managed to smile at him, somehow overcoming the unexpected urge to cry.

'Hannah,' he said at last. 'You're Hannah.'

That part of herself that remained cool and lucid registered his use of the formal *'vous'* as her greatest triumph.

'Hannah,' he repeated, 'it's incredible . . .' He shook his head.

She abruptly turned away, incapable of controlling her trembling fingers. Facing the bookseller, she got out another piece of paper, and was able to say in a nearly normal tone of voice: 'Would you kindly have the books delivered to this address. Here are fifty roubles.'

The bookseller insisted this was too much.

'In that case, open an account for me with what's left over. I buy a good number of books.'

They went out of the shop together, she and Taddeuz. Or rather she managed things so that she went out first and he followed her. She had had every last word and gesture of this meeting planned for a very long time now: if she had been friendlier inside the bookshop, they might only have chatted there and he might have let her go easily. This way, since she had declined any immediate exchange, he was bound to come after her, intrigued. 'It's all happening the way I planned it,' she thought triumphantly, recovering nearly all her self-control.

Taddeuz was talking, still expressing his amazement. He had not known she was in Warsaw, and certainly had not expected to see her 'so changed' – and particularly in a bookshop, buying volumes of poetry, when he himself read so much poetry. And this he said with a shyness she thought affected, only the ploy of a wily seducer . . .

Oh Lizzie, I was so stupid that time in Warsaw when, at sixteen, I finally met Taddeuz again! I had worked out all kinds of incredibly complicated, nearly machiavellian ruses, and I was so proud of them. I credited Taddeuz with a cunning, an experience of women and of life that he was a very long way from possessing. I even went so far as to think, poor fool that I was, that I had tempted him with the fifty roubles I brought out in the bookshop. In other words, I made a mess of everything. As far back as then. Just as I'm going to make a mess of the rest of it . . .

Shyly he asked if he could address her as *'tu'*, as was perhaps more appropriate to childhood friends:

'After all, I've . . . I knew you when you were . . .'

'I'm eighteen,' she volunteered adding a good twenty-two months to her age. 'And of course we can address each other as "*tu*" . . .'

She walked along with her head lowered and guessed what was going on inside his. Surely he was remembering their first encounters beside the stream. She knew the dangers of such reminiscences: any second now and he was going to come to the barn, his own cowardice, Yasha's death. And indeed he very soon slowed his pace and began to stiffen: 'That's it, it's all come back to him,' she thought, 'now's the time to speak.'

She said hurriedly:

'I've cut my ties with my family, Taddeuz, and with my village. I'm living on my own now, thanks to a legacy my Uncle Bunim left me. It's extraordinary suddenly to find oneself with so much money. I don't know what I'm going to do with it. Travel, perhaps. Have you ever been to Vienna, or Paris?'

He seemed to recover himself too: no, he had never been away save to Prague, the previous summer, when he had visited an aunt. From his tone of voice Hannah sensed she had underestimated his remorse; stricken by conscience, he was probably quite tempted to dump her there and then. With the sole aim of gaining time, she quickly began talking again. In her panic she expanded on the details of her inheritance, elaborated on her travel plans. She said that she had not yet received her capital, that for the present she was allowed only an income of two hundred and forty roubles a month (she knew this to be precisely four times the amount Taddeuz received from his mother); it would be months before her wealthy uncle's estate was settled.

As the minutes went by the risk of Taddeuz leaving her receded. He expansively replied to her unnecessary questions about his lodgings, his studies, how he passed the time. And what about books, she asked. Had he read Lermontov? (*A Hero of Our Time* was one of the titles that had caught her eye when she visited his room in Praga; she had noticed that there were a great many pieces of paper between its pages, as though the book had been annotated.) From that point on their conversation took on a warm almost conspiratorial turn.

They arrived at the Vistula escarpment behind the Radziwill Palace. Hannah began to walk along a steep path and soon stumbled, not very certain herself whether she had done so deliberately. Taddeuz caught her just in time, but kept his hand on her arm even after she had regained her balance . . .

'I almost didn't recognize you, Hannah.'

His voice was deep, low, almost rough, and his eyes searched Hannah's. The gentle pressure of his fingers urged her to turn around and face him . . .

'Hannah . . .'

'He's going to try and kiss me,' she thought. This too she had anticipated; it was the reason why she had chosen this path beneath the trees, where they would be alone. She had tried very carefully to prepare herself for this occasion by rereading all the pertinent books – including *Les Liaisons Dangereuses*, which she'd read five times – but they remained mysterious on many essential points. And Rebecca, whom she had questioned, had not been a great deal of help either. Nevertheless, she had already decided on her strategy: if he did attempt such a thing she would gently disengage herself, like a *grande dame* (the expression came to her in French); above all he must not take her for a *fille facile* . . .

For once, however, she discovered her calculations to be inaccurate. For while she did disengage herself, there was nothing gentle about it; she practically leapt away from him, unable to control herself. 'You fool,' she scolded herself, 'you're lucky you didn't find yourself up a tree, flying away like that!' She failed to notice at the time – and here was a crucial error – that Taddeuz was not very adroit either.

In the ensuing moments she took refuge once again in literature, moving on to Stéphane Mallarmé, though she had never read so much as a line he had written – all she knew was his name. From there she raced to de Musset, with whom she was no more familiar, whose first name she gave as Albert.

'Alfred,' Taddeuz corrected her.

'I was referring to your brother,' said Hannah, quickly trying to cover up her mistake.

'Oh really?' said Taddeuz, who seemed genuinely surprised.

The rest of their meeting went more smoothly, especially once she had abandoned the subject of literature, where she was decidedly on rather slippery ground. When she talked instead of travel and of her forthcoming inheritance she became much more at ease; she knew with absolute certainty that she would one day be very rich and that she would travel, following the routes she had drawn in her atlas three years ago.

The cathedral bells had long since struck six and she was still talking, inexhaustibly.

'Hannah,' he said suddenly, 'I don't even know your surname . . .'

She stared at him, dumbfounded. She had been so engrossed in her lies that she had not noticed that he wasn't listening any more. He too was staring at her, but with an unmistakable gentleness. She believed it to be feigned and she continued to think him insincere when he began to tell her that he felt very lonely in Warsaw, that he was very happy to have bumped into her, that he hoped to see her again . . .

I was so stupid, Lizzie, so stupid, I really thought he was trying to make me feel sorry for him. Since I'd been lying, he must have been lying as well; that's how I thought at the time . . .

He spoke in a gentle voice, with a shy, almost apologetic smile.

'Yes, we could perhaps see each other again,' she said, her tone of voice implying that such an idea had only just occurred to her.

She smiled. 'Why not?'

As she had been the one to choose the direction they should follow all the time they were walking, they emerged in the Old Market Square at exactly the hour she had intended. A barouche had in fact just appeared and was drawing near the couple. Pinchos was dressed in a liveried uniform that came very close to fitting him, apart from the hat which slipped over his eyes. All the same he raised it as he opened the carriage door for Hannah.

'I have to go now,' she apologized, and again pretended to think. In the end it was she who suggested when they should next meet – not the next day, or the day after that, as Taddeuz proposed, but the following week. Unless of course she had to go and visit that factory in Lodz that her Uncle Bunim had left her, in which case – but she did have so much to do as a result of this inheritance!

They agreed to rendezvous at the bookshop in Holy Cross Street, seven days later, at five o'clock.

The following week, she turned up, intentionally, a good twenty minutes late. Knowing Taddeuz could not possibly afford such an extravagance she asked him to take her for a hot chocolate on the terrace of one of the cafés in the Saxe Gardens; she announced that she would pay for the drinks. He smiled without replying and himself gave the waitress one rouble and six kopeks when she set down their hot chocolates. Hannah thought: 'I know what he's up to: he's making an investment, so to speak, and only when he's squandered the little money he has will he accept as his due the five hundred or one thousand roubles that I shall give him.'

For this second meeting she had prepared a very detailed description of the factory in Lodz and of the buildings in Warsaw she was going to inherit, but as soon as she started speaking he interrupted and asked her about herself, about what she liked, about her daily life in Warsaw. She deduced that he was trying to pretend not to be interested in her money. Such hypocrisy upset her, though she did not find it entirely surprising, especially as she was particularly tired that day: having got up at three o'clock, she had spent the day running from Goyna Street to the Arsenal. Dobbe had given her a very hard time over a mistake made by Rebecca that had cost them one rouble and nineteen kopeks; furthermore, on the strength of his co-ownership of the second shop, Leib Deitch had tried to get rid of Maryan Kaden whom he considered too friendly with the clients. (The real reason for Deitch's hostility towards Maryan – as Hannah was well aware – was the boy's fervent loyalty to her.)

And then there was Pelte Mazur.

He was proving something of a nuisance, though not giving her any concrete cause for concern. Hannah was not the kind of person to be afraid of a man like Mazur; besides, she had taken precautions, and been careful not to mention his name to Mendel Visoker, whom she knew to be capable of killing the Wolf and probably only too happy to do so. On three or four occasions Mazur had planted himself in her path on Goyna Street, forcing her to make a detour. He had stopped playing that idiotic game the day that Hannah had ground a cheese – which she had had ready for the purpose – into his face, an act that had delighted the entire street. Since then however the pimp had been following her on occasion; two, even three weeks could go by without a sign of him and then suddenly one night she would realize he was trailing her, always at a distance.

Mazur – who as it turned out had been a knife-thrower in a circus – did not appear at any point during Hannah's second meeting with Taddeuz, but she saw him, or thought she saw him, the third time they met, when she and Taddeuz visited the elegant Visitandines Church.

There was no sign of him at their fourth meeting, or the fifth,

when Hannah finally agreed to go back with Taddeuz to his room
in Praga.

'And this is the terrace,' he said.

She walked with him through the French doors; the room was
actually cooler than the terrace, on to which the late-September
sun, now due west, was shining directly. It caught Hannah full in
the face so that she had to screw up her eyes to make out Warsaw
on the opposite bank of the Vistula. She was no fool, however, and
she knew the sun had nothing to do with her discomfort. She was
about to make love with Taddeuz. She had known for years – in
fact, she had always known – that this was the way things would
happen, and the time had come.

Her hands were trembling a little. She laid them on the wooden
balustrade and forced them to relax. At the same time, she took
several deep breaths, willing her lungs and heart to resume a
regular rhythm. She could feel the warmth spread through her
belly as she moved away from the balustrade.

'Your flowers could really use a watering.'

'It would have been difficult to come up with a more ridiculous
remark than that,' she thought immediately after speaking. She
turned around. Taddeuz was standing back slightly from the
doorway, out of the sun's warmth, and he was staring at her. He
seemed to be waiting for something. What was she supposed to
do? They had been alone, in his bedroom, for more than half an
hour and he had not made the slightest move even though they
had several times found themselves very close to each other, she
breathing in his smell, which she had so well remembered. They
had stood side by side for what had seemed to her an interminable
length of time, for at least twenty deliciously cruel minutes, while
he had shown her his books, a hundred or so in all, one by one.
The silence, which became denser by the moment, began to oppress
Hannah even more than the sight of the big four-poster bed had
earlier.

*There again, Lizzie, it didn't occur to me that he might be horribly
intimidated, virtually paralysed by his real love for me, by the genuine
respect he had for me. I thought him so full of experience . . .*

She walked across the terrace and back into the room; he stepped
aside just as she reached him. She interpreted his retreat as a
rejection and at once – with that lightning quickness with which

her feelings so often changed – she felt ashamed, angry, desperate. He did not want her, that was clear. He was rejecting her even when she had given him every reason to believe that she was ready to give him everything. She stood motionless in the middle of the room, wide-eyed and overwhelmed with despair. When she had first entered his room she had put her hat, her Irish lace gloves, her pearl-encrusted purse (the pearls were fake but looked completely genuine) on a blue velvet armchair. Practically with her eyes closed she took a first step towards the armchair, then a second. In those brief moments she had a very clear picture of herself hurtling downstairs to Marta Glovacki's astonishment, then running down the street like a mad woman to the Praga Bridge, from which she would hurl herself into the river . . .

Only then did she feel the hand on her shoulder. Prompted by some last vestige of pride, perhaps too by feminine instinct, she tried a little – a very little – to resist succumbing to its pressure. Taddeuz's other hand circled her waist. He drew her against him.

One part of her was aroused, almost unable to breathe, overcome by an extraordinary sense of triumph. But at the same time that impersonal part of her that always remained outside her situation was set into motion. She had promised herself this much: she would miss nothing, not a single detail, of the first time she made love to Taddeuz, the first man she would give herself to and the only one she ever intended to give herself to. She finally relaxed and let herself go, all the while fully aware of what was happening. Taddeuz's fingers had travelled from her waist to her breasts. And she could feel his body too, now pressed against her own, its relief charted against her back. There were some things that her books, even Monsieur Laclos's, had failed to mention . . .

She knew that he was supposed to undress her with great tenderness, but nothing of the sort happened. After he had clasped her in his arms, she was the one who had to turn around to face him so that she could rest her head against his chest, to feel that strange part of him whose strength she had been for so long unaware of. Taddeuz's arms held her like a wolf trap. He had bent down to press his mouth against her own, but she was not convinced that this was what people called an unforgettable kiss. It felt more like being suffocated. She freed herself and immediately wanted to laugh, especially when she saw the expression on his face: he thought she was rejecting him.

If I had only known, Lizzie, if I had only known what a mixture of shyness and pride could be like . . .

'Help me, would you . . .'

She spun round and presented him again with her back, with the thirty-nine silk buttons that ran down her red-and-black dress. But he seemed not to understand. What dream was he lost in? Was he mixing her up with someone else, she wondered? His arms came around her again, clumsily caressing her breasts. She squeezed her eyes tightly shut, torn between the desire to laugh and to scream out in exasperation. Only at that moment did it occur to her that he might not be toying with her, that perhaps he didn't *know* what to do.

'The buttons, please, Taddeuz.'

A minute later Taddeuz for all his willingness had only undone four buttons. 'Thirty-five to go,' she calculated to herself, 'we'll still be here in three days' time!' And she was shaken with laughter, a laughter she couldn't suppress. He froze.

'What's wrong?'

'Nothing. Go on.'

He didn't move, then he withdrew slightly. Quietly he asked: 'I'm a complete fool, is that it?'

A few seconds went by.

She turned around slowly and confidently. For the first time since finding him again by the stream she saw him as he really was. He was exceptionally beautiful, as she had always known, but there was in the depths of his blue eyes a sad and pensive tenderness. He seemed already resigned to defeat.

'I'm a complete fool,' he repeated, a look of stubbornness on his face. 'And laughable as well.'

'That's not true,' she said, annoyed that he should be so quick to give up.

She no longer felt any desire to laugh.

He stared at her, still immobile, though he allowed his clenched fists to relax slightly. She sat down on the bed and gently drew him to her, indicating that he should sit beside her.

'Kiss me,' she murmured.

She lay back and held Taddeuz's face between the palms of her hands, exactly as she had dreamed of doing a thousand times.

'Gently . . .'

Their lips barely touched. Their mouths played lovingly with each other, moving on to explore other regions of the other's face.

Occasionally, for a split second, Hannah stopped thinking entirely and felt her flesh thrill to his touch; she had never known before this tingling. 'He's kissing me, Taddeuz is kissing me' – the words floated to the surface now and then, before being swallowed up again by the pleasure that washed over her. There was nothing bookish about these sensations, they weren't coming to her second-hand like those Rebecca had described to her.

She made no attempt to undo the buttons on her dress herself. She knew that she would not be able to; generally Rebecca helped her to undress. She was intoxicated with love and weak with expectation. Taddeuz's embraces were becoming increasingly urgent and would soon turn into desperate manoeuvres to discover more of her. A wave of anger flooded over her: this wretched dress was a stubborn obstacle between the two of them! The next time she would buy a different style of dress, a simple one, one that a woman and a man could slip off at the appropriate time without having to behave like novice acrobats.

Taddeuz could no longer restrain himself. His body pressed against hers with a violence that frightened her a little. She knew that in a moment he would be inside her, and she knew that she wanted him, whatever happened; she wanted him now and for ever, all her plans, all their adolescent ignorance aside. She lay back on the bed and herself pulled up her dress and the petticoat she wore underneath, making Taddeuz raise himself slightly to allow her to do so. Amongst all the layers of material around her she found the cord drawn round her waist that held up her lace-trimmed bloomers and she untied its knot with great difficulty. She did not bother with her garters and stockings; this was the way he would have to take her.

And yet before he responded to her actions Taddeuz did something very odd, something she would never forget. He took off his shirt in a swift and graceful movement that contrasted entirely with what had gone before and what was to follow. For a moment he remained still, then he took hold of Hannah's hands, drew them to his chest and placed them on his heart. From the depths of her tiredness, her expectation, her pleasure and disappointment, through her dishevelled hair, Hannah saw him, looking miraculously strong and handsome, capable of anything, heartbreakingly so. She closed her eyes.

She did not see him free himself and try to penetrate her; she knew nothing of his appalling dread of hurting her, of making her

bleed. She took his throbbing penis in her hands and guided him
to her, sensing he was on the verge of tears. Then she was conscious
only of the tearing of her hymen, which seemed to be repeated
with every movement he made. She had expected this pain and
thought she was prepared for it, but she had never imagined it
would be so keen and so constant, so likely to redouble in intensity
whenever she thought it had subsided. Hannah bit her lips so as
not to cry out, and to prevent herself from begging him to stop.

More than anything else she would remember her sense of failure
that evening; every one of her subsequent meetings with Taddeuz
in his bedroom in Praga, from the end of the summer throughout
the winter of 1891, would be similarly branded with it. She barely
knew if she even desired him any more. And yet she did, she
wanted him as she could not, even in her wildest imaginings,
dream of desiring another man. But very little came to replace the
pain.

'So very little, Lizzie. I felt almost nothing when he was inside me. It
was as though my love for him was in abeyance. I thought there was
something wrong with me, and it's true that in a certain way there was
something wrong with me; the Hannah that I was then, when I was in
Warsaw, lived on a level of uncompromising need and fanaticism. She
wanted to have everything and didn't know how to give . . .'

In order to open the second shop Hannah had had to find someone
to lend his name to it, someone Polish. She could not be registered
as the shop's manager because of her age; and Dobbe, after having
agreed to do so, had later refused to fulfil this role. The Hayrick
gave her difficulties in walking and her reclusive character, as the
reasons for her refusal. Eventually the store was opened in the
name of one Sluzarki, who had been suggested by Leib Deitch.
Deitch suggested him again, in December 1891, when she needed
an official manager for a third shop.

With this third concern, a new and much more important stage
began in Hannah's development. This shop was not a grocery store,
or a delicatessen, but a dress shop, a women's dress shop. Maryan
Kaden was to be the only person who knew anything about the
enterprise, and he knew what he knew indirectly. Even Rebecca
would always remain completely unaware of the store's existence,
a surprising fact given the two girls' closeness. Kaden first learned
of the project in mid-October, when Hannah asked him if there

might not be someone reliable on the Polish side of his family who would be willing to spend a few hours in a shop, who looked respectable, and who would agree to sign papers without attempting to make sense of them. Kaden eventually came up with some distant uncle or other, who had been out of work since getting mixed up in politics at the time of the 1862 anti-Russian rebellion. The uncle was eventually taken on as manager by the two business partners at the end of what Maryan was to remember as an extremely bitter argument between Leib Deitch and Hannah.

There were two partners this time, not three: Dobbe Klotz was left out of Hannah's plans entirely, a fact that would not be without repercussions.

So the third shop opened in December 1891, towards the beginning of the month. Unlike the shop in which Hannah had bought her first dress it was of modest size, employing only two saleswomen, whom Hannah herself hired. It was located a stone's throw from Cracow Avenue, right in the centre of town.

It was relatively easy for Hannah to manage to see her project through without revealing anything at all about it to Dobbe Klotz; for months she had been dividing her time between the two grocery stores, and it would have been impossible for anyone to keep close track of her whereabouts.

As for the manner in which she managed to persuade Leib Deitch to become a partner in this new enterprise, Maryan remained wholly ignorant. He would simply remember the figure of two thousand four hundred roubles, the sum total of Hannah's personal investment and he would recall that Hannah had been her own first client, choosing a chic, red and black dress for herself. It was slightly décolleté and it buttoned down the front.

The first signs that Hannah was beginning to wear down physically were visible as early as mid-October. Rebecca noticed them, and became worried. 'It's nothing but a little tiredness,' explained Hannah. And indeed, as the weeks passed, the young businesswoman's state of health seemed to improve. Better still, from December on, her narrow face took on a radiance that Rebecca interpreted as the happy result of Hannah's liaison with Taddeuz.

In a way she was not mistaken.

And then at the end of 1891, Rebecca Anielowicz herself became engaged, which kept her fairly preoccupied. She was to marry the son of a very wealthy scarf manufacturer from Lodz who was willing to overlook her rather meagre dowry, thinking only of the face of his betrothed. The wedding was to take place the following spring.

It was agreed that Rebecca would stop working for the Klotzes from the first day of January 1892.

So she was not there when it happened.

6

PELTE THE WOLF

On the evening of January 6th Hannah returned to Goyna Street much later than usual, at about midnight. She went quietly to her room, but somehow or other – probably because she had spent hours listening carefully for Hannah's return – Dobbe heard her and heaved her bulk up to the fifth floor.

She found Hannah already in bed, with the blankets drawn to her neck. The oil lamp burned beside her.

'You've forgotten to put out the light,' said Dobbe.

No reply. Hannah's eyes were, and remained, closed,

'I know you're not asleep,' Dobbe insisted, as she stepped into the bedroom, something she had not done since Hannah had moved in. Climbing those stairs did not really agree with her heavy legs, swollen by fifty years of shopkeeping. Apart from the bed the room contained a little table, a chair, and an improvised wardrobe consisting of a piece of string and a cretonne curtain. The halo of lamplight fell on some papers and books on the table; more lay on the floor. Dobbe sat down on the chair to recover from her climb.

'I want to talk to you, I know you're not asleep.'

'*Not this evening,*' said Hannah slowly and with enormous effort.

There was something very odd about her voice; though the lamp wick was low and cast only a little light Dobbe Klotz could make out blotches on her temples and a dark stain on the pillowcase. The collar of Hannah's dress poked out over the edge of the

blanket, revealing that she had got into bed without undressing.
Dobbe turned up the light.

'Are you hurt?'

'I . . . fell . . .' said Hannah, in the same syncopated manner.

'You're lying,' Dobbe replied simply.

Slowly, heavily, Dobbe stood up and came towards the bed: she
saw a bleeding bruise at Hannah's temple and another on her jaw.
And that was not all. When she lifted the blankets the Hayrick
found the girl's dress in ruins. Hannah held her eyes closed and
continued to lie motionless. She was deathly pale. Dobbe's fat
hands tried to prop her up, but they succeeded only in exacting a
plaintive little cry.

'Someone beat you up!'

Dobbe pulled the covers back: Hannah's dress and chemise were
in tatters about her chest, her breasts exposed, one of them scored
with a fine gash. The lower part of her dress was covered in blood.
Dobbe lifted it up; Hannah had nothing on underneath.

Dobbe did not ask any questions: she was certain she knew what
had happened. The folds on the muzzle that served her as a face
tensed in a fierce expression of rage. She suddenly became aware
of the cold in the room and despite the young girl's moans wrapped
Hannah tightly in the blanket; picking her up, blanket and all, she
carried her downstairs. On the first floor she put Hannah in her
own bed, which she then dragged over to the stove.

'Who raped you, Hannah? Who was it?'

Hannah opened her grey eyes a fraction.

'Don't say anything about it to Mendel Visoker, Dobbe, I beg
you . . .'

Dobbe removed her dress and chemise, cutting them loose from
neck to hem with a knife. She bent over the naked body; her flat-
tipped fingers touched the drying semen on her pubic hair.

'Open your legs.'

Hannah seemed not to have heard. Dobbe forced her thighs
apart and bent over to examine her more closely. A very thin cut,
undoubtedly one made by the blade of a knife, ran from her
abdomen to her groin. Dobbe heated some water on the stove and
washed the young girl twice over.

'Can you hear me, Hannah?'

'Don't say anything to Mendel . . .'

'Who did this to you?'

'Don't say anything to . . .'

She was losing consciousness. Dobbe feared, when Hannah's eyes rolled up, that she might even be dying, but the small face quickly grew taut with the effort to remain conscious.

'Dobbe, I'm in pain, very great pain . . .'

Dobbe began to cry. She placed her giant hands around Hannah's hips resting her cheek against the naked belly. Hannah screamed. Panic-stricken Dobbe leapt up.

Hannah said: 'I'm pregnant, Dobbe.'

Towards one-thirty in the morning Hannah seemed finally to have fallen asleep under the effect of the laudanum that the Hayrick had forced her to swallow. Dobbe had covered her up with all the blankets and quilts she could find, and she continued to keep the stove well fuelled.

At precisely the point at which she decided she had done everything she could, Pinchos made an unprecedented appearance, his nightcap on his head. Blinking like an owl, he did not say a word. His eyes alone questioned Dobbe.

'Bugger off!' she advised him in a rage.

He retreated to his cellar.

Though Hannah still occasionally moaned very quietly in her sleep like a sick child, she appeared to Dobbe to be asleep. After watching over her for another half-hour she decided it would be safe to leave Hannah on her own. For the second time that night she climbed the five storeys to the attic, pulling herself up by the handrail and stopping on every landing to rest her legs. In Hannah's room she noticed nothing remarkable, until she saw the blood in the washbowl, which was far too copious to have come only from Hannah's wounds.

And until she saw the empty wardrobe, where the one hundred and thirty-two rouble red-and-black dress was no longer hanging . . .

And until she saw the streaks of blood on the lower edge of the pillowcase. Dobbe lifted the pillow and underneath it discovered a small cut-throat razor with a bone handle. It was half open, and its blade sticky with blood; so too was the handle.

'She used it!' Dobbe was overcome with a proud and savage joy. 'I hope she slit his throat with it!'

She seized the razor and dropped it in the wash bowl: she then removed the pillowcase, as well as the blood-stained sheet and blanket. She would wash everything and remove all traces of Hannah's misfortune. In the state she was in, in the grip of such extraordinary hatred, the idea that Hannah had doubtless killed a man caused her little concern. She was about to leave the room, the linen rolled up in a ball under her arm and the bowl in both hands, when her eyes fell on the little table, the only part of the room that might conceal any further mystery.

She ended up by opening its drawers, of course, having put down the wash bowl. Inside she found a bundle of manuscript pages, all penned in the same broad masculine handwriting. They were poems written in Polish, but not signed. Dobbe glanced through them, looking for some clue as to who the author might be but found nothing. Only then did she turn them over; inscribed at the bottom of the first page on the right, in Hannah's small cramped handwriting were the words: *6 September 1891 – Taddeuz made love to me for the first time.*

The remaining sheets were dated at roughly weekly intervals, but otherwise they were left blank. The most recent was 30 December. On only one other occasion did Hannah add a commentary: *28 November – I'm a little frightened.*

Dobbe's huge paws trembled then ventured further into the drawer. Her first discovery was a fat leatherbound notebook. Dobbe opened it and found mostly figures inside . . .

Oh Lizzie, I only wrote 'I'm a little afraid' when I discovered I was expecting Taddeuz's child. And I was worried not so much about my condition – I was so proud and happy to be carrying his child – as about the consequences it would have on my life as it was then, with all those millions of things I had to do, those three shops I had to look after, the other shop I wanted to open. It's true, I worried too about what Taddeuz's reaction would be. Of course I hadn't said anything to him. I didn't want him to think I was trying to force his hand by making him marry me just because I was pregnant. And as he always does what's right, he certainly would have married me instantly . . .

. . . The figures were written in columns, a dozen to each page of the leatherbound notebook, numbered from one to twelve. It did not take Dobbe long to realize that the first column recorded the turnover of the shop in Goyna Street; the second, Hannah's personal share of the receipts calculated on the basis of the agreement the two women had made early on; the third, the turnover or to be more precise the profits, of the store in the Arsenal; the fourth, Hannah's share of these same profits.

All this was in a handwriting that was so tiny and cramped as to be nearly illegible. The regularity of it was unnerving, but it was not so much the meticulous care taken over these entries that alarmed Dobbe. Nor was it the fact that on the day she had made her agreement about sharing the profits from the shop in Goyna Street Hannah was obviously already thinking of additional shops and had kept her books accordingly. What made Dobbe Klotz's blood run cold, what set her teetering on the brink of madness, were her other two discoveries that Hannah had opened a third shop without telling her anything about it (and this shop was already extremely profitable, although this detail was of no importance to Dobbe), and that Hannah was regularly paying money to this Taddeuz, about whom Dobbe knew nothing at all apart from the fact that he had got Hannah pregnant and that she was afraid of him. There were no two ways about it: Hannah had opened a column which she had headed TAD, the figures inscribed in it – between ten and twenty roubles on each occasion – corresponded exactly to the dates that appeared on the backs of the sheets of paper the poems were written on.

To a third discovery Dobbe – carried away by her anger – paid scant attention. Wrapped in a soft moiré ribbon was a piece of dark wood inlaid at one end with two tiny fragments of red glass that looked like eyes.

Dobbe locked the bedroom door and made her way downstairs carrying the linen and the washbowl. She found Pinchos standing at the foot of her bed.

'What are you doing here?'

'Cried,' said Pinchos.

A moment later, as if to clarify his laconic explanation, Hannah cried out again. The sound escaped from deep in her throat and was cut short by a moan. At the same time the upper part of her body tensed and arched up.

'Doctor,' said Pinchos.

'No.'

'Dying,' said Pinchos.

'*No!*'

For the first time in a quarter of a century Dobbe's eyes met Pinchos's.

'Get out,' Dobbe snarled.

Pinchos did not budge at first. He continued to stare at Dobbe with devastating intensity, all his strength burning in the black eyes that were normally so gentle and veiled. Then he turned away.

'Pinchos?'

He paused with his back to her.

'She's been raped,' said Dobbe. 'She's sick, but especially inside her head.'

He did not move.

'In her room was a little razor with a bone handle. You used to have one just like it.'

No response.

'Did you give it to her, Pinchos?'

He made no sign that he had heard his wife.

'You did give it to her. So you must have known she was in danger of being attacked, and by whom.'

Still no sign.

Still holding the blood-filled washbowl, she continued dramatically:

'I think, I hope, that she killed him with this razor. Pinchos, Hannah isn't in my room, you haven't seen her tonight. Yesterday evening she came to tell us that she had to return to her *shtetl* because her mother was ill and that she was going to stay there as long as she was needed. You don't know anything else.'

She still received no response from her husband, who, she suddenly realized, was completely dressed, wearing his phylacteries and a prayer shawl.

'*Pinchos?*'

Finally he motioned to her vaguely with the back of his hand and left the room. About half an hour later Dobbe heard his footsteps in the courtyard, where he harnessed his horse as he usually did before making his rounds. She heard the sound of the cart and horse in the alleyway and then out in Goyna Street. The sound grew fainter and died away.

Hannah continued to moan and stir restlessly in her sleep. Occasionally she cried out in a pain that Dobbe Klotz in all good faith mistakenly believed to stem from psychological rather than physical causes. It was for this reason that she increased the doses of laudanum to ten grains, eighty drops – in other words to a little less than the dose she took herself when her legs gave her too much pain. The drug had its effect: the cries ceased, replaced by a gentle moaning which would at least not be heard either in neighbouring apartments or, more importantly, in the shop. The

Hayrick would thus be able to conceal Hannah's presence in her room for as long as necessary, and to keep Hannah for herself.

Not for a moment, I'm sure, did she suspect that she was in the process of killing me, Lizzie . . .

On January 7th Maryan Kaden did not, to his surprise see Hannah all day. He was not alarmed; his confidence in her was absolute. He finished his usual day's work as driver of the delivery cart for the shop in the Arsenal and at nine o'clock, when the shop closed, took up the surveillance of Taddeuz, relieving another child from duty. Taddeuz was at home, probably busy reading or writing. Having assured himself that the student would not be going out again in the course of the evening, Maryan went home to his mother and his eight younger brothers and sisters, all of whom lived on his wages.

Three more days went by with no sign of Hannah. Maryan began to grow anxious, especially in view of other events: on the afternoon of the tenth Leib Deitch appeared at the shop in the Arsenal in person, which was a rare occurrence. Without wasting any time, he told the young boy that he was fired as of the following day and that he would be replaced by a man Deitch himself had hired.

'Yes, of course your lady friend agrees,' Leib Deitch replied to Maryan's question. 'She and I discussed the matter before she went away.'

Maryan had lived through enough difficult situations to have developed a sturdy disposition. But worse was yet to come: when he went to see his uncle at the dress shop in Cracow Avenue he learned that Deitch had visited earlier in the morning and insisted his uncle sign papers which seemed to indicate Deitch had bought out the entire business.

That same evening, Maryan paid a hesitant visit to Goyna Street. He was surprised to find the dairy closed although it was barely seven o'clock. As Maryan did not know either of the salesgirls he resolved to question Dobbe Klotz herself, though he did not look forward to doing so: the fat old woman had always made him feel ill at ease. He went down the corridor and knocked on the door to the private apartment. Dobbe soon appeared but instead of asking him in she dragged him back out into the street. Yes, she said, it was true that Hannah had left Warsaw for a few days, perhaps longer; Dobbe had received a letter from their friend to say she had arrived safely back at her *shtetl* and was still very concerned about her mother's health.

Out of pride Maryan neglected to make any mention of having lost his job, though he assumed Dobbe knew about it. He did not want to beg, especially not of this giant shrew whose face was even more impassive than usual and who looked very much on edge.

He went away.

It was Pinchos who must have got the doctor to come, Lizzie, and it probably cost him a fierce confrontation with Dobbe. In any case, he saved my life by calling to my bedside a doctor who had studied in Vienna with the famous Semmelweiss. I don't think any ordinary doctor could have cured the puerperal fever that followed my miscarriage, especially with the pelvic fracture I had, and all those kicks I'd been dealt. I have no recollection of the first few days, but in my delirium I must have said a great deal too much. My first memory was of the doctor beseeching me not to move about in bed so that my fracture could mend. And I remember the shadowy figure of Pinchos, who came to watch over me in silence while Dobbe worked in the shop. He would watch me with those big sad eyes of his, which said so many things it was wholly unnecessary for him to speak . . .

But mostly it's Dobbe that I recall; she was omnipresent. I was extremely weak, and it was she who fed and washed and caressed me, with those enormous male hands of hers. Sometimes when I wasn't too stupefied by all that laudanum she was giving me I would catch her eye and see her great internal anger; I know now but didn't know then that she was plotting her revenge which she believed to be our revenge. I asked her if I could see Rebecca and Maryan Kaden. She told me that Rebecca had gone to join her fiancé in Lodz but that she would ask Maryan to come as soon as I was better. The days went by, though I easily lost count of them; in fact more than three weeks elapsed but Dobbe led me to believe I had been unconscious only for a few days.

She did not mention Leib Deitch and what he was up to. And of course she didn't say anything about Taddeuz. I didn't know at the time that she knew all about him, or thought she did, thanks to her search of my bedroom, and thanks especially to that little fool Rebecca. Nor did she tell me about the letter she was about to write to Mendel Visoker.

I only learned of its existence on February 23rd, after everything had happened and it was already too late.

*

It was about January 20th when Maryan was lucky enough to get his job back unloading goods on the Vistula docks. It was work that kept him busy mostly at night and therefore left him plenty of time during the day. Accordingly he took on additional work as a porter in the Yanash Market; since he was expecting Hannah to return any day, he also continued to make sure that Taddeuz was watched, as she had asked him to.

And so it was that he witnessed the incident that set things in motion. In need of a confidante he went to see Rebecca, who was indeed getting ready for her wedding but – contrary to what Dobbe had said – who had not yet left for Lodz. To Maryan's great disappointment, Rebecca was no better informed than he: Hannah was presumably back in her village looking after her mother.

'She'll be back soon enough,' Rebecca gaily concluded, never one to worry. Maryan listed for her the things that disturbed him, about both the management of the shop in the Arsenal and that of the dress shop (Rebecca was put out to learn only now of its existence), but she paid him little attention: business and Leib Deitch's plots left her stonily indifferent, and she thought Maryan deadly dull to begin with. She did prick up her ears however when the boy mentioned Taddeuz.

'Taddeuz Nenski? And what's our fine friend Taddeuz up to?'

(Consumed with curiosity, one day she had literally torn out of Dobbe's shop to catch a glimpse of the student. Up until then she had thought that Hannah had been exaggerating a bit. But no; Rebecca had been transfixed by the sight of him, the handsomest boy a girl could ever dream of, handsome beyond belief. And so elegant . . .)

Maryan Kaden described the scene he had witnessed. Two days earlier Taddeuz had been invited to dinner at the Wlolstkas, the home of the wealthy lawyer with the unmarried daughter, whom Hannah had particularly asked him to keep an eye on. After dinner he had seen the student walking in the gardens of the house on Marshalkovski Avenue, arm in arm with the young lady, who looked completely smitten by him.

'I managed to speak to one of the Wlolstkas' servants,' said Maryan, 'and there's talk of an engagement. And there's something else too: Hannah gave Taddeuz an address he could use if he wanted to get in touch with her. I went by the place: there are two letters for Hannah from the student, but the caretaker wouldn't give them to me. Besides, I wouldn't know what to do with them if she did.'

What Rebecca, the future Becky Singer, would remember above all was her own anger and indignation. She knew virtually everything about the intrigues her friend had been plotting, and she had even played a crucial role in them herself.

'How was Nenski dressed when he went to see his betrothed?' she asked.

In a fine suit, shirt and new shoes, and in a coat with a velvet collar, Maryan told her with his customary attention to detail. Rebecca gritted her teeth. It was clear that Hannah had given Taddeuz money, and lots of it, in the form of a loan.

If Taddeuz was now able to strut about Marshalkovski Avenue, courting a young lady and cutting such a fine figure that there was talk of an engagement, it was all thanks to Hannah's money.

And that being the case, discussing the matter with Dobbe Klotz seemed to Rebecca the only thing she could do.

Pelte Mazur was killed during the night of February 23rd 1892 after a six-week hunt for him; the former knife-thrower was no victim of an accident.

It was about nine o'clock on a particularly cold night, when Mendel Visoker – who had been out of town and did not even know of the hunt – laid eyes on the house where Mazur had taken refuge. The house was on the outskirts of town, well beyond Muranow Street. There was nothing attractive about the place even though it was in the country surrounded by fields and orchards: it was within shotgun-range of the massive brick Citadel, which served as a prison.

Mendel first noticed the tracks of the cart in the fresh snow, then he saw the cart itself, fairly well hidden among the trees. He wasn't called the drayman for nothing and he easily recognized the cart, as he could have had it been one vehicle among a thousand. He began to follow the footprints.

In the viburnum thicket he began to sense the presence of a human being even though he saw no one. He said in a low voice:

'It's me, Visoker. Please don't kill me.'

Then, after several seconds, he slipped between the branches. At the heart of the thicket was a sort of hideout, and as he'd expected he found Pinchos Klotz huddled up inside it, small and frail as a child. He did not so much as turn to look at Mendel, who shook his head.

'There's really no sense to it. And how were you thinking of killing him, on your own?'

He got no reply, and for a moment Mendel thought that the little fellow had quite simply died of cold; by his reckoning, Pinchos must have been lurking in the thicket for about twenty hours, his arms crossed on his chest, his hands tucked under his armpits, slender stalactites of ice hanging from his ear locks while he kept his eyes hypnotically fixed on the house a hundred metres away.

'Did you know I was going to come?' asked Mendel.

A movement of the head told him no.

'Did you know your wife had written to me?'

A second movement of the head told him no.

'Is Mazur really in that house?'

'Barn,' said Pinchos.

Mendel Visoker had stepped off the train from Danzig to Warsaw five hours earlier. Dobbe Klotz's letter had reached him on the morning of February 22nd. She was lucky to have caught him; two days later and he would never have received it. In his jacket pocket was a ticket for a journey that would take him from Danzig to Sydney, via Hamburg, Amsterdam, London, Lisbon, Port Said, Aden, Colombo, Singapore and Port Morseby. In recent months the desire to leave had been mounting inside him, like a toothache. The old demons that had haunted him since childhood had returned, and his travels across the wide Russian plains no longer satisfied him. He had received another letter from his cousin Schloimele singing Australia's praises more enthusiastically than ever, and he had made the decision suddenly one evening, lying between those two Lithuanian ladies of his who were a little too fat, a little too old and who moaned a little too much. Mendel instantly discovered how much more readily one could change one's life than one could one's suit or café, and within a few hours he had sold his *brouski*, the horses, his share in one or two businesses; he had closed his account with the Baltic Bank and bought a ticket.

He was due to leave Danzig on February 25th, for Amsterdam, where he would stay several days, waiting for a boat that would take him to London. From England he would set sail for the open sea, on the morning of March 11th aboard the *Tasmania*.

It was in the midst of all these plans, while he was mentally beginning to put Poland and the Ukraine behind him in the same way that he had left so many women, that he received Dobbe's letter. He worked it out: if he were to go quickly and return by train, spending only twelve hours in Warsaw, he would have plenty of time to kill Pelte 'the Wolf' Mazur and to get away without running any risk of ever being caught.

Dobbe Klotz's letter came to the point without any preamble:

To Mendel Visoker: she has been raped and beaten up. She has been badly kicked about. She was pregnant and this was certainly the reason for it. She had a miscarriage and almost died. I had hoped she'd killed the man, but she did not. And that crazy little fool Pinchos disappeared two weeks ago. Come. The man is a Pole by the name of Taddeuz Nenski.

Mendel had immediately burned the letter, not only as a matter of caution, but because he knew full well that Hannah's rapist was not Taddeuz.

When he got off the train he went to Goyna Street and found Dobbe but not Hannah, who was sound asleep. He set off in pursuit of Mazur finding within three hours the trail that it had taken sixty-year-old Pinchos Klotz weeks to uncover. He left a fair amount of destruction in his wake, but since he was going to disappear the next day . . .

'It was Pelte Mazur who raped her, wasn't it, Mr Klotz?'

A nod.

'And beat her up?'

Another nod.

Mendel smiled: he promised himself the great pleasure of killing the Wolf. He looked across the field at the barn, of which only the roof was visible.

'And he's inside?'

A third nod.

'Has he got knives on him?'

Pinchos signalled that he did from under his black hat and his wardrobe of kaftans, all of which he wore for protection against the cold though he looked no sturdier bundled up as such.

It had begun to snow again, deadening all sound. Mendel estimated that it must be about nine-thirty. He had just under eleven hours, more than enough time. He stood up.

'I'm going inside, and I'm going alone. You'd only get in my way and end up in prison.'

Pinchos shrugged his shoulders. Mendel landed a kindly little punch on his hat. Pinchos fell to the ground, face down in the viburnum and the snow.

Mendel's knock was met by a man who spoke Polish with a German accent; from the description a whore on Krochmalna Street had once given him, Mendel easily recognized him as a former weightlifter named Hermann Erlich. There was also a woman in the house, albeit one with a beard: she had travelled with the circus as far as Spain.

To the very polite question that Mendel put to him, Erlich replied that neither he nor his wife had seen a sign of Pelte Mazur for ages. The ex-weightlifter's eyes glinted when he announced he had no idea where Pelte was and that in any event he was such a good friend of his that he would certainly kill anybody who tried to pick a quarrel with the Wolf.

Mendel smiled. He had been misinformed, that was all, and they should forgive him for disturbing them. He turned away slightly, then let his fist fly –

Once, twice, three times. It was certainly the first time he had seen anyone remain on his feet for so long. But the weightlifter eventually sank to the ground, with the whites of his eyes showing.

Visoker was also obliged to knock out the bearded lady who seemed to have it in mind to cut him in two with a cleaver, but he did so more gently.

Silence fell, Mendel blew out the only candle. He removed his shoes and pressed himself up against the wall.

Then he shouted: 'Pelte? I'm here. Keeping my promise.'

At first there was no sound from the barn, which adjoined the house by the wall against which Mendel was leaning. Then Mendel caught a very quiet footstep. He knew perfectly well that Mazur was trying to get out through the door to the barn.

He shouted out mockingly: 'You needn't bother trying that: I've blocked it. You'll have to come out this way. I'm waiting for you.'

After about thirty seconds' silence the panel in the wall separating the barn from the house swung open. Mendel could see nothing in the total darkness, but he heard the tiniest creak, followed by Mazur's breathing.

'Visoker?'

'Who else?' said Mendel with a laugh.

'I didn't rape her.'

'Oh no?'

'I didn't do it. She had a razor, she used it before I was able to.'

'But you tried.'

'I was drunk.'

'That doesn't change very much, my friend. I told you not to lay a finger on her. And then you went and kicked her about.'

'I was drunk. Mendel, for old times' sake . . .'

'First,' said Mendel very calmly, 'I'm going to break both your wrists. And only then will I break your neck.'

Something whistled past him; a knife embedded itself in the bread box that Mendel had been holding up at arm's length in front of him.

'Missed,' said Mendel. 'And you don't have thirty-six knives on you.'

'I've got more.'

Mendel was now on the other side of the room, crouching down, as well he should be: a second knife flew into the wall just above his head.

'Missed again.'

He crawled away just as something cut into his back, a little above his belt. But the blade had only nicked his flesh.

'Another miss. And you've only got three knives as usual.'

'I've got more.'

'I don't think so,' said Mendel.

Total silence. At this point Mendel was under the table, close enough to the unconscious bearded lady to be able to smell her rather nauseating body odour. And a few signs told him that the lady in question and, what could be more of a problem, her herculean husband, were coming round.

'I'm going to make a bet,' he shouted. 'I'm going to bet that you haven't got any more knives on you. I'm coming for you, to break your wrists. And then your neck.'

Visoker was as good as his word, as he always had been and would be all his life. He began walking slowly towards the part of the room where he felt Mazur was still lurking. As he took his fourth step he smelled the Wolf's presence. He hit out, making contact, but not hard enough to inflict much damage. And he felt another gash along the length of his right bicep. 'The bastard had another knife!'

He rushed forward and grabbed Pelte by the shoulder. His hand came down, circling Mazur's wrist; the room was filled with the sound of bones shattering. It was at that moment that the outside door opened and a tiny figure burst into the house, yelling.

'That crazy Pinchos Klotz!' thought Mendel. His attention was distracted only for a moment, but for long enough to allow a knife to sink into his left side.

'I had *two* more knives,' screamed Mazur, while his other wrist was broken. And he continued to scream as Mendel's hands came around his neck, crushed the cartilages, then with a quick twist broke his vertebrae.

Mendel fell to his knees. 'Well, I can't let myself die here, for God's sake!' He took hold of the handle of the knife that was plunged into his hip and pulled, panting in excruciating pain. Behind him strange things were happening; he could hear inarticulate cries and the sounds of a struggle. Almost immediately, there was light again and he just had enough time to see the woman come rushing at him, brandishing her cleaver. She impaled herself on the knife that Mendel held in his hand, falling on top of him and knocking him to the ground.

There was an otherwordly stillness in the seconds that followed. Mendel eventually freed himself from the woman's body and sat for a moment with his back against the wall, surveying the room in which nothing stirred.

'Oh my God!'

The long farmhouse table hid from his view both Pinchos and the weightlifter, but neither of them seemed to be moving.

'Oh my God!' repeated Mendel. Bracing himself against the wall he got back on his feet.

Pinchos Klotz lay on the floor with a broken neck, just like Pelte Mazur. But unbelievably, either before he had died or in doing so, the little fellow had managed to sink a butcher's knife into Erlich's chest, right up to the fingerguard. 'No doubt he was hiding it under all those wretched kaftans . . .'

Erlich was not yet dead, but he was not very far off. When he tried to speak the red froth that Mendel had often seen on the lips of dead men appeared on his.

'I didn't intend for you to die,' Mendel said to him gently. 'Nor your wife. I didn't intend that. But what can I do about it now? If I put you on to a cart or a horse, by the time I get you to the Citadel or into town you'll be dead. It won't do any good and you'll suffer a bit more pain, that's all. Do you understand?'

The dying man slowly blinked his eyelids, as if to signal that he had understood. Mendel shook his head. The incredible surge of anger that had carried him along since Danzig had subsided. In its place he felt an equally great sadness.

Mendel walked over to the woman who had died instantaneously – Mazur's knife had penetrated her throat. He then rummaged in the wardrobe, brought out all the candles he could find, lined them up on the table and lit them. He tended his three wounds, assuring himself he would indeed survive.

'Two things are possible, Mendel, either your time has not yet come, or else you're nothing short of immortal.'

He stripped to the waist and applied fresh snow to his wounds until they had more or less stopped bleeding. Then he bandaged himself with the aid of Hermann Erlich's spare shirt, which was more or less clean and which he tore into strips. He dressed again, putting on a kind of greatcoat that he found hanging on the coat-peg. It had the advantage of not having any knife rents in it, so he would be able to board the train without attracting any attention.

'Are you dead?'

Erlich did not respond, but Mendel observed that there was still a flicker of life in him. He sat down on the floor at his side and grasped his shoulder.

'For the coat I'm borrowing,' he said, 'I'm leaving you fifteen roubles. I'm no thief. Anything else, but not a thief.'

He slipped the bills into the dying man's pocket and waited. It vaguely occurred to him to arrange the scene of the massacre to make it look as though he were innocent. But that would be a waste of time: with all the destruction he had left behind in his not particularly subtle search for Pelte Mazur, there would never be any doubt that he was the Wolf's killer, and therefore the killer of the other three as well.

'You've no choice but to get on that damned train, and on to that damned boat, before anyone finds all these bodies.'

Mendel, who had been talking out loud, realized that he was doing so for no one's benefit but his own: his companion had breathed his last. He closed the weightlifter's eyes and left the house, shutting the door behind him.

Seven hours later, he stood on the snowy Vistula docks. He spotted Maryan Kaden and signalled to him to drop what he was doing.

'I can't leave work just like that,' retorted the boy.

'How much do you earn, son?'

'One rouble thirty kopeks a night.'

'Here's five hundred, from Hannah and me; you can pay it back twenty years from now, on the same day, at the same time. Now get in.'

Maryan climbed up on to the seat of Pinchos Klotz's cart, to the back of which was tied Mendel's hired horse.

'One question, to start with,' said Mendel. 'Is there the slightest possiblility that our friend Taddeuz could have done Hannah any harm? Think hard.'

Young Kaden thought for a long time, and eventually shook his head.

'Not that I know of. Of course, that's apart from . . .'

'Apart from what he did to her in bed, I know. Nothing else.'

Maryan told the story of the lawyer Wlolstka and his daughter, of the fine suit Taddeuz had worn to Marshalkovski Avenue. But Mendel very quickly stopped him: he already knew this much, and even knew a little more of what had been going on.

'Do you have any idea where Taddeuz might be?' he asked.

Maryan began to give the address in Praga but once again Mendel interrupted him.

'I already know about that too. I was there earlier this evening. He wasn't there and his room was empty. He left about two weeks ago, and his landlady didn't know where he was going. Do you know anything she doesn't?'

'No, not really,' said Maryan. He too had noted Taddeuz Nenski's disappearance two weeks before. And Taddeuz had not simply left his rooms; he had given up attending lectures at the university, and he had stopped going to the bookshops. It was as if he had completely vanished from Warsaw. 'People say he was in trouble with the police.'

Mendel stopped the cart.

'Right,' he said. 'Now listen. It's not completely beyond the bounds of possibility that something tiresome might happen to me within the next two hours. I have, as you might say, caused a bit of a commotion in this damned town. But I have also learned a few things. And if I run into trouble, you'll have to be sure to tell Hannah exactly what I'm going to tell you. She's spoken to me about you, apparently you can be relied on . . .'

Maryan looked up at Mendel with a seriousness that pleased the older man.

'Leib Deitch, first of all,' Mendel began. 'I went to see him and got him out of bed. We talked, he and I. He suddenly remembered he owed Hannah four thousand roubles. Here they are, with all the paperwork in order. You'll give them to her. If she wants any further details, all she has to do is to visit him in the hospital. He's going to be there for some time: he broke a bench with his head. Okay?'

'Right,' said Maryan, taking the money and the papers.

'Now this is more serious. Pinchos Klotz is dead.'

Mendel told him about the massacre, leaving out nothing.

'. . . And as for Dobbe, it's quite clear that she's mad. She's been hounding Nenski. She's created what one might call an alliance between the rabbis, the president of the consistory, the Catholic priests, and above all a Russian state prosecutor whom she has probably paid well to bring proceedings against a Polish student. She's masterminded one hell of a plot to prove that Taddeuz not only raped and beat up a little Jewish girl whom he had already seduced and got pregnant – and whom he wanted to kill because she was pregnant by him – but on top of that he had revolutionary papers hidden in his room. She has had him expelled from the university, turned away from the Wlolstkas' home, disgraced everywhere, in short. She also paid money to a certain Glovacki woman, the boy's landlady, so that that woman would say the most incriminating things imaginable. And now the secret police are after him.

'Dobbe's almost ruined herself with all her scheming, but she's also had her revenge, on the pretext of avenging the girl. Do you understand that, son? This is what you must tell Hannah: that Dobbe Klotz was really acting on her own behalf, prompted by a madwoman's jealousy. That it suited her down to the ground to believe that Taddeuz was guilty. That the more tender and loving Taddeuz was, the guiltier, the more vile he was in Dobbe's envious eyes. Do you understand?'

'I think so,' said Maryan.

'. . . And you're also to tell Hannah that Dobbe is damned dangerous and that she . . .'

Mendel stopped. In explaining as best he could to Maryan what had happened he had just seen something clearly himself. The intuition that had been gnawing away at him since he had received Dobbe's letter in Danzig appeared perfectly accurate. Despite his fatigue, his injuries – in his 'conversation' with Deitch his own wounds had reopened – there was still something he had to do, which young Maryan could not possibly handle. He consulted his watch and saw that it was well past five o'clock.

'You've still got about one and a quarter hours, Mendel; that ought to be enough to go and find her, snatch her away from Dobbe and put her somewhere where she'll be safe, and then get on that damned train. The boy just wouldn't be able to do it. And anyway, you're responsible for her whether you like it or not, you have been for the past ten years, from the moment you took her in your arms and cried over her . . .'

He smiled at the still-attentive Maryan.

'Correction. After tomorrow, you won't find Hannah at Goyna Street, she'll be somewhere else . . .'

He gave him Kryztina's address in Mirowski Street where Hannah had turned up on her own on that memorable evening the previous year.

'Goodbye, son. And God be with you – if He exists.'

As he drove along he kept an eye out for police.

'It's all very well being immortal, Mendel, but there are limits. People are going to recognize you around here, and it can't be long before someone runs over to the Erlichs' place to see whether you didn't break a few vases there . . .'

It was snowing more heavily than ever by the time he reached Goyna Street. The dairy was closed and in darkness. He knocked on the apartment door and found himself face to face with Dobbe Klotz. He had little strength left, and was finding it hard to think straight even though he knew exactly what his plan was.

'Well, it's done,' he said.

She fixed him with her rhinoceros eye: 'You found him?'

'Found him and killed him,' replied Mendel. 'That was what both you and I wanted, wasn't it?'

Dobbe pitched her huge bulk in the middle of the doorway; he had to push her aside slightly to get into the front room. With a slight hesitation she asked:

'The Polish student, eh?'

'She's given herself away,' thought Mendel instantly. 'She *knew* the student had nothing, or virtually nothing, to do with the whole affair, and yet in her letter she told me to go after him . . .'

'Who else?' said Mendel. 'And he defended himself.'

He showed her his wounded arm, the red stains on his palm and wrist. As he did so he walked into the back room, where Hannah had been sleeping deeply when he had called eleven hours earlier. Although Mendel had tried to wake her, she had not stirred; Dobbe explained this was because of the medicine the doctor had given her. He could see the change straightaway: Hannah turned when he came in, her eyes open wide in disbelief.

'Mendel, oh Mendel!'

He took a lamp to her bedside and was immediately horrified by her thinness and extreme weakness; kneeling beside her he wondered how he could possibly have thought of leaving for Australia without seeing her again.

Tenderly, as he had done to no one before, he kissed her forehead. Then he whispered: 'Don't say anything, I'm going to take you away . . .'

He also said out loud:

'The Poles are after me, they're going to come here, and they may take revenge on her. The best thing is to put her in a safe place . . .'

. . . just as he took the full brunt of a blow on the back of his neck that made him collapse on top of Hannah.

'You're lying, Visoker,' said Dobbe. 'You're lying. You haven't laid a finger on the Pole. You were with Pinchos, you have his cart.'

She struck him again, on his side, though he managed to roll in the other direction.

'You men are all the same!' shouted Dobbe, hitting him again with what turned out to be a rolling pin.

In other circumstances this assault would have made Mendel laugh: he had been attacked by rolling pins, by offended, jealous women often enough in his life. But Dobbe was a completely different kind of creature. She was trying to kill him, and she was better equipped to do so than most men. He curled up a little tighter and managed to block her arm once, then again; he stood up reeling, and without a moment's hesitation drove his fist into her. The blow made him feel even more dazed, but not as much as it did Dobbe, who fell to the ground.

'It's just not possible,' thought Mendel vaguely, 'I really am on my way to knocking out half the population of Warsaw.' He did not have the heart to laugh any more however; he felt terrible, his whole body in pain.

He dragged the unconscious giantess into the storeroom and locked her in. To his surprise, he turned around to find Hannah out of bed, standing barefoot in her nightdress, staring at him with grey eyes that had regained almost all their sharpness.

'I know,' said Mendel, 'it might surprise you. But I haven't gone mad. I'll explain. We have to leave, I haven't much time.'

He gathered up all he could find in the way of blankets and quilts, including a fur coat in which he started to wrap her.

'I can walk,' she said.

'So much the better. Except that now isn't the time.'

He was about to take her in his arms when she backed away warily.

'So you don't trust me any more, Hannah?'

For a few seconds her eyes held his.

'Yes,' she said, 'I do.'

And she rested her cheek against his chest, as she had ten years earlier, at the time of the horsemen and the pogrom.

Warsaw was waking up as they approached Mirowski Street, even though it was still dark and the snow continued to fall. Mendel had spoken very quickly; he had told her all the essentials.

'Maryan will explain the rest and give you the money.'

Warily he looked around again. There was no doubt about it: two pimps were following them, and they were not the only ones. The whole brotherhood seemed to be convening out of nowhere to make him pay for the deaths of Mazur and the Erlich couple.

'All things considered, I'd far prefer the police, who'll at least wait a while before putting the noose around my neck.'

He looked back at Hannah and his heart contracted: she looked shocked, with that wide-eyed stare she had in her moments of suffering.

With tears in his eyes, he said: 'At least he's alive, Hannah. God knows where he's gone, but he's alive.'

'I wrote to him as soon as I could.'

'You can be sure Dobbe didn't send him your letter. I'd swear that he isn't in Poland. Can you really walk?'

Almost furtively, he consulted his watch again; two minutes past six: 'It's going to be a close thing, Mendel. Unless the blasted train's late – just a matter of luck. But I'd really like to sleep for a bit, I'm not much use to anybody any more.' The cart turned into Mirowski Street.

'It's all falling apart,' said Hannah with haunting calm. 'I've lost everything, made such a mess of everything. Everything.'

Mendel's pursuers – there were at least twenty of them – had gained ground. 'And they'll pounce on me as soon as I've parted with the little one,' he thought, 'since I'll have to stop when I say goodbye to her forever.'

Extraordinarily enough, considering her condition, Hannah too turned around, calmly, and saw the villains chasing after them.

'Are they after you, Mendel Visoker?'

'They're just out for a stroll, that's all.'

'They're going to kill you.'

'I ought to have died ten years ago,' replied Mendel, laughing. 'Ten years ago, on the outskirts of some unspeakable *shtetl*, knocking the heads of some Cossacks with a wagon shaft, on account of some snotty-nosed kid.'

He looked straight ahead, where his eyes now fell upon young Maryan Kaden, who was walking towards them very fast, followed by two policemen on horseback. Mendel stopped the cart and closed his eyes. He sighed, then smiled. Suddenly everything was very clear to him.

'Hannah, don't interrupt, there isn't time. I bought a ticket for Australia. Take it and use it if you like. Or sell it. Take my money too; the warders will steal it from me in any case, you might as well have it.'

She shook her head with her usual fierceness. This time he was not going to indulge the girl however; he stuffed the ticket and the wallet into her hands, picked her up with one hand and lowered her to the ground.

'Go to Kryztina, she's a good woman.'

'I'm going to make a deposition and tell them everything, to explain why you killed Pelte Mazur.'

'They may just send me to Siberia. And I'll escape from there sooner or later, don't worry. Now move!'

He was so exhausted he could hardly keep his eyes open. His side and the back of his neck were hurting like hell. The horde of pimps on his trail had come to a halt ten metres back: the police and young Kaden stood a few steps away, straight on.

'For the love of God, Hannah, get the hell out of here. Go wherever you like. Become very rich. Show them what you're made of, what a damned fine woman you are. But I won't be around any more, remember that.'

As he spoke, he smiled down at Maryan Kaden, who was also shaking his head very sorrowfully.

'All I could think of doing was to call the police . . .' said the boy.

'My own son couldn't have done better,' replied Mendel. 'If I had a son. And, in any event, one of two things is possible . . . One of two things is possible . . .'

He couldn't remember the rest.

Visoker was sentenced to twenty years' imprisonment and deportation for life. The lawyers who cost her a king's ransom did a devil of a job, preventing him being hanged, in spite of the state prosecutor who made a great issue of presenting the massacre as a sickening and depraved quarrel among pimps.

She watched him being taken away in chains, and two days later set sail for Australia.

7

THE INDIAN MAIL

She had been in Australia for six weeks, but had only just arrived in Sydney.

In the end she had not sailed on the *Tasmania*, the ship Visoker should have boarded in March; her state of health did not allow her to leave so soon, and she was in any event determined to find out what was to become of Mendel. She had done everything she could to help him during his trial; she had even considered following him, if not to Siberia, then at least as far as St Petersburg or Moscow. She had not been able to carry out a single one of her ideas for his escape, as she had been refused all visas to travel in Russia because she was too young, because she was Jewish and female, because she had no blood kinship with the convict. She assumed that the heavy hand of Dobbe Klotz lay behind the Tsarist administration's steadfast opposition to her request.

The same Dobbe Klotz had written six letters to her: Hannah had not opened any of them.

All the time Mendel was in prison in Warsaw, waiting for his trial, she tried in vain to see him. She also laboured to get notes to him by greasing the palms of one or two of the warders, but not to much better effect; she doubted he ever received them.

And she did not stop there. Since she was not able to go herself, she paid for one of Maryan Kaden's cousins to travel to Prague, to make sure Taddeuz was not at the home of the aunt with whom he had spent the previous summer. Her spy returned on schedule, convinced that the student had not returned to Prague. Hannah sent Maryan himself to Taddeuz's own village; he had not been seen there either. As Visoker had predicted, Taddeuz seemed to have left Poland. Hannah thought – and would go on thinking for a long time to come – that he had taken refuge in Vienna or Paris.

Mendel was found guilty of murder and sentenced towards the middle of April; he began his journey to the penal colony three weeks later. It was only then that she was able to catch a glimpse of him, as he was taken out of his cell. Mendel saw her at once and gave her a big smile, his white teeth gleaming beneath his black moustaches. He raised his handcuffed wrists as high as he could, like a triumphant Roman gladiator. And he cried out: 'Happy birthday, Hannah!' as if he knew that she had herself forgotten that she had just turned seventeen.

She had not sold Mendel's boat ticket, only postponed the dates of departure, feeling quite determined to leave Poland where she had made such a mess of everything. It seemed to her that by completing his journey she was fulfilling Mendel's wish and his dream that she was following the route he had marked out for her, and that by doing so she would continue to enjoy the protection he had given her for the last ten years. She counted up her savings: twenty-six thousand roubles, of which twenty-two belonged to Mendel. She saw in this sum the possibility of preparing a fabulous welcome for him when he escaped. She was convinced of Mendel's indestructibility, certain that he would manage to find his way to her, even from the far reaches of Siberia. And in what other corner of the world could he be more sure of finding her than in Australia, where the secret police certainly would not come running after him? Moreover, with this initial capital she would make profits beyond the bounds of possibility, which would not be without significance when she laid hands on Taddeuz again . . .

From the first days she had spent with Kryztina in Mirowski Street, she had taken it into her head to learn English. As soon as she had been able to walk about with ease again, she had gone to the British Embassy, where she had obtained the help she wanted and the books she needed. She also obtained the kindly support of Mrs Leonora Carruthers, the wife of a diplomat, who for two hours a day over the course of two months made her repeat *I am, you are, he is,* and learn her irregular verbs. She was dazzled by her pupil's progress. During the same period Hannah read for ten or twelve hours a day; she did not have a good deal else to do. She devoured the whole of the embassy library and read the newspapers daily, taking in every word from the first line to the last.

Leonora Carruthers and her husband helped her to get a passport to London and then Australia, though she was obliged to lie about her age, claiming to be twenty. She left the Carruthers in tears (which is to say that *they* wept) and several days later she arrived in London, from Danzig, and took the Indian mail.

From Bombay to Singapore, Singapore to Perth, Perth to Melbourne, she travelled three decks above the ordinary emigrants in the second-class berth to which Mendel's ticket entitled her. She had hardly left her cabin during the voyage, exhausting the ship's library, beginning with Dickens, and refusing to disembark at any ports of call for fear of being left behind.

At eight thirty on the morning of July 16th, 1892, the four-thousand-ton steamship, *China*, of the Peninsular and Oriental line, rounded Cape Otway. It sailed into Philip Bay, where there was a bush fire burning, or at least such was the explanation offered Hannah for the glimmering red glow on the mainland by one of the junior officers, who, like fifteen or so of his colleagues, had tried everything to get Hannah into his bunk during the crossing. The *China* waited eight hours for the high tide at Point Lonsdale to subside, adding a final delay to a voyage that took seventy-one days in all.

She walked the streets of Sydney, completely penniless, as she had been for six weeks now. Less than three hours after landing at the Melbourne port of Sandridge and arriving at Flinders Street Station she had been robbed of the eight hundred and ninety-seven pounds sterling and fourteen shillings she had so often counted. She had carried her big carpetbag herself – a porter would have cost an entire shilling! – and with a heavy heart had asked how much it would cost to take a taxi to the city centre, three kilometres away. She would have willingly walked the distance but she was ashamed of her stinginess, especially in front of the other passengers and the young midshipman who was so disappointed not to have been allowed to as much as kiss her.

She had been advised to stay in the Oriental Hotel on Collins Street. As soon as she was told the price of a room, however, she did an about-turn and checked into a little boarding house in Swanston that was not terribly expensive, and where the price per day included the evening meal. By then it was too late in the day to deposit her money in a bank; she was told the boarding house had no safe.

She was impatient to see Melbourne properly and – not wanting to carry around her carpetbag, which was weighted down by books – she had locked it inside a wardrobe and gone out without unpacking. She had not gone far, venturing no further than Bourke Street, whose praises the midshipman on the *China* had sung, assuring her that it was the equivalent of the rue de Rivoli in Paris, though Hannah had some difficulty imagining what the rue de Rivoli might be like. She found a few very ordinary shops, and this put her in a much better mood; if that was the competition she was going to have an easy time of it. The lightness in the air and the liveliness of the town too made her spirits rise.

'I'm going to make my fortune here,' she said aloud.

When she got back to her room an hour later, she found her door had been forced open. And while the bag was still in the wardrobe, the money – most of which she had left in Mendel's old wallet – had disappeared.

She was barely seventeen years and a half, she was penniless, and she was on the other side of the world, twenty thousand kilometres from her *shtetl*.

8

LOTHAR HUTWILL

Mrs Smithson, the landlady of the Swanston Street boarding house, was an ascetic woman with grey hair and yellow teeth. Her husband was evidently the captain of a ship and somewhere at sea, but in all the time Hannah was in Melbourne, she never saw this husband, and even began to think that he was imaginary.

Mrs Smithson took the defensive as soon as Hannah spoke, swearing that it was absolutely impossible that such theft could take place in a house like hers. Her only boarders were honest, single women, two or three elderly couples, and a small number of Anglican clergy . . .

But she soon became convinced otherwise by the tremendous despair of a white-faced Hannah, who in her panic forgot her English, and was holding forth in a mixture of French, German, Russian and Yiddish. Mrs Smithson and Hannah searched the room once again, with no more success. The room was located at the far end of a second floor corridor; at the end of the corridor was a window. The rollers on the windows were broken, and Mrs Smithson was forced to admit that perhaps, after all, the larrikins had struck again.

The constable at the police station was of the same opinion. 'Larrikin' was an unfamiliar word to Hannah. The constable explained to her that it referred to a typically Australian kind of hooligan, who operated in gangs and whose audacity knew no bounds.

'You should never have left so much money lying about,' he chastised her.

Hannah told the constable what she thought of his advice – in Polish so as to be sure he didn't understand what she said.

The policeman did not think there was any chance of finding the thieves, much less of recovering the money.

At about nine o'clock that evening Mrs Smithson brought her tenant some tea; she found her lying stiff as a board on her bed, staring at the ceiling with swollen eyes. What aggravated Hannah most – aside from her own unbelievable carelessness – was that the money was not hers, it belonged properly to Mendel. This was what disturbed her most, more even than her own plight.

She did not sleep all night, but at daybreak she recovered most of her energy. As soon as she could, prompted now by a cold anger at her own stupidity, she went to find out how to get from Melbourne to Sydney and how much the journey would cost. At Spenser Street Station she was told she would first have to take a State of Victoria train to a place called Wodonga, where she was then to travel by stagecoach for fifteen to twenty hours, depending on the state of the road, before being able to take advantage of the New South Wales railway network. The journey would take three days and cost forty-five pounds fifteen shillings.

Her first idea was to try to borrow the money from the young midshipman on the *China*. She could see the drawbacks of this solution: he was certain not to keep his wandering hands off her, and she would hardly be in a position of much power.

She swiftly abandoned that plan, as much because she was put off by the idea of being fondled, as because – she suddenly realized – he was bound to be insolvent.

Throughout the seventy-one days of her voyage from Danzig to Melbourne she had debated very seriously the question of whether or not to remain physically faithful to Taddeuz. With the first sticky heat of the Mediterranean, and the slow passage through the Suez Canal, she had decided that she would not. It was simply a matter of common sense: it would be two years, perhaps even three or four, before she would have made a great enough fortune to be able to marry Taddeuz and bear his children. And it would be silly not to use the time to prepare herself for their marriage. It seemed perfectly clear to her that she should present herself to Taddeuz with every possible advantage, of which knowing how to make love was not the least important.

It was clear that she would need someone experienced to educate her. Though a sailor, the midshipman was certainly not capable of such a course of study; after all, he had not even succeeded in seducing her.

The midshipman having been ruled out as a potential donor, she began to consider the suitability of the passengers in whose company she had completed the last part of her journey. She had told them all she was going to Sydney to join an uncle of hers who owned a long list of gold mines, but nonetheless, she would have to give her story a new twist.

She walked to the port, hoping to find her companions' Australian addresses in the shipping company's registers. This was to no avail; the elderly couple she was most counting on lived in a town to the west called Adelaide; almost immediately upon arrival, Wittaker, the man with the heavy moustaches, had set sail again for Tasmania; Reverend Forbes, his wife and their four children had returned to their house in Donnybrook. And so it went on. No one remained but the Flemings, the young English newlyweds who had given an area in Melbourne as their place of residence, but who had been very vague. Hannah spent two days walking round South Yarra, calling on every cottage by the river, to no avail. Each time she returned to Swanston Street in greater agony, her feet, no longer accustomed to walking, covered with blisters.

For the time being, Mrs Smithson was giving her board and lodging on credit, as she considered herself partly to blame for the theft committed on the premises. But it was obvious that this could only be a temporary solution.

Hannah looked for work but very quickly gave up on the idea. The average salary was eight or nine shillings a week; at that rate it would take her two years to save the rail fare – on the condition that she did not eat and that she slept under a tree.

Only on the fourth day did she think of sending a telegram – she had never made use of such modern technology – and the idea came to her only by chance, when she happened to walk past the General Post Office. She still needed to find the money to pay for it, however, and that afternoon sold one of her five dresses for two pounds ten shillings, to a milliner in Bourke Street. She then sent her message of distress, which was perhaps not as accurate as succinct:

Mr Schloimele Visoker, 173 Glenmore Road, Paddington, Sydney. Desperately need fifty pounds. Mrs Mendel Visoker, Smithson Boarding House, Swanston Street, Melbourne.

Six days passed, during which Mrs Smithson grew increasingly sullen, envisioning herself forever burdened with a non-paying tenant. Or virtually non-paying; Hannah generously gave her a few shillings for her keep after the sale of her dress. With the remaining two pounds she opened a bank account, the first she had ever had.

She spent a good deal of her wait walking all over town, which was also her way of getting used to exercise again. She walked from the 1880 Exhibition Hall to the two museums on either side of the Municipal Library. She visited all the monuments in Melbourne, the Botanical Gardens and the Fitzroy Gardens when the weather permitted, and the library when the southern winter became too humid. She read the local authors: Henry Sawery, Rowcroft, Vidal and especially Rolf Boldrewood, whose *Robbery Under Arms* delighted her. But the days went by and brought with them no word from Cousin Schloimele.

'I shall ask Mendel to give him a good dressing-down,' she thought.

On the twelfth day she sold a second dress, though she did so on completely different terms from the first, having learned her lesson. She went again to see the milliner on Bourke Street, wearing her pride and joy, the dress with the thirty-nine buttons.

'I've just realized something terrible. On that dress that I sold you last week, I think I left a cameo given to me by my grandmother, the Comtesse de Laclos, whom I shall be seeing again shortly, as I'm returning to France next Monday. . . What a pretty shop you have here, one would think this was the rue de Rivoli — of course you know the rue de Rivoli . . .? One of my former chambermaids opened a shop there last year. A fine girl. I gave her a little help to get started — the equivalent of three hundred pounds. Would that be enough to do the same in Australia? Yes? And how much would one need to buy something bigger?'

She managed to leave the shop with the address of the woman who had bought her first dress, a certain Margaret Atkinson, who lived in the posh quarter of St Kilda. Hannah went directly to the house, where she gave her name as Anne de Laclos. She told Margaret Atkinson more or less the same story as the one she had served up to the milliner: she was French; she was on a pleasure trip with her father; she was getting rid of a few of her clothes on his insistence, since the author of her days felt that one hundred and twelve dresses were decidedly too many. She did wonder why she always had to lay it on so thick.

The second dress was sold to Margaret Atkinson – who had thirty at most – for twelve guineas. Hannah joined Mrs Atkinson on the veranda for a cup of tea as her two children played nearby, under the supervision of their governess.

It was these children, and a few words uttered by her hostess, that finally gave Hannah the idea she had been looking for, though at the time it was no more than the embryo of an idea.

Margaret Atkinson spoke of a trip she was about to undertake with her family, to New Zealand, where her husband had some major financial interests. Laughing, she invited Hannah to act quickly if she wanted to sell her any more 'Parisian dresses'.

'I can come back tomorrow,' suggested Hannah. 'Another of my dresses would suit you splendidly.'

A time was agreed upon, and Hannah left, walking down the length of the very impressive garden. 'I shall have one like this in twelve to eighteen months' time,' she told herself.

She continued to turn over and over in her mind the idea that had occurred to her at the Atkinson house until it gained in substance. She walked back to Swanston Street, stopping only once on the way: to deposit eleven pounds in her account at the Union Bank of Australia, bringing her savings to a total of thirteen pounds.

She made a quick calculation: if she sold her three remaining dresses, including the one with the thirty-nine buttons for which she could get at least twenty-five guineas, either to Margaret Atkinson or to someone like her, she could raise well over forty-eight pounds. She might have to walk about completely naked, of course, but she would have the forty-eight pounds.

All of this was sheer speculation; she knew very well, deep down inside herself, that she would never sell the first dress she had ever owned, not even if she were dying of starvation. Even though – or perhaps because – Taddeuz hadn't succeeded in removing it from her in the bedroom in Praga. . .

It was almost with indifference that she asked Mrs Smithson whether Cousin Schloimele had sent her any money. Naturally, he had not. She gave her landlady a pound, reproaching herself a little for her extravagance.

With some of her remaining shillings she bought the least

offensive pair of shoes she could find in Bourke Street; they were
made in America and came very close to fitting her tiny feet. With
a scrap of material from an old skirt stuffed into them they were
more than adequate, and they brought her feet, which were
covered in blisters, a good deal of relief.

Hannah's idea took shape in the night. The next day she lost no
time in selling – for sixteen guineas – her third dress, a satin one
which she calmly stated was a Worth (having seen the name of the
great Parisian couturier in a back issue of the magazine *L'Illustra-
tion*). Hannah then explained to Mrs Atkinson that she was not
only to leave a few dresses in Australia.

'My chambermaid would like to stay and settle down here. She
has a kind of cousin, or an uncle, I'm not quite sure which, living
in Sydney. Before going back to Europe, I'd like to help the poor
girl find a job. You know what it's like: one grows fond of one's
servants. And she's still very young. I wouldn't like to send her to
just anybody – I'm responsible for her, in a way. She can look after
children, or handle secretarial work, she's very good at reading and
writing and knows four languages; she's nineteen and her name's
Hannah. I'm only sorry to be losing her, and of course I shall give
her the most favourable references.' Would Mrs Atkinson by any
chance know of a family?

The agreeable young woman from St Kilda promised to do her
best.

Hannah did not content herself only with this story. She went
next to Spenser Street Station and, having told some cock-and-bull
story, was given first-class reservations on trains to Wodonga and
Sydney. The railway clerk whom she selected as her victim was a
tall young man, almost as sweet as the midshipman on the *China*
and even more soft-hearted. When she told him she was looking
for her father, who had gone gold-digging, deserting his wife and
eight children, he completely swallowed her story. The clerk was
moved to tears and invited Hannah to dinner. Naturally she
accepted; that would be one less meal to reimburse Mrs Smithson
for. With his help, she also drew up a list of the wealthy families
with children who would shortly be heading North, to escape the
Melbourne winter, a list she kept up to date with daily visits to the
station. On her fourth visit the railway clerk asked her to marry
him, but she was able to put an end to his interest by revealing the
dreadful truth: she was already married and the mother of two
children and it was not her father she was looking for but her

husband. (It should be said that he was was even more moved by this version than by her original story.)

She completed her list by making enquiries at the reception desks of all the big hotels in Melbourne.

One week later, twenty-one days after she had disembarked, she hooked her first fish: a clan of extremely wealthy Brazilians who, as it happened, needed a governess for their four children. They were preparing to leave for Brisbane. But her hopes were quickly dashed: the Brazilians were planning to travel by sea, sailing via Sydney but without stopping over there. Moreover, they had with them not ordinary servants but slaves, so recently emancipated that they seemed unaware of their liberation.

Two more weeks went by.

'There was no sense to it, Lizzie . . . What I did in Sydney I could have done just as well – and perhaps even better and more quickly – in Melbourne . . . But I'd set my sights on Sydney. It was almost as if there were a competition between Australia and myself, a challenge to meet: I wasn't going to give up at the first setback. I think that was the real reason for my obstinacy, much more than the fact that I was sure Mendel would find me more easily in Sydney than Melbourne . . .'

On the thirty-fourth day she struck lucky.

All the alarms went off at once, or at least on the same day: she heard the news from the railway clerk at Spenser Street Station, from the receptionist at the Oriental Hotel in Collins Street, and she read it in the personal columns of the *Melbourne Argus*. A certain Mrs Eloise Hutwill was looking for a chambermaid before returning to her estate at the upper end of the Murray Valley. The estate in question lay near a place that went by the exotic name of Gundagai, in New South Wales. As for the Hutwills, Hannah's inquiries revealed that they were very rich, a couple with no children, of Swiss-German origin. The family had settled in Australia thirty years before, having brought some vine cuttings with them in their baggage: their wealth rested in vineyards (their renowned Albury wine had won a prize at the Paris Exhibition in 1878), as well as in mines.

Acquiring this precious information almost cost Hannah the job; by the time she turned up at the superb house in Toorak, on the left bank of the Yarra, there were at least ten or twelve applicants already waiting. During the next hour, while they were all made to wait patiently, Hannah set about getting rid of the competition.

The main danger seemed to her to come in the form of a sturdy blonde girl, who was no more crafty than the others, but who must have known German, since she came from Schleswig-Holstein. In rather hesitant German Hannah expressed her surprise at Hildegarde's interest in this position when she should have been in St Kilda, at the home of that young lady who lived in the magnificent colonnaded house with her two adorable children, and was looking for a governess who spoke the language of Goethe and was capable of teaching it to her offspring for the exorbitant salary of twenty-five shillings a month . . .

Hildegarde left like a streak of lightning, armed with the address in St Kilda. The way was clear, or at least Hannah thought so. When her turn came to be interviewed by Eloise Hutwill, she found herself face to face with a plump little woman who had thin lips and pudgy fingers covered in rings. With a feverish, harsh stare she questioned Hannah first in English and then in German, hardly bothering to read her references, all of which Hannah had written herself.

At the back of the salon in which the interview took place was an open door half in shadow, which led into an even darker, neighbouring room. Hannah was instantly convinced that there was someone on the other side of that door, someone she could not see but who could see her and on whose decision the job depended.

'I like my chambermaids to be elegant,' said Eloise Hutwill. 'Will you please walk from the chest of drawers over to that armchair. . . Turn around, I want to see you from behind. Now in profile. Come and stand next to me . . . Undo the top of your dress . . . Yes, I want to see your breasts, I detest chambermaids who pad their chemises to give the impression they have a generous bosom. Bend down . . .'

Having unhooked the top of her dress and lowered her linen chemise as far as it would go, Hannah bent over, facing the half-open door at the end of the room.

'Button yourself up again,' said Eloise. 'Go and wait next door. Someone will come and let you know what the reply is.'

The reply was yes. Hannah was engaged, for eighteen shillings a week, a wage well above – even suspiciously above – the normal rate.

She also received – another extravagance that astonished her – ten pounds to buy some new clothes, a hat and some shoes. These instructions were conveyed to her by a housekeeper with an impassive face who was clearly of German origin too, and who spoke rudimentary English. She let Hannah know that her two red-and-black dresses were far too distinguished for a servant; she had the most clear-cut ideas on the kind of clothes that were suitable, and nothing but square-necked black dresses with grey collars would do.

'And lace underwear . . .'

She lifted Hannah's skirt, right up to her hips, and nodded her head.

'That will do. You're dressed like a lady – just who do you think you are? You're to be here, with your baggage, and ready to leave, the day after tomorrow, in the afternoon. Do you have any family in Australia?'

'My five brothers,' said Hannah. 'Each one bigger than the next. Real giants, all of them.'

On August 19th she paid Mrs Smithson the thirty-two shillings she still owed her. She packed her chambermaid's clothes into her carpetbag, on top of her own dresses, and slipped in a razor with a mother-of-pearl handle that she had bought the same day.

The next day she boarded the train for Wodonga at Spenser Street Station. This was her second train journey (she had already travelled from Warsaw to Danzig), but the countryside that flashed past was of an Australia unknown to her. At first sight it was not very alluring: after the factories in the suburb of Footscray, the scenery became flat, empty, and deserted. As far as the eye could see, barbed wire fences marked out paddocks, inside which were nothing but sheep, and more sheep . . .

Hannah felt no more kindly towards her employer. This was not only because Eloise Hutwill simpered, because she affected an exasperating little-girl style of behaviour although she was well over fifty, or because she insisted on being sprinkled with eau de Cologne at every available opportunity. It was above all because she talked, in a shrill voice, in her incomprehensible Swiss German. She droned on and on about her considerable Australian fortune, which belonged to her, to her alone, and none of it – should anyone be interested – to her husband.

He had still not entirely materialized; Hannah had caught one glimpse of him from a distance in the house in Toorak, and another time at the station as he stood beside Eloise, while she directed the loading on to the train of her employers' seventeen trunks. Oddly, he was not travelling in the same carriage as his wife.

The train stopped at Wodonga, on the banks of the river Murray, after passing through a petrified forest of eucalyptus trees. In Wodonga they boarded an omnibus drawn by six horses in which they were to cross the river and reach Albury, the first town in New South Wales. The customs check was routine; it was only when travelling in the other direction, into the Colony of Victoria, that the formalities were strict. Hannah made a note of this, and of the twenty per cent tax payable on imports. She quite naturally registered details of this kind, even when she did not yet have the slightest idea how she could make use of them.

Only at that point did Lothar Hutwill join them, having parted with the group of men with whom he had been travelling so far. He was a slim, elegant man, nearly as tall as Taddeuz. He was clearly younger than his wife – by Hannah's calculations he was about ten years younger – so he would be about forty. As his pleasantly ironic eyes met Hannah's she was immediately convinced that he had been the person in the darkened room in Melbourne, assuming someone had really been there. He had therefore witnessed her performance in her qualifying exam.

He spoke to Hannah in German, in a very pure German. He was polite and friendly and talkative, and when they sat down to dinner at the Exchange Hotel, he insisted that Hannah sit at their table – 'We're in Australia, Fräulein, not in Europe. Social distinctions do not exist here, *per se* . . .' He was amusing and cheerful, and told a story about the town councillor in Ballarat, to the west of Melbourne, who received a request to import thirty Venetian gondolas to adorn one of the city's lakes. He had protested, saying he could see no reason why taxpayers' money should be wasted in this manner; why not simply have a couple of these creatures sent over from Italy, a male gondola and a female gondola, and leave the rest to nature?

Hannah laughed. There was in Lothar Hutwill just a tiny trace of Mendel Visoker – '*The same way of smiling with his lips beneath his moustache, and especially with his eyes, Lizzie . . . He was forty-two then, and seemed to me very old and yet at the same time still quite young, with silvery hair at his temples and that suntan of his . . .*'

They spent the night in Albury. Hannah very quickly discovered that the proprietor of the hotel was Jewish, and though his

Romanian Yiddish was only just comprehensible to a Polish ear, she gathered a great deal of information. He knew the Hutwills well, they stayed at his hotel three or four times a year. He did not have a very high opinion of Mrs Eloise, who drove him half-mad every time she visited by being so demanding. On the other hand, he gave a more qualified appraisal of Mr Lothar.

'Be careful, *faygeleh*, it's common knowledge, in Sydney as in Melbourne; their chambermaids are intended for the master, and they engage as many as five or six a year . . . All right, all right, but no one can say I didn't warn you . . .'

The next day, the 21st, a brougham awaited them at the hotel entrance. It was driven by a red-haired devil of a man, an employee of the Hutwills, who answered to the name of Micah Gunn. The carriage had only two proper seats, faced by an uncomfortable-looking bench. Lothar gallantly opted for the latter, leaving the velvet padded seats to the two women. Eloise very soon fell asleep, snoring with her mouth open, the sweat trickling down her cheeks, half-waking now and then and demanding to be sprinkled with eau de Cologne.

'Where did you learn German?' asked Hutwill before long, his knees touching hers. Hannah said the first thing that came into her head: that she had lived in Vienna (she hoped he had never set foot there, which seemed to be the case). She then quickly turned the conversation to a subject that was of greater interest to her: how to make a fortune in Australia.

He smiled knowingly. 'You're intending to make your fortune?'

She held his gaze, and he was off, talking about the Hutwills' property holdings, their vineyards, through which the carriage was travelling, and their mines – gold mines, but also copper mines, iron and coal mines, all in New South Wales, in the inland part of the colony, around Bathurst, Lithgow, Cobar. Though she did not always appreciate the way her employer leaned over her as he spoke, Hannah was grateful for the diversion; fifteen hours had gone by, broken only by very short stops. Hannah would remember this as the worst journey she had undertaken; the countryside was mountainous, the air increasingly hot and humid, the night bringing only a little coolness. It was two o'clock in the morning on August 22nd, when the carriage crossed a bridge and when Lothar Hutwill announced with some satisfaction:

'The Murrumbidgee.'

The bridge was endless, nearly a mile long, and at the end of it Hannah caught a glimpse of multi-coloured river lights.

'Gundagai,' said Hutwill.

Twenty minutes later the brougham drove down an avenue lined with eucalyptus trees. Servants came rushing forward, their lanterns swinging. Eloise was literally carried to her rooms, her snores sounding as though all the bellringers in Warsaw were in action.

As for Hannah, she staggered to the room shown her. She did not have the strength to get undressed, but fell asleep in a heap, her last and only thought that she was now only one day's journey from Cousin Schloimele.

The touch of a hand around her ankle woke her.

It was broad daylight. Lothar Hutwill was sitting on her bed, dressed in a splendid cream-coloured suit and a scarlet silk waistcoat, a gold nugget set with a pearl pinned in his cravat. He anticipated her question.

'Ten o'clock in the morning. And my wife has no need of your services, she won't wake until tomorrow at the earliest. She sleeps that long every time we make the journey.'

'Your hand,' said Hannah.

'I won't touch you anywhere else. Not if you don't want me to. Do you want me to?'

She was lying on her side. She turned on to her back and stared at him, her body still heavy with sleep. Thin wooden screens, such as she had never seen before, were drawn across the windows, filtering the sunlight. The heady scent of eucalyptus hung in the still air of the bedroom.

His hand climbed a little way up from her ankle, under her skirt. It ventured above her knee, and lightly brushed the inside of her thigh.

'Someone has already tried to rape me,' she said. 'He didn't succeed. He got his stomach cut open with a razor.'

'And you have a razor?'

He sounded amused, even while he looked attentive and serious. She was not the slightest bit afraid of him, even while the hand beneath her skirt resumed its progress. With great delicacy it came to rest on the curve of her belly, palm open, fingers spread; she could feel the warmth of his touch through the silk of her lace knickers.

'You'll never have need of a razor with me, Hannah.'

His fingers exerted a gentle pressure on her belly. Languidly, she thought: 'You want him to make love to you, Hannah, you want him to undress you, very gently, very delicately. He's certainly capable of it. But if you succumb now, you won't be able to ask him for money later.'

She herself was surprised by her own conclusion; no conscious rumination had preceded it. Where did she get the idea that sooner or later she was going to want to borrow money from him?

'Take away your hand, please.'

He nodded his head, smiling. He had a smile that formed slowly, preceded by a slight contraction, a puckering of his upper lip. And he did as she asked.

Then he said: 'Are you Jewish? I heard you talking to the hotelkeeper in Albury.'

'I just know a little Yiddish.'

'I see.'

She could not tell at all from his voice whether he believed her or not. Then he began talking about himself. He had been born in Switzerland in a place called Solothurn, and he had never considered emigrating to Australia. He had even begun studying philosophy at the University of Heidelberg. One day he had received a letter from the other side of the world, asking him if he wanted to take over for his cousin Joachim, who had broken his neck in a disagreement with his horse. Lothar took Joachim's place in every capacity, including his place in his cousin's widow's bed.

He paused at this point in the story, his brown eyes wandering over Hannah's reclining body. His eyes stopped on the arm she kept tucked under the pillow; he was clearly wondering whether she was holding a razor or not.

'Fifteen years ago,' he went on slowly, 'Eloise wasn't what she's become. Or it didn't show. You guessed that I was there when the prospective chambermaids were asked to parade in Melbourne, didn't you?'

'Yes.'

'You've been told that Eloise's chambermaids are hired only for my benefit?'

'Yes.'

'And yet you embarked upon this journey.'

Her reply was again yes.

'You intrigue me,' he said. 'And you interest me even more. May I touch your breasts?'

She shook her head.

'I've already seen them, after all,' he remarked. 'It's an agreement my wife and I made nearly ten years ago: she chooses my mistresses herself, which is just a way of ensuring my fidelity. She chooses her chambermaids according to my tastes, or to what she believes to be my tastes. Which is to say, she never gives the job to anyone she thinks might please me. Fortunately, I've managed to persuade her that I only like buxom women, which is why she chose you: you were the thinnest and smallest of the lot. Would you sleep with me if I gave you five pounds?'

'No,' said Hannah with a smile.

'Ten?'

'Not for ten either.'

He laughed. 'I'd have been surprised if you'd said yes. You asked me so many strange questions when we were travelling in the carriage. Strange coming from a woman, I mean. Do you really intend to make your fortune in Australia?'

Her answer again was yes.

Silence.

Then he asked: 'Do you think you're capable of it?'

'Mmmmmm,' she said, staring at him.

'Any idea what you're going to do to earn so much money?'

'Not yet.'

Another silence.

'I've no money of my own, Hannah, as she's bound to have told you. Every shilling I spend, I get from her. I can spend almost as much as I like, as long as I account for every penny. If you'd accepted that ten pounds a moment ago, it would have been Eloise herself who paid you. Although ten pounds would undoubtedly have seemed to her to be far too generous a . . . consideration. Is there someone waiting for you in Sydney?'

'Not really.'

'A man?'

'Not the kind of man you're thinking of,' she said.

She stretched – keeping her arm under the pillow all the while – and added: 'I'm thirsty.'

It was true that she was parched, but she was really trying out an experiment. And it worked exactly as she hoped and expected:

Lothar stood up, leaving his wide-brimmed hat on the bed, and came back with a glass of water.

In the meantime, Hannah had sat up. She drank while he remained standing, facing her. She took her time, quite wide awake now, although bruised all over from the twenty-one hours in a carriage. Her languor had vanished, her mind was now calculating away, analysing everything. Not for a second had she doubted what she would do once she reached this godforsaken place in the Australian interior: she would abandon her chamber-maid duties and make her way to Sydney by the shortest route possible. She had clung so much to the idea that she had ended up devoting very little time to the other question, which was actually more important: what would she do in Sydney when she eventually got there? Obviously raising sheep, or digging for gold or copper or coal, was out of the question. She knew she did not have the necessary constitution. What was more, it would take fifteen years, at best, to get rich that way. Besides, she was a woman, which meant, in principle, that there were only two things she might easily do to achieve her aim: work as a prostitute on an industrial scale, or marry a man with a good deal of money, who would share it with her providing she kept her looks. These were not acceptable alternatives. But a man like Lothar Hutwill, who seemed to be saying he would not be against the idea of killing his wife as long as she gave him a little help – this was even more trouble than she had counted on.

She put down her glass, having made its contents last as long as possible. She was not at all sure that she had accurately interpreted his words. Perhaps he wasn't planning to kill his wife after all.

'Do you confide in all your chambermaids like this?' she asked.

'No,' he said with a smile.

'Only in me?'

'Only in you.'

There was a sound of horses outside. Hutwill drew out a fob-watch and consulted it; she used the occasion to study his hands.

That's what I always notice first about a man, Lizzie, before his lips, his eyes, his smile or his teeth: his hands. I like them to be fine-looking, well-cared for, reasonably strong but long. They can tell you a great deal, whether they're clenched, or unnecessarily active, or on the contrary very still. I've always been a little disturbed, but even more attracted, by a man with fine hands who knows how to keep them under control. Lizzie, remember always to be wary of a man whose hands are both still and supple . . .'

Lothar Hutwill's were, after Taddeuz's, the most remarkable hands Hannah had ever seen.

'I must go,' he said gently. 'I'll be away for two or three days. I'm going to Adelong, twenty-five miles south of here. We drove through it last night but you were asleep. A pity: Eloise has two gold mines there. And since you are so interested in making your fortune . . .'

He extended his arm and, with the tips of his index finger and middle finger, closed her eyelids.

'Your eyes are real shotguns, Hannah. We'll be seeing each other again soon, of course . . .'

She watched from her window as he mounted his horse and rode away, flanked by two men who appeared to be bodyguards. They wore guns slung across their shoulders and strange hats, the brims of which were raised and pinned to the crowns.

For the next quarter of an hour she stood looking through the jalousie. The eucalyptus avenue was on her right; to the left, she could see the river. The house was large, extended on one side by wooden sheds that must once have served as stables. There was not a living soul to be seen anywhere; she wondered where that great red-headed beanpole Micah Gunn was . . .

It all seemed too easy. Lothar had taken the trouble to tell her that he would be away, that his wife would not call for twenty-four hours; he had even left a map of the country. Even so, she found the idea of having to steal a horse slightly worried her. It would not really be stealing, she told herself; in Yass, where she planned to catch the train for Sydney, she would leave the horse with someone trustworthy, who would return it to the Hutwills. And anyway, what else could she do? If she did not leave today she would have the implacable Eloise on her back tomorrow.

She counted her money yet again: she still had twenty-five pounds and eighteen shillings left from the sale of her dresses, plus another one pound five shillings saved on the advance she had been given in Melbourne. She hastily washed and changed, putting on a durable royal blue dress which she had bought especially for the trip. She stuck the safety-pin into it that she had bought with her escape in mind: she would use it to pin her skirt together between her legs, when she had to sit astride a horse like a man.

She nearly forgot the razor, which she retrieved at the last minute from its place under the pillow, where Lothar Hutwill had suspected it to be. With her carpetbag clutched in her hand (she was still carrying twelve or fifteen books in it, including *Vanity Fair*, several Dickens novels and her beloved Choderlos de Laclos), she ventured out into the corridor.

It was empty.

As was the staircase. Silence reigned in the house. When she reached the ground floor, she opened a door and found herself in a very fine study that appeared to be Lothar Hutwill's. On the tabletop, placed in a prominent position, were two leatherbound books that had obviously been read many times: Nietzsche's *The Gay Science* and *Thus Spake Zarathustra*.

'It's almost as though he was inviting you to take them, Hannah . . .'

She settled instead for a sheet of paper that conveniently happened to be lying on the desk, next to a pen and inkwell.

In German, she wrote: *I'll leave the horse in Yass. I'll repay you the advance on my wages and the expenses of my trip to Gundagai as soon as possible.* She hesitated, very tempted to add something else by way of reply to Hutwill's statement that they would be seeing each other again soon. In the end she contented herself with an improvised signature: a double H, consisting of four heavily drawn vertical lines tilting slightly to the right, all crossed with a single, rising horizontal line – a signature she created that day, in her distraction, and one that would become famous.

She returned to the hall to find it still as silent and deserted as before. She got her bearings and set off again, dragging the bag – which already felt as heavy as a dead donkey – along with her.

She reached the stables without meeting anyone at all, much less a groom. All the same she found eight or ten horses lined up in front of their mangers. She could remember Mendel saying: 'You always mount a horse from the left, you young fool . . . And you talk to it, Hannah, you tell the animal that you love it, that you're counting on it, or you don't get on it.'

She chose what she thought was a mare, without being very sure. The horse pleased her, with its gentle glistening eye. She wasted a good thirty minutes trying to saddle it, breaking a fingernail in the process and starting to swear.

Part of her expected to find Hutwill and all his men outside with tears of laughter rolling down their cheeks; she still could not shake off the impression that he was setting a trap for her.

She finally succeeded in girthing her horse more or less correctly, and hung her bag on the cantle; she then allowed herself to sit down to recover. She was bathed in sweat and exhausted after holding the heavy saddle at arm's length for so long.

'Listen to me . . .' she said to the mare in a low voice. 'You might have knelt down, the way camels evidently do. In any case, we're going to leave together, at least I hope so. I'm counting on you, I'm immensely fond of you, I'd like to believe that as a female you'll show a bit of solidarity. If you could keep me on your back, that would be a great help. I'm not very adept as a horsewoman . . .'

She got no reply.

She then realized she had addressed the horse in Yiddish. A fit of nervous giggles welled up inside her. She took the animal by the bridle and, − language barriers aside − was delighted to see the mare following her. A minute later she was outside under the blazing sun, quite certain she had not been seen. Avoiding the avenue, she made her way through a grove of gum trees, the mare in tow. Only a quarter of an hour later, with the help of a felled treetrunk, did she hoist herself on to the mare's back and into the saddle.

Feeling extraordinarily proud of herself, she set off on the road going north.

And at that moment discovered that Micah Gunn was following her.

He stopped whenever she stopped, and he set off again immediately she did. There could be no mistake about it: that was his red hair, and scarecrow figure, and he had no other motive than following her. She seriously considered hailing him, and explaining that, with the full consent of Lothar Hutwill, she had simply ridden out to have a look around. But he remained always at a distance, motionless on his big golden bay, and the one time she tried to ride towards him, he instantly retreated. One of two things was possible, as Mendel Visoker would say: either he was carrying out orders he had been given, or he was doing this of his own volition. In which case he might try to have his way with her in the first Australian thicket they came across . . .

She subscribed more to the first hypothesis than the second, but all the same she took out of her bag the mother-of-pearl razor and slipped it down between her breasts. 'With my penchant for cutting people open,' she thought, 'I ought to have become a doctor!'

Two hours went by, then another two, without any change whatsoever in Micah Gunn's interest. The countryside was magnificent, even to Hannah's anxious eyes. The road followed the side of a mountain, overlooking the Murrumbidgee Valley, and the air was invigoratingly cool.

Micah Gunn continued to trail her, always maintaining a distance of about three hundred paces. He got no closer or further, even when she rode through a little cluster of houses, grouped around a white church, which she would later learn was the town of Jugiong, even when the road narrowed and threaded its way through a patch of trees. This haunting, silent presence at her heels began to wear on Hannah's normally steady nerves. More than that, she felt exhaustion stealing over her, and she could feel the sores forming on her legs from the heat of the saddle. To her aches from the day before were added uncomfortable pains in her stomach: on top of everything else, her period had started!

She became a little more weary with every mile, to the point where she could see Micah Gunns everywhere. At one moment she found herself talking deliriously about Taddeuz to the mare, who seemed to prick up her ears in interest.

Judging by the setting sun, it must have been well after six in the evening when, rounding a final bend in the road, she glimpsed the arches of a metal bridge, which looked exactly as Lothar Hutwill had described it: she was at Yass. It was at first an immense relief to slip out of the saddle, but she very quickly had to face up to reality: the mere act of walking was torture.

What was more, she could tell she was making a fool of herself. She staggered into the foyer of the Commercial Hotel in the midst of a great hullabaloo. She was the only woman in sight, which further heightened her sense of wretched abandonment; the fact also fuelled her anger, which fortunately sustained her as far as the reception desk, which she was barely tall enough to peer over.

'You ill?' asked the receptionist.

'No more than you are, moron,' she shouted over the din around her. 'I'd like a room, without a man in it, if possible, and I want to know the times of the trains for Sydney and how much a ticket costs.'

He obliged, kindly. And he asked if she wanted to dine. She said no without even thinking: the place was full of men awash in beer, some of them gathered round an out-of-tune piano singing refrains which she understood not at all. She was in a hurry to do only one thing: to be on her own, lying down, flat on her stomach!

Her room was just above the big hall, and she lay in bed there for hours, her eyes wide open, assaulted by hunger and nausea and fever, not knowing what hurt most – her muscle aches, her blisters, or her menstrual cramps. Once again she found that she was talking to herself:

'You wanted to come to Australia. Well, here you are. And it's no country for women, if such a place exists anywhere. And you think you're going to make your fortune here. You must be joking. Look at you!'

As if to confirm her new opinion of herself she crawled to a wall mirror, from which a dishevelled face stared back:

'You'd scare off a kangaroo.'

Sleep finally overcame even her self-loathing, however, while less than two metres below her, the squalling of drunken voices continued unabated.

When she emerged from the hotel the next day, still sagging at the knees, Micah Gunn was sitting on the steps, waiting for her.

She had drunk a little warm tea and immediately vomited it up again, each convulsion causing her more pain than the last. After a night's relaxation she could not tell which of her muscles hurt most. Putting one foot in front of the other had become an act of heroism, and her stomach ached so much she wanted to scream. Impassively, Micah Gunn watched her approach, calmly filling a short pipe with tobacco from his leather pouch. He had repulsive fingers; like the rest of his body, they were thin and bony, with spatulate fingertips. His eyes were an astounding yellow-brown that seemed abnormal and unhealthy, in contrast with his vital red hair.

'Are you going to be watching me for much longer?'

'Yep.'

He lit his pipe; the acrid smell of the so-called tobacco he was smoking almost made Hannah vomit again.

'And how far will you follow me?'

He shook his head, without releasing his clay pipe.

Hannah thought she would like to kill him.

'Are you going to stop me from getting on the train?'

'Nope.'

'Have you been given orders concerning me?'

'Yep.'

'Because of the horse I stole?'

'Nope.'

'Orders from whom?'

He emitted an indescribably foul-smelling puff of smoke as a reply. Was he even capable of saying anything other than 'yep' and 'nope', she wondered? Hannah toyed with the idea of murder: were she a man, she would smash his nose with some jolly good punches, and make him swallow his pipe, tobacco and all. Where was Mendel when she needed him?

'I've something to say to you,' she told him. 'You're the most stinking, rotten scum in Australia. If I don't insult you further, it's only because I don't know how to say *schmuck*, *momzer*, *putz*, *schmensch*, *oysvorf* or arsehole of a *Tierisch* in English. Have I made myself clear?'

'Yep,' said Micah Gunn, looking delighted.

Hannah incomprehensibly felt a great desire to laugh.

'Let's change tactics,' she thought, 'otherwise I'm going to have this moron on my heels for the rest of my days. Which, among other things, will allow the Hutwills, Mr and Mrs, to get their hands on me again and perhaps send me to prison for theft. Or worse still, involve me in their settling of marital scores . . .'

'For a start, the horse,' she said. 'Did you get it back?'

'Yep.'

'Now let's talk business. Would you stop following me if I gave you two pounds?'

'Nope.'

'Five pounds?'

'Nope.'

'Ten pounds?'

The yellow eyes registered interest. Hannah had twenty-six pounds and three shillings. The train fare to Sidney cost five pounds ten. She had to keep reminding herself – what a ridiculous system – that there were twenty shillings to the pound.

'Twenty,' said Micah Gunn.

'Fifteen.'

He shook his head.

'I'm going to collapse,' thought Hannah, 'I'm going to collapse with my arms stretched out on either side, in the middle of this road at the end of the world, and I shall have come all this way for nothing.'

'All right, twenty,' she said. 'But on one condition: I'm going to give the money to the hotelkeeper, who will give it to you only after the train's left. Two hours after it has left.'

Drained of strength, blood creeping down her thighs, she dragged herself to the station. Occasionally her vision grew blurred.

'Five pounds sixteen shillings,' bellowed the clerk employed by the New South Wales railway.

'I was told the price was five pounds ten.'

'Last year, it was. But not since the new rates came in.'

She clung to the ticket office grille, overcome with faintness. She was burning with fever.

'Are you sure you can travel, miss?'

'Positive. Mind your own business.'

Before her were *two* ticket clerks, sometimes even three; she seemed suddenly to have four hands and two purses. She proved incapable of counting out her money, and in the end it was the clerk who had to pick the fare out of her notes and coins.

'You should go back to bed and take the train another day, miss.'

'Go to hell.'

In her present state, aggressiveness was the only possible refuge. The clerk handed her the ticket. The train would leave at five o'clock in the afternoon, he told her, assuming there was no delay. It was eight in the morning. She counted and recounted the seven shillings she had left with a drunkard's obstinacy; she still had to pay for the hotel.

She went back to the Commercial Hotel, now empty of its raucous bushmen. She was charitably allowed to keep her room until her departure. She dragged herself up the stairs, barely finding the energy to wash her blood-covered legs before collapsing on the bed. She had no sooner lain down than she heard a knock at the door; she had to get up and remove the chair she had jammed under the doorhandle. She opened the door to a young girl with chapped red hands who had brought her an Australian breakfast; an enormous steak topped with three eggs swimming in grease. It was enough to make anyone vomit, which she did, even though her stomach had been empty for a good thirty hours.

'Take it away!' she cried belatedly, as the girl scurried down the hall.

She put the chair back in position and returned to the bed, not allowing herself to fall asleep for fear of missing the train.

She did not miss it, miraculously enough. Someone – in the fog that enveloped her, she could not tell whether it was a man or a woman – helped her carry her bag to the station, took the twenty pounds to be given later to Micah Gunn, and hoisted her up on to the wooden bench in one of the carriages. She found herself in the company of three or four bearded giants who smiled at her, showing their rotten teeth. They all smelled very strongly, in fact they stank, from their crotches. They treated Hannah with an awkward kindliness, insisting on offering her a seat and a makeshift bed, fashioned out of their jackets. And they promised her she would be safer with them than in her mother's arms.

For the first time in her life, she felt a desire to surrender herself to events, to give up her struggle. She fell asleep the moment the train started, as the husky voices of her strange bodyguards singing 'Waltzing Matilda' as though it were a lullaby, reached her ears.

She was in a deep sleep when the train stopped at Mittagong. When she opened her eyes again, she was at Redfern, Sydney's central station. From her companions' embarrassed explanations she finally understood that the train had come in a good three hours before, that they had appealed to the railway company to let her sleep, and that she could now put away the razor with which they had evidently let her sleep since leaving Yass, even though they had been afraid she might cut her own throat with it. They clubbed together to give her money for a hotel room and even put something in her purse; she now had a whole pound. She kissed their prickly cheeks, one by one, holding her breath as she did so, and she refused any further help. Now that she had arrived in Sydney her uncle, who was very rich, would take care of her.

It was true that she felt much recovered; she could at least see clearly and she had recovered all her self-command.

'I'm in Sydney, which was my destination, and everything will be all right from now on,' she thought.

They had not parted for more than three minutes and she had hardly emerged from the station into the streets of Sydney when she sensed she was being followed. Turning around, she saw Micah Gunn behind her at a distance of about one hundred paces.

She walked and walked, all the benefit of the rest she had managed to get during the train trip lost in the course of her wandering. The idea of getting into a taxi had seemed to her crazy; there was no point in wasting her only pound. And because she did not know the town, she had been obliged to walk round and round in circles. Oddly, the persistent presence of Gunn at her heels had helped her, in so far as she had felt egged on, driven to excel. She felt she would rather die than give that schmuck, that red and yellow dung-heap, the pleasure of seeing her give up!

She then had a very heartening idea. Her arms were aching so from the weight of the bag that she decided to leave it in the middle of the pavement. Sure enough, her plan worked: she watched as Micah Gunn hesitated, then unperturbed, picked up the bag and began to carry it himself.

At about five o'clock in the afternoon she finally came into Glenmore Road, in the district of Paddington, the address given to her by Mendel. Schloimele's house was number 173. It was a Victorian-style, one-storey building, with a small garden in front completely buried under hydrangea bushes. It was painted white all over, apart from the front door, which was peacock blue. Hannah rang the bell once, and while waiting for an answer, turned around in time to see Gunn deposit her carpetbag at the garden gate, then walk off, looking for all the world like someone whose mission had been accomplished.

Nothing stirred in the house.

Despite her exhaustion, a tide of rage began to well up inside her, just as it had two years earlier in front of the double doors of the private mansion in Krolewska Street in Warsaw. 'Except that you're no longer capable of giving any kind of kick to anything at all,' she thought. 'A slight puff of wind and you'd be blown to the ground . . .'

The door finally opened; a little girl with red-blond hair and big green eyes stood before her. She must have been nine or ten years old. She stared at Hannah, clutching a doll to her chest.

'I'd like to speak to Mr Schloimele Visoker,' said Hannah.

'Who?'

'Schloimele Visoker.'

And in the half-mist into which she was beginning to slip, the two scenes became confused, this one and the one in Krolewska Street, when she had asked to speak to one Taddeuz Nenski.

'One moment, please,' said the little girl with great maturity. She left the door open and returned in a moment with a tall, red-haired woman a good deal past forty, with the same green eyes. For the third time Hannah pronounced Cousin Schloimele's name. The woman shook her head.

'The previous tenant was called something like that, I think. But his first name was Sam.'

'Has he moved?'

'You could say that,' replied the woman. 'He went to America, at least a few months ago.'

In any case he no longer lived at 173 Glenmore Road.

'A relative of yours?'

'A friend,' said Hannah, struggling to keep her eyes open and to remain on her feet. It was all too much. She had suspected that Cousin Schloimele, that unspeakable fool, had had a reason for not replying to her telegram, but she had not imagined this.

'Just a friend,' she said again. 'Thank you very much, ma'am. You have a very pretty house.'

She did an about-turn, after a fashion, and walked down the path that wound its way through the hydrangeas, in the direction of the bag that had been left at the garden gate. She lifted the ten- or fifteen-ton weight, and with a thud, she fell to the ground.

When she opened her eyes again, she found herself lying on a fine calico sofa. Sitting quietly on the other end of the sofa was the little girl, who was holding her doll upside down and solemnly observing her.

'Are you awake?'

'I think so.'

'Mother said you must be hungry. Are you hungry?'

'Not at all.'

'I think,' said the little girl, 'that you tell strange fibs and that you're really very hungry.'

Hannah managed a smile.

'Why are you holding your doll with its head upside down?'

'I'm waiting for her to burp. I've just been feeding her. Her name's Frankenstein.'

'And yours?'

'Lizzie MacKenna,' replied the little girl.

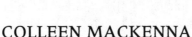

9

COLLEEN MACKENNA

The MacKennas had been in Australia for eleven years. They came from the Indies; Dougal, the father, had been born in Bombay in 1843, had completed his studies as a civil engineer in England, and had married an Irish girl from Galway, a Catholic like himself. She had agreed to accompany him when he returned to India in 1865 to build bridges across the Ganges, but she could not get used to India, to its sweltering heat and mosquitoes – particularly after the loss of two of their children to fever – and had insisted they leave. Rather than return to England – where neither of their hearts really lay, Dougal had taken a position in the public works department of the Australian colony of Queensland. The Mac-Kennas lived for years in Toowomba and Brisbane, but as the railway lines and the bridges began to extend south they moved into a new area and settled in Sydney. There they had raised a second family of which Lizzie was the only girl.

Her four brothers lived with her in the house in Glenmore Road. Evidently there was a fifth brother, Quentin, about whom Lizzie knew very little apart from the fact that he existed and that his name must never be mentioned. As it happened, she would never meet him.

All this Hannah was to learn shortly, though it would be of little interest to her at the time. What mattered that day was only that she was finally seated at a table, eating boiled beef and vegetables, subject to the gaze of seven sets of eyes. Everyone had been introduced to her with a naturalness that seemed to imply she had been invited to dinner; she felt just a little overwhelmed meeting all the Australian MacKennas at once like that. Dougal and Colleen, the parents, sat at either end of the table; in descending order of age came Rod, the eldest, who was twenty-six; Owen, who was twenty-four; Patrick, twenty-one; Alec, nineteen; and Lizzie, nearly ten.

For Hannah, this sudden immersion in a real family came as something new and surprising; she had not experienced the same since she was seven years old. This family, what was more, seemed to her to live in incredible luxury, eating off an embroidered tablecloth with a baffling profusion of knives, forks, spoons and glasses. Their average height alone was impressive: the youngest of the boys, while not as tall as his father, or his eldest brother, was already taller than Mendel and nearly as tall as Taddeuz. She felt like a fox terrier invited to share a meal with an assembly of St Bernards.

'Lizzie, you've often told me that I intrigued you all, you and your family, the day you first welcomed me into your house in Glenmore Road. I was more than intrigued: I was discovering a different world. I was coming straight from a closed world that perhaps wasn't called a ghetto at the time but that certainly was one. I'd known only overcrowding, overpopulation, promiscuity, and the consequences of these things: a remarkable spirit of solidarity but also a lot of pettiness, narrow-mindedness, a resistance to anything new, escapism into the past. The Jews of Poland and Russia, who alone were to account for three-quarters of the Jews in the New World, had grown accustomed to living that way after all the abuse they had suffered. The most intelligent – and some of them were fiendishly bright – wasted their talents studying Holy Script. This made them intellectually extraordinarily sharp, but to no real purpose; their learning was of no significance outside the little world in which they lived.

'When I arrived in your house, the first thing I found was a real family. But above all I found people with enormous confidence in themselves, who wouldn't for a minute think to be afraid of the society in which they lived, because they felt that their society had to adapt to them and not the other way round, that it was there to serve them.

'I was unbelievably fascinated, Lizzie . . .

'. . . fascinated, but on my guard: the ten years since the death of my father had taught me not to trust anybody. Apart from Mendel, of course.'

*

'A little more tea?' asked Colleen MacKenna.

'No, thank you.'

'What about some tart?'

'No, really. That was a wonderful meal.'

Silence.

Suddenly Hannah had a lump in her throat; for the first time in her life she felt shy. Incredibly shy. Fortunately, in the half-hour since they had finished eating and moved into the drawing room, Dougal had done a lot of talking, allowing Hannah to remain silent. He had rambled on endlessly about the bridges he had built, and about railway gauges, which evidently differed from one Australian colony to another, which was not very practical when the Continent's systems had all to be connected. People had been a lot more intelligent about it in India, from the Khyber Pass in Afghan country right down to the Coromandel Coast. These names meant nothing to Hannah and she had no better understanding of the string of technical words Dougal used – words like trolley-wheel, stanchion, ballast, and trellis work – but she was captivated by his enthusiasm.

After the moment of silence the conversation had taken a new turn, giving her no more chance than before to add her tuppence-worth, assuming she even wanted to; this was not the case, as she was falling asleep where she sat. Dougal MacKenna did not have a very high opinion of the Australian colonists. Most of them, according to him, were direct descendants of the convicts who had landed in Port Jackson, or – and this did not say very much more for them – of Dampier's pirates. He railed against the future Aussies, while to Hannah's sleepy surprise – for she would never have expected a son openly to contradict his father – Rod defended them, quoting Lawson, Furphy and Paterson, even insisting that the day would come when Australia would break its ties with England.

'I must leave, now,' said Hannah, taking advantage of a short lull in the discussion.

She stood up and – to her embarrassment – found as she did so that all the men in the room did likewise. She had been in the MacKennas' home for a little over three hours and so far had managed not to say very much about herself. She had treated her hosts to one of her usual stories: she told them she was French and lived in Paris, that her name was Anne de Laclos and that she had come to Australia on holiday, that she was only visiting Sydney in order to call on her old Russian teacher, Sam Visoker. But since he had gone to America she would simply have to take the next day's train back to Melbourne, where her parents were waiting for her.

'And which hotel are you staying at?' asked Colleen MacKenna.

'The Imperial,' said Hannah, who had no idea whether or not there was an Imperial Hotel in Sydney.

A gleam lit up Colleen's green eyes.

'And you're planning to walk there carrying that big bag? How old are you?'

'Twenty-one. I'm used to travelling alone.'

Colleen began to laugh.

'You're obviously going to sleep here. There's a very big bed in Lizzie's room. If you can manage to keep her quiet, you'll probably be able to get a good night's rest. *J'insiste, mademoiselle.* Rod? Take Hannah's bag, please.'

Rod obligingly grabbed the carpetbag and carried it upstairs. Hannah began to tremble. It was quite true that she did not know where to go and that she would not get very far with one pound, but mostly she was overwhelmed by this friendliness. Apart from Mendel, she could not remember anyone having treated her with such sympathy. She lowered her head and then looked up, surveying the clan whose eyes were upon her.

'My name was never Anne de Laclos. My real name is Hannah. I'm Jewish and I come from Warsaw.'

Colleen smiled calmly.

'We'll have plenty of time for more tea tomorrow. Lizzie, get yourself to bed. At once, please. You've got school tomorrow. Not another word.'

And clearly, this 'not another word' was directed just as much at Hannah.

At eight thirty in the morning the following day the house was astonishingly quiet, not in the oppressive way the Hutwills' had been, but with the peace and quiet of a home in which everything is in order. Hannah went downstairs, wearing one of her remaining red-and-black dresses but no shoes; her walk through Sydney the day before had made her heels bleed once again.

'I'm in here.'

The voice came from a room on the left at the foot of the staircase. Hannah crossed the threshold to find Colleen MacKenna sitting at the kitchen table, her hands wrapped around a mug of tea.

'It's the same every morning,' said the Irish woman, 'everyone at action stations, then suddenly it's as calm as Galway Bay or the lakes of Connemara. Did you sleep well?'

'Like a log.'

'I had no end of a job stopping Lizzie chattering when I got her out of bed this morning. She was so excited she was jumping about like a flea.'

'I didn't hear a thing.'

'How long have you been in Australia?'

'Five weeks, nearly six,' replied Hannah, suddenly determined not to tell any more lies.

'Tea? Help yourself. Be careful, it's very hot.'

Silence. The green eyes fell on her naked feet.

'In Warsaw we always walk around barefoot in the morning, when we come out of our huts, and before we start gnawing at the roots of plants, dressed in our animal skins.'

'How old are you really?'

'Seventeen and four months. My birthday's in April.'

'No relations in Melbourne?'

'None.'

'In Australia?'

'No one. I know Sam Visoker's cousin, that's all. His name is Mendel. He's in Europe.'

'Money?'

Hannah hesitated, not because she wanted to lie, but because she did not want to appear in need of the MacKenna stunning generosity.

'One pound,' she said finally.

'One or two pieces of toast?'

'Two, please.'

'Butter and marmalade? Unless you'd like steak and eggs? That's what people eat in the morning here in Australia.'

Their eyes met and they exchanged smiles.

'We'd better do something about those blisters on your heels. They could turn septic.'

'St John's wort,' said Hannah automatically, with her mouth full. 'Or better still, woodruff. With woodruff, you need only crush the freshly picked plant on the wound and it will heal in the twinkling of an eye. But I wonder if it grows here in Australia.'

Colleen MacKenna was one of those women with very long legs, comparatively narrow hips and a heavy bosom. She was not particularly pretty, and probably never had been. With her bright-red cheeks and a mixture of awkwardness and assurance in her gestures she always looked as though she had just come in from striding across the Irish moors. She looked like a woman who had borne eight children and lost two; she looked tired, with blue rings round her eyes.

'Lizzie, I loved your mother from the moment I first saw her. Of all the men and women I've ever met, she was one of the very few people, if not the only one, who made me believe I could have been different had I only met them sooner. She taught me tenderness, the little that I have, and kindness, the few grains of it that I possess . . .'

With her mug at her lips, Colleen asked: 'How is it you know so much about plants?'

'My mother. She taught me nothing else.'

'Is she still alive?'

'I don't know,' said Hannah, tempted to lie, 'I haven't seen her for two years at least.'

There was no other sound in the kitchen apart from the ticking of the clock. The smell of toast still hung in the air, even though Hannah had long devoured her breakfast.

'I've got a free hour ahead of me,' said Colleen quietly, with just the right degree of detachment in her voice. 'But you know, you don't have to tell me anything at all.'

They were seated face to face, at either end of the long table.

Hannah began to tell her story.

She left out nothing, relating the events in the impersonal, vaguely sarcastic tone of voice that she always adopted when speaking of things very close to her heart. This was her way of filtering out emotion, of controlling the volcano inside her.

She told Colleen all about her father, whom she would later speak of to no one but Lizzie, about the stream and the Temerl barn; about Mendel Visoker on his *brouski* with the wagon shaft; about the *shtetl*, and Taddeuz; about going to Warsaw and meeting Dobbe Klotz; and about the three shops, about Pelte Mazur, and how it all ended. (She only realized then, and confessed as much to Colleen, how much remorse she felt about Pinchos. She had not seen him again, but Maryan Kaden – who had accompanied the body back to Goyna Street – had told her that his eyes had remained wide open, that no one had been able to close them.)

Of the long journey that had brought her to Australia she had little to say. She blamed her disorientation, and her fatigue, for her own uncharacteristic carelessness in Melbourne. The money had not even been hers; she was only looking after it until Mendel showed up.

'So I don't have any choice,' she said. 'I have to get very rich, very quickly.'

'Because your friend Visoker is going to escape from Siberia and come to find you?'

'Yes,' Hannah replied simply.

'What confidence!'

'Complete confidence.'

'I wasn't just referring to your faith in Visoker, but also to your certainty of becoming "very rich".'

'Very quickly,' added Hannah.

'Any idea how you're going to set about it?'

'Not yet.'

'You're going to make your fortune here in Sydney?'

'I had too much trouble getting here to go anywhere else.'

They smiled at each other. Hannah described her stay in Melbourne, her encounter with the Hutwills, and finally Micah Gunn.

Colleen put down her mug. 'And that red-head followed you all the way here?'

Hannah nodded.

The Irish woman rose and left the kitchen. Hannah heard her open the door on to Glenmore Road and saw her return.

'No one there.'

'Perhaps I dreamt it.'

'You don't really seem the sort of person who has hallucinations,' said Colleen with some concern.

Her green eyes searched Hannah's face and noted for the first time her pallor, her drawn features, the bags under her eyes.

'Are you ill?'

'I've never been ill in my life.'

'Already a very long life . . . Indisposed perhaps?'

This English word was not yet part of Hannah's vocabulary.

'I was asking whether you might not have your period?' explained Colleen gently.

'Since yesterday.'

'Early?'

'By several days.'

'It must be because of the journey, the dislocation. Come,' she said with a smile. 'And not another word.'

'Not another word. Just do as you're told,' she repeated once they had reached Lizzie's bedroom upstairs.

She made Hannah lie down and undressed her.

'This dress is far too old for you, although it's pretty, very pretty in fact. But too old for you all the same. Wasn't there anyone around to tell you that?'

She removed Hannah's layers of chemises and petticoats and washed her thoroughly.

'And it never occurred to you to visit your mother before you set sail? No, don't say anything, I know it's none of my business. Now you're going to get some more sleep, young lady. Or some rest at least. Don't argue. If there's anything you want, call me, I'll be somewhere in the house . . .' She brushed Hannah's forehead with her lips. 'You have a bit of a fever, which is only to be expected under the circumstances . . .'

It was extraordinarily pleasurable to be in a bed, especially one as soft as this, with piles of pillows and feather cushions, and clean smelling sheets. For Hannah, this was a new sensation. She reflected on the almost frenetic pace of her journey since the day she had left her *shtetl* on Visoker's *brouski*, and she realized there had not been a day, not a single day, when she had not been carried along by her own momentum. Since the Temerl barn, she had not once put her trust in anyone other than herself, apart from Mendel in any event. 'And anyway,' she thought, 'I never asked him for anything, except to take me to Warsaw. And I'd have gone there sooner or later without him . . .'

She stayed in bed for three days. She would hear the MacKenna men leave in the morning and return in the evening, occasionally lowering their booming voices to whispers, as they were doubtless instructed to do by Colleen, who reigned over her giants with calm authority. Now and then Hannah felt genuinely remorseful; she was troubled by the Irish woman's remark about her mother, whom she had indeed not thought to go and kiss before leaving for Danzig.

'I certainly wrote to her,' she reminded herself, 'but I can't say that my letter was brimming over with affection. Anyone would think I was some kind of monster. Take Simon: he's my brother, after all, even though he's a moron. And have I ever shown any concern for him? Not a bit of it. I forgot his existence while I was in Warsaw with Dobbe. I have sent no news since my arrival in Australia. I haven't even thought of writing to the Carruthers, and they were so helpful. Your egotism is monstrous, you're definitely abnormal, Hannah, a real bitch . . .'

It was in a way Colleen's firm kindness that made her endure these moments of great depression. Once or twice, she even went so far as to question her love for Taddeuz; since she had made her love for him the very foundation of her life, this amounted to complete heresy. She was, in short, experiencing a clear-sighted-ness about herself that was not entirely comfortable.

Her only visitor as she lay in bed was Colleen, who would talk to her about Ireland, about her father and brothers, all ardent supporters of Irish independence and of the Fenian movement that was born in the United States. Three of Colleen's brothers were living there now.

'I'd have gone to join them there if it had been solely up to me, Hannah. But all things considered, Australia isn't such a bad place . . .'

Hannah was told this on her third day in bed, at which point she had already begun her dialogue with Lizzie, that would last all their lives. It was usually conducted in whispers once the lights were out at night; with her still-hesitant English, Hannah felt more at ease with the child than with anyone else. *'And you weren't exactly an ordinary child, Lizzie . . . You had almost as ready a tongue in your head as I did . . .'*

'Why did you call your doll Frankenstein?'

'I didn't. It's her name. It was her name before she was given to me.'

'And who gave her to you?'

Santa Claus, the Christmas before.

'It's a strange name for a doll,' said Hannah, who had not at that time read Mary Shelley's novel.

'Do little girls in Poland play with dolls too?'

'I didn't,' replied Hannah.

The next day she went out for the first time in four days. She rode in Colleen's carriage, a kind of tilbury stanhope, on two wheels, drawn by a single horse; it was by driving round in this, holding the reins the way Mendel had taught her, that she got to know Sydney. She was not much impressed by the town itself and though she found its setting magnificent she was not particularly responsive to its landscape either. At most she noticed that the streets were narrower, and also a little older, than those in Melbourne; that they were less rigidly geometrical in their layout. It was mostly the shops she wanted to see . . .

She and Colleen drove down to the large circular quay, where the big steamers of the Orient Line and the Pacific and Orient Company were moored, surrounded by sailing boats of all sizes redolent of adventure, some of them carrying exotic cargoes. They drove along the picturesque streets of Miller's Point, so reminiscent of the Baltic with its seamen's taverns and chandlers' shops it could almost have been Danzig.

'Do you really want to work, Hannah?'

'I can't stay with you forever.'

'There's no hurry.'

A group of children, ragged but happy, recognized the Irish woman and gathered round the carriage with outstretched hands. Over their blond heads, Hannah could see the tip of Darling Harbour and Pyrmont Bridge. Colleen drew out a wicker basket covered with a red-and-white chequered cloth from behind her and began distributing muffins and scones to the children.

'I was forgetting,' she said, 'you have your fortune to make . . .'

'And very quickly,' replied Hannah, returning her smile.

She kept her eyes peeled, but she saw not a sign of Micah Gunn.

The last of Colleen's baking disappeared. 'I haven't any more,' the Irish woman explained to the urchins. Hannah smiled at a tiny child of five or six whose bright eyes amused her.

'What's the equivalent of Bourke Street here in Sydney?' she asked.

'I don't even know where Bourke Street is.'

'In Melbourne. It's the most elegant street, where the finest shops are.'

'In that case, George Street . . .'

With a click of the tongue, just the way Mendel would have done it, Hannah got the horse moving again. 'I'm not so bad at it, after all,' she thought, as they advanced at a walking pace, entering the great carriageway in the centre of town.

The question came unconsciously out of nowhere to Hannah, and she asked it without really thinking. Seeing the change in the Irish woman's face, she realized she should have kept it to herself.

'Who said anything about Quentin to you?' said Colleen.

'Lizzie.'

'What exactly did she say?'

'That she had another brother, a fifth brother, as well as Rod, Owen, Patrick and Alec.'

'What else?' There was a kind of sad harshness in the Irish woman's voice.

'Nothing else,' said Hannah, hating herself for having broached what was obviously the Great MacKenna Family Secret. 'Colleen? Let's pretend I never said a word . . .'

They both fell silent, though Hannah had the feeling that Colleen came very close to confiding in her. In the end she said nothing, the whistle of a train pulling up alongside the platform in Redfern Station emphasizing the silence. On the pavements, bushmen in their headdresses mingled with bankers in top-hats and frock-coats, while the road suddenly grew crowded with steam-powered omnibuses.

Hannah stopped the carriage and she and Colleen stepped down on to George Street, the memory of Quentin's name and the secret Hannah had touched upon gradually forgotten. They soon began chattering away like old friends, all awkwardness dispersed. The atmosphere in Sydney promoted their high spirits; the air was warm and light, and many of the women strolling about were elegant and carefully groomed, outfitted in hats and corsets such as women in London must be wearing, their dresses bulging with bustles, their faces protected by veils.

'And you still have no idea how you're going to make your fortune?'

'Not yet,' replied Hannah, although the idea was gradually taking shape.

She began her research two days later, after an unusual weekend at Glenmore Road.

The day before, she had accompanied the MacKenna clan to Mass in St Michael's Church in Cumberland Street. Colleen had asked her on Saturday about her own religion, curious as to whether Hannah gave any thought to it or observed its rites. Colleen knew nothing at all about Judaism and would doubtless not have been surprised to learn that it advocated witchcraft, black mass, even human sacrifice.

'Those aren't the kind of problems that have held much interest for me,' Hannah replied cautiously, not wanting to offend the convictions of a woman for whom she had the highest regard.

Colleen had insisted. Was it not true the Jews had priests they called rabbis, and that they prayed every day in temples?

'We've got loads of rabbis, there's no question about that, more than we know what to do with. And plenty of temples as well. But . . .'

'It doesn't interest you very much . . .'

It was at that point that Hannah, almost despite herself, allowed free rein to her very sharp tongue.

'It doesn't interest me at all. It's a religion for men, like all religions, for that matter. I'll take an interest in religion the day there's a chance I could become a rabbi, an imam, or a pope, and that isn't going to happen tomorrow. Anyway, I've no need of a crutch to help me walk through life.'

No sooner had she finished speaking than she immediately began to reproach herself for her bluntness.

'I could see quite clearly that I'd shocked your mother, Lizzie. Worse than that: I'd upset her. I bitterly regretted it. And at the same time I was amazed at myself, never having thought much about religion and not being aware that I had such a strong opinion on the matter. You weren't listening or, to be more precise, you pretended not to be listening. You struggled away with your needlework – you were starting on that tapestry which, if I'm not mistaken, you still haven't finished now, fifty years down the line. But by way of apology for my irreverence I asked your mother if I could go with you to Mass the next day. I was curious.'

It was the next day that she began to pursue her idea. The shops in the George Street neighbourhood seemed to Hannah, who would always have a keen eye for such things, more interesting than their Melbourne counterparts. In the first place, the buildings they occupied had a patina, not one comparable with that of the shops in Warsaw, but much more so than the newer buildings of Melbourne. In short, there was everywhere what seemed like a rather comforting European atmosphere. And the people themselves seemed different: they were more nonchalant, warmer, perhaps less concerned with money since they had acquired their wealth earlier. They had a marked tendency to be interested in trinkets and baubles: you only needed to look in the shop windows to see that more jewellery was sold here than in Melbourne. And above all, it seemed that people were prepared to pay more for their purchases, a fact that was of great interest to Hannah.

She also took careful note of the great specialization of many shops. She was accustomed to Warsaw, and especially to the Jewish quarter there, where the traders sold absolutely anything. She was astonished to find so many shops that sold only one product, compensating for this exclusivity with higher prices. She found a shop that sold nothing but ladies' hats, another specializing in corsets, a third that sold pipe tobacco but not cigars, a fourth given over entirely to stationery.

'I hadn't yet been to London, Paris or Vienna, Lizzie, and even in Warsaw I had done little investigating. I had no experience, though I had already some familiarity with the commercial advantages of snobbery. I knew there are only two ways of succeeding in business: by selling in large quantities at a low price things that everyone needs, or by selecting one's clientele with the greatest of care and persuading these people to buy things they have absolutely no need of at exorbitant prices . . .'

As soon as she had told the MacKennas that it was her firm intention to work, and to become independent, despite their hospitality, Dougal and Colleen offered to help. They could, they told her, find her all kinds of desirable jobs. Dougal was a member of several clubs: one for the managers in public works and Australian railways; another that united former residents of India; an Irishmen's club, a Catholic league, and a cricket club that kept him busy at the weekends. Colleen was equally willing to mobilize an attack force consisting of charitable organizations, and Rod, who had just joined the Colonial Secretary's office having completed his law studies at Sydney University, was only too happy to help put Hannah's stay in Australia on a slightly more secure footing.

It was difficult to resist such a tidal wave of kindness. But Hannah managed to do so with a patience and gentleness that were not much in character, finding it rather difficult to imagine herself as a teacher, a governess, or a librarian. Instead she visited all the shops in the centre of Sydney, one by one, and drew up an exhaustive list of them. She crossed out and eliminated from her list all those that were too big, too old-fashioned and which, in her view, had no future; she passed over all the shops that had anything to do with food (she had had more than enough of cheeses!), with the wholesale trade, with hardware; she excluded any business that was unabashedly male-orientated.

She still had no idea what she was going to sell, but it became more and more obvious whom she would sell to: to those tall

Australian women, all of them a head taller than she was, with the huge feet and the big red cheeks, the ones who had come to this country on the other side of the world, a country made by and for men, where they could not find the feminine luxuries of their native Europe.

By the third day, only eight shops remained on her list. One of these sold mostly umbrellas: she ruled it out. Having eliminated a shoe shop and a few dusty, ill-located establishments she was down to four, all of them women's dress shops, just like the business she had started in Cracow Avenue. She finally selected one, run by two Australian sisters of Welsh origins. Her research revealed that one was married, the other a widow: both were as shrivelled as plum-pudding raisins and timorous as bustards. It took Hannah two days to persuade them to employ her. They sold lace, embroidery and buttons, all of it very quaint and antiquated. There was no hope of actually developing a business like theirs, or of repeating the kind of arrangement she had made in Warsaw with Dobbe Klotz. Hannah's weekly wages of seventeen shillings was the maximum she could expect from this job, and to extract even that much from the two sisters she had had to tell the most extravagant lies.

It was for very different reasons that she had been drawn to this rather dreary haberdashery, situated on the ground floor of a two-storey house that backed on to George Street. Its main entrance lay at the end of a paved inner courtyard; the whole place, including the vaulted, high-ceilinged side buildings, had for a long time served as an entrepôt for wool. Its entrance was large enough to accommodate the huge drays drawn by six or eight horses that had years before made their way from the bush into the centre of town.

Hannah wrested an agreement from the Williams sisters on September 16th, 1892. She had been in Australia for two months; approximately one hundred days had elapsed since she had left Danzig and Poland.

Her plans were falling into place. And they would, she was sure, easily make her rich.

10

---•---

THE HOUSE IN BOTANY BAY

'Oh, and I nearly forgot,' said Hannah, 'I must have told the Williams sisters I was a tiny bit Welsh, on my mother's side . . .'

'And you'd rather I didn't go contradicting you . . .'

'They wouldn't have given me the job otherwise.'

'And just how did you explain that despite your Welsh mother you still don't know English very well?'

'I was brought up in France.'

'I see. By whom?'

'A Russian governess living in Florence – the Williams sisters adore Italy even though they've never been there – who took me in after my father, a French count, had abandoned my mother and me. And my mother died of starvation in Paris. The Williams sisters also adore Paris, though they haven't been there either; in fact they've never left Australia.'

'Well, that's all very clear,' said Colleen.

'It is, isn't it?'

Hannah was packing her belongings into her carpetbag. Colleen MacKenna was standing behind her, not far from the door of Lizzie's bedroom. She coughed, a dry spasmodic cough.

'You ought to do something about that cough of yours.'

Hannah was packing the dress with the thirty-nine buttons last, but she was unable to change the subject.

'What else?' asked Colleen.

'What other lies have I told that you'll have to cover up for me? Practically none.'

'Practically . . .'

'I told them you could vouch for me. The reason being . . .'Hannah still did not turn to face the Irish woman '. . . that you're my aunt.'

'Oh Lord!' exclaimed Colleen.

Hannah put the dress down, turned and said very quietly: 'That wasn't a lie, that was a wish. And . . .'

Colleen's green eyes glared at her. 'Yes?'

'I should like to have said that you were my mother. And what's more, I should like it to have been true.'

In the silence that followed she thought, 'That's what's so awful about you, Hannah. You really believe what you've just said, but at the same time you know very well the effect that little speech will have on her, how she'll be touched by it. Now she'll agree to cover up your lies. You're sincere all right, but only when it serves your purposes. You use your sincerity like a weapon and you're starting to manipulate people again, even after it cost you so much in Warsaw . . .'

'A distant aunt, of course,' she said. 'And only by marriage, since you're Irish and my poor mother was Welsh.'

Hannah had been at the MacKennas' for exactly twelve days on the morning this discussion took place. During that time she and Colleen had talked for hours on end, especially during the first four days, when they were on their own in the house in Glenmore Road and Hannah did not move from her bed. She had got to know Colleen MacKenna well, to form some idea of the kind of unconditional love she had for her husband, Dougal, and for her giant sons, apart from the mysterious Quentin. She had seen enough to realize that Colleen was very lonely, that she had reached the age when there is no longer a great deal to live for, other than a familiar daily routine, the same porridge in the mornings and the same Irish stew once a week, the same enormous loads of wash . . .

She looked up to see, as she had expected, tears in Colleen's eyes.

'I'm not really going away, Colleen. I'm staying in Sydney, after all.'

All the same, she too felt emotional. She walked over to the Irish woman, stood on tiptoe and hugged her close, realizing as she did so that as far back as she could remember she had never made a gesture of tenderness like this – especially not a sincere one! – towards anyone. Never. Not even towards Shiffrah, her mother.

She sent the letter the next day, on September 18th. By way of address, she settled for *Mr Lothar Hutwill, Gundagai, New South Wales*. She did not know the name of the estate on the banks of the Murrumbidgee, and thought in any event that the Hutwills must be well enough known to people in the area for those three lines to suffice.

It took her a week to find a place to stay. Not that lodgings were scarce in Sydney but, as with everything else, she had a very clear idea of what she wanted. A room with a family was out of the question, as was a boarding house. She was determined to have complete freedom of movement. And she did not want to repeat the mistake she had made in Warsaw, where she had worn herself out travelling from Goyna Street to the Arsenal to Cracow Avenue. In the end she was lucky, which is to say that her six days of knocking on doors ten hours a day finally paid off. She found two small rooms on the first floor of a building erected at the time of the gold rush forty years earlier. They had the much-sought-after advantage of a separate entrance and were less than a minute's walk from the haberdashery.

Her downstairs neighbour was an import-export company, the owner of which was a certain Mr Ogilvie, who had himself lived for many years in the two rooms he rented to Hannah. At first, he had refused point blank to rent her the apartment, first of all because he claimed to occasionally use it himself, secondly because he did not want a young single girl moving in, even if she were a relation of the MacKennas. He had weakened a little when she volunteered this first reference however, and he weakened even more when – putting on a fine show of indignation – she told him he ought to be ashamed of himself for thinking for one minute that she might be contemplating moving into his property in order to trade on her charms and that she had never in her life been so humiliated. It was enough to make her weep, and she began to do so.

His resistance broke entirely when, her grey eyes blazing, she asked him – now that she could see clearly what his vile game was – whether he was not making very improper suggestions. What did he take her for? And he was a respectable, married man, if people were to be believed! Was he not trying to lead astray a defenceless young girl, who would not be surprised, after all she had just heard, if he were to pounce on her lecherously, and by the way how much was the rent?

Twelve shillings a week? She laughed. That was a figure worthy of a would-be satyr, piling usurous greed upon lewdness!

She offered him eight, with a schedule of rising payments: eight shillings for the first six weeks, ten for the next six, fifteen shillings from the thirteenth week . . .

'Work it out, Mr Ogilvie. On that basis, in six months you'll receive three hundred and eighteen shillings – in other words fifteen pounds eighteen shillings – instead of three hundred and twelve. You'll make six shillings more this way; you really have nothing to complain about. No, no, please don't thank me, business is business. Of course, in exchange for that additional payment it's natural I should ask for something in return: I won't pay the first week in advance. How can I? I've only just started working and I still haven't received my first wage packet. So, it's settled then. I'll pay you in arrears – thank you for being so understanding, it's clear that we see eye to eye. And I'm prepared to commit myself to staying here at least six months, you just have to add a date to the lease. That is the right word in English, isn't it? A lease? I thought so . . .'

For three or four crucial minutes Ogilvie had not been able to get a word in edgeways. He stood open-mouthed, like a fish caught the previous day.

'And another thing,' continued Hannah, unrelenting. 'When I walked through your warehouse just now I noticed that you do a fair amount of business with France and Germany. Do you speak French and German? No? Do you have anyone working for you who does know German or French? No? I do. I know both those languages, I can speak and write them. You'll surely have letters to write: look no further, I'll do it. Ten pence a letter. That's all, because we're friends already. No? Ten pence is too expensive? Let's say eight, and have it done with. While we're on the subject, I also know Russian. And Polish. By the way, could you leave the bed in the flat, as well as the table, the chair and the cupboard? That way, after all, you won't have to pay any removal costs. Come now, Mr Ogilvie, let's have a smile, you've just found the best tenant you could ever dream of having . . .'

'*It was fun in those days, Lizzie, I enjoyed myself immensely. Men at the time – and I'm not so sure they've changed a great deal in sixty-odd years, frankly – were staggered and even appalled to discover that a woman could count as well as they could, sometimes better and more quickly. And the more money they had and the higher up the social ladder they were, the easier it was. These men were familiar with only two kinds of women: their wives, whom they considered too delicate to know anything about money, and prostitutes, with whom they would go and smoke a cigar, or whatever . . . For them there was nothing in between, particularly for the Anglo-Saxons. They were the best of all. You could wind them around your little finger as easily as you could toss a pancake. There were two types: the pioneers, from Australia or America, who had been terribly deprived of women – did you know that in your native Australia they started out practising polyandry, sharing a woman between five or six men? It's no laughing matter, it's the simple truth. Then there was the British Empire type, straight out of university, whose knowledge of "females", as they put it, was confined to their mothers and sisters. That kind of Anglo-Saxon couldn't come to terms with the idea that he must have been conceived in a bed, thanks to a woman. What's more, they often married late in life, taking virginal young girls as wives. That poor man Ogilvie, for instance – you knew him, but you won't remember, you were too young. He worked like one of the damned in order to make his fortune, and only when he had secured his position in the world did he send back to the Highlands for a Caledonian maid. To whom I'm sure he made love respectfully, without even removing her nightdress; he's probably never seen her navel. Naturally, when the poor devil ran into me, I threw him completely, with no more than my sharp tongue.'*

When she moved into Ogilvie's apartment, with all the pride of a person who has found her first home, Hannah had three shillings and four pence in her pocket. She had spent most of the pound she had when she arrived in Sydney, on an apprentice haberdasher's dress and on some new shoes, as well as tuppence on postage for her letter to Lothar Hutwill. Colleen offered to lend her a little money, but Hannah refused. She had already developed a great distrust of loans, a distrust she would always retain. By eating only one meal a day she managed to survive the week until she received her first wage packet.

She began to discover the virtues of the English week; as she had calculated, her work in the haberdasher's store kept her busy only ten hours a day, five and a half days a week. Compared with her hours in Warsaw, she felt she had all the free time she could have wished for.

And in which she might get some real work done.

*

The day she posted her letter to Lothar Hutwill, she went to Sydney University. The admissions officers thought her completely mad, explaining there was no way they could accept her as a student if she had none of the prerequisite qualifications. She made further enquiries and then went to the National Model and Training School in Spring Street.

'I'd like to attend classes in business English, medicine, botany, pharmacology and book-keeping.'

The secretary was bald and wore a pince-nez, a detachable collar and oversleeves; he looked like an old featherless eagle, and was as impassive as a rock.

'Are you sure that's all?' he asked.

'For the time being, yes,' said Hannah without a smile. 'I'll come back and see you, if I need to. And I haven't any money. I hope the classes are free.'

With an almost imperceptible glimmer in his eye, he explained they had been free since the Education Act was passed fifteen years earlier.

'I'm making a friend here,' Hannah said to herself.

'I've another small problem,' she said. 'I'm not free during the day. Are there any evening classes?'

'There are. Reading and writing classes, as well as classes to teach English to the poor wretches who don't know the language.'

'I already know how to read and write – by the way, you look very much like Alfred Jingle, in *The Pickwick Papers*. And as for English, as far as I'm aware it's English we're talking right now.'

'Quite right,' said the secretary, peering at Hannah over his pince-nez as though he suspected her of robbery. 'Would you by any chance have read Charles Dickens, miss?'

She thought: 'I'd bet my third-best lace petticoat, the one that's darned, that this fellow considers Dickens the greatest writer in the world. Why not give him pleasure?' Aloud she said: 'I've done nothing but all my life. I have the greatest respect for him and for all his fine works. As a matter of fact, that's how I learned the little English that I know.'

'He's your spiritual father, in a manner of speaking?' the secretary asked.

'That's putting it mildly,' said Hannah.

He paused. 'Who's Barkis?'

'The carrier in *David Copperfield*.'

'Miss Squeers?'

'The daughter of Wackford Squeers, headmaster of the school in Yorkshire, in *Nicholas Nickleby*.'

'Incredible!' said the secretary.

'I'm not telling you anything you didn't already know,' Hannah retorted.

The man stood up, like an extension ladder paying itself out. Hannah almost expected to hear him creak. He closed the grille on the counter window, took off his oversleeves, and opened the door to his office.

'Come in and sit down, please. You remember, I'm sure, the names of Mr Pickwick's three friends . . . It's a really elementary question . . .'

'Tracy Tupman, Augustus Snodgrass and Nathaniel Winkle. I adore Sam Weller too.'

'Incredible!' repeated the secretary. With obvious regret added: 'There are no evening classes in medicine, pharmacology, chemistry or botany. But as for book-keeping, I could find someone for you . . .'

'I could give lessons in exchange – German, French, Polish and Russian. As well as in Yiddish and Hebrew, if that would help.'

'Incredible. For botany, there's Mr James Barnaby Soames, he's said to have the finest herbarium in Australasia. He studied here before going to London. He honours me with his friendship and would perhaps agree to see you once a week, in the evening at about six o'clock . . .'

'I'm a respectable young girl,' said Hannah, very sweetly.

'I'd sooner die than doubt that for a second,' said the secretary tersely.

He then disclosed that his name was Ezekiel Rudge – 'just like one of the Great Man's characters, isn't that an extraordinary coincidence?' Hannah admitted that she was literally stupefied. In a whisper Rudge then broke the news to her: during a trip to England that he had made in 1868, he had had the unparalleled honour of attending a public reading given by the writer.

'I saw him with my own eyes.'

'Incredible,' said Hannah.

'In any case, Mr James Soames is a gentleman, of more than seventy years of age. You can trust him as you would me.'

Another gleam of humour flashed through his glasses.

'No comment?'

'None,' said Hannah with a smile.

'As for medicine, I'll think about it, and I'm sure I'll find someone for you. It's the chemistry that worries me . . .'

He pointed an uncommonly long index finger at Hannah.

'The title of the novel he was writing at the time of his death?'

'I haven't the foggiest idea, I'm desperately sorry to say.'

'*The Mystery of Edwin Drood*!'

Ezekiel Rudge was triumphant. But he was not fooled, either by himself or by the game they had been playing. As he adjusted his pince-nez, he asked whether he might make so bold as to ask an indiscreet question of the girl before him. Yes, replied Hannah. What, he wanted to know, would prompt someone so young to take an interest in so many different sciences simultaneously?

She told him, in the greatest detail. She explained how she was going to make one hundred thousand pounds in less than two years.

Silence.

'Incredible,' said Ezekiel Rudge finally. 'Absolutely incredible.'

James Barnaby Soames was an old pink-faced gentleman who did indeed have a marvellous collection of plants in his villa at Pott's Point. And not only under glass: his two-hectare property was a dream garden. This inoffensive little short-sighted man had, it seemed, travelled thousands of miles across Australia, as far north as the Torres Strait. He had seen the Coral Sea, the Gulf of Carpentaria, and the Great Barrier Reef. He had sailed all the way to Tasmania and ventured as far as the frontier of the terrifying Simpson Desert. Of course he knew Brisbane, Melbourne, Adelaide and Perth, and with only two aboriginal guides – 'who are no more anthropophagous than you or me, unless you yourself happen to be a cannibal' – he had walked the length of the Australian Cordillera and its Blue Mountains.

He and Hannah would see each other four times a month, as long as she remained in Australia. He would impart to her everything he knew of botany, a not inconsiderable amount, though it would prove insufficient for her unusual purposes.

The doctor that Rudge found for her was of German origin and, like many Australians at that time, a recent immigrant. He had studied in Vienna and would combine what he was to teach her of medicine with all that he could tell her of a city she had been swearing she knew well without having visited ever since she had arrived in Australia. As he could not answer all the questions she put to him, he advised her to go and see the Frenchman Berthelot when she returned to Europe.

'What if I wrote to him?'

'I doubt that he would reply. But he might recommend a few books you could read . . .'

Hannah wrote the letter, specifically asking the renowned chemist to suggest several titles for her to read on the subjects she listed. To be sure that her grammar was correct, she blithely copied out whole phrases and expressions taken from her precious Laclos.

No chemist could be found as Ezekiel had feared. But a pharmacologist was, he announced triumphantly ten days after their initial meeting in Spring Street. The apothecary was also German, from Bavaria, and he had the red face, whiskers and paunch to prove it. As soon as he was sure, first of all that she would not sleep with him no matter what he did; secondly, that she did not intend to give away his manufacturing secrets; and lastly, that she would not encroach on his territory by producing remedies and liniments, he told her all he himself had learned about plant-based medicines. He showed her how to use a mortar and pestle, a phial, a pill box, spatulas and retorts. He taught her the names of oils and how they were made. And he also began to point out to her – in between two sausage and cabbage hotpots – some useful similarities between the flora of Europe and that of Australia.

In the end the question of book-keeping was settled as well. Ezekiel's twin brother, an accountant with P & O, the Peninsular and Orient Line, happily took on the job. His first name was Benjamin, which Hannah told him meant 'son of the right hand' – in other words, 'child of fortune' – in Hebrew. 'Whereas Ezekiel means "to whom the Lord lends His strength".'

The brothers, both bachelors, invited her to dinner at their home. They lived in an area called Petersham, in a wooden house dating back to the early days of the colony. Each of its rooms was a museum, filled with numerous editions of Dickens, for whom the Rudge brothers shared the same veneration.

The dinner took place in mid-October, when the days were beginning to grow longer as spring approached in the southern hemisphere. At about eight-thirty Ezekiel and Benjamin – whose faces were identical – accompanied Hannah home in a cab hired expressly for the purpose. They thanked her once again for her visit. She was three-quarters of the way up the staircase when she turned around to say goodbye – and when, as the carriage disappeared into the night, she saw the familiar shock of red hair.

Micah Gunn was standing in the shadows; he now stepped forward two paces into the foggy light cast by a gas streetlamp on the far side of the road. He raised his arm to indicate he had a letter in his hand.

She hesitated on the staircase.

'I won't come near, miss,' he said. 'I ain't gonna hurt you . . .'

Seeing that she did not move, he crossed the street, placed the letter on the second step of the staircase, and retreated to a spot about ten metres away. She of course came down and unfolded the sheet of paper, read it, and looked up questioningly at Gunn. By way of reply, he moved away, disappearing for a moment from Hannah's field of vision. She heard the sound of horses. In an almost ghostly fashion, a luxurious barouche with a black leather hood emerged silently out of the fog.

The carriage came to a halt at the foot of the steps. Its two horses were led by Micah Gunn, who was the only coachman. Hannah could at first see only the hands of the man seated behind him; they were long and handsome, one calmly resting on his knees, the other on the side of the door.

Hannah remained undecided for a full minute, then stepped down into the street.

'Twenty-seven pounds and seven shillings for the train fare, first class, from Melbourne to Wodonga. Eloise and I, or to be more precise about it, I and Eloise, have decided not to charge you for the journey from Wodonga to Gundagai, since you travelled in a private carriage that would in any case have made the trip without you. On the other hand, as far as the five pounds given to you as an advance against your wages as well as the expenses incurred during your attendance on my wife, it seemed right to charge you five pounds eighteen shillings.'

'That's thirty-three pounds five shillings . . .'

'You're as quick as ever at counting. Then there's compensation, both on moral grounds or simply because Mrs Hutwill ended up without a chambermaid, thanks to you, in the middle of the bush, far from all civilization . . .'

'. . . and her husband without anyone to indulge his skirtchasing instincts.'

'The poor man.'

'Ten pounds?' suggested Hannah.

'To cover damages plus interest? One hundred at least, taking into consideration that Eloise meant to lodge a formal complaint and send all the police in Australia after you. For two or three weeks after your precipitous disappearance, she was convinced that you had stolen some of her jewels, as well as some cash. She even drew up a list of what you had taken. Had it come to her word against yours, you'd have ended up with your ankles in chains.'

The two fine horses trotted along, pulling the barouche swiftly southwards on a road that ran alongside the Pacific. Hannah told herself he was trying to intimidate her, that he was having fun at her expense.

'Be that as it may,' he continued, 'Mrs Hutwill was absolutely furious to learn that you'd no sooner arrived in Sydney than you embarked on a ship bound for New Caledonia, where those devilish Frenchmen are, and from there sailed to China, thereby escaping her vengeance.'

'So I'm in China right now.'

'Evidently. You travel at the speed of greased lightning. You may already be amongst the Russians, or at the feet of a maharajah in India. May I call you Hannah?'

Hannah's pulse quickened slightly.

'Yes.'

'Make no mistake, Hannah. She – Eloise, I mean – is assiduous in her hatred and dogged in her vengefulness. I really did have to carry out a full-scale investigation, the effects of which I managed to moderate better here in Sydney than in Melbourne. She nonetheless made some headway; she learned, for instance, that you are Jewish, and she hates Jews.'

'But you don't.'

The smile appeared slowly, reaching his eyes.

'I'm also a member of an oppressed minority, the category of prince consorts. Eloise is the one with the money, all of it. Our marriage contract was very clear on that point. You were indeed ingenious to write that letter to me on New South Wales Railways notepaper, and to sign it D. MacKenna. If you had not taken the precaution of doing so, I should have had some difficulty in explaining why you were writing to me, and why you were still in Sydney, contrary to the detective's report on you.'

'You paid someone to say I was in China, or with the King of Siam?'

'Male solidarity played a part in it.'

Hannah looked up at Micah Gunn, who sat above them, to all appearances completely deaf to the conversation going on behind him. In the last two or three minutes it had begun to rain, a fine warm spring rain. Pointing to the red-haired man, Hannah asked:

'You told him to follow me?'

'Yes. Micah does whatever I ask him to.'

'Absolutely everything.'

'Absolutely.'

'Did you know I was going to run away from Gundagai?'

'I didn't know. However, you were anything but a real chambermaid. Even in Australia a chambermaid doesn't express interest in the revenues of a mine or a farm, in the customs duties imposed in the colony of Victoria, in the way banks are run, the conditions of credit they offer, and the comparative possibilities for economic growth in Melbourne and Sydney. To tell the truth, I've never met a woman capable of understanding a single word about any of these things – they're men's concerns. To be equally frank, I've known few men as eager for information on these topics as you, or as capable of absorbing it so quickly. Those I have known did not measure five feet tall with their shoes on; they did not weigh barely six and a half stone; nor did they wear clinging dresses. Above all they did not have huge grey eyes, the memory of which could haunt a man for weeks and months . . .'

Silence.

Hannah thought to herself: 'This is the first real compliment a man has ever paid you. And it isn't at all disagreeable, in as much as it is sincere, which it must be since he didn't go so far as to say you were pretty. And in as much as his aim isn't simply to get you into bed instantly and plough into you as though you were a field of potatoes.'

At the same time, as she reasoned so lucidly she began to feel breathless. The bodice of her dress suddenly felt tight over her breasts.

The barouche slowed down.

'When we arrived at Gundagai, before I left for Adelong, I gave Micah orders to make sure you weren't after Eloise's jewels, and that you weren't the scout for a bunch of larrikins. If you did run away he was to follow you, but assuming you took nothing with you he was to leave you in peace.'

'I didn't take anything.'

'Except the horse. Micah almost died laughing, watching you saddle and mount it.'

'That was mean of him.'

'He couldn't very well give you a hand. He followed you to the MacKennas in Glenmore Road. Were they the people you knew?'

She told him about Cousin Schloimele 'Sam' Visoker.

'That explains everything,' said Lothar.

The barouche stopped.

'Hannah,' said Lothar. 'I didn't want to run the risk of waiting for you at your place, in that apartment you've rented – on very strange terms – from Tom Ogilvie, who happens to be one of the people I do business with. And I didn't want to ask you to meet me in a hotel, where we would have been seen together. Eloise tolerates my escapades with her chambermaids, she encourages them, in a way, as you realized. At least she knows with whom I'm being unfaithful to her, and I suppose she doesn't feel compromised by it, since in her eyes they're only servants.'

She almost said: 'Which I'm not.' But she was not sure she even wanted to take part in this conversation.

'Officially, which is to say as far as Eloise's suspicious eyes are concerned, I'm in Sydney on business, even though it's Saturday. I arrived this morning, and I've had two perfectly genuine business appointments. This evening, at my club in George Street, I dined with the owner of a schooner – perhaps you don't know, but that's a sailing boat. This one's a real beauty. It was built in the United States and I haven't been able to put it out of my mind ever since I first saw it several months ago, speeding past the lighthouses at Queenscliff in Melbourne, the wind in its sails. It's the most wonderful craft anyone could dream of. Eloise has finally agreed to let me have it – just as a man gives way to his wife's desire for furs or diamonds – and has given me permission to buy it. The deal was concluded this evening. Tomorrow I shall be leaving for Brisbane, where the schooner is anchored . . .

Hannah looked at him with some surprise. Though she still did not know him well, she had only ever seen Lothar Hutwill demonstrating courtesy and a quiet irony. When speaking of this boat, his voice and his demeanour became perfectly boyish.

'Men are sometimes so surprising, Lizzie. We appreciate their qualities but more often than not we love them for their shortcomings. Or their weaknesses. And the weakness Lothar Hutwill revealed to me that October night as he told me of the lies he'd told his wife, when I'd thought him so

*sure of himself, affected me more strongly than all the strength I credited
him with . . .'*

He smiled once again.

'I don't mention this boat without good reason. Eloise made the
necessary credit facilities available to me; my buyer sold me that
boat for a little under the price we'd agreed. I don't suppose you
were expecting any advice from me on the enterprise you referred
to in your letter. How much do you need?'

'One thousand five hundred pounds,' said Hannah.

The rain fell more heavily than before, large fat drops beating
down on the leather hood. Hannah's eyes met Lothar's and she
followed his gaze. Twenty or so metres away, the veranda of a
white house loomed up out of the darkness.

Lothar Hutwill, in a voice once more calm and gentle, said: 'This
house doesn't belong to me – I mean, it isn't Eloise's. It belongs to
a friend of mine in Sydney with whom I breakfasted this morning.
He has offered to lend it to me before. I've never accepted. This
time I did.

'You're under no obligation to come in, Hannah. If you prefer
Micah will take you home and bring you the fifteen hundred
pounds in cash on Monday morning.'

'We'll make a contract.'

He laughed. 'If you like.'

She closed her eyes, but immediately opened them again. While
reproaching herself for the feelings that came over her she could
not help but take an irresistible pleasure in them.

'We'll make a contract,' she said. 'A private agreement, if that's
the right way of putting it, so that your wife knows nothing about
our partnership.'

'Because we're to become partners, are we?'

He smiled, with more than his usual irony.

She looked out at the house, now at closer range. It had a
veranda similar to ones she had seen in Melbourne; it reminded
her of the home of the woman she had sold her dresses to in St
Kilda. But as soon as she'd crossed the veranda and walked through
the main door, Hannah stepped into another world. The whole of
the ground floor consisted of a single room, measuring a good
fifteen metres square, with a low ceiling and eight or ten very
slender columns that were practically invisible. Everything in this
huge space was black and white: black floorboards, black door-
frames and windowframes, black beams, and a black staircase

leading to the floor above. The rest of the floor was a uniform dazzling white.

Until then, Hannah had known only the luxury of abundance – profusions of furniture, carpets, wall hangings, all of it staggering under the weight of braids and tassels and furbelows. This elegant sparseness left her flabbergasted – and unnerved. The only colour came from the pictures on the walls, most of which were charcoal sketches. The few paintings were brilliant in colour but haphazard in their composition; they seemed the works of a tormented mind.

'Impressionist,' explained Lothar Hutwill. 'I should have warned you, this house belongs to a most original painter. He did a portrait of Eloise, but when she saw the result she had a fit and refused to pay him. Have you heard of the Impressionist school?'

She shook her head: no.   .

Something else about the appearance of the place heightened her anxiety, particularly in view of what she knew she was about to do in it. There were no curtains on the windows.

There was an entire row of them, almost touching one another, running along the wall at the far end of the room. They had neither curtains nor shutters. 'In other words,' she thought, 'from the outside, in the darkness, people must be able to see us as clearly as in broad daylight!' She felt herself begin to panic.

When they had entered the room, she had sat down at his invitation. She turned down the glass of wine he had offered her, however; she had never before had a drink and this seemed a bad time to begin. She refused as well his offer of a cup of tea. He laughed.

'Just as well. I don't in any case know how to make it.'

He sat down – not beside her, which confounded her greatly – and stayed put, as though he were paying a formal visit, his hands resting flat on his knees, his hat, cane and gloves lying beside him. He looked at her very calmly, so that she felt the need to seek refuge in the only topic of conversation that seemed to her inoffensive: the money he was willing to lend her . . .

For a few seconds she forgot her confusion, that of a young girl at her first assignation.

'What do you mean? Don't you want us to be partners?'

'It hadn't even occurred to me. I'll lend you the money and you can give it back to me when you think best.'

'With nothing on paper?'

The gleam in his eye became more marked.

'I've the greatest confidence in you, Hannah.'

He crossed his legs, with great attention to the crease in his trousers. As usual, he was dressed with the utmost elegance. His face was even more tanned than it had been in Gundagai, so that it contrasted magnificently with the silvery hair at his temples. His hands were beautiful.

'He is waiting for me,' thought Hannah, with what was almost mounting rage. 'He is waiting. He doesn't have Taddeuz's inexperience; this is something else.'

She said: 'You haven't even asked me what the fifteen hundred pounds is for. Is that also because of your confidence in me?'

'I'm asking you now.'

'Beauty salons,' she said.

'For women?'

'For kangaroos.'

'*Touché*,' he said. 'Ask a silly question and you get a silly answer. And how are you going to set about it?'

'I'll make creams; one to start with. To prevent wrinkles or get rid of them.'

'Does it really work?'

'I haven't a clue. My mother used to say it did. She made enough to pomade the whole of Poland, the whole of my *shtetl* at least . . .'

'Your what?'

'*Shtetl*. It means village in Yiddish. My mother used to say that her pomade provided protection against the cold, in winter, and it did. If you put a little on your lips and cheeks, you never had a problem with chapped skin. And it smelt wonderful.'

'You may have noticed that it's not very cold here in Australia.'

'But there's a lot of dust, and wind and salt air from the sea.'

'Is your mother here?'

'I should be very surprised if she were. But I know the formula. You need some plants and fruit. And one or two other little things.'

Beneath his nonchalant air, he had a very quick mind.

'Are you planning to make these potions yourself?'

'Mmmmmm.'

'By setting up a factory?'

'Mmmmmmmm.'

'With fifteen hundred pounds?'

'I don't need a big factory.'

'Everything is already worked out?'

'Everything.'

'Are you going to employ a staff?'

'Yes.'

'And where are you going to find Polish plants in Australia?'

'Do you know someone called James Barnaby Soames?'

'By name. He's a kind of explorer, a slightly eccentric old man.'

'He's also a botanist. The best and the kindest in all of Australia. I gave him a list of the flowers, fruits and plants I need and he has traced the Australian equivalents. He's found some, a sufficient number in any event. Enough for me to be able to make a cream very like my mother's and . . .'

She stopped. The look in Lothar Hutwill's eyes was not that of a man with his mind on a business discussion. He was hardly listening to her any longer. She saw this and began to pace back and forth before him as she talked, relishing the sheer pleasure of anticipation. Lothar Hutwill's eyes followed her, fixed upon her intensely. She knew it was not her conversation that fascinated him now – it was her breasts and hips, her whole body he was imagining, undressing. This was a new and powerful sensation for her, like a rising fever, one she was prepared to make rise even higher . . .

And while this was going through her mind, she continued her technical exposition:

'I've not only studied botany, I've also consulted a doctor, and his books. I've learned a lot of things about the skin, the way it's made, why it becomes unhealthy and when, and what you can do to keep it in the best possible condition. The doctors – those I've seen, at least – don't know a great deal about what they call dermatology. I'd need to go to Europe, to France. But I've learned a good deal. I'm also interested in hair, and nails, in teeth and the reasons why they fall out or turn yellow like horses' teeth. And why some people's breath could kill a mosquito in full flight. I don't yet know all that it's possible to know . . . I only began studying a month ago. I've also been working with a pharmacologist, who teaches me what he can. It isn't much. And the same goes for book-keeping. Two evenings a week. Next, I'll see about banks, the way they work, the services they can provide and to whom . . . and by the way, Lothar, there are no curtains on the windows.'

She said these last few words in the same tone as before, in her clear, distinct voice, admittedly with a slight catch in it, but still under control. It took Lothar Hutwill a second or two to react.

Feeling rather pleased with herself, she realized that she had taken
this man who was so sure of himself by surprise.

'So?' he said at last.

She stared at him. The rhythm of her heartbeats quickened
again.

'I suppose,' she remarked calmly, 'that on the other side of those
windows there's a crowd of your friends from Sydney who've
come to watch the spectacle?'

'And I suppose I even charged them admission . . .'

'Or just Micah Gunn.'

Silence.

Even at this point he remained totally still, which made Hannah
increasingly uneasy.

'But, after all,' she tried to tell herself, 'this is what you wanted,
isn't it? You knew when you came here, and you knew it all the
time you were talking, you knew it even before you saw him, that
you expected this man to teach you how to make love, a slightly
more difficult subject than book-keeping or botany. So, one of two
things is possible: either you leave straightaway, or you let him do
it.'

'Do you want me, Lothar Hutwill?' she heard herself say.

'Terribly. And do you want me?'

One of two things is possible: either . . .

Lothar Hutwill still had not moved.

'Do you make love as well as Mendel Visoker?' she asked finally.

Surprised or not, Lothar Hutwill did not bat an eyelid; he was
trembling, however.

'I don't know Mendel Visoker.'

'He's . . .' began Hannah. 'I'm going to sleep with you,' she said.
'But certainly not because of the fifteen hundred pounds.'

'I'd stake my life on that, Hannah,' he replied very gently.

She knew he would. She also knew that beneath his imperturbability he was in as much turmoil as she. And it was awfully good
to know all that.

'Do you wait like this with every woman?'

He shook his head. 'No. No, certainly not.'

'Why with me?'

A short silence.

He said in a slightly hoarse voice: 'You're extraordinarily direct.'

'Why with me?'

Another silence.

His hands tensed a little. They were three or four metres apart, he still seated while she stood in the centre of this huge black and white room.

'The bedroom is upstairs,' he said at last. 'Any other woman would have been there by now. No, what's happening tonight has never happened before . . . What I mean is that I never thought I would ever be playing a game like this. If it is a game. You're very strange.'

'What do you expect me to do?'

She held his gaze.

'Get undressed?'

'Only if you want to.'

'Get undressed in front of all these curtainless windows?'

She did not expect an answer, and there would not be one. She removed the long pin holding her wide-brimmed hat in place, then tossed the hat aside. This untidiness was a new pleasure. She then threw back her head and opened her eyes wide. She knew she was a little frightened – just enough. Her fingers relaxed one by one and she started to undo the buttons on her dress. Lothar Hutwill still had not moved. Hannah read in his eyes all the things that a woman could love: desire, respect, confidence, dread. 'Not only are you shameless,' she thought to herself, 'but what's more, it's as though you knew instinctively all the right gestures.'

She stopped when she reached her waist. Then looking deep into Lothar Hutwill's eyes, she sat down to unlace and take off her ankle boots, making a note to herself that she was more than ready.

She stood up, looking much smaller now that she was barefoot. She finished unbuttoning her dress, slipping it off her shoulders and letting it drop to the laquered floor, with a wriggle of her hips.

Slowly she took off her four petticoats, then the first of her chemises. She was in no hurry. She removed the second chemise, and stood before him, her breasts bared. She could feel that her nipples had hardened.

Unfastening the knot holding her lace knickers round her waist, she let these too drop to the floor.

She was left in her stockings, which she rolled down unhurriedly, having unhooked her rose-trimmed garters.

With her foot she nudged the pile of clothes away.

Finally she loosened her hair, which tumbled down to the small of her back.

She could not have been more naked. She waited.

She barely had time to glance at the windows, whose dark panes reflected like so many mirrors, before Lothar Hutwill was beside her. Taking her in his arms, he carried her upstairs.

She cried out, she moaned, but she of course still managed to keep the promise she made to herself: to take note of everything, analyse everything, learn everything.

Lothar Hutwill had crossed the threshold of the bedroom with Hannah in his arms. Slowly he had laid her on the already turned-down bed. Then he had left her alone for a few moments, just long enough for her to grow scared, really scared, in this dark room. Both a woman and a little girl, she was about to let tender words escape her lips – asking him to come to her, not to leave her on her own. She said nothing. And he came to her.

His mouth explored her entire body. She felt his breath on her, still regular but from time to time punctuated by a husky sigh. She listened to her own breathing, her gasps whenever a caress took her by surprise. After his mouth, it was his chest that he gently pressed close to hers. Her fear had dissipated.

There was a natural, slow rhythm to his caresses, and yet he never let her rest; she felt carried away by wave upon wave. Suddenly he was inside her and she felt a burning sensation, but different from what she had felt with, with . . . She thrust the name to the back of her mind and allowed herself to be swept along, matching the violence of his lovemaking. 'So this is what it's like,' she thought, 'this is what it's like . . .' saying the words to herself over and over again, all the time he was inside her, until her body and mind formed a ball of fire that exploded. She no sooner thought she had regained her calm than he moved deeper inside her and there was another explosion, more cataclysmic than anything she could have imagined, reducing her to a series of cries and moans, and to an incredible happiness that she had waited so long to experience.

She was slowly regaining consciousness when he murmured that he wanted to take her again, and when in her new voice she said yes, and again he was inside her and again she knew, she would not forget.

She felt marvellously weary and languid. She smiled, the darkness protecting her.

He was not moving any more either, quiet on his back beside

her, both of them surrounded by this salty sea smell and the smell of lovemaking that she knew, briefly, from the room in Praga. Eventually he drew her to him and she nestled in the curve of his waist, against his hip, her cheek resting on his chest.

'Of course there wasn't a living soul on the other side of those windows,' he said.

'Not even Micah Gunn?'

'Certainly not. But if I ever found out that he was, I'd kill him.'

'I don't care.'

'I do. He wasn't there. I love you.'

'No,' she said, very distinctly.

A pause.

She felt his whole body stiffen.

After a few seconds he asked: 'May I light the lamp?'

'No,' she said, without understanding why.

'Then may I ask a question?'

She smiled mischievously in the darkness, playfully licking his chest with the tip of her tongue.

'I know very well what you're going to ask me, Lothar Hutwill. And the reply is still no. No love between us. Ever.'

'Another man?'

'Mmmmmm.'

'And that's definite?'

'Yes.'

'In Australia?'

'No.'

'Now he's going to sulk like a child, despite his age,' she thought. 'That's a man all over, for you.' She felt incredibly light-hearted, a light-heartedness nothing could dampen.

She then remembered the fifteen hundred pounds, which were very heartening in themselves. There was no connection between the money and the last few hours, however, she was quite sure of it. She had slept with him because Mendel had refused to sleep with her years before. There was in fact something of Mendel in Lothar, not a great deal but a tiny trace, if only in the smile beneath the moustache, in the laughing eyes, and in that confidence, the confidence of a large man with a very soft heart.

The patter of rain continued outside, its rhythm reinforcing the silence between the two of them. Lothar's breathing had calmed after the quickening Hannah had noticed in it when she told him there could never be any question of love between them. She sank

into a deep sleep, already very drowsy when she replied to his last
question: yes, of course she would see him again, in this house or
elsewhere, when she had the time and he could get away from
Eloise for a while. They would have to see each other after all so
that she could report to him on the state of their business.

When she awoke he was no longer beside her. Wrapped in a sheet,
she explored the house. She was less surprised to discover that she
was alone than she was to find that the wall of windows looked
out over the Pacific. Below there was a dizzyingly vertical drop;
the black-and-white house was perched on a rocky cliff more than
one hundred feet high.

She remembered that it was Sunday and that she was in no
hurry whatsoever. There was no boat visible on the horizon, and
she saw no sign of life from the veranda when she looked down
the road in both directions. She instinctively dropped her sheet,
intoxicated with her liberty, with the sense of having a house to
herself. She hardly worried about how she would get back to
Sydney; this was the first time she had ever really been alone,
away from everything, and she wanted to savour it all. It was after
all also the first time she had taken a lover, or to be more precise
that she had made love with a man she did not really love, the first
time she had ever got such great pleasure from it.

In the kitchen she prepared a perfect breakfast: tea, some biscuits
she found in a cupboard, bread and butter with jam. She ate it
looking out over the ocean. Then she filled the English bathtub, in
which she could almost lie full-length, with hot water and climbed
in.

She relished every minute of that late morning, as pleased with
the solitude as with the exhilarating sense that the world already
belonged to her a little, and would belong to her even more, thanks
to Lothar's fifteen hundred pounds.

She was more than a little disappointed when she heard the
barouche return. From the window she saw Micah Gunn sitting on
the box, waiting for her very patiently, his whip poised. When she
finally announced that she was ready – she kept him hanging
about for the sheer pleasure of it – he took her back to Sydney. He
told her that he had delivered Mr Hutwill to the Brisbane train and
that he would bring her the money, as arranged, the next day.

Which he did, and from then on, Hannah was adequately
equipped to make her fortune.

11

QUENTIN MACKENNA

In the last week of October 1892 she wrote a third letter to Mendel Visoker. She held no great hope of his ever receiving it, any more than he might the previous two she had written, the first from Melbourne to tell him of the robbery, because she felt that he ought to know, the second the day she had met the Hutwills and had finally managed to resolve the problem of the journey from Melbourne to Sydney. In that letter she assured him she would find his cousin Schloimele, and that she would tell him that he had better have had good reason for not having replied to her telegram; he would help her to get back the money Mendel had entrusted to her and that she lost through her own stupidity.

She posted the first two letters to the governor of the Siberian penal colony, in a place called Irkutsk miles from anywhere. The name was familiar to her from Jules Verne's *Michel Strogoff*; she had furthermore verified it in her atlas. She figured that it would take three or four months, at best, for her letters to reach Lake Baikal; whether they would actually reach Mendel was another matter. All the same she was as sure he was alive as she was that the sun would rise in the morning.

In her third letter she wrote:

'I'm in Sydney. Everything's working out marvellously, except that Cousin Schloimele has gone to America, the fool. But I've made other arrangements: in six months, twelve at the outside, I shall begin to make my fortune and I'll be able to pay you back all your money. You will have

*it when you escape, which you may have done already, after all. With
heartfelt love and kisses, Hannah.'*

'And that's that,' she said to the Bustards, Harriet and Edith,
otherwise known as the Williams sisters. (Why, she wondered, are
they both called Williams when they've both been married, presumably not to the same man? That's a puzzle that needs
explaining.)

'Have I made myself clear?'

The two haberdashers bobbed their heads and rolled their eyes;
they claimed they had not understood a word. Hannah felt well-
disposed, almost affectionate, towards them. The nickname she
had given them was, in her view, a friendly one, just as Dobbe's
nickname had been.

'Very well,' she said. 'I'll go over it again, perhaps a little more
slowly. This building we're in, which was left to you by your father,
will sooner or later be demolished. The road outside is going to be
widened – I obtained this information from the Colonial Sec-
retariat. The City of Sydney will buy the place from you, and you'll
be compensated. But what good is that? You'll be driven out of
your home and consigned to a distant suburb on the north bank,
maybe even to St Leonards, amid a crowd of flea-ridden immigrants, perhaps even Jews and Chinese. I have a solution. Thanks
to the inheritance my Welsh grandmother Ethelind Llewelyn left
me, I can rent from you everything to the left and right of the
carriage entrance in the courtyard: the ground floor and upstairs,
as well as the arches and the yard. There's no change as far as
you're concerned. You can continue to live where you've always
lived. What am I going to do with the buildings I rent from you?
Renovate them, paint them, make them as good as new again.
Turn your courtyard into the loveliest garden in Sydney. I shall live
in the west wing, the east wing will house my beauty salon.
Upstairs will be my laboratory. The arches and the garden will
become a tea shop. As everyone knows, you make the best scones
and muffins in Australia. If you would agree to run the tea shop, I
should be honoured. You would officiate over high tea as my
directors. And I would pay you, whereas at the moment the
opposite is the case.'

Silence. She thought to herself:

'Once again you're being manipulative, you little beast! However, you haven't told the charming Bustards any lies. It's true – or

else Rod MacKenna has been telling you stories, which would be surprising, as he's got about as much sense of humour as a boiled egg – quite true, that there are plans to demolish this block of flats in order to build new ones. It's also true that it won't happen for another fifteen years or more, but what harm if I'm anticipating history?' She smiled at Harriet and Edith.

'You're going to be rich, and you won't be obliged to leave the place where you've always lived. Next year, I promise you, you'll have enough money to make the trip to Europe that you've always dreamed of, to Great Britain, Wales, even Italy if you like.'

Earlier that day, as promised, Micah Gunn had brought Hannah her fifteen hundred pounds. They were delivered very discreetly, in the heart of a bouquet of twenty-one roses. To avoid again making the mistake she had made in Melbourne she had hurried with her money – and with Micah as an escort, though he followed her only at a distance – to the Bank of New South Wales. It had been founded in 1816, and was in the opinion of both Rod MacKenna and Tom Ogilvie, the most solid. It was on Rod's recommendation that the bank agreed to open an account for her, even though she could not see over the counter, a small impediment when it came to watching the cashier count out bills.

Hannah bowed her head very politely in deference to the two elderly ladies, hoping to convey all the conviction, charm and friendship in the world with her huge grey eyes.

Only when the Bustards had finally recovered from their initial alarm and said yes, did she finally ask them about the name they shared.

'It's because we married two brothers,' they explained.

'I should have thought of that,' Hannah conceded. 'What a dimwit I am.'

She had dozens of estimates submitted and went through them as carefully as she might read Laclos. She knew exactly what she wanted and was particularly concerned with what she called the right wing, where the tea shop was to be, as well as some other adjoining rooms that would be used for a kind of club which she had decided would be strictly inaccessible to men.

She would locate the beauty parlour above the tea room; she had very clear ideas about this too. Tom Ogilvie had recommended a foreman to her who was married and not very young, just as she had wanted. He was a sturdy sixty-year-old of Scottish origin,

passionate about doing a job well. A former master carpenter in
the Navy, this Watts had an almost mystical love of wood. His wife
was a little unassuming-looking woman, of a strong character. She
painted watercolours and did not even raise an eyebrow when
Hannah began to talk to her about Turkey red.

Robbie and Dinah Watts agreed to supervise the renovations. He
would take charge of all the exterior work on the building and she
would see to the details and surface decoration; in short, she would
add the feminine touch that Hannah prized above all else. With
them she made her only business mistake, carried away by her
wild excitement at getting things started.

'It's now October 20th. I want everything to be finished within
six weeks and I'll pay you an extra two pounds a day if it is.'

When she saw their faces, she immediately realized her stupidity.
She lowered her head, then looked up, smiling meekly.

'Please forgive me, Mrs Watts, and you too, Mr Watts. I know
that you'll do everything humanly possible, and that you'll do your
best. I should have known that straightaway. May I call you Dinah
and Robbie?'

In those few moments the look in her eyes was almost hypnotic,
all the more so since she was as sincere as she could be. The two of
them smiled back. Dinah, who was old enough to be her grandmother, quite brilliantly. They thought the project both original
and ambitious, especially as it had been conceived by someone so
young, but they both also thought it feasible. And they would be
happy if she would come and have lunch with them one day, at
their little house up in Willoughby, with its wonderful view and its
modest garden. They would do everything in their power to make
her happy, as long as she told them exactly what she wanted . . .

Beneath the arches and in the small garden that was to be
created in the courtyard, she wanted a café terrace that would
recall that of the Saxe Gardens in Warsaw. It would be the first of
its kind in Australia, aside from the hotel cafés, and it would be
private, closed to the general public, and invisible from the street.

'It must be the prettiest garden in Sydney, with flowers all year
round, and water flowing everywhere with little fountains, and
moss, and several aviaries – on the condition the birds don't make
too much noise and drown people's conversation. It must smell
lovely, and it must be cool, and it must be tasteful. I'll want screens
and canopies, charming little nooks in the greenery. And remember
to put cushions on the seats . . .'

The terrace would extend under the arches of both wings, so as to offer shelter when it rained. And the arches in turn would open on to rooms to the right, for when it was cool outside.

'In all the rooms I want white, nothing but white, with a Turkey red floor, the same red as my dress, Dinah, if you can find the same shade. And black skirting-boards everywhere . . .'

At this point Robbie Watts suggested that ebony would suit her purpose perfectly; he could not bear the idea of painting wood. Hannah endorsed his suggestion, despite the additional cost.

'And on the walls, Dinah, I want delicate watercolours, pictures of London, Paris, Vienna, with all the grace of those cities.

'For the door on the first floor, which will open on to the beauty parlour, the same . . . what did you call it? . . . the same ebony. Could we put wood-panelling upstairs, Robbie?'

They could, he replied. It would perhaps overwhelm a whole wall, but it could easily extend to chest height, and be finished off with an amarinth moulding. Amarinth was a kind of mahogany, he explained, which would not be far off Turkey red in colour.

'And all the rest will be white, including the ceiling,' said Hannah. 'With copper lamps. The furniture will be soft, feminine, fragile, but deep enough to allow one to sink into its plushness. No one will be able to get up once they've sat down, they'll want to spend the rest of their lives where they are. I also want some musical boxes, as delicate as the watercolours, their silvery notes tinkling in every room. Dinah, it will be true upstairs just as downstairs that only women will be allowed entrance, not a single man. Apart from the firemen perhaps, if the place were to catch fire one day. And even then! I want . . . how can I put it? . . . the sensual atmosphere of the harem. Does that shock you, Dinah?'

'You're a tiny bit surprising . . .' answered Dinah with a smile; the Scottish woman apparently understood Hannah better than she could have hoped.

'As for the three rooms at the back, Robbie,' continued Hannah, 'where the wool used to be stored, I want them to be separated from the beauty parlour by another heavy door, even more massive than the first. Mysterious, intriguing, secret, so that all the women in Sydney, Australia and the rest of the world will wonder what lies hidden behind it. On the black wood of this door, in gold letters, I want the word *Laboratory* to be inscribed. That will be my kitchen.'

She burst out laughing at the expression on the Scotsman's face, delighted as well with her own stroke of inspiration. If she closed her eyes she could almost hear the subdued hubbub of the crowds of women who were bound to come running breathlessly to her establishment, as she would make them beautiful and happy.

She explained that by 'kitchen' she meant the place where her creams would be made, or at least where her clients would think her creams were made. For a while she would manufacture her products behind the mysterious door but the moment when success would force her to set up her factory elsewhere could not be far off. Twenty or thirty young girls would work there, all having sworn to reveal nothing of their work, as much to prevent imitation of Hannah's products as to maintain the mystique she considered essential to her advertising.

'In the meantime, Robbie, you'll have to make me a provision for direct access to the kitchen from the street, so that my ingredients can be delivered without having to pass through the courtyard. What would you say to having a contraption which can be hoisted up on a rope – that's it, a goods lift, I didn't know the word in English.'

She reeled off further details and specifications, at high speed, releasing the inventory of dreams that had been so long crowded inside her head.

This session took place on 20 October. Two days later, convinced that she had found in the Watts the best possible agents to give concrete shape to her enterprise, she embarked on her expedition westwards.

She again had a very clear idea in mind, though she could not have expected to meet the person she was soon to encounter, and who would simplify her plans many times over.

'Quentin MacKenna.'

She had been watching the countryside go by, when she looked round and saw him appear out of nowhere, in a wooden carriage on the Great Western Railway.

He was slightly shorter than his four brothers, and less sturdy as well. In fact he was actually rather emaciated looking. He had Colleen's green eyes, but the resemblance ended there. He had a perfectly individual way of crinkling his eyelids to screen his eyes, and he wore an expression of very aggressive insolence. Cleanliness was evidently not one of his obsessions, as it was with the other MacKennas. His blond beard was untrimmed and he was dressed in the faded canvas trousers and shirt and hat of the bushmen, stained with months or years of sweat. A fine white scar ran down his suntanned face, from his forehead, through the arch of his left eyebrow, and down his cheek to the corner of his mouth. A curious curl that made him look as though he were permanently sneering sat on his lips. His green eyes were penetrating, cold and hard.

'And what am I supposed to do?' said Hannah. 'Go into raptures?'

'You ought to, I'm worth it.'

He narrowed his eyes even more.

'Defensive, eh? I was warned of that.'

'Defensive to a point you couldn't begin to imagine. Who warned you?'

The train had left Sydney and passed through the little town of Penrith only moments before. It was now crossing a very fine metal bridge, strung over a river forty metres wide.

'The Nepean,' said Quentin MacKenna. 'That valley and the Hawksbury Valley are quite similar to Europe. You'll find most of the plants you're looking for there.'

How could he already know the reason for her journey?

She repeated her question: 'Who warned you?'

'It wasn't Rod, or any of my brothers, my father even less so. He hasn't spoken to me for more than ten years and he's forbidden every living MacKenna to remember my existence. I'm the disgrace and bane of my family. It's true that I've something of the devil inside me: I left school, and by the same token left the clan, when I was twelve years old. I went to sea as a cabin boy. After that my life is a long catalogue of ignominious behaviour. A few hopes were raised when I joined up at sixteen to fight the Mahdi in the Sudan under Kitchener – the Sudan's in Africa. But I deserted, more or less. When I came back to Australia I was put in prison, not so much for having killed two or three men but on account of other misdemeanours. I was given the benefit of the doubt – in any case, I was the only survivor – and I went looking for gold. I didn't find any. End of story. The day before yesterday I saw my mother for the first time in three years. She loves you immeasurably. I hope you love her too, at least a little bit. I'm capable of feeling affection for nothing in the world apart from my mother and my sister, in so far as I'm capable of feeling affection at all. My mother told me she thought you were mad to set off the way you have. I thought so too, and wanted to get to know you. Now may I sit down?'

He did not wait for a reply, but sat on the seat next to her. Very calmly he said: 'Another fraction of an inch closer with that razor and you're going to rip my trousers open. And I only have one pair.'

Hannah was completely astounded. She gave him a searching look.

'Are you really Colleen's son?'

'And therefore your cousin, since she's recently become your aunt, it appears. My mother showed me where you slept, with my sister Lizzie, whom I've only seen from a distance – I'm not allowed near her. Yes, of course, it's a torment to me, could you doubt it for a minute? You want more proof that I really am Quentin? Let's see . . . You have a black-and-red dress with forty or fifty buttons, which my mother told you was very pretty but too old for you. Another thing: yesterday morning Lizzie was grappling with her needlework, rather reluctantly I must say, and she was putting yellow wool in the mane of what she believes to be a lion. Her blond-haired doll is called Frankenstein. In memory of me. I bought it for her six years ago when I came out of prison, when I learned for the first time that I had a sister. I gave the doll its name, which I thought best expressed my fundamental nature. Convinced now?'

He scarcely seemed to notice that she had sheathed the razor and put it away in her purse.

'Another thing about the romantic Quentin MacKenna,' he said in his drawling voice. 'I'm not a complete man. Ever since the time when I was attacked in a particular part of my anatomy with a knife I have been unable to touch a woman, even if I was madly in love with her. Do you understand what I'm talking about or are you one of those virgins who guards her supposed treasure between her thighs as though it were the Crown Jewels?'

As she made no reply he turned towards her. He met her grey gaze, holding it for a long time, then nodded his head.

'All right, so you aren't just anybody, I had an idea you might not be. My mother is not a woman who would love just anybody. If I were a complete man, I'd want you, even though you're not really beautiful. Now, tell me what kind of plants you're looking for.'

*

'It's so strange, Lizzie, that it should be me telling you about your brother. He was a bit crazy, it's true, but less so than people thought. He could be unnerving. He unnerved me at first, though not too much; the man capable of terrifying me hasn't yet been born. But he aroused my interest more than most because there was something highly unusual about him. And to think that for two years I got him to pick flowers for me!'

Outside her train window the countryside was changing. Until then, it had actually borne some resemblance to Europe – in any event to the Europe of Hannah's imagination, Western Europe. But after they crossed the Emu Plains the scenery became hilly, the orchards and farms disappeared. The single railtrack reinforced by dry-stone walls on both sides climbed its winding way up the slopes, often perching atop viaducts.

At Hannah's side, Quentin MacKenna rifled through Professor Soames's ink drawings. Now and then he would comment: 'That one I've seen . . . And that one . . . and that as well. In the Blue Mountains.'

He came to the index cards she had patiently put together, over the course of many evenings. For a few moments he was dumbfounded, then he began to read aloud:

'Sweet almond, wheat germ, elderberry, hawthorn, rice, gentian, soy, cucumber, hops, maize, camomile, sesame, mallow, burdock, marjoram, hyssop, witch hazel, liquidambar . . .'

He broke off: 'Liquidambar, for God's sake!' then continued: '. . . wormwood, basil, speedwell, melissa, strawberry, eucalyptus, periwinkle, artemisia, chelidonium, dandelion, saponaria, grapefruit, wild pansies, marsh mallow, roses, arnica, citronella, lavender . . .'

'Ordinary lavender,' interjected Hannah, suddenly feeling very much like laughing.

'. . . carrots – carrots! – fumitory, thyme, mint, coltsfoot, lemon, euphrasia, poppy, nasturtium, daisy, myrtle, mullein . . .'

'To make infusions with.'

'. . . birch, rosemary, juniper, alchemilla, savory, vervain, cress, borage, artichoke, nettle, St John's wort, chicory, aniseed, lime blossom, calendula . . .'

'Marigold.'

'. . . couch-grass, fenugreek . . .'

'That's ordinary trigonella.'

'That explains everything . . . Sage, centaury . . .'

'In other words, cornflower.'

'. . . hawkweed, fennel, walnut leaves, oregano, cheese rennet, tormentil . . .'

'That's a variety of potentilla. Your mother has another kind in her garden.'

'As for oils, apricot oil, sweet almond, sesame, wheat germ, coconut . . . You need palm oil?'

'And coconut milk too. It's very good for the skin.'

'. . . hazelnut oil, maize, pistachio, castor oil, cypress. You should have stopped off in the Nepean and Hawksbury Valleys, they would seem a gold mine to you.'

'On the way back.'

'Where are you going?'

'Cobar.'

'Why?'

'To see the mines.'

'To buy one?'

'Why not? Though not immediately, of course.'

'You are indeed eager to make your fortune.'

'There's no eager about it. I will make my fortune.'

'And there's no room for any discussion, eh?'

'None at all. It's as good as done.'

He looked at her and said: 'Go to Cobar, then. But you'll be disappointed.'

'That's my problem.'

'True.'

His indifference intrigued her, especially because it was so obviously genuine. He never laughed or smiled – the closest he came to either was that sardonic sneer, which seemed to her more and more an expression of hopelessness. Examining him in profile, and from quite an angle since, even seated, he towered above her, she looked for further resemblances to Colleen. She found them in the determined set of his chin, in his quiet authority, both of which made her think of Mendel, of the obvious loneliness of these two renegades. He continued reading.

'And seaweed and clay, apples, cow's milk and . . . *vaseline*?'

'That's made from an oil that comes out of the ground, called petrol.'

'Where the devil did you learn all this? If you really are seventeen, this is obviously the work of the devil. To get milk out of you, one probably has to squeeze your nostrils rather than your breasts.'

'I don't advise you to touch either. As for the vaseline, a doctor told me.'

'And . . . *lanolin*?'

'You get it from the suint in sheep's wool. And don't tell me there aren't any sheep in Australia.'

The train had made a series of stops at the little towns of Woodburn, Lawson and Mount Victoria, and now – after a series of bends, viaducts and even a tunnel – it crossed the Blue Mountains, descending once again into the Lithgow Plain.

'And you're going to slap all that gunk on some poor woman's face?'

'I'll make up different concoctions. And then yes, they'll pay, and a high price too, to be larded with them.'

And I hope not too many of the women die of the treatment, thought Hannah to herself, her humour tinged with a degree of anxiety.

Already the cereal-sown plains of Bathurst and Orange could be seen in the distance.

Quentin pulled out another card, one with only two names on it.

'Why "yarrow" with a question mark after it?'

'Yarrow water. It's rather peculiar.'

She wondered whether to tell him and decided she would.

'I want you to give me your word that you won't repeat this.'

'My word isn't really worth a great deal.'

'On the contrary, I'm sure it's worth a lot. A lot more than that of most men or women. Yarrow water is made with cow's urine, or from dung if need be. And not from any old cow; it must be a cow nourished in the open air in clean green meadows.'

'Heavens alive!' exclaimed Quentin MacKenna. 'And what's this *schmuckbez*?'

'That's Yiddish. A *schmuckbez* is a *schmuckbez*, there's no other word for it. That's what my mother used to call it and I haven't yet managed to translate it.'

There could be no doubt that the bizarre, nearly amorous friendship that was to unite them for a short time had its origins in that moment, as they met each other's gaze and saw the laughter in each other's eyes, while the train plunged on into the heart of Australia.

*

She would never really understand why she had gone to Cobar; it was perhaps only because Lothar Hutwill had spoken of it. She imagined gold lying around in pre-cut ingots on the ground.

But there was no gold at Cobar, and there never had been. There was nothing but copper. The real gold mines, or what remained of them then, were located near Bathurst and Ironbark and they had passed her by while she was deep in conversation with Man-Eater MacKenna.

Perhaps she had taken the trip because she knew that once she got back to Sydney she would have to work like a slave, perhaps she had undertaken it out of her instinctive need to venture towards the unknown. This travelling to the edge of the great deserts, the Sturt and Simpson and the Desert of Stones, was like advancing to the edge of a precipice.

She and Quentin spent hours discussing her plans, which is to say that she talked as he listened, his eyes narrowed to a slit. Hannah's ambitions were of no particular interest to him; it was clear that he did not give a damn about them. It was Hannah he was interested in, and his was not the kind of interest a normal man might have in such a perfectly curvaceous young woman. His attitude towards her at least was different.

At first, armed with her usual mistrust, she was sceptical about his infirmity, assuming it was some kind of ruse to catch her more easily off guard. It did not seem to be so; with complete shameless-ness, she looked down at his lap and had to admit that something did seem to be missing, he was indeed flat as a pancake where most men are not. She felt sorry for him, but was careful not to reveal even the slightest trace of pity. At that point in her life she had very few points of reference as far as men were concerned, but she knew – with Mendel's virility in mind – that it would be cruel to so much as refer to Quentin's handicap.

Oddly, the idea of employing him as Chief Herb Collector – as it seemed Colleen had suggested – did not immediately appeal to her, although she would normally start wondering what use she could make of a person the moment she met them. She was not sure she was capable of imagining Quentin MacKenna travelling the length and breadth of Australia harvesting herbs for her, particularly after he told her his life story, deliberately trying to shock her, she was sure.

Having become a cabin boy when he was twelve years old, he

had sailed to New Zealand. Then all over the Pacific, from the
Sunda Strait to the Strait of Malacca, then west, on several
occasions, calling in at Valparaiso, San Francisco, Alaska. There,
like everyone else, he became a gold-digger for a while, finding
little in the way of gold, but enough to travel across America and
get to New York. He had spent a year or two teaching the
Manhattan natives how to play poker, squandering his winnings
on women; from there he had gone to Europe. What did he live
on? Robbery mostly, which did not require a work permit. He one
day found himself in the company of some dancers in Cairo, where
he was faced with the threat of being hanged for some fairly
obscure incident, so he made his way to Aden to join the expeditionary force being sent to fight the Mahdi in the Sudan. He was
wounded, and he more or less left the army, although he was not
convinced it had not been the other way round. At Jibouti he had
boarded yet another ship, one bound for the Pirates' Coast in the
Persian Gulf, and he had ended up in the Indies again, where he
discovered to his surprise that his parents had emigrated to Australia. He was anxious to see his mother again: 'The others could
have dropped dead for all I cared, though I didn't know I had a
sister on the way.' He stayed in Malaya and in Sumatra – unless it
was Borneo, his memory was a bit vague on that – where he and
four other men chartered a schooner to trade copra in the islands.
That worked out well for a while, dissolving into a drinking session
that would last from one port of call to the next, and then
somewhere, in an archipelago of which he never learned the name,
there was a fight on board, probably over a Kanaka woman. They
had been drinking heavily, and so his memory was foggy, but at
nightfall the fishermen of Cairns, in the colony of Queensland, saw
what you might call a ghost ship suddenly appear, sailing on
nothing but a jib. At the helm was a single survivor – Quentin
MacKenna himself. He had a gaping wound in his stomach and he
had been emasculated. There were gashes on his face, which was
covered with bluebottles. He was three-quarters dead, unconscious
and completely delirious. His only companions were the corpses of
nine men and women. Two of them, both women, had been neatly
cut up with the blade of a knife, properly quartered like animals
destined for the butcher's shop; bits of them were missing.

   All of which gave rise to a few suspicions about his morality.

                                    *

Quentin did not skimp on the details of the carnage on board the
schooner. In fact Hannah suspected him of exaggerating, out of
some morbid pleasure and a desire to degrade himself further. The
place where he chose to tell his story only increased the sombre
horror of it: they were passing through the oppressive lonely area
around Cobar. The map she had acquired showed nothing but a
blank for this part of the continent with no relief or river marked
on it. There was only a little town that did not amount to very
much; it looked like some kind of mirage in the desert.

Hannah had tired quickly of the mines, and had wanted to press
on a bit further west, so they had hired two mounts at the Shear-
Legs Hotel, in Cobar, and headed out. They had been riding for
nearly four hours, and were by now feeling shaken by the
incredible silence. She had rediscovered the feeling that had seized
her many years before and that she had nearly forgotten, that of
the day she had ventured away from the banks of the stream with
Taddeuz, into the ocean of wheat and rye fields. She finally
stopped, although very tempted to go on a little further, and it was
while they both sat motionless in their saddles, facing the limitless
horizon, that Quentin had begun to tell his story, to explain why
he was called Man-Eater MacKenna throughout Australia and
even as far away as New Zealand.

'Although the term's not quite accurate, Hannah. I've only ever
eaten women . . .'

So he really had eaten human flesh! she thought. He had used
his knife to cut off bits of arms and legs, pieces of stomach perhaps
and to eat them raw. That's why Dougal MacKenna had banished
even the memory of his name . . .

'Hannah?'

She was a bit afraid of him, and above all felt repugnance for
him.

'Hannah? Did you know that no one has ever crossed Australia
from east to west?'

She was still imagining him, in a little too much detail, stuffing
himself with human flesh oozing with blood. Quentin had dismounted and stood with his back to her, his long blond hair falling
down past his shoulders. He was looking straight ahead. She stared
at him in amazement.

'Cross Australia? What for?'

'Neither from east to west, nor from north to south,' he said as if
she had not spoken. 'About thirty years ago an Irishman by the

name of Robert O'Hara Burke tried, with some Indian sepoys and camels. He died in the attempt, which wouldn't have mattered if he hadn't failed. All the other expeditions have failed as well.'

'And you'd like to try?'

He lowered his head, then looked up again.

'I'm not going to try. I'm going to do it. Just as you're going to make your fortune.'

She looked at the map. About one hundred miles away from the place where they had stopped – they were already thirty miles from Cobar – was a river. But beyond that . . .

Quentin must have heard the sound of the map being unfolded. He added:

'I wouldn't leave from here, I'd go from Brisbane. I'd follow a straight line, on foot, without deviating, sticking all the way to the twenty-sixth parallel. Can you see it on your map? Sturt Desert, Simpson Desert, Great Victoria Desert, and the Gibson Desert. I wouldn't stop walking until I could dip my feet in the Indian Ocean. Look at your map: a long way north of Fremantle and Perth, that big indentation in the coastline called Shark Bay, have you got it?'

'Yes.'

'I shall end up there. I'll build a star out of stones to mark the spot, when I get there.'

She began to work out the length of the journey. It was at least two thousand five hundred miles, four thousand kilometres, as long as you went in a straight line and didn't have to skirt any mountains. It was not much more crazy – perhaps it was even less so – than wanting to be extraordinarily rich from the moment she had climbed up on to Mendel Visoker's *brouski* and left her *shtetl* . . .

'And when do you plan to leave?' she asked.

'At the end of the summer, or next summer. Do you want me to find those goddamned plants of yours, yes or no?'

She thought for a moment that she should put a sign on the door of her beauty salon which read: 'All the creams that are going to be slapped on your faces have been made with plants picked by Quentin MacKenna, the notorious eater of human flesh.' That would be enough to ruin business and leave her to live in exile among the Papuans.

'Yes,' she said, 'I'd very much like you to find those goddamned plants of mine.'

'A lady doesn't say "goddamned plants".'

'Whatever a man can do, I can do too. In any case, I don't want
to be a lady, I only want to be myself.'

'That's supremely arrogant.'

'Yep.'

'I'll need some illustrations, Soames's drawings, I mean. And I'll
need what you call the list of equivalents. It surely can't be possible
to find all those plants whose names I've just read here in Australia.
Of course, I could go and see old Soames himself, although . . .'

'Yes?'

'Although it wouldn't be very good if people knew I was working
with you. It would reflect badly on you. No, don't say anything.
I'm sure it's already occurred to you. My mother says you've a
devil of a brain. May I at least go and see old Soames? Not so much
for his drawings as to ask him where I'd be likely to find this
rubbish of yours. He knows Australia better than anyone else.'

'Go ahead.'

He nodded.

'I'll also need to have some idea of the quantities you want of
each plant, whether you want them freshly picked or dried. And
where you want them delivered.'

'At Ogilvie's. At his entrepôt. He's agreed. He's not happy about
it, but he's agreed.'

'I'll have them sent by train, on the Great Western. Someone
will have to take delivery of them. I shan't appear.'

'I'm not ashamed of you,' she somehow managed to tell him.

'It's kind of you to say it, but I don't give a damn. I'm going to
enlist the help of two or three groups of Abos that I've lived with
recently. I speak their gibberish and they're not as stupid as people
take them for. I'll need a bit of money.'

'I was thinking of giving you sixty pounds to start with. And
after that I'll pay you . . .'

'Young lady, if there's anything of less interest to me than money
it would be bloody interesting to find out what it was. I don't need
your goddamned money for myself. It's just to pay for some tafia
rum for the Abos and cover the transportation costs.'

'Send the stuff carriage forward. Great Western has agreed to
handle it. And the same goes for the Cobb Company stagecoaches.'

'You think of everything, eh?'

'Yes.'

He laughed. 'Listen to her,' he said. 'She doesn't even say, "I try

to think of everything," she says, "Yes, I think of everything."
According to my mother, you're fiendishly intelligent.'

'But she loves me.'

'She loves you. Hannah?'

Silence.

'Hannah, I saw my mother's face and I heard her cough. She
hasn't got much time left.' She hoped he would stop there, but he
did not. 'It's not her I'm thinking about but little Lizzie. I'll die of
rage – if I haven't already died of something else by then – if, after
my mother's death, I learn that my bloody fool of a father and
those bloody fool brothers of mine, especially Rod, are looking
after her. Is she bright?'

'She's wonderful. I love her like a sister.'

'And that's how I already thought of you, Lizzie. Even then.'

'Tell me about her. Anything. Whatever comes into your head.'

Hannah told him how they had chatted together during those
eleven nights when they had shared the same bed, about the great
fits of giggles they were often seized with. She recounted some of
the childishly funny things Lizzie had said. And she was suddenly
taken aback by the strange and violent love Quentin so obviously
felt for a sister he had never seen, except from a distance, in hiding.

*'Don't cry, Lizzie, it's all so long ago now, in another time and another
life . . . Quentin's been dead for more than thirty years and I'm not sure
I should have spoken of him to you . . . Don't cry, Lizzie . . .'*

In that indifferent voice of his he asked: 'Will you look after
her?'

'I give you my word, a man's word,' said Hannah with a lump in
her throat.

He remounted, his green gaze narrower than ever, almost
invisible behind his crinkled eyelids.

'When shall I start sending the consignments of those goddamned plants?'

She couldn't help it, she had already figured that out too.

'After 10 November I shall be ready to make the first pots of
cream.'

'Goddamned cream.'

'That's the stuff,' said Hannah.

Cobar did not leave her with an indelible memory. Other than
being the place where she made her agreement with Quentin
MacKenna – an agreement which, in her eyes, signalled the start

of an adventure — Cobar remained a town in the middle of a treeless plain. Three or four thousand men lived there at the foot of a couple of dozen tall furnaces. Only two things made an impression on Hannah: the horse race — the first she had ever seen — organized in front of the Shear-Legs Hotel, and the bizarre steel cage in which the miners were lowered into the ground.

She made the return journey to Sydney in two stages, stopping at Bathurst and in the Nepean Valley. Quentin did not sit with her during this trip, though he continued to accompany her. Evidently he had chosen to keep his distance again, as much because he did not want to compromise her, she guessed, as out of his taste for solitude. At both stops she hired a horse-drawn carriage — only after ferocious negotiations over the price on each occasion — and drove around the countryside, paying no attention to the gold mines at Bathurst, which she could have had a look at.

She equipped herself with some jute sacks and filled them with whatever she happened to find, so that by the time she got back to the station they were almost too heavy to drag along. She had found all her cultivated plants with no problem; in the private gardens of farmhouses she had found heaps of salvia, periwinkles, cornflowers, nasturtiums, marigolds and roses. There was no difficulty either in obtaining cow's milk, almonds, dandelions, or pine cones; even fennel, parsley, cress and borage. An abundance of eucalyptus was to be had and she even found a lime tree transplanted from its native Normandy by a family of French colonists, who regarded it as their pride and joy.

On the way back to Sydney she was overcome with a fit of uncontrollable laughter when she imagined Quentin MacKenna leading a horde of Aborigines, each one more of a cannibal than the other, out into the bush, wreaking havoc on the Australian flora. And she thought of herself, with her pestle and mortar, turning a haphazard mixture of whatever she had been able to find into a cream that could just as well disfigure the ladies of Sydney — if not kill them outright — as it could make them beautiful.

The two huge, red-faced farmers' wives sitting next to her stared at her while she sniggered, unable to contain herself. She wondered how she would feel about being hanged for applying homicidal facemasks.

Quentin travelled back the whole way with her, protecting her from a distance, though she could find no sign of him when she left the train in Sydney and loaded her two enormous bags on to a cab.

She had been away for eleven days in all. She was now ready to begin.

12

12

THE SANDALWOOD BOXES

The building works had progressed at a speed that delighted her; she was particularly thrilled to find that her 'kitchen' was ready. The room had been whitewashed and the problem of access overcome; a staircase with a single flight of steps set flush against the wall now led upstairs from a neighbouring street. Next to it a hole had been cut into the wall which would give on to the goods lift; this would operate in two days' time. The three rooms of the laboratory were already fitted with long tables, and with numerous cupboards, as well as with two of the six sinks she had requested. Not only could she start work, but she soon discovered that the other rooms were also well on the way to being finished. Robbie Watts had doubled his work teams, deploying his men – he had seen it done in the shipbuilding yards – in two teams working in succession. In this way the Scotsman kept the building works going twenty-four hours a day, using gas lamps, or even ordinary flares, to provide work light at night.

The paving stones in the courtyard had been taken up, and pipes had been laid to service the central fountain and the eight smaller watersprays in the rockgarden. The paths had been marked out and laid with flat stones; it was already clear how they would intertwine and lead to arbours. The flowerbeds, designed by Dinah, had already been marked out as well. And the first miniature copses had been planted in the cartloads of fresh soil that had been brought in; small shrubs were beginning to take root. Several rooms, both on the ground floor and upstairs, were in the hands of painters, and in two or three others the panelling and marquetry were already under way. Hannah was delighted with it all.

'Robbie, this is incredible! You'll be finished well before December 20th!'

He groaned in exhaustion. The only thing he hated more than receiving compliments was having anyone, even a partner, breathing down his neck, keeping an eye on what he was doing.

Hannah locked herself inside her kitchen less than two hours after getting off the train. On the red-lacquered tables she spread out the contents of the two bags she had filled in Bathurst and in the Nepean Valley; she spent the next thirty hours sorting out her plants. She emerged on only two occasions: once to ask for a messenger whom she sent with a list as long as an almanac to the Bavarian pharmacologist, and again when the messenger returned, staggering beneath his load, and she ran out to greet him and his load.

Dinah ventured to bring her some tea and several cakes, but the only response she got were a few indistinct, almost ferocious grunts, those of a bear from the Carpathian Mountains whose winter sleep had been disturbed. She was not even convinced Hannah recognized her.

It was late in the morning on November 5th that Colleen MacKenna decided to force her way in to the laboratory, though she did so as cautiously as one might indeed enter a bear's den. On a tray she carried a peace offering of bacon and eggs, toast and tea, prepared at her request by Harriet Williams. She found Hannah sitting on the ochre-coloured rubblestone floor, her skirts hitched up to the middle of her thighs, her legs apart, her hair a mess, wildly stirring some substance in a copper saucepan she gripped fiercely between her knees.

'Straight from the canteen,' said Colleen.

'Not hungry. Thanks all the same.'

The huge misty eyes suddenly turned to steel; they seemed to register the tall Irishwoman's presence, and scanned her face.

'Have you ever put a cream, any kind of cream, on your face before?'

'Good heavens, no,' replied Colleen laughing. 'Do I look like an American Indian? Nothing but soap and water.'

Hannah smiled, with the humour of someone whose worst fears have just been confirmed. On the table were no fewer than twenty-seven different receptacles – a saucepan and a bowl, several fondue dishes, saucers, and basins, some ordinary earthenware plates – each of which contained a different substance and each of which was numbered. Evidently, they marked the successive stages in Hannah's research. She pointed to the copper saucepan between her knees.

'This is number twenty-eight. It smells worse than the others. The lunatic who slaps this on her face and walks down George Street will clear the place sooner than a leper with his bell,' pronounced Hannah, her voice trembling with rage.

She suddenly fell back and lay stretched out on the floor, with her knees up. She let one arm fall at her side, the other she folded over her face.

'Oh shit!'

'A well-brought-up young girl does not swear,' said Colleen.

'An intelligent young girl does not spend two days crushing herbs in a mortar. Nor does she go roaming around the countryside like a rabbit. She doesn't go to Australia either. She seeks out and finds a very, very rich man, and makes sure she's given diamond rivières on every possible occasion. If she's really intelligent.'

Colleen leaned over the copper saucepan on the floor and sniffed warily.

'I must admit it does smell rather vile.'

'It's a re-creation of my mother's recipe: cow's milk, nut shells, fresh mint, tormentil roots and fir cones all crushed in wheat oil.'

'It may still make a good pudding, assuming you pour whisky over it and serve it flambé to kill the fumes.'

'. . . It's my mother's recipe except that I don't have any fresh mint, and I used potentilla instead of tormentil, and Colonial pine instead of fir cones. As for the nut shells, they didn't survive the journey very well, or else they're Russian nuts that dislike Polish women. And I must have put in too much suint, to replace the oil.'

With this she removed the arm from her face and stared at the white ceiling.

'To be frank, Colleen, I feel a bit like crying . . .'

Colleen MacKenna walked up to one of the tables, where she had deposited her tray. She pulled up a chair for Hannah.

'Just get up, sit down and eat. And not another word.'

'Hannah.'

In silence the girl lifted herself off the floor and into the chair.

After examining the breakfast as though it might poison her, she began to eat.

In a low, rather subdued voice Colleen asked: 'Did you see him?'

'I saw him. He's very handsome, in his own way.'

'Were you able . . . to come to an agreement?'

'He's going to work for me at least until next summer. Perhaps longer. He'll collect everything I need from the countryside. That's what you wanted, isn't it?'

The Irish woman nodded. She said very quietly, with infinite tenderness: 'He's like someone who's fallen down a very deep, very dark well, with nothing holding him any more. I hoped that if he met you . . . you being so full of life . . .'

'He loves you. You and Lizzie. He loves you without a shadow of a doubt.'

'But not enough to want to live with us. Did he tell you what he would do when he got fed up working for you?'

Hannah hesitated.

'*Hannah?*'

'He's going to cross Australia, on foot. And no doubt on his own. From Brisbane to Perth.'

Colleen sat down.

'He wants to die, Hannah, doesn't he?'

'He might succeed. Only madmen succeed. Other people don't try to do anything.'

'He's going to die.'

'In a way he's already dead,' thought Hannah, 'and the worst of it is that he knows.'

She was very hungry, as it turned out, and she bit into the bacon with an appetite that embarrassed her. She felt guilty too about not being able to tear herself away from the wretched creams. She felt moved, genuinely and painfully moved, by Colleen's despair, but all the same her mind was on her recipe. She suddenly realized she ought to try to add some oregano, which she did to no effect. For four more days she worked day and night. In that time Colleen and the Watts were obliged literally to tear her away from her kitchen and force her to get a few hours of sleep; this usually amounted to three or four. On the sixth night, as she dragged herself off to her little apartment in Ogilvie's building, she caught sight of Micah Gunn. He had parked his carriage some distance away, as she and Lothar Hutwill had agreed he always would, and he was waiting impassively on his coachman's seat, his whip pointing skywards. He made no attempt to catch Hannah's eye, looking like someone who had never seen her before. Gunn's being stationed there meant that Lothar was in Sydney and was waiting for her somewhere, in secret, perhaps at the black-and-white house; it was up to her to choose whether to get in or not.

She passed by the carriage without stopping, too tired to think, and was within a few seconds sinking into a sleep crowded with retorts and mortars. In her dreams she heard the carriage departing: the clear sound of the horses' hoofs rang out in the night as it did.

Less than four hours later she reappeared in the courtyard. It was brilliantly illuminated by flares; masons, carpenters and gardeners were all getting under each other's feet. She shut herself away in her laboratory and at last obtained her first successful result: a cream with a lime and cornflower base. The mixture was scented with roses and mint, both of which Dinah had managed to find for her. She used a pulp of raw apples and refined lanolin as a binding. It was her seventy-ninth concoction.

Hannah tried the cream on herself, forcing herself to keep the white mask on her face for a six-hour stretch. When she removed it she found not only that she was still alive and in no way disfigured (she had been ready for anything) but that her skin was rather softer than usual. Her complexion was clearer, a little more radiant, her pores – she saw in the huge magnifying glass lent her by James Barnaby Soames – nearly invisible. She retained the blue rings round her eyes, but these she knew were due simply to her state of exhaustion.

She cleaned her skin with an eau de toilette she had made with spring water and surgical spirit, in which she soaked marigold heads, rose blossom and vervein flowers for two days and two nights, and to which she added a dash of green lemon. She was quite content with the results: the skin on her face was smooth and soft, her usual pallor was heightened. 'Another one hundred and fifty years of intensive care and you'll see yourself become almost pretty, owl-face,' she said to the mirror.

There seemed no point in waiting any longer; she put number 79 into production.

Dinah found her three young girls recruited from an orphanage; these were to be her first workers. And because she knew from experience that such things were important, she invested in a horse-drawn carriage which she hired by the hour, to ensure that her young girls travelled safely, morning and evening, between the laboratory and St Leonards. Determined to keep an eye on every detail, she similarly made arrangements for them to have a healthy lunch every day. She reached an agreement with a family boarding house nearby, where she was able to obtain a discount, paying fourpence instead of six, for the midday meal, and where she intended to eat with her assistants.

It took her a little longer to solve the problem of what containers to sell cream number 79 in. Ogilvie had suggested marmalade pots, of which he had plenty in stock. In the end these turned out to be too big; she knew that the less cream she included in each pot the more highly priced – and prized – the contents would be. In the end she made friends with a Chinese merchant, and bought from him – after only five hours' bargaining – a batch of tiny terracotta vases that had originally contained tiger balm, an ointment the merchant imported from Singapore. Once the vases had been immersed in boiling water, and swabbed in alcohol to dispel any lingering smell, and once the Chinese labels had been removed, they proved the perfect little containers, with their charming lids, their moiré waxed undersides, and their Turkey-red ribbon ties.

In Hannah's opinion the elegant containers of cream number 79 were worth five guineas a piece. She figured she could comfortably sell about twenty-five pots of cream per week, as soon as the business had got under way, by about January 1893 by her calculations. After about six months she thought that production and sales – given a few ideas she had come up with – should double if not triple.

In the debit column of her notebook she listed the expenses relating to her workers – their salary, food, and transport, the red and black overalls and the lace caps they would wear in the shop – as well as the cost of collecting the plants, flowers, fruits and other ingredients, the expense of buying and preparing the pots, the rent paid to the Williams sisters, the overheads on her kitchen, and finally her own salary. In this last she noted one pound a week. Adding all this up she discovered – between two outbursts of rage and nervous giggles – that each pot was going to cost her more than four pounds each to produce. In other words based on a sale of twenty-five pots, she would make a weekly profit of roughly twenty-two pounds.

She knew however that she had to pay back Lothar Hutwill his fifteen hundred pounds, as well as a reasonable sum in interest. He had not of course asked to be reimbursed – and would certainly not be expecting to be paid back with interest – but on the only loan she would ever accept Hannah was absolutely determined to play by the book. What was owed was owed, whether she was a creditor or debtor; she would never make any compromise on that point. Clearing her debt with Lothar would also allow her to dissociate the two aspects of their relationship: she wanted to separate as quickly as possible the fact that he had lent her money and that she had wanted him as a lover.

With twenty-two pounds' income every week it would take her, she calculated, seventy-six weeks or 18 months to repay him her debt of sixteen hundred and eighty pounds, including the interest.

That was far too long; she knew she would not feel free – to break off relations with him or to leave Australia – until she was clear of this debt.

There remained the possibility that she might sell more than twenty-five pots of cream a week, but she might also sell fewer. Nevertheless, if sales and production were to increase, the unit cost would drop and the profit would be that much greater; she realized that if Mendel were sitting before her, listening to her calculate, he would be dying of laughter.

The obvious solution was to sell something else. She decided on eau de toilette, and at once put her formula into production. Again she was faced with the problem of containers; it was clear she would never find a small and elegant bottle in Australia, and so she had the idea of using wooden phials. The only kind of wood that would suffice was sandalwood, which Robbie Watts had very nearly used for the moulding finish on the panelling, and which he thought he could turn on the lathe. He thought he could produce some tall rectangular bottles, with wooden screw-on stoppers.

More than ever Hannah got more than she had counted on: the sandalwood turned out to have its own fragrance, which combined with that of the eau de toilette and miraculously gave birth to a different product, better than the one Hannah had started with. And there was even a difference in chemistry depending on whether the sandalwood was white, lemon-yellow, or red.

She ended up with three toilet waters instead of one, and naturally decided to sell them as different products, at different prices, from one guinea for the white, to two guineas for the red. She was ready to bet that the red would outsell the others, if only because it was dearer, and despite the fact that its contents were virtually the same as the others. (She had simply added some orange blossom to distinguish this eau de toilette from the others, and to clear her conscience, which was fairly accommodating anyway.)

She made further calculations and felt comfortable anticipating a profit of sixteen pounds a week, from sales of the sandalwood phials.

This brought her to a grand total of thirty-eight pounds a week, hardly a fortune in her eyes. She knew she would need something else . . .

Quentin MacKenna's first deliveries reached her in mid-November. He did not, however, send a letter, and she had to imagine for herself how he had managed to find her the same lavender her mother had used. He also sent her some seaweed still moist with sea water, as well as ingredients she had despaired of ever finding, such as arnica blossom and St John's wort.

Thanks to this delivery she embarked on the preparation of a second face-cream. She had decided, for no particular reason, that this potion would eliminate wrinkles. In it she combined arnica, sage, mallow, carrot, cucumber and, again in imitation of her mother's recipes, apple pulp, honey and sweet almond oil. This became preparation number 91. Hannah did not give it a name any more than she had given a name to the earlier cream, because she could not find one she was satisfied with, one that conveyed the proper sense of sophistication and feminine mystery.

She would charge six guineas for a pot of number 91, which would be lacquered in black and Turkey-red so as to be distinguished from the pots of number 79. And she could count on making a weekly profit of twenty-six pounds on this new addition to the line. 'Plus thirty-eight, equals sixty-four. I'll be lucky if I'm rich in seventy-five years . . .' she sighed.

She considered perfecting a third cream, then a fourth toilet water. She wondered what type of product would best complement her line. Should she make something more luxurious and more expensive? Or, on the contrary, should she package some of the wretched cream in Ogilvie's jam jars, some of the eau de toilette in ordinary glass bottles, and charge a reduced price for these 'inferior' products? If she followed up the second of these possibilities she would be able to enlarge her market considerably.

In the end she pursued neither idea, eager to see if she might first earn some money at last and – most importantly, even at the expense of all else – establish a brand image.

By about November 20th she was ready. She was pleased to find that Dinah had picked a real winner at the orphanage in one Meggie MacGregor: this fat, insipid-looking girl had an innate sense of organization, and the temperament of a chef, although she rarely said a word. A few days was all she needed to identify every flower, fruit, leaf and branch in the laboratory; she could soon handle a pestle and mortar better than Hannah herself. Nearly overnight Hannah found herself before a stock of one hundred pots of each type of cream and one hundred and twenty bottles of eau de toilette.

Leaving the manufacturing to the girls, Hannah busied herself putting into operation one of the very first ideas she had had – and doubtless one of her best. She knew the most important thing was neither the manufacturing, nor the creation of the beauty salon, but the impression she created on her public. To this end Hannah hired a cabinetmaker, recommended to her by Robbie Watts, to make some very handsome sandalwood boxes with rosewood marquetry. These were lined with black velvet; each included compartments designed to hold one pot of each of her creams and the three bottles of eau de toilette. She ordered fifty boxes in all, and on the upper left-hand corner of every lid she had engraved the double H of her first name in fine gilt lettering.

She set the retail price of each box at one hundred guineas.

'It's sheer madness,' declared Colleen. 'You'll never sell them. What woman in Australia would part with that kind of money?'

'None probably. But their husbands will, for a Christmas present or a wedding anniversary gift. And for more imperative reasons. Do you want to bet on it, Colleen?'

She went to see Rod MacKenna in his office in the Colonial Service, even though she did not like him very much. More than anything else his idiocy offended her; it was the characteristic of many men extremely capable and intelligent in their professional capacity, but thoroughly stupid the rest of the time. And he was particularly shortsighted with regard to women. All the same, Hannah reckoned Rod could be very useful indeed.

Standing before him, her nose on a level with his fob watch, she explained what had brought her to his office.

'It's really very simple, I want you to provide me with a list of the twelve richest married men in Sydney . . . no, wait a moment, the twenty richest, but they must be married. The men whose wives have influence in the best circles in this town. No, I have absolutely no interest in knowing whether they love their wives or not. You know everybody, don't you? What with the important duties you perform, your justifiable ambition and your exceptionally good judgement . . .'

Rod admitted that he had all these qualities and a few more besides. He also said he would draw up a list. Hannah's second request was more embarrassing; she allowed that, in politics, it was always a delicate matter asking journalists for a favour, but . . .

'Rod,' she said, 'Rod, come now . . . You'd be doing *them* a favour by telling them that something as out of the ordinary as an exclusive beauty salon catering to the élite is about to open in Sydney, a salon to rival any in London and Paris, offering creams made here in Australia with the age-old secret recipes of the gypsies of Hungary. That news is worth gold to journalists.'

Her ploy worked. A short time afterwards she was amazed to receive visits from two society page columnists, one from the *Bulletin* and the other from the *Sydney Morning Herald*. Wearing the dress with the thirty-nine buttons, making the most of her grey eyes, and even playing on the slight accent she still had when speaking English, she hypnotized them with the most barefaced lies, stopping at nothing: She was Viennese, the daughter of a count who was a cousin of Archduke Rudolph. 'Alas, yes, the one who died tragically at Mayerling. I knew the poor boy a little, Marie Vetsera was my childhood friend. What a tragedy. I still weep over it, three years later. Please forgive my understandable emotion, these are such painful memories . . .'

She also told the columnists that she was twenty-seven – 'I don't look it? You needn't look for an explanation: it's the creams!' – and that she was in possession of a secret formula belonging to a gypsy queen who had died not long before in her parents' castle.

'Can you believe it? She looked thirty or thirty-five, but she was at least seventy-five or eighty, and she'd met the Emperor Napoleon . . .'

Could her creams make women look younger, asked the journalists.

She laughed and simpered: 'Not to the point of returning them to childhood. But they'll certainly take off ten or fifteen years.'

She gave them a guided tour of her kitchen, introducing them to what she called her pastrycook apprentices, who were not on these afternoons her usual orphans but three ravishing misses who were less adept, but who looked adorable in their pretty lace collars and figure-hugging red-and-black overalls. (The reporters were men, after all, and pallid Meggie and her crew – despite all their talent – could not be trusted to make the same impression.)

Finally, and most importantly – having sworn the reporters to the utmost secrecy – which she knew they would immediately violate – she told them that fifty de luxe boxes, containing a sample of each cream and each eau de toilette, would be sent out shortly as presents to the fifty most elegant women in Sydney, these fifty having been selected after a very long survey.

The reporters went away charmed, bursting to tell the news.

'And what do you think will happen, Colleen?'

'You mean you've actually sent out only twelve boxes? And the women who haven't received one are going to torment their poor husbands to buy them one, just to prove to their friends that they appear on your supposed list? Hannah?'

'Yes, Colleen, darling?'

'You're fiendishly cunning.'

'Thank you, Colleen.'

'. . . And you were in my kitchen that day, Lizzie, do you remember? It was your first visit to my laboratory, you'd been dreaming of coming to see me there. And you laughed, oh, how you laughed!'

The remaining thirty-eight boxes were sold in three days, at one hundred guineas apiece. She could probably have sold five times as many but she deliberately limited the number available, wanting to direct her future clients towards the creams and toilet waters she sold separately, the manufacturing cost of which was, happily, quite a bit lower.

On this score she was not disappointed: thirty-nine pots and seventy-nine phials disappeared in ten days, and her beauty salon had not yet opened!

Hannah went over the accounts again: after paying the cabinet-maker, she would have brought in fifty-three pounds on the sandalwood boxes. She had also made sixty-seven pounds eleven shillings on the individual items sold, which added up to a total of one hundred and twenty pounds eleven shillings. She had done this in ten days, which meant an income of twelve pounds a day, or, she thought with some disappointment after all her efforts, four thousand pounds a year.

The publicity that resulted from her story about the boxes had, however, made Hannah's name known throughout the city. Every day a procession of luxury cars drove past the carriage entrance, now painted Turkey red with a black outline; her dreadful lies about Marie Vetsera and Mayerling had caused a stir in every drawing room. Sydney's women were waiting for nothing more than her official opening, when they would be able to question her about the princely drama she had witnessed.

She knew she was a devil of a liar. But what else could she do? She was not going to remain in Australia for twenty years, and she was already getting old, nearly eighteen. Taddeuz would not wait half a century for her, nor would Mendel, in the event that he had not already escaped . . .

It was now nearly mid December and summer in the southern hemisphere was reaching its height. In the preceding weeks Hannah had received two letters from Lothar Hutwill, neither of which was signed, both of which were in a hand not his own. Both contained the same laconic message, in English, although he and Hannah generally spoke to each other in German or French: *I absolutely must see you.*

On two occasions already she had declined the invitation by pretending not to notice Micah's carriage outside her door. The third time, on December 12th, feeling that she needed a short respite before the official opening of her salon, she decided she would take a break from this uninterrupted period of work. When she was certain the street was entirely empty she nodded to Gunn and took a seat in the barouche.

13

I'M A TIGHTROPE WALKER

'Tired?'

'Yes.'

She was lying down, her eyes closed. Only the roof of the black-and-white house was visible over the rocks behind her; straight ahead, in front of Hannah, was the Pacific, dotted with the white sails of boats that had put out from Botany Bay.

She lay flat on her back on a sort of wharf that extended from the cliff, and that towered one hundred and twenty feet – about forty metres – over the ocean. The Pacific was visible between the alternating black and white planks of wood; she could feel the void below her, and thought her present state of suspension perfectly representative of her life in Australia: she was a tightrope walker.

She felt good. She was hot, but comfortably so, under the heat of the Antipodean sun whose pleasurable effects she was only just discovering that day. She had allowed Lothar to remove all her clothes; her head rested on his thigh.

'Are you afraid of the drop, Hannah?'

'No.'

The false pier jutted out about five or six metres, although they had hardly ventured more than a foot or two beyond the edge of the cliff.

'Who built this thing?' she asked.

'My friend.'

'He's mad.'

'Completely.'

'But I like madmen. Will I meet him, one day?'

'He'll want to paint your portrait.'

'Why not?'

'Nude.'

'Why not?'

The night before when she had stepped out of the barouche, she had found the house deserted and dinner for two waiting. She had watched Micah Gunn set off again and, while she waited, had inspected the rooms more thoroughly than on her first visit. Upstairs she had found a studio crowded with canvases, most wearing dust-sheets for protection. Every one of them was covered with exactly the same kind of daubings as the ones hung downstairs. Hannah didn't know anything about painting, aside from the references to da Vinci and the Baron Gros she had come across in her reading. After hesitating for a moment she removed a few sheets and began to examine the canvases one by one. The signatures on the paintings were often difficult to decipher but she was able to make out a few French ones – Cézanne, Degas, and Renoir – as well as a Dutch name, Van Bogh or Van Gogh, and an Italian-looking one, Pissarro. She was fascinated by what she saw – as much by the canvases as by the luxurious circumstances in which she first made their acquaintance – and an abiding passion for painting was born in her instantly.

'Why is it that there isn't a single painting in the house by your artist friend?'

'He burns them as he paints them.'

Her eyes opened wide in amazement. 'Why would anyone do a thing like that?'

'In his opinion,' said Lothar, 'his works are worth nothing. He lived in France for ten years and brought back a shipload of paintings by some of his artist friends over there. Since then, he's been trying to imitate them, without, according to him, much success.'

'Is he rich?'

'Very.'

Lothar had turned up only towards midnight the previous evening. He apologized a thousand times for being so late: he had been detained at a business meeting, the official reason for this trip to Sydney. They had supper together, during which she tasted both

wine and champagne for the first time in her life. She had liked it
a good deal, though it made her feel off-balance. She and Lothar
then spent a long time making love, with results just as extraordinary as before. In the course of the evening, Hannah discovered
that a woman could take the intiative in bed, that she could also
lead the game, that she could create and impose her own rhythm;
that she could, in a way, dominate her partner; that there was
much pleasure to be had in both roles.

When she woke the next morning, Lothar was not in bed. She
had found him ultimately in the kitchen, where he was burning
his fingers trying to fry bacon. She took over from him – though
she was not very adept with the frying pan either – and suggested
they have breakfast in the sunshine. That was how they had ended
up on the impressive lunatic gangway suspended over the ocean.
Lothar had refused to set foot on it, but she had walked out a
metre or so, insisting he follow her – 'Only if you strip naked, so
that I'll be risking my life for good reason.' came the reply.

In the twinkling of an eye she had thrown her nightdress to the
sea breeze and watched it drop into the blue-black of the Pacific,
relishing the wind's caress on every centimetre of her body.

And now, after an evening and a morning together, she felt she
could finally indulge her curiosity. As she looked out at the water,
her head on Lothar's thigh, she asked slowly:

'Why were you so keen to see me?'

'I wanted you so much.'

'Surely that wasn't the only reason,' she said patiently.

Silence.

Eventually he said: 'Eloise.'

He told her the whole story, which came awfully close to the one
she had so dreaded hearing.

He told her how he had lied to Eloise about the actual price of
the schooner, adding two thousand pounds to the amount it
actually cost, and how Eloise, with that malevolent mistrust of
hers, had made enquiries and learned of the difference. He told her
about the fierce questioning that had followed; how he had lied
again, claiming to have gambling debts. At first she had believed
him. And then . . .

Hannah stood up in a single, feline movement. One of the two
Hannahs that coexisted inside her registered that it was a marvel-

lous thing to be naked under the sun, unhampered by all those idiotic things a woman has to wear for the sake of propriety.

The other Hannah trembled with rage. She was angry enough to kill someone, or at least to feel a very strong desire to. The far end of the gangway was nine planks away. She advanced along it until only three or four remained. Controlling her voice as best she could, she said in a distant, very detached tone:

'Let's see now. Your Eloise has discovered that I'm still alive . . . Does she know that I'm still in Sydney?'

'Not yet.'

'She'll find out. And according to you, I should be in China. She'll find out that I've started a business. Right?'

'Yes.'

'She'll deduce that you lied to her from the start. And most important, that I was the one you gave that wretched fifteen hundred pounds to. Or even two thousand.'

'Yes.'

Hannah took another step forward. She was only two planks from the end of the pier.

'She'll remember that I had virtually nothing when she hired me as a chambermaid. And above all that I left without allowing her the pleasure of giving me the sack. And she's bound to infer that I'm your mistress, that I used her, and you, and of course her money . . .'

She took another step forward; the pier had begun to vibrate beneath her feet like some living creature.

'And when she sees that I'm making a fortune — that I'm doing my utmost to get people to talk about me — she'll of course turn up in Sydney like a Fury, making accusations against me . . .'

The vibration travelled up her legs and her back, through her whole body, synchronizing with her own enraged tremblings.

'Now, what could she say? She could accuse me of having stolen from her the money that I used to start up my enterprise. And she would say, no doubt, that she had not wanted to lodge a complaint at the time, out of pity for me. But there is a limit, and she would feel it her duty to warn the honest ladies of Sydney — and all Australia while she was at it — against this little Jewish hussy. That wouldn't be very good for business. You've thought of all this, Lothar?'

'Yes.'

'I'm sure you have. Quite sure.'

She advanced one final step and stood on the pier's edge, looking down between her erect nipples, between her pink toes, to the Pacific Ocean far below, while the lunatic gangway swayed gently beneath her.

'What a god-awful place the world is,' she thought, 'what a goddamned stinking hole, as Mendel Visoker would say . . . I miss him so much, especially in circumstances like these, when his great fists would come in so handy! A man in my place probably wouldn't even have been robbed when he landed in Australia, for the simple reason that he would have had countless pockets to put his money in. He wouldn't have needed to line his dress with bills, would not have looked silly and bloated because of it. He wouldn't have had any problem finding work, and once he had made his fortune he would have prided himself on the fact that he had worked at thirty-six different jobs . . .'

'For the love of God, Hannah, don't stand there!' Lothar Hutwill's hoarse voice interrupted her. 'You're terrifying me.'

'I'm not frightened any more by this gangway than I am by any human being, whoever he might be. And I never will be.'

'. . . but apart from working as a prostitute, how else would I have obtained the money so quickly? Would a bank have lent it to me? They would have eyed me up and down, back and front, and hearing my idea would have simply curled up with laughter. A woman wanting to go into business – the very idea! They may have that woman Victoria on the throne, but it doesn't go any further than that. That moustachioed old lady can't even go into their clubs, queen though she is. As for me, I've no chance at all!'

'Hannah, please!'

She looked down one last time between her breasts, half-closing her eyes so that the auburn hair between her legs blended into the indigo blue of the Pacific.

Feeling somewhat calmer, she retreated, step by step. The vibrating subsided, as did the trembling. She swivelled around, to face Lothar, who looked completely panic-stricken.

'It's all so petty, Lothar.'

Her rage had completely subsided, she was thinking clearly again. She was virtually certain he was lying to her: Eloise knew nothing, he had made it all up. And the reason for doing so was not all that difficult to work out – assuming of course he really was lying.

She knelt down, stretching backwards as she did so, her breasts thrust forward. The cool wind played between her thighs. She touched the moist lips of her vagina, holding Lothar's eyes unwaveringly with her own.

'Make love to me. Here. Now.'

She asked him to open all the windows of the large downstairs room, which he meekly did. She went upstairs and spent as long as her attention would allow splashing cold water over herself. She also washed her hair, mostly to gain a little more time.

Eventually she went downstairs again to find him dressed, sitting on the semi-circular seat in front of the bow window, holding a book in his hands but looking out to sea.

'Hungry?'

He shook his head.

'I am,' she said. She went to the kitchen and made herself a sandwich consisting of cold steak, ham, cured bacon, salted butter, and lettuce, all piled as high as she could manage between two slices of the white Anglo-Saxon bread that she hated so much.

'Fantastically hungry.'

'So I see.'

He finally looked around; she guessed he was about to speak. Although her mouth was full, she said:

'Don't say anything.'

'There is a solution.'

She did not want to hear what he would say next.

'There is a solution that would settle everything,' he said in a subdued voice.

'Not that.'

'I love you.'

She bit into her sandwich with a carnivorous appetite, her sharp little teeth cutting through the meat easily, leaving half-moon shapes in the bread that were very pleasing to the eye. As far as Lothar Hutwill was concerned, she was beginning to feel annoyed and irritated by him. Why should he get her mixed up in his problems with Eloise? If he could not put up with his wife any more he had only to leave her, and forget about her money; he could make his own way. The little affection Hannah might have had for this man quickly died.

She reminded herself that it was not at all necessary to love someone in order to make love with him; that perhaps the opposite was even true: if you loved someone too much, the pleasure might be lessened, or in any case different. That would explain Taddeuz, and that room in Praga anyway . . . 'I love you and I can't do without you, Hannah.'

Using her thumb and index finger, she removed the rind of the bacon from her mouth, and placed it on the side of her plate.

'That's no reason to kill someone, Lothar.' She paced up and down the huge room.

'I wouldn't kill her myself,' he said from behind her.

'I see. Micah Gunn.'

'He's already killed before. Twice at least. I'm the only person in Australia who knows. He'll kill Eloise if I tell him to, he can't refuse. Anyway, he hates her. And I'll be away when it happens.'

She spun around and stared hard at him. It was one thing to have expected this suggestion, another to hear such calmness in the planning of a murder.

'It wouldn't worry me, Hannah,' he went on. 'And for Micah too, everything would work out. He knows that he runs the risk of being recognized at any moment. I'll give him a thousand pounds and he'll set sail for America. And I'll be able to marry you then.'

'Nothing simpler, in fact,' Hannah replied sarcastically. 'And after that we'll live in luxury, on Eloise's money. This is all foolish talk.'

She sat down on the far side of the room, a good fifteen metres away from him. It was almost midday and inevitably it was a Sunday.

'In the first place, Lothar, I shall never marry you. Never. Even if Eloise were to die from natural causes, and even if you had all the money in China. If I'm ever to get married, I shall make my own choice. Besides, I've already made my choice, and I'm not about to change my mind.'

A kind of wild hilarity was erupting inside her. This whole affair was not only tasteless, it was ridiculous.

'. . . Secondly, Lothar Hutwill, I'm going to write one or two letters and put them in the hands of people I can trust. In these letters, I shall describe how you offered to kill your wife for me, with or without Micah's complicity, so that you could then marry me. If anything happens to Eloise, whether she has a riding accident or chokes on a piece of Westphalian ham or commits suicide, those letters will go to the police. I shall also say that I tried to reason with you and that I thought when you were telling me your plans you were only playing a game. And it has been just a game, nothing more.'

He studied her with his usual calm, his lovely long hands as relaxed as usual. She suddenly realized the danger that tranquillity concealed; he must have been plotting to kill his wife for some time, although he probably was not capable of killing her himself.

'And I'm going to give you back your fifteen hundred pounds. Sixteen hundred and eighty, including interest.'

'That's not necessary, Hannah. Especially not the interest.'

'I'll give you back every last pound.'

She slipped her hand down the front of her dress and brought out a wad of notes.

'Here are one hundred and twenty pounds. I owe you another fifteen hundred and sixty.'

As he made no move to take the money she placed it on the table in front of her.

'I think the repayments will be made very quickly, in a matter of a few months.'

He did not bat an eyelid; his calm was beginning to worry Hannah a little. She had just ruined his plans for murder, condemned him to a life with Eloise — he might well be thinking of strangling her in his despair.

She moved away, heading for the staircase. In the bedroom, she checked to see if her hair was dry; she began to comb it, forcing herself to take her time and not to hurry on any account. Soon she saw in the mirror that he was standing behind her, his brown eyes boring into her disconcertingly.

'Do you want to break it off with me, Hannah?'

'Of course not. Whatever gave you that idea?'

She held his eyes and smiled at him.

'So we're going to see each other again?' he asked.

She turned around and kissed him, caressing his cheek.

'Not with Micah Gunn's assistance. I shall soon have enough money to buy my own carriage.' She examined his hands. 'You're the most wonderful lover I could dream of having, how could I deprive myself of you?'

She continued to embrace him, clinging affectionately to his neck. She was herself surprised at the pleasure these caresses gave her, especially when she had so firmly decided never to see him again.

After a few minutes, she sensed that he had finally calmed down by the way he began to return her kisses. The danger was past.

She moved away from him.

'I wonder what I did with my boots. We were so impatient last night . . .'

He gave her a regretful smile. She took the risk of turning her back on him and got down on all fours to retrieve her boots, which had been tossed to the far end of the room the night before. Sitting on the floor, she put them on. When she looked up she discovered that Lothar had left the room, as soundlessly as he had entered. With her hat and purse in hand, she followed him downstairs; he was not in the large ground-floor room either. She eventually caught sight of him at the bottom of the rock steps that led to the crazy gangway. He headed out towards the planks and Hannah was seized with another anxiety: what if he were to jump? How could anyone be so old and at the same time so childish?

'I'm leaving now, Lothar, I've such a lot of work to do,' she called out.

She received no immediate response.

He was halfway out along the planks when he said: 'Micah will take you back.'

'I feel like a bit of a walk. I used to walk a lot in Poland . . .'

She opened her mouth to shout, convinced he was about to jump. But he stood motionless on the final plank, just as she had done earlier. To her great relief she saw him sit down, his legs dangling in space. Then he lay flat on his back, covering his face with his forearms.

She knew now he would not kill himself; he would only have done it with her there, as a sort of punishment.

She left the house. Micah Gunn was nowhere to be seen; in fact, the estate was entirely deserted. She began to walk; the gangway was invisible from the path along the clifftop except at one point, thanks to a rocky overhang that projected further than any other outcrop. She stepped out on it and could see, two hundred metres below, both the crazy pier, absurdly suspended over thousands and thousands of kilometres of Pacific Ocean and Lothar Hutwill lying motionless upon it on his back.

Half an hour later a group of picnickers travelling in two horse-drawn carriages gave her a lift back to Sydney.

Before settling down to do her accounts, she wrote a letter to Quentin MacKenna, telling him the whole story. She took the precaution of only using initials, and made a point of writing: *It's Red I'm most worried about.* He would understand; she had already told him about the Hutwills when they were travelling on the train together. She did not know where to reach Quentin exactly but delivered his letter to James Soames, who had told her that Quentin called upon him occasionally.

The opening of the complex which had preoccupied her for months took place on December 14th, six days before the date she had originally aimed for.

It was a triumph. This hardly surprised her: a good idea and lots of hard work could not fail to result in success. And apart from the Saturday night and Sunday morning she had spent in the house in Botany Bay, she had devoted more than twenty hours a day, seven days a week, to her business since returning from Cobar.

The figures spoke for themselves: two hundred and eighty-three pounds profit in the first week, three hundred and ninety-one in the second.

She decided to spend Christmas Eve and day alone. She made these plans instinctively and only later understood her motives for doing so: she would spend the end-of-year festivities on her own every year until she found Taddeuz again. And then she would spend them alone, always alone, with him.

All the same the MacKennas begged her to join them, worried that she would feel lonely, and later offended by her refusal of their invitation. On the evening of the 24th, at about six o'clock, Alec MacKenna came to fetch her in the buggy, accompanied by Lizzie, both of them polite but insistent. She continued to say no, equally politely, but with a great deal of stubbornness. Not even Lizzie's tears could shake her resolve. It was not that she was terribly busy – though she did have her interminable accounts to review – she simply wanted to be left on her own. To sleep. Despite her rugged health, she felt tired, a bit lonely and abandoned, and she wanted a chance for once to wallow in her disorientation. She felt almost nostalgic for Europe, five months after arriving in Australia, even though she was beginning to make her way in her adopted continent. Images, sounds, smells haunted her; she was unaccountably certain she would never again see a whole universe – the universe made up of Goyna Street and Krochmalna Street, the Saxe Gardens, the Vistula and its embankments, not to mention Mendel.

Not to mention Taddeuz and the room in Praga.

She woke up in the middle of Christmas Eve to find herself shedding tears. At first she could not understand why, and then

she remembered her dream: she had dreamed that Taddeuz was in
Australia, that she had seen his tall figure among the merchandise
and drays on the Circular Quay in Sydney Harbour. He was coming
towards her, wearing his wonderful smile, but just as she was
about to run into his arms, he turned away from her forever,
because, in the dream, she had had fifty lovers at least, and because
she had posed in the nude for several painters.

Hannah was not completely taken in by her depression. She was
well aware that it would pass – she had given way to it deliberately,
and she had hardly had fifty lovers. Besides, what else was she to
do? Her rational side reminded her that it was precisely because
she had achieved her primary objective with those wretched
creams that she was flagging, losing her drive. It was always like
this after a victory: exaltation was very quickly followed by a sense
of emptiness.

She tried to get back to sleep, but without success. She lay in her
bed, her eyes staring into the darkness, torn in two: one Hannah
calculated very lucidly that the business in Sydney was only a
beginning; she was still a long way off the one hundred thousand
pounds sterling that she had as a target; she still had millions of
things to do – while the other Hannah wanted to bury her face in
the pillow and cry her heart out, like a little girl whose doll had
been broken.

In the end she lit the lamp. Of the dozen books she had carted
around in her carpetbag all the way from Warsaw, there was only
one that was not in French, German or English, only one that
could satisfy her feelings of nostalgia. And furthermore, it was rich
in memories: in Russian. She started to read Mikhail Lermontov's
A Hero of Our Time, opening a page at random. A few lines caught
her eye almost at once, lines the author put in Pechorin's mouth:
*If I am to die, I'll die! The loss to the world will not be large and, anyway,
I myself am sufficiently bored. I am like a man who yawns at a ball and
does not drive home to sleep, only because his carriage is not yet
there . . .*

She was struck by the quotation, not because it expressed her
own sentiments, which it did not at all, but because it made her
think of Taddeuz. Taddeuz, she feared, might say such things, or
think them, sooner or later.

* Nabokov's translation, published as a World's Classic paperback by OUP,
1984

It was by now three o'clock in the morning. This was the time when she usually got up, on the days she bothered to go to bed at all, that is, which had been only about one in two or three for the past forty-six days. Nothing needed doing urgently today, however; and she was faced with the absolute silence of the Sydney night. It was precisely because of this calm that she caught the sound of the excessively quiet footstep on the wooden staircase of the Ogilvie warehouse, the staircase that led to her apartment.

She stared at the double-locked door, groping under the pillow for the handle of her razor. The footsteps came to a halt; she could hear someone breathing on the other side of the door. Hours seemed to go by. Then she heard what sounded like fingernails scratching on the wood.

'Quentin . . .' he murmured.

14

HAVE YOU KILLED
SOMEONE?

He looked around the two rooms, his eyes crinkled and his face slightly tilted back. He nodded.

'It doesn't look as though you go in for creature comforts.'

She had locked the door behind him, and relit the lamp she had blown out before letting him in. She stood with her back to the door, the lamp in one hand, the other hand pressed behind her between the wood and her body, the razor still in her palm. Quentin was dressed in the same stained shirt and trousers. He was wearing tawny-coloured leather boots, over which he had turned up the bottoms of the his trousers. One of the sleeves of his shirt had been torn and clumsily mended with big stitches and a patch of material of a different shade of blue. There was a yellowish bruise on his left cheekbone; his right hand was bleeding.

'Are you hurt?'

'Put that bloody razor away.'

She put down the weapon and the lamp simultaneously, on the chair that served her as a night table.

'Hurt?'

He seemed to notice his hand for the first time.

'It's nothing. Just a scratch.'

'You've been in a fight.'

'It happens.'

Not a hint of a smile.

He added: 'No one saw me come here. I can leave if you like.'

He looked even more emaciated than she remembered. He seemed exhausted but she could also tell from his eyes that he had been drinking. Rather heavily, she would wager.

'Give me your hand.'

The blood was coming from a deep gash in the palm of his hand.

'It looks as though you grabbed hold of the blade of a knife.'

No reply.

He swayed slightly. She made him sit down on the bed and only then she noticed that his shirt had a long tear in it, just above his leather belt. And he was bleeding there too.

'Take off your shirt.'

'. . . get stuffed.'

He offered no resistance when she unbuttoned his shirt, only shutting his eyes tight now and then.

'Have you killed someone, Quentin?'

The wound was a long, not very deep slash. The knife had been applied to the abdomen but the blade had then slipped to the right, cutting through the flesh, but not to the organs.

'Someone tried to cut open your stomach. You took hold of the blade in your hand and pushed it aside. Is that it?'

He fell back and lay stretched out on her bed, staring at Hannah. She went to fetch some water and a cloth and began to clean his wounds with her usual imperturbability.

'I've only got tea.'

'No.'

A long silence followed this refusal; she assumed he had fallen asleep. Then he suddenly started talking again, mumbling a bit. He wanted to talk to her about 'her goddamned plants'; had she received all the consignments he had sent, and could she not cut down 'her goddamned list'. Surely she did not need all those 'goddamned things'; now that her 'goddamned business' was off and running she must have a better idea of exactly what she 'goddamned needed'?

All this he said without drawing a breath.

'Yes, to all your questions,' she replied. 'I'll make another list, more precise and shorter. Lie down. You smell as bad as three skunks. Don't you ever change your shirt?'

'I don't have another one.'

With Hannah's help, he dragged himself up until he lay stretched out in the middle of the bed.

He reminded her of a stray cat, a very big, very thin stray cat, a cat that everyone throws stones at. She felt a bit like crying again. She fought back the tears by busying herself, the way she always would.

'Take off those trousers as well. I'm going to wash the lot and try to darn the holes, although I'm no wizard at sewing and patching. And not another word,' she added, smiling to herself.

She managed, with much difficulty, to get his boots off. Thank God his feet were more or less clean. With the same determination she unbuckled his belt, unbuttoned his fly, seized the trouser legs and pulled, all in a single, rather awkward movement. She froze, feeling herself turn scarlet. She was horribly embarrassed.

He stared at her.

'Satisfied?'

His penis was mutilated; virtually non-existent. The scar was an old one.

She shook her head.

'Quentin, I wasn't even thinking . . .'

She immediately resumed her frenetic activity, filling the tub with water, piling the clothes into it, washing them twice over with vigour. Finally she plucked up the courage to say:

'If you'd let me give you a bit of money, you would at least have been able to buy some new clothes. You can almost see through these.'

She got no reply, and turned around to see that he had fallen asleep with a touchingly childlike expression on his face. Her eyes lingered on him for a moment, then she hung the trousers and shirt to dry next to her own knickers. She could do nothing else, unless she were to go over her accounts again; she had been over them six times already.

She decided to lie down on the bed. It was either that or sit on the only chair in the room. Nudging Quentin over a bit, she managed to make a bit of room for herself. She picked up Lermontov, but after a moment he murmured something about the 'goddamned lamp'. She turned it out, put down the book and curled up in the small space he had left her.

It had been light for several hours and it was still entirely silent when in his sleep Quentin stretched out his arm and flung it across her chest. Without moving she studied the bony hand with broken fingernails resting on her stomach, a hand that was at first inert but gradually came to life, the fingers creeping up her body to her left breast. The hand unhurriedly withdrew. From the rhythm of his breathing, she realized that Quentin had just woken. He opened his eyes, looking as though he did not understand where he was.

'Have I been here long?' he asked, seeing her.

'You arrived last night at about three in the morning.'

According to the church bells, that had been six or seven hours before.

'I was drunk. Forgive me.'

'It doesn't matter. Really, it doesn't. I was alone too.'

'My family wouldn't have you?'

'I wanted to be alone.'

He rolled over, ending up on his stomach.

'Who undressed me?'

'Who do you think?'

'Where are my clothes?'

'Washed. They stank to high heavens. It wouldn't do you any harm to have a wash yourself. There's some water next door. In the meantime, I'll try to cook you something. I'm a very bad cook.'

'We do like giving orders, don't we?'

'We do what's necessary.'

She got out of bed, drawing the Indian robe she wore over her nightdress tighter around her. She took stock of her frugal provisions: five eggs, a tin of beans, a piece of bacon, a bit of milk, some tea and a pound-bar of chocolate. For herself this was ample enough fare for a week at least. But a man would eat a lot more, certainly.

'Are three eggs enough?'

'Whatever you've got.'

He had slipped like a shadow into the small room next door; she could hear him pouring water and splashing it about. It was a new experience, and a pleasant one, to have a man in her home who needed her. She decided to throw into her only frying pan the beans in tomato sauce, the eggs and the bacon.

Quentin came back wrapped in a sheet, looking very much like a bearded blond Hindu, his face as tanned as his body was white.

'I'll go as soon as it's dark,' he said between mouthfuls. 'I can't very well emerge from your house in broad daylight.'

She started to say that she was not at all concerned when they heard the sound of a carriage and soon afterwards footsteps on the wooden staircase. At least two people were on their way up. There was a knock at the door.

'Hannah? It's me.'

It was Lizzie's voice. Hannah did not move a muscle as her eyes plumbed Quentin's. She shook her head. There was another knock.

'Hannah, are you there?'

Silence.

Hannah made as if to get up, determined to open the door, but Quentin's hand reached out and stopped her. *Don't answer*, his green eyes signalled. The seconds elapsed in silence. The visitors descended the staircase; then soon they heard the sound of the carriage departing.

'I'd have sooner knocked you out cold,' said Quentin.

'You ought to see her and, more important, you ought to talk to her.'

'There wasn't the slightest chance of his agreeing, but I tried, Lizzie, I did my best.'

He did not bother to reply, wolfing down what remained of his breakfast with the greatest indifference to the kind of meal she had served him. He did not say a word about the letter she had written to him about Lothar Hutwill and Micah Gunn; now that she saw him, she felt bad about it and was sorry she had called on him to help. What the devil could he do? She really had to get out of the habit of looking for Mendel Visokers everywhere, who would solve problems of her own making. With some luck he had never received the letter and she would be able to retrieve it herself at Soames's.

She told him she was going out for an hour or two; and went to her laboratory for no good reason. The city felt entirely deserted.

She returned to the apartment to find that he had fallen asleep again, his finger marking his place between the pages of *Vanity Fair*, the only English book in her possession. He could not have read more than three pages. She pulled a chair up to the table and began to compile a revised list of the products she needed, specifying exact quantities. Then, to keep herself busy, she mended the tears in his shirt as best she could, using pieces of an old apron for patches. The only thread she had was black or Turkey red, and the result of her needlework was — as she had expected — lamentable.

And so the bizarre afternoon passed. She eventually settled down to read again, first Lermontov, then Lichtenberg, in German, drawing closer to the window as the light faded, and glancing over at the sleeping Quentin after every fifteen or twenty pages. She noticed the shadows creeping over his face and his long muscles, tense as cables, beneath the extreme thinness of his body.

'You made me a promise, about Lizzie.'

She had not been aware that he was awake, and could not have said how long he had been watching her.

'I'll keep it.'

He nodded.

'Tea?'

A movement of the head told her no.

She put down her book and asked: 'Are you really going to walk all the way across Australia?'

'Do you have a map?'

She did. He spent the next hour explaining the route he would take and how he would travel. The project was six years in the planning. The idea had come to him while he was still in prison, after the carnage on the schooner. He had at first thought of using camels, which at one time were brought from the Azores. But he had finally decided to make the trip on foot; he would do it alone, without so much as the company of an Aborigine friend or two, from whom he had learned how to survive in the desert. He would take as long as he needed – twenty, thirty, forty months, more if necessary.

The only window in Hannah's room faced south-west. They could see the sun turning red as it set.

'I asked you for a more accurate list.'

'It's ready.'

'You'll continue to receive supplies, with or without me at the other end of the line. I've made arrangements: a bloke called Clancy will take care of the consignments. You just have to give him one pound a week, thirty shillings at most, no more . . .'

When Clancy made contact with her, she thought, it would mean that Quentin had started out or was on the point of beginning his long walk.

Silence.

The light was behind him, since he had raised himself almost to a sitting position in bed. She could hardly see his eyes, but she guessed what was going through his mind; her thoughts were not much different.

'I'd love to,' she said.

'Are you so sure of what I was going to ask?'

'I think so, yes.'

'Out of pity.'

'So far you haven't been too self-pitying. Don't start now, please.'
He nodded.

'There's no doubt I'm being told to shut up here. Tough, eh?'

'Yes.'

'I pity the man you've decided to love, that Pole of yours.'

'That's certainly none of your business.'

'All right. I never said a word.'

'Now?'

'Yes, please.'

She untied her robe and took off her nightdress, facing him in
the declining light.

'Could you loosen your hair?'

She did as he asked.

'Turn around slowly.'

She obeyed, and she lay down beside him in response to his next
direction. He did not touch her, although there was no more than
a centimetre's distance between his left hand and her hip. They lay
perfectly still for several minutes until the last rays of sunshine left
the room. Only then did he get up and dress; he was ready to
leave.

'Two things,' he said. 'About the Hutwills, first of all. They've
gone back to Melbourne. I managed to speak to one of their
servants at Gundagai. You're quite right to think that, left to his
own devices, he's incapable of killing his wife. I also found out that
they were about to leave together for Europe, where they'll be
staying for at least a year. Eloise has never opened any sort of
investigation of you, she doesn't even know your real name, and
she doesn't care. You're of no interest to her. He lied to you, and
you had him rather well sized up.'

'And the second thing?'

'Gunn. He's dead.'

'Was he the person you were fighting?'

'You needn't concern yourself with that. Without Gunn, your
man Hutwill is harmless, that's the only thing that matters. What's
the name of that bloke in Siberia?'

'Visoker. Mendel Visoker.'

'If he ever reaches Australia, I'd be interested to meet him.
Clancy will know where to find me. Hannah?'

'I know,' she said. 'Lizzie.'

'There's nothing else.'

In two steps he was at her bedside. He bent down and kissed her very lightly on the lips.

'Thank you.'

After he had gone, at about ten o'clock in the evening, she wrote her fourth letter to Mendel.

I've done it, Mendel, I'll soon have more money than I had when I arrived. I shall soon very nearly be rich. It doesn't make me as happy as I'd expected. True, this is just the first stage, a very small achievement. My idea of using sandalwood boxes, which I told you about in my last letter, or the one before, produced astonishing results, and surprised even me. It's satisfying to see a project you've dreamed of come into being. It even goes to your head a bit (not for long, don't worry) when people do exactly what you've predicted. Especially when you're no taller than a chair, and you're a girl and not yet eighteen. You can laugh, but the Brat is feeling fairly pleased with herself, all things considered . . .

At that point she wavered for a moment, not knowing whether she ought to tell him all about her involvement with Hutwill. She decided against, thinking it would only add to the pain he must already be coping with in Siberia.

She contented herself with mentioning Quentin, without going into much detail, telling Mendel that when he arrived in Australia she would arrange a meeting with him: *and he is not my lover, so don't go getting any ideas on that score!*

She wrote that it would take another few months to put the business on a steady footing, but that after that, she would embark on a second, more ambitious phase.

In other words, everything's going well, Mendel. Lots of love and kisses, Hannah.

In any case, he might never read her letters, she thought. She might just as well be writing to God, for all the response she expected to get.

She made three hundred and thirty-nine pounds' profit between Boxing Day and the last day of 1892.

She was alone again on that day, the last night of the year. Again she declined an invitation from the MacKennas, as well as those from the Ogilvies, the Williams sisters, Meggie MacGregor, and the Rudge brothers, who were all saddened by the idea that she should want to be alone at the birth of the New Year. As usual, Colleen, more than anyone else, came closest to persuading her to change her mind. The Irishwoman's illness was growing more and more visible, and Hannah had a great deal of trouble disappointing her.

Only two hundred and nine pounds during the first week of 1893.

She had been prepared for this slump, but it was irksome nonetheless. The holidays themselves accounted for the record profits made in the last weeks of December, so it was natural that there should be some sort of decline with the new year. Particularly as almost all the women in Sydney must now have at least one of her creams, not to mention an eau de toilette, at the rate things had been selling. Hannah knew she had more or less flooded the market, but she also knew her pots were tiny, and that sooner or later everyone would need new supplies.

She found the most comfort in the success of the tea shop. After the first few days, during which they were paralysed with shyness, the Williams sisters had very quickly adapted to their new roles as manager-hostesses. Of course they went into a panic when Hannah told them she intended to charge between ten and thirty times cost for their muffins, scones, raspberry turnovers, buns, crumpets, Dundee cakes, rhubarb pies, pink meringues, plum puddings and Victoria puddings – not to mention the seventy-one different kinds of tea on the menu – but in the end they bowed to her insistence.

Better still, so far as Hannah was concerned, the Bustards had undergone a transformation: they had become fanatically snobbish, barring entry into the establishment to two or three women whom they considered insufficiently distinguished. These prohibitions caught people's attention. Boadicea's Garden – named by the Bustards after a kind of English Joan of Arc, who fought against the Romans – became known as a highly aristocratic venue. For the first few weeks Edith and Harriet insisted on making the pastries themselves; Hannah had to battle to pry them away from their ovens. They rejected the first two candidates, sent by Colleen, for the position of cook, and condescended to take on the third only after having submitted her to a rigorous three-day examination. They greeted with equal suspicion Hannah's suggestion of a further addition to the kitchen staff, but eventually yielded to the appointment of an assistant pastrycook.

When it came to taking on a second pastrycook, some seven weeks after the opening of Boadicea's Garden, they were more easily persuaded. The newcomer was a recent immigrant, only just arrived from her native Austria. She was exceptionally good at making Viennese specialities: from *Sachertorte* to *Milchrahm Strudel*, including *Zwetschenknödel*, *Mozartkugeln* and Salzburg *Nockerl*, Carinthian *Kouglof*, Tyrolese *Hupfauf* and little pastries with almonds and currants, also from the Tyrol.

The Bustards conceded that it was all very exotic.

Hannah began to think of herself as a public liability, stuffing these Australian women with pastries while she buffered them with creams, but she also thought that it had been a bloody good idea (her language was becoming more and more colourful in this land of pioneers; she would all her life retain a penchant for strong words) to open a tea room. Unlike the sales figures for her face creams and toilet waters, those for cakes of every sort were for the time being on a constantly upward curve after a modest start. By the end of February they accounted for one third of Hannah's total profits, and soon another assistant joined the kitchen staff. The Williams sisters could no longer manage waiting on tables by themselves; four girls were engaged as apprentice waitresses, and six by March 1st.

Another vacancy arose: Hannah needed a driver-deliveryman to drive her cart, which was of course black with a Turkey red facing. Because there was no longer room to seat all her clients on the premises during the more popular hours, Hannah had agreed to accept orders for home delivery. She wished Maryan Kaden were there and for a while thought of writing to him, asking him to join her and convinced that he would come. But apart from the fact that she would have to pay his passage, which was not yet quite within her means, she remembered that he had to provide for his mother and his countless brothers and sisters, whom he would not be happy to leave in the lurch. She made a mental note to think more about Maryan at a later date.

The figures for both January and February 1893 were impressive, despite the additional salaries that had to be paid. Hannah wrote everything down in her indestructible leatherbound notebook, which still contained the entries, balance sheets and records of her early days with Dobbe Klotz in Warsaw. By the end of February, she was bringing in more than two hundred guineas a week.

This was, she figured, about one hundred and forty times her wages as a chambermaid. It was, indisputably, progress. But at her present rate it would take her ten or twelve years to reach her target, and in the meantime she feared Taddeuz would have had time to get married six times over, time to give his wives fifty-four children. She told herself she would have to move a good deal faster, and at such times she almost succumbed to despondency, but the path she had to follow continued to be very clear to her: she would make her fortune, build up a huge workforce, return to Europe, find Taddeuz, marry him, make him happy – and incidentally make herself happy – and live with him until their deaths, one spring day, when they were very old. (She was willing to concede that this might take place in autumn; this was the one point on which she had not yet made up her mind.)

It was all very simple.

'I don't think I shall live to see next Christmas,' Colleen said calmly, as she might have said she expected it to rain the next day.

'That's not true. People don't just die like that, not unless they give up.'

'What an amazing person you are, Hannah. You really believe that living is just a matter of will power, don't you?'

'Yes. Or at least that it costs nothing to try. If you've got any chance at all, you might as well do all you can for it.'

She did not believe in paradise, she said. Nor in hell, nor in any other life in the hereafter. And she already knew that she would die a very old lady, when she started to get a little too tired. In a hundred years' time.

Having said this, she fell silent, because Colleen coughed and coughed, seized with another fit. She also fell silent because she could see that she caused the Irish woman a great deal of sadness by revealing herself to be so lacking in any religious feeling.

They were together in the interior courtyard, on the first floor, looking on to the main part of the building which contained the tea room, the beauty parlour and the laboratory. These rooms had been stripped and whitewashed by the Watts's workmen, but no other refurbishment had yet taken place and they remained uninhabitable. Hannah was keeping them for her own use, when she was a bit richer. This room would be her bedroom, adjoining a future bathroom she told Colleen; that would be her office, and that her library; and here would be another small apartment, very nicely arranged . . .

'For Lizzie,' Colleen said softly.

'I hate hearing you talk like this, you're not dead yet.'

'Quentin told me about the conversation he had with you about

Lizzie. I'd make the same request he's already put to you, Hannah. I've spoken about it to Dougal. He's practically agreed already, and Rod too. So everything's settled apart from your agreeing to it.'

From down below in the garden the chattering voices of the ladies of Sydney rose up, as if contained in the sound of running water.

'That was how I adopted you, Lizzie. It was very simple and almost inevitable. Rather like taking in a dog without a master . . . Do stop barking, please: here we are, two old ladies taking tea at the Ritz, sixty years after the fact, and we're supposed to be respectable . . . '

One thousand eight hundred and fifteen pounds. On January 15th, in keeping with the agreement she had made with Lothar Hutwill – an agreement she had actually imposed on him, so little did he care about money – she delivered the sum of eight hundred and eighty pounds in person to a banker by the name of Edward Rudston Greaves. This brought the amount she had repaid Hutwill to a total of one thousand pounds; she still owed six hundred and eighty. She figured she could clear the rest of her debt by the middle of next February, but instinct told her that this would not be very financially sound. The profits on her beauty products had unhappily reached a ceiling; she could see that she had come to a stage it would be difficult to go beyond. Without the ever increasing profits from the tea room and the cake shop, her takings would have levelled off, if not dropped by this point. The only solution seemed to her to invest in something else, which would mean settling her debt to Hutwill a little less quickly. With the remaining part of her profit she would start new enterprises.

E. R. Greaves looked about forty-five; he held an important position at the Bank of Australasia. Whether he was consummately skilled in the art of dissimulation, or completely unaware of Hannah's relationship with Lothar Hutwill, he seemed prepared to accept her money with no questions. It was to be credited to a secret account belonging to his friend and client.

'I shall come – or someone else will come – and bring you sixty-eight pounds every week for ten weeks,' explained Hannah. 'Or rather, no, another idea occurs to me; you can tell me whether it makes sense. I open an account with you, you pay me ten per cent – that's the minimum, I believe – and every week you withdraw from my account sixty-eight pounds and credit the amount to your other client. On reflection, I'd rather have twelve per cent. You can refuse. There are other banks.'

Greaves said yes.

'As far as statements are concerned,' said Hannah, 'one or two a week will do. Let's say on Tuesdays and Fridays. I like to know how my affairs stand and I'm quite good with figures. Thank you for being so obliging. I shall have one hundred thousand pounds within eighteen or twenty months and I'll need someone to entrust the money to . . . Yes, that's right, I'm expecting to come into a small inheritance. May I ask a question?'

Greaves allowed as how she might.

'What would you give for someone's chances of walking from Brisbane to Perth, following a straight line?'

He gulped, disconcerted by the abrupt change of subject.

'Crossing the central desert? Absolutely nil. No one's ever done it.'

Well, a few had already tried. He reeled off the names of a Polish count, called Strzelecki, who discovered and named Mount Kosciusko in 1840; of a certain Angus Macmillan, who, one year later, reached Corner Inlet; of a Prussian called Leichardt, who in 1848 headed due west from the banks of the Darling River and had yet to return; and of a John Forrest who made the trip between Perth and Adelaide . . .

'But Adelaide is in South Australia . . . west of Melbourne, and Forrest's trek cannot in any way compare with an attempt to walk from Brisbane to Perth.'

He cited the names of other luminaries, all of whom had disappeared. He thought you would have to be mad to undertake a trek like that, even with the new horseless cars people were talking about.

Hannah smiled; only madmen were interesting. She had one last question: where were Mr and Mrs Hutwill at present?

Undoubtedly in Melbourne. Until June or July, when they usually returned to their estate at Gundagai. But Greaves believed that the couple would be leaving for Europe at that time.

And he thereby confirmed the information she had been given by Quentin MacKenna.

Hannah reviewed her accounts when she got home, and concluded that by the end of May she would be in possession of two thousand six hundred pounds, plus the interest paid by the bank. She would also be, at last, out of debt.

In her fifth letter to Mendel she wrote:

If you were to turn up tomorrow, I could feed you the most wonderful things, even though you're a bit of a glutton, with that cupboard you have for a chest . . . Oh Mendel, my depression is over, I'm in a true fighting spirit. And I've a battle to fight. When the devil are you coming to join me?

She set out for Brisbane on April 29th 1893.

15

NO ONE FLIRTS AS MUCH
AS I DO

She had a berth on the Australian Navigation Company's steamship *Alexander*; she was the only woman on board, and enjoyed being treated as such, more than ever before. She was delighted to see for the first time the exotic, mangrove-lined coastline outside Sydney, as she was to meet her first millionaire. Naturally he expressed a wish to visit her cabin (he was less artful than he might have been in conveying this), preferably at a time when she would be there, and preferably, he implied, at a time when she was in a horizontal position. She countered his attack with ease – he was a jokester, and in any case he was horribly old. She already had plans of her own for the ruddy-faced Clayton Pike after all, who owned a couple of million hectares crammed with sheep and the occasional cow, not to mention some gold mines near Gympie and some considerable interests in a number of trading houses. Furthermore, this giant of a man was an elected member of the Queensland Parliament. She knew she could not have found a better victim.

She claimed to be Swiss, from a region she invented on the spot that she named Vierwaldstättersee. She told Pike a heartbreaking story that would have brought tears to a wallaby's eyes about a catastrophic shipwreck off Papua in which she had lost her whole family – and she watched him burst into laughter.

'You don't believe a single word of what I'm telling you, do you?'

He admitted he did not. He himself had been something of a fibber in his youth, and felt a bit sad at having no reason to lie any more, truth having overtaken fiction – proof of how decrepit he was now. He was one of those men carried along purely by the indomitable belief in themselves, whether they displayed a Texan joviality or the cold austerity of the Jewish or Presbyterian money-men from America's East Coast. These men were capable of taking the craziest gambles, but were at the same time prepared to argue for ten days over a dollar. They also all shared the belief that a woman was either a mother or something pink and flirtatious that emitted frightened squeals when required to.

Hannah could see nothing wrong with flirting; on the contrary. One of the first things she had turned her attention to, after her profits had seemed assured, was her wardrobe; in her view clothes were an investment as well as a source of pleasure. Out of some fabulous silk crêpe imported from China she had three identical copies of the famous dress with the thirty-nine buttons made to measure. Out of some no less sumptuous lampas she had another dress made, with a décolletage that plunged revealingly low; she had ordered a fifth dress of satin-smooth Pekin, uniformly Turkey red. Some black shot-silk with red and white lace trimmings was used for her sixth, which had a décolletage as breathtakingly low as the lampas dress, and some Indian tussor was purchased for the last three, all of them white, as she intended to wear those outfits only in the sun with a flowery wide-brimmed hat. She had bought six hats and ten pairs of shoes, including some flat-heeled French shoes that felt like slippers. As for her underclothes, they now amounted to a mass of frothy faille, grosgrain, foulard, and needle-point or bobbin lace, as well as a profusion of Dacca muslin, efflorescent if not completely transparent.

'There's surely no one in the whole of Australia who flirts more than I.'

As for being pink and wailing, however, that was quite another matter. She was often going to have to confront these ambitious men – of whom Pike was a most distinct southern prototype – and convince them right off the bat that she could hold her own on their territory. She would also, on occasion, want to make it clear she could get the better of them. This did not mean that she could not be pink and squealing, so long as it won her the advantage . . .

From behind his cigar, like some Russian artilleryman watching the charge of the Light Brigade at Balaclava, Clayton Pike listened to her while she told him her story. She left little out including the trick with the boxes. He laughed, but she could see clearly that it had made him think. He had not thought her quite so Machiavellian. At this point she judged it wise to hold back a bit on the trap she had been setting; for a good hour she went through her little-girl routine, acting enthusiastic, ambitious, cultured but naïve.

As the *Alexander* entered the mouth of the Brisbane River on the third day of its voyage, Hannah was measuring each of her words. And Clayton Pike was becoming more and more aware of the fact that she was a woman.

Finally she sensed that the moment had come when his mistrust had been laid entirely to rest. She ventured more closely towards her trap.

'Pike,' she said (she had decided to skip the 'Mr', not only because he called her Hannah, but also because 'Mr Pike' did not seem sufficiently egalitarian), 'Pike, you have a fortune of something like five hundred thousand pounds, but you're also . . .' – here she pretended to assess his age, when in fact she knew, thanks to the steward, that he was sixty-three – 'you're also fifty years old. I'm eighteen. I'll make a bet with you. I have now made over two thousand six hundred pounds. I bet you that in a year's time I'll have twenty-five thousand. At least.'

'A year to the day?'

'To the day, to the hour. Without any loan or inheritance. And without robbing people in the streets with a revolver. Twenty-five thousand pounds that I'll have earned all by myself.'

'With proof to hand?'

'All the proof you want. You'll have the right to check my books.'

'Who will arbitrate? A bank?'

'Whichever one you choose.'

'The Union Bank of Australia, in Melbourne.'

'All right.'

'You know it?'

'Never heard of it.'

'It's a big bank.'

'Good luck to it.'

'And if you make the twenty-five thousand pounds?'

'Then you'll pay me twenty-five thousand pounds. In exchange . . .'

'What if you've already got the money?'

'My account is with the Bank of Australasia in Sydney. I'll give you access to it. I don't have any other. I've only been in this country since a year ago July. You can verify everything I've told you about myself, including the story of being robbed by larrikins. If I were to be so much as a pound short, or even a shilling, I would in exchange give you every penny I own, in Australia and the rest of the world. In three hundred and sixty-five days from now, I mean, to the minute.'

Silence.

The Light Brigade was clearly advancing on the undaunted Russian artillery.

She thought she had done it; in any event, she was having fun.

Pike removed his cigar from his mouth and exclaimed, or rather began to exclaim: 'Well, I'll be . . .' but broke off, because he could not bring himself to swear in front of a lady.

'As far as I'm concerned,' said Hannah, with her most charming smile, 'you can go right ahead and say "damned" or "buggered", if it makes you feel better. Yes or no, Pike? Do you accept my bet? You wouldn't be afraid of me, would you?'

She leaned forward a little, the more to dazzle him with her décolletage; she was, not coincidentally, wearing her lampas dress.

They shook hands on their wager – her tiny little hand in Irish lace mitts disappearing in his huge Australian paw – beneath the shade of a twirling parasol.

'He would not have bet if I'd been a man,' she thought as she held out her hand. 'Being a girl can sometimes be damned useful.'

Pike invited her to stay with him while she was in Brisbane, although she had intended to stay at the Imperial Hotel.

'And while my intentions are entirely honourable,' he added, not without a degree of embarrassment, 'I would prefer that we didn't speak of this bet in front of my wife, Hannah. She might not understand . . .'

'I give you my word as a gentleman,' replied Hannah with a laugh.

Pike lived – with his wife, five children, and seven grandchildren – at Kangaroo Point, Brisbane's preferred address. He introduced Hannah, as they had agreed, as the daughter of one of his business contacts in Sydney. She was given a warm welcome as was usual in Australia, and such as she would not come across anywhere else but America. Her hosts wanted to organize a ball for her, even though she told them she did not know how to dance. More to her liking, Pike lent her a carriage and a coachman who was to serve as her escort and, better still, he placed all of his contacts, both in town and throughout the colony of Queensland entirely at her disposal.

The afternoon after disembarking, she went by ferry from Petrie's Bright to the centre of town and met the real estate agent recommended to her by her host. She visited ten or twelve likely properties with him, and chose one the next day, in Queens Street, on the first floor of an attractive brick building with flowerboxes in all its windows. On the ground floor was a French dress shop, whose proprietor turned out to be as French as Hannah was Austrian or Swiss.

She figured that three rooms would suffice for the first branch shop. She made arrangements for them to be painted white with a Turkey red floor and ebony-black skirting-boards; she had brought with her on the *Alexander* samples of the ebony planks and the red paint from Sydney, as well as several watercolours that would hang on the walls once they had been finished. She lost no time in choosing some white-lacquered rattan furniture; the only thing left for her to do was put flowers in the rooms.

So far everything had gone the way she liked things to: quickly. It then took her five entire days to recruit an agent, however. And had it not been for the network of social contacts that the Pikes deployed on her behalf, she probably would not have found one at all, at least not without camping out in Brisbane for months on end. She ultimately hired two representatives, as she was not able to decide between the two best candidates and because they seemed to complement each other, one being very good with figures, while the other seemed better suited to selling. Their names were Evangeline Pope and Mary Carr, and both of them were sailors' wives, which meant they were only fleetingly occupied by their usually-absent husbands. She told them, in excruciating detail, exactly how she wanted them to sell the face creams and toilet waters that she would send them from Sydney in monthly consignments, and how they should dispense beauty advice. When they objected that they knew nothing about such matters Hannah bellowed, 'So? Do you think I do?'

They would be paid, she told them, a percentage of sales.

And she told them she would see to the publicity herself. She quite simply used the box technique again in Brisbane, with an additional asset this time in Clayton Pike, who had interests or firm friendships in the local press, notably among the editorial staff on the weekly publication *Queenslander*. Evangeline, even more so than Mary, appreciated Hannah's tactics and soaked up her advice like a sponge – what was more, she understood it.

Hannah reckoned she could bring in one hundred and thirty pounds profit per month in Brisbane for the first ten months; after that the profits should increase. She decided to take every precaution with this satellite enterprise, however, and she consulted a senior executive with the Bank of Australasia, whom she made responsible for keeping an eye on the agency's books and informing her should things stray at all from their expected course.

'Why one hundred and thirty pounds?' asked Clayton Pike.

'There are 240,000 inhabitants in Sydney, who bring in eight hundred pounds a month, taking a month to be only four weeks. Brisbane has a population of 40,000. One sixth of eight hundred is one hundred and thirty-three. Do you want to reconsider the terms of our bet, Pike? To raise the stake?'

He did not.

At the ball that was finally held in her honour, she categorically refused to dance, pleading a slightly sprained ankle for the occasion. Again, she had no clear reason to have done so, just as she had instinctively insisted on being alone for the end-of-year festivities. It was true that she did not know how to dance, but she also knew she could learn. This was something else: a kind of vague dream taking shape, which she would nurture for seven years.

She returned to Sydney on May 14th, but stayed only two days, having booked a place on the first train to Melbourne. In Sydney, acting on Clayton Pike's advice, she managed to persuade Benjamin Rudge, Ezekiel's brother, to give P & O only part of his time as a book-keeper, and to devote his free hours to keeping financial track of her business affairs. He needed only supply her with a weekly statement of accounts since she trusted him – insofar as she could trust anyone.

She knew Pike was right. It was high time she delegated the day-to-day running of her business; she herself had better and more important things to do. She entrusted Meggie with the supervision of the production process: by mid May, 1893, eleven girls worked in the laboratory and this number would rise to eighteen during the next six months. For fifteen pounds a month, Dinah Watts took charge of the general running of the beauty parlour and tea room, supervising Edith and Harriet Williams, who could not see

much further than the ends of their sharp noses as far as money
matters were concerned.

After all this planning, Hannah still found time, two hours before
her train left, to race out to the MacKenna house and kiss Colleen
and Lizzie. The Irish woman had lost a spectacular amount of
weight during the two weeks Hannah had been away. At times she
could not breathe; she would turn pale with the grinding pain in
her chest.

'I warn you, Colleen, if you're not here when I get back . . . '

'Not another word, Hannah.'

Only because of the train connections she spent a night in Melbourne; she certainly did not intend to linger there. Melbourne
was too big a challenge, one which she did not know how to tackle.

She took a room at Mrs Smithson's, in the family boarding-
house where she had spent her first nights in Australia and where
she had been robbed. She could not resist the temptation of
showing off her wealth a bit, after the pathetic circumstances of
her visit only nine months before. Taking into account the money
she had invested in Brisbane, her travel expenses and the greater
cost of her wardrobe, she still had a little under two thousand
pounds.

The next day she set off for Ballarat and Bendigo. All she knew
about Ballarat was what Lothar Hutwill had told her, when he had
spoken of the male and female Venetian gondolas. But once again,
she used numbers as her guide: there were at least fifty thousand
inhabitants in the first of these two towns, thirty-odd thousand in
the second. More important, some two hundred million pounds
sterling's worth of gold had been extracted from the ground around
them.

Clayton Pike had given her the name of a friend in Ballarat, a
certain Lachlan, the proprietor of a number of things in the area,
particularly of a few vineyards. Lachlan did not turn out to be
terribly interested in her; Hannah quickly registered his indifference when she announced her intention of repeating on his
territory what she had already achieved in Sydney and Brisbane.

But fate would play its part, as would Hannah's constant vigilance, that permanent state of alert that kept her ready to leap on
the smallest opportunity. Six months earlier, in Melbourne, Lachlan had hired a young French couple to work for his vineyards,
largely because they were from the Bordeaux and Burgundy
regions. By coincidence, Hannah entered Lachlan's office just as

these compatriots of her beloved Choderlos de Laclos and Jules Verne were leaving. She was delighted to hear French spoken in Lachlan's waiting-room – and to understand it – and as soon as her own tepid interview with Australia's wine-grower was over she ran after them . . .

Their names were Régis and Anne Fournac and neither of them was yet twenty-five. They had been in Australia, where they intended to settle permanently, for eight months, and were considering opening a business. They had no specific idea in mind, and were vacillating between a restaurant or a dress shop like the one Régis' older brother had opened in 1887 in Melbourne, in Bourke Street. (Hannah remembered the shop and better still its windows well, as they had often made her gape in admiration.) The Fournacs had a little capital – about sixty pounds – that they had put aside since they had come to work for Lachlan.

It also turned out that before emigrating to the southern hemisphere they had worked in Paris, he as a salesman at the Bazaar de l'Hôtel de Ville, and later at le Printemps, she as an assistant cashier in a shop in the rue de Faubourg St-Honoré. Hannah saw them as a Godsend. She spoke to them in a French she had learned in books and had never spoken before, sometimes employing expressions that made them drown in laughter. She liked the couple a great deal, so much so that she almost distrusted her luck; and the feeling was mutual, despite their suspicion and reluctance, so typically French, to get involved too quickly.

She explained in great detail how her business operated, and how she would envisage an association between herself and the two of them. She would send them her products, and they would have an exclusive franchise for all territory west of Melbourne, which was to say Ballarat, Bendigo and – why not? – Adelaide. Was that not where they had been planning to settle anyway, she guessed correctly?

Anne's clear eyes sparkled. She sniffed at a pot of '79'.

'And this will remove wrinkles?'

'Not that one, the other one. At least I think so.'

She decided she would tell them the truth, and admitted that she had created the two creams herself, and did not really have the foggiest idea what they might be good for. The only thing she was certain about was that they were harmless. She had been using them every morning for months herself – this was a slight exaggeration – and had no unwelcome results.

Looking like someone who had been invited to dine with the
Borgias, Anne Fournac ventured to dab a little on her cheeks.

'It smells nice, I'll say that for it.'

Hannah agreed that Perth and Fremantle could be included in
their area; the two towns were situated miles from anywhere, on
the Indian Ocean, and she had never herself intended to establish
anything there. If the Fournacs were keen, however, why not?
And if they really insisted on investing some of their capital in the
venture she had no objection: they would put down fifty pounds
and she three hundred. They would get eighteen per cent of the
profits; within six months at the outside, they would, she guaranteed them, be making between seventy and one hundred pounds a
week. And that would quickly become two hundred a week, of
that she was sure. What was more, if they agreed to certain
conditions, which she was quite willing to specify, they could all
three agree to allow their joint profits for the first eight months of
trading to accumulate, or, if they preferred, to reinvest the money
as soon as they had reached five hundred pounds. And with this
capital they would branch out from the sale of beauty products
into running tea rooms, where people could buy the best pastries
in south-west Australia . . .

'It would be good if one of you . . . all right, both of you . . . were
to come to Sydney to see how it all operates . . . Very well, I'll pay
your travel expenses – and your living expenses, while we're at it.
No, the suit and the dress you'll have to pay for yourselves!'

At that point both Fournacs burst out laughing and explained
that they only wanted to know how far her generosity extended.
They were joking. They wanted to be real partners, footing their
share of the bill, no more, no less.

'But there is one question, Hannah: where did you learn your
French? Now and again, it sounds really strange!'

She was at first a bit disconcerted by this French mockery with
which she had no experience, but she eventually joined in their
laughter.

In Sydney they were to call on Dinah Watts, who would tell
them what they needed to know. No, she probably would not be
there herself. She would most likely be in Melbourne.

She had high tea and dinner with the Fournacs, encouraging
them to talk about Paris, and she spent the following morning
giving them a little more training. She categorically insisted on her
shop décor, which they were to respect down to the smallest detail

— white, Turkey red and black-lacquered wood, if not ebony, which might be too expensive to start with.

She had planned to spend four or five days in Ballarat, if not more; then to go on to Bendigo and finally to Adelaide, in order to set up her agencies in these three towns. Running into the Fournacs like this was almost too good to be true; they had solved all her problems in one fell swoop. And the more she tried to fuel her distrust with endless questions, the more the replies the French couple gave confirmed her opinion that she had found two real gems.

They went to the station to see her off, disappointed not to board the train with her, so well did they get on together. They still had a few things to take care of before they could be released from their contract with Lachlan, however. And they needed to find a place to live, as well as to take stock of the territory further west, principally in Adelaide. From there, it was agreed, they would send her a report.

Much as she loved the Fournacs' company, Hannah was relieved to be on her own for the next few days. She thought that while she had been out looking simply for agents, she might well have found something much better: a comprehensive solution on an Australian-wide scale to the problem of representation. If Régis Fournac's brother even remotely matched up to their description of him this would be the case. The possibilities were so attractive that she preferred to be alone to consider them in depth.

On the train back to Melbourne, she reviewed her accounts yet again. She had fifteen hundred pounds left, very nearly the amount she had borrowed from Lothar Hutwill, which she had now completely repaid. In fact she had much more than that: she had set out for Brisbane a month ago now, and on the first day of June, as had been agreed between Benjamin Rudge and herself, the profits for the month of May would be collected and deposited in the account they would open at the Union Bank of Australia.

The revenues for the month should total eight to nine hundred pounds, which gave her a grand total of more than two thousand three hundred pounds. And that amount seemed quite sufficient to allow her to embark on a Melbourne offensive . . .

Régis' older brother, Jean-François Fournac, was thirty-one years old. Having read *The Three Musketeers* nine times, Hannah immediately thought of him as d'Artagnan. He had d'Artagnan's moustaches and the same sardonic cheerfulness in his nut-brown eyes. His shop in Bourke Street was uncommonly elegant, and he proved to be a terrific salesman. He had the requisite cunning, an extraordinary, imperturbable affability and a dash of familiar insolence that added spice to his otherwise unfailing courtesy. His seven sales assistants danced to a mere glance from him.

Hannah decided to put him to the real test; she walked into the shop as an ordinary client. And she actually bought something: a crêpe-de-Chine blouse with leg-of-mutton sleeves and a frill of lacy muslin, for which she paid an extravagant seven guineas.

'I shall have to remember to ask him for a rebate if we go into business together,' she told herself.

But she took more than two hours to make her purchase, deliberately driving the sales assistants to a state of exasperation with her demands, and she kept a cold hunter's eye on Jean-François while he circled about. He finally realized what was going on and asked:

'Am I mistaken or do you have something other than a simple purchase in mind?'

What happened then, in that moment, affected her entire future in Australia, but equally, and more importantly, the rest of her life. Just as she was on the point of entering into negotiations with Fournac, she saw herself already on the way back to Europe, beginning her search for Taddeuz, finding him, marrying him, having his children, settling down for good.

The vision was fleeting but bold enough to colour all she was about to say.

It was now June 2nd. She had been in Melbourne for four days, not having raced into Fournac's shop the moment she stepped off the train. She had carried out every possible study, she had calculated and reflected.

Above all, she had met Polly.

16

POLLY TWHAITES

Wittaker, Wittaker and Twhaites was a Melbourne law firm specializing in commercial practice. Clayton Pike had given Hannah the name and address; he had advised her to become a client of theirs.

'Hannah, if you were the kind of woman to be satisfied with becoming a well-to-do shopkeeper . . .'

'Which I'm not. I want to be richer than you.'

'There's no limit to your insolence. But go and see these people. They'll be able to help you.'

She did as he suggested. Paul Twhaites, the third partner, had been in Australia only one year. He was thirty-four and had previously worked in London and New York, where he had accumulated a sizeable amount of capital, some of which he had used to buy a third share in the eminent practice. Pike had told her this, recommending she see Paul Twhaites and no one else.

'He'll suit you down to the ground.'

Pike could not have known how right he was. 'Polly' was short, almost portly, blond, pink-faced. He wore a winningly surprised look in his eyes, but it was clear that he had a crafty, fastidious mind. He was not satisfied with hearing Hannah talk of her ambitions, but wanted to know everything that had led up to her arrival in his office.

Then suddenly he was saying that he did not want a fee for his consultation; he would take a token shilling at most. On the other hand he wanted her to make a very firm commitment: from now on she was to call on him in respect of all her business ventures, in every area and in every country. He was to be her accredited legal adviser.

She stared at him in amazement.

'Because you think I'm going to succeed?'

'I haven't the slightest idea. But I'd be curious to see a woman going into this jungle, her only weapon a stunning pair of eyes, big as saucers. By the way, will you marry me?'

'No. And what if I don't succeed?' she asked, not missing a beat.

'I'll have seen you try, and that in itself is no everyday matter in a country where entertainment is in short supply. So, I'll advise you, free of charge, for six months . . .'

'Eleven.'

'Why *eleven*, of all numbers?'

She told him about her bet with Pike, and about her plans to leave Australia after she won it.

'It was Pike who gave me your name, Mr Twhaites.'

'Call me Paul.'

'Call me Hannah.'

'Hannah, I'm actually the best lawyer in this hemisphere . . .'

'In all modesty.'

'In all modesty. I've understood you correctly, haven't I? You're going to make as much money as possible, as quickly as possible, here in Australia, and then go back to Europe?'

'Exactly that.'

'I'm bored to death here as well. Are you sure you don't want to marry me?'

'Positive.'

'We'll talk about it again in twelve months' time, when you've won your bet with Pike. All things considered, I'd rather marry you when you were rich to the tune of fifty thousand pounds. I'm not the kind of man to refuse a woman on the grounds that she has money – there are limits to my snobbery. My fee, if you please.'

He wrote out a receipt for one shilling in settlement of his fees for the period lasting until May 2, 1894 at eleven o'clock in the morning, the day her bet with Pike was to be settled. His desk top was a thick sheet of glass, completely bare, with no writing case, no paper, not the smallest personal object on it. He looked at Hannah with his guileless, doll-like eyes, then made a gesture she would become familiar with: the chubby index finger and middle finger of his left hand advanced across the glass in a childish imitation of someone walking.

'Now, let's talk about this possibility of an association with the Fornacs . . .'

'Fournac. Jean-François and Marie-Claire.'

'Whom you haven't yet met.'

'They don't even know I exist.'

'But you're confident of being able to persuade them.'

'Absolutely.'

Pressing together the tips of his little pink fingers, he said: 'Well now, there are several possibilities . . .'

The idea of exchanging shares in her two companies – one for beauty products, the other for the chain of tea rooms, companies he helped her to set up formally – for shares in the companies set up by the Fournacs was his. Admittedly, there was one small difficulty, apart from the fact that the Fournacs of Bourke Street knew nothing about these far-reaching projects: even though they were directly involved, they had not yet formed a company.

'I'll persuade them to set up one, even two if necessary,' said Hannah.

'This extraordinary confidence of yours is completely disarming.'

'Do you want to bet? Let's bet your fees on it.'

'I'm not Clayton Pike. What would become of me if I were to lose that shilling? Taking risks is out of the question. Let's suppose you've persuaded the Fournacs . . .'

Twhaites had to do battle with Hannah to overcome her fierce reservations about giving away shares; she did not want to give away anything at all, however little, of what she had created and what was properly hers.

He eventually came up with the decisive argument, the only one likely to strike at the heart of her stubbornness.

'You're not going to spend your whole life in Australia, Hannah.'

'Certainly not. I've just told you that.'

'You hope to go back to Europe, and soon.'

'Yes, but . . .'

It was when she understood what he was trying to tell her, what he had seen before she had, that she made her decision. Everything became clear to her: she was not simply going to find success in Australia and then, with her newly-acquired fortune, set off for Paris, Vienna and London in order to find Taddeuz and Mendel. Why not try to go further with her 'goddamned creams'? Why not repeat elsewhere what she had achieved on this far side of the globe?

She could, she thought, become the richest woman in the world, or if not the richest then at least the first to have earned all her money herself. Taddeuz would write his books, and she would make the money. They would both be famous all over the world . . .

'Hannah, I think you'll go infinitely further than you yourself anticipated. Why do you think I want to link my fate with yours? This shilling that I'm staking on you is going to bring me the money to buy two castles in Kent. And it'll be devilish good fun to watch you on your way up. Say yes, for pity's sake. There are three or four million Australians. It won't be long before your businesses here reach a ceiling. These concessions to the Fournacs – Good God, when I think that they don't know anything about it yet! – will seem very insignificant to you when you look back at them from France or England. We won't make any partnership agreements with them for anything but a well-defined geographical area; at most it will include New Zealand. The rest of the world will be yours . . .'

She gave way. How was anyone to resist a person who revealed you to yourself? With Polly's help, she officially founded her first two companies. He insisted there be two for the cosmetics alone; 'You can never take too many precautions, Hannah. What if one of your creams were to disfigure a single woman? You'd be sued. If you lost the case, you'd lose everything. Two companies divide the risks. And then you'll have to patent your products. I'll take care of that. Not just for this country: all over the planet. That would be the last straw, if someone were to steal your magic recipes. Just sign here.'

And this was the way she had spent her first four days in Melbourne. Only afterwards did she set foot inside Jean-François Fournac's shop.

First he had looked at her with the solicitousness of a good vendor, then with surprise, then with the mistrustful coldness of a horsedealer, then with a sort of dreamy self-interest.

'And you want me to rent you a part of my shop?'

She replied that he had understood very well what she wanted, that it would save time if he would stop pretending he did not understand, that she already knew his brother Régis and sister-in-

law Anne, that she had been able to appraise his wife Marie-Claire
at their second shop in Little Collins Street.

'I bought some things at your other shop too, including an
adorable pair of white drugget shoes with diamond-encrusted
buckles, made in Ireland. You and your wife stock the loveliest
garments in Australia. I myself represent the height of luxury and
refinement in another area. We were made to become partners.'

She did not expect him to give her a reply straightaway. Such
transactions are not made on the spur of the moment, and she
would not in any event have wanted partners capable of making a
rash commitment. Furthermore, she knew how much he relied –
quite rightly – on his wife. People had sung her praises to Hannah:
she was the one who attended to their finances, while he concentrated mainly on manufacturing garments copied from sketches he
selected from Parisian magazines, as well as on others he designed
himself. Hannah already knew she was going to buy a new
wardrobe of dresses from him, on the condition that he offered
them to her at a special price. 'By the way,' she asked, 'could you
not reconsider the price of the blouse I have just bought? Seven
guineas was after all a bit excessive ... if we are to become
partners, the two of us, the least you can offer me is a forty per
cent discount and ...'

'Could I get a word in?'

'You just have. No, don't say anything. I know what you're
going to tell me. You don't know me from Adam, and I could be
an adventuress. I am. But an honest one. And I've money behind
me. I've a business lawyer, one of the most highly thought of in
his field. He studied law at Oxford and he's practically a cousin of
Victoria – the woman with the moustache who always sits down
without ever looking to see if there's a chair for her to sit on – he
knows no one better than he knows her. What's more, Mr Clayton
Pike, the richest man in Australia – well, nearly – can vouch for
me equally, he's a friend of mine – in the most honourable sense
... the poor man, he's really decrepit.

'That's not all. I've already invested three hundred pounds in
your brother Régis, which is proof of my sincerity and of the
seriousness of my intentions. And of course, in Sydney, where I'm
better known than in Melbourne, people everywhere will tell you
that I'm in the process of making a fortune. While I'm thinking of
it, the best thing would be for you and your wife to go there and
see what I've already achieved. And that's just the beginning.

Within a year, my business in Sydney will be worth thirty, perhaps even fifty, thousand pounds. Because there's also my agency in Brisbane.

'As far as our partnership is concerned,' Hannah went on, 'nothing could be simpler. Your lawyers will sort out the details with mine. Don't let us get involved in any sordid discussions, please. Let's not fight against the friendship that's growing and growing between us. I hope you're going to invite me to have dinner at home with you this evening. I passed by the block in Collins Street where you keep your eight rooms. Very pretty. I see no reason why you shouldn't buy the whole street inside two years, three at the outside, once we've made our fortune together.

'And we could extend this partnership of ours to Tasmania and New Zealand. I was told you get orders from women there, and that you send them the dresses you have made up by the fifteen seamstresses in your workshop. Just think, together we could develop the network you already have, from Perth to Auckland, acquiring a monopoly on all women's luxury products; together we would represent the heights of style. How could we fail? It's impossible. I can guess what question's bothering you: you want to know where the creams and toilet waters I've been talking about are. The answer is: at the station in Flinders Street, right here in Melbourne. My assistant Meggie MacGregor has arranged for one thousand pots and three thousand bottles to be sent to me. It's a start; We'll increase the deliveries in future. Well now, that's everything. Did you want to say something?'

The Gascon eye undressed her with a smile:

'Nothing more. We've covered all the questions, it seems to me. While I think of it, would you consent to come to dinner this evening? My wife, Marie-Claire, would be very happy to meet you.'

'What a good idea!' laughed Hannah.

The invitation was issued – and accepted – easily, but the negotiations proceeded less benignly. The Fournac delegation – both brothers and their wives – did indeed visit Sydney at their own expense. What they saw there completely reassured them, but it nevertheless took seventeen days to reach an agreement, which was ultimately sealed at a solicitor's office, in the presence of both parties' lawyers. In the end Hannah agreed to give the Fournacs forty per cent of the receipts on the beauty products throughout the whole of Australia and New Zealand (but strictly nothing outside these two territories), and forty per cent as well on the tea rooms already opened and those yet to be opened, which were in future to be grouped together in a third separate company. As for the different concessions Hannah had already granted the younger of the Fournac brothers, this matter was to be resolved in an agreement between the two brothers.

In exchange for what she believed to be great generosity on her part, Hannah insisted on and got the same percentage share in all the Fournacs' business activities, present and future, in all areas (Régis was dreaming of restaurants), in all territories. It was understood that the elder Fournac couple would do their utmost to develop the sector that Hannah called 'Toiletries and Trimmings'. The ultimate goal was nothing short of a war machine that was prepared to set up garrisons in every town of notable size in Australia, New Zealand, and the rest of the world.

When the negotiations were completed, Hannah found herself with five companies: she had a majority shareholding of sixty per cent in three of them, and a minority holding of forty per cent in the other two. (The Fournacs had divided their enterprise so that ready-to-wear items would be included in one firm and jewellery, trinkets, scarves, handkerchiefs, hats, gloves and fine lingerie would be included in another.)

In her mind she now had an empire and, best of all, she owned an empire that she would be able to leave as often and as long as she liked. She asked Polly his opinion of the Fournacs.

'Intelligent, sensible, ambitious and very resourceful. The type who'll be sterling millionaires by the age of fifty. You'll need to watch them.'

'Could you set up some kind of system for keeping an eye on them, with or without your involvement?'

'The Wittakers could do it, to the last penny, day in, day out.'

'Where do I sign?'

The idea of a chain of shops, or a series of identical boutiques, was Hannah's, and at that time, it was a novel one. She wanted a wide-reaching network and a certain corporate omnipotence, assuming that the tea room's clientele would be drawn to the beauty salon, which in turn would bring in customers for the clothes shops. She saw it as a natural business synergy.

She also insisted on – and managed to assure – a uniform design of all the beauty parlours and tea rooms, down to the waitresses' uniforms, the paintings, the smallest pastry. A client from Melbourne who might go to Sydney, Brisbane, Wellington or Auckland – and later to Europe or America – ought to feel at home there, in a familiar haven, a privileged refuge. She had read in the *Sydney Bulletin* that an American by the name of Gray had invented a coin-operated telephone two years earlier, in 1891, and she immediately wrote to find out about the possibility of equipping her tea rooms and beauty parlours with the devices, so as to put them in closer contact with one another without having to bear the burden of the communications herself. She thought about installing a telephone network as well so that she might receive reports of each branch's performance, or keep track of a client after she had moved away, or keep a record of how regularly clients availed themselves of her services.

Wearing a stiff collar and the striped tie of his English college, Polly rowed on the Yarra-Yarra in Melbourne. Hannah sat facing him beneath the shade of a wide-brimmed hat and a parasol, dressed in one of her white tussah dresses. The light played on her narrow triangular face, swallowed up by those huge grey eyes and dotted with tiny freckles; she looked like the subject from one of the paintings in the black-and-white house. Polly was saying: 'You could conquer the world, Hannah, with those eyes of yours.'

'Polly,' she said, twirling her parasol with her fingers peeping out of her mitts, 'you're even crazier than I am.'

'That's a claim I would never make, my dear. But it's true that I believe in you more than you believe in yourself. Now, tell me more about this wild giant Mendel Visoker . . .'

It was Polly who urged her to borrow money from the banks, even before the contract with the Fournacs was signed.

Niet, came her reply, in Russian and in every language she could speak, including Aramaic.

'I don't want to borrow money, Polly. I can't bear it. I was once in debt and that won't happen again.'

'How much do you have at your disposal? Three thousand, maybe a litle more with the June income? The chances are it won't be enough. The Fournacs will want to see you invest more than that.'

'Too bad.'

'Do you know what a credit limit is?'

'A waist measurement that people reduce according to temperament.'

'Very funny. That isn't how bankers understand the term. I'll explain what they mean by it, although I wonder whether it's wise of me. With that head you have on your shoulders you'll soon know more than I do about these things and I'll be of no further use to you. You'll get rid of me.'

'Poor, poor Polly!'

'Hannah, when I look into your eyes, I sometimes see the beads of a Chinese abacus flashing past. You know how the Chinese do their sums? Tschung-tschung, two and three are five, seven and four are eleven, I take everything and keep the change – that's you all over.'

'Am I going tschung-tschung right now?'

'You're making eyes at me, which will end in a shipwreck. I've seen some amazing things in Europe and America . . . In Paris they have light shows, created by a certain Reynaud, in which the characters move; they seem to be alive, not as in photographs of Niepce or Eastman. And in America someone called Edison has developed a machine called a kinetograph . . . Yes, moving pictures. If these gentlemen put you in their pictures you'd be able to see your parasol twirling and you smiling, making fun of me. Your eyes are like magic lanterns, Hannah . . . Good gracious, it strikes me that what I've just said is rather pretty! How long is it since I last asked you to marry me?'

'Two days.'

'The answer's still no?'

'As ever.'

'Hannah, a credit limit is the amount of borrowing a banker allows a select client beyond the client's immediate, actual means, and it's determined by the degree of confidence the banker has in the client, based on an informed estimation of the client's assets, the warmth of the client's friendship with his banker, the range of his social contacts, or a mutual passion for cricket. At the Union Bank of Australia in Collins Street, there's a short-sighted beanpole of a man whom I was at college with. Although he's a banker, he sometimes shows glimpses of intelligence. I'm afraid we're cousins, distant cousins, thank God. His name is Arbuthnot. In your case, I should be able to persuade him to allow you as much as twenty-five to thirty thousand pounds.'

'No.'

'You'd have virtually no interest to pay.'

'No.'

'And how are you going to persuade the Fournacs to invest more than you?'

'I'll pay each month, as the money comes in. With my money.'

'They won't like it.'

'I don't give a damn.'

'What language! I'll try to win them over.'

'Row the boat, Twhaites.'

'Yes, boss.'

The beauty parlour opened in Bourke Street, not very far from the recently erected building in which the various departments of the colonial legislature had been brought together. Contrary to the way things had been done in Sydney, the tea room was established in Melbourne on different premises in the centre of town. The face creams and toilet waters were no longer sold alongside the cream strudels. This first tea room was in Little Collins Street; the second, located a few paces from the Treasury Building, was identical save that it had a terrace, one that resembled the cafés in the Saxe Gardens in Warsaw.

The success of all three shops was almost immediate, which came as less of a surprise than it had in Sydney. This time she had support of a kind she had not enjoyed before. With a virtuosity born of experience, Hannah had once again repeated her trick with the complimentary boxes, Robbie and Dinah Watts came and joined her, bringing with them one hundred and twenty boxes, of which ninety were to be sold instantly. Clayton Pike arrived from Brisbane on a special train for the opening together with his wife, his daughters and daughters-in-law, as well as female friends from all over Queensland with whom he organized huge parties at which Hannah was the guest of honour. (She again refused to dance, complaining of a sprained ankle again.) The elder Fournacs themselves had a vast network of clients, who numbered among them the most important people in Melbourne. They alone invited about two hundred guests. Finally, Polly drew from his inexhaustible reserve of cousins nothing less than the Governor's aide-de-camp – 'he was the most stupid person in the family, we made a soldier of him.'

The spate of openings took place at the beginning of July, which was perhaps not the best time, but Hannah could wait no longer, what was done was done. And still she went over her accounts again and again: the least she could hope to gain in the short term from her association with the Fournacs was about three thousand pounds a month, after the first weeks' launch period. Polly was inclined to expect four thousand, being an inveterate optimist.

'Probably even more, Hannah, by October or November. You can't imagine how much you're answering a need by setting up your companies. And in a year's time, you'll be able to start paying my fees; I'll in turn be able to stop asking my Aunt Lucinda for money. The poor woman, how she's going to miss me! No, no, that one-shilling advance is quite enough, I assure you . . . And the extraordinary pleasure I get from watching you operate satisfies me most of all. You're in the thick of the jungle and for the time being you're making progress without encountering any resistance. Hannah, in France they tell the story of an Englishwoman who followed a circus, day after day, in the hope of seeing the tiger eat its tamer . . .'

'And am I the tamer, Polly?'

'A tamer who's not even five foot tall and rustles with lace. And whom I have not yet lost hope of marrying one day, although I don't really believe any more that will happen . . .'

She offered Clayton Pike the chance to cancel their bet, her chances of winning being now rather great, in her view.

'And besides, I'm certain that if I lost, you wouldn't accept my money . . .'

With a roar of laughter, he boomed: 'A bet's a bet, you silly Polish goose! I'd follow you to the islands of Papua to claim my money!'

'My eye! And in any case, the game's spoilt because of you. You're cheating – by helping me to win. That's a fine attitude! You wouldn't have done any such thing if I'd been a man.'

He laughed even more loudly. It was quite true she was a woman: he had noticed this himself, and if he were forty years younger he would have done quite a bit more than notice.

'Oh no Pike, I wouldn't consider it,' she said, following his eyes. 'I'd be cradle-snatching. Anyway, I like men the same way I like cheese: mature.'

She kissed him on both cheeks and thought: There's no question but he adores me, and so much the better, it's so darned useful. Besides, I like him too. As a sugar grand-daddy, of course. I should have kissed him on the mouth, while I was at it; the thrill would have kept him happy for weeks.

Her only anxiety during these early days in Melbourne quickly disappeared: the Hutwills had well and truly left for Europe. They would not be back for some time.

She went boating with Polly and received invitations from all quarters, to balls where she refused to dance and to the best restaurants in town. How pleasant it was to be moderately success-ful, she thought, even – and perhaps especially – when one was not overly pretty. She looked at herself in mirrors less and less often, doing so only to check that her clothes were perfectly elegant. For the rest, she had abandoned all hope: she was stuck with her owlish looks.

It was July 25th when the letter reached her; she had been in Australia for one year and nine days. She had not been back to Sydney for three months, apart from a forty-eight-hour stopover on her return from Brisbane.

And the letter made her cry as she had never before cried in her life.

Colleen was dead.

17

WALTZING MATILDA

Before her stood the MacKenna giants, Rod, Patrick, Owen and Alec – dressed in black, in line to one side of the ground-floor room in the house in Glenmore Road. Dougal was seated; across from him Hannah felt isolated and dwarfed in the wing-backed chair she occupied. Dougal was explaining that Colleen had insisted over and over during the last weeks of her life, in the intervals between her dreadful fits of breathlessness, that Lizzie should be entrusted to Hannah's care.

'She loved you very much, Hannah. As much as if you'd been her own daughter, or a sister . . .'

He went on to say that he was not only concerned with respecting his late wife's wishes and the promise he had made her. He was also aware of the fact that the MacKennas did not have a single female relative in the whole of Australia, or in the Indies; only in Ireland – in Belfast as far as his side of the family was concerned, in Galway on Colleen's side – were there any aunts who might bring up the little girl. Which meant that unless she was to be sent to a boarding school in Melbourne . . .

'You were in your bedroom upstairs that day, Lizzie. You were waiting for the verdict. You'd started crying when you saw me arrive, you'd thrown yourself into my arms, refusing to let go, begging me to take you with me . . . In a way, I was the victim of a terrible conspiracy, involving your entire family . . . All right, all right, Lizzie, it's perhaps not

altogether necessary to break that vase over my head. I very much wanted to take care of you, I admit it.'

Of course, said Dougal, neither he nor any of his sons – the youngest of whom was ten years his sister's elder – would agree to be completely separated from Lizzie. They would, if the truth be told, prefer to keep her with them always. If they agreed to let her live elsewhere, it was with great sadness in their hearts. But in a house without a woman . . .

'Perhaps Lizzie has something to say about it,' suggested Hannah calmly, inwardly quite irritated by all this shilly-shallying, but also afraid of overstepping her bounds. 'She's nearly eleven, after all. And she's a sensible girl.'

Dougal agreed.

'She wants to go with you,' Rod admitted.

All that remained was for her to give some assurances of her suitability as guardian – unofficial guardian for the time being; she would become Lizzie's official guardian only later, if everyone was agreed.

Hannah wondered how long this pantomime was going to go on, but she all the same explained with some patience how her business projects were developing. She called on Rod to testify to what she said; she described the expansion of her business in Melbourne and the scale of her ambition. She mentioned the names of Clayton Pike and Paul Twhaites, Robbie and Dinah Watts, and the Williams sisters in Sydney.

She said it was in Sydney that she would live in the future, in the apartment she was renovating above Boadicea's Garden. There was no more respectable place; Lizzie would live with her and a very proper governess named Charlotte O'Malley, who was Irish, as her name suggested, and who had been engaged by Dinah. In addition, there would be a servant, also female. She herself would take care of the young girl's studies and also keep a careful watch on Lizzie, as agreed, for the possible manifestation of the first signs of tuberculosis, if indeed it was tuberculosis that had carried off her mother, in the event that the illness had been passed on to the daughter. She told them that any and all of them would be able to see Lizzie as often as they liked, for as long as they liked . . .

'And one more thing,' said Hannah. 'In twelve or eighteen months' time I intend to go to Europe. Would you consider allowing Lizzie to accompany me?'

With the assent of the MacKenna men on this last matter, she stood up and climbed the stairs to the bedroom.

'It's all agreed, we're going to live together,' she told Lizzie as she took her in her arms. They were almost the same height despite the difference in their ages, and time would obscure the latter.

'Let's go very quickly, Hannah. Before they change their minds.'

'Frankenstein's upside down. Her knickers are showing.'

At the shop Hannah found a letter from Lothar Hutwill that had been waiting for her for several weeks. He announced that he and Eloise were setting sail for Europe; this was no longer news to Hannah. He also wrote that Micah Gunn had completely disappeared, as Hannah was probably already well aware; he wondered if she might have something to do with this. She always had an answer to every problem after all, did she not?

Another note signed with a single initial, arrived three days after Lizzie and Hannah moved into their quarters in the new apartment. It said only: *God bless you, Hannah, for keeping your word.*

This was the last sign of life Hannah would see from Quentin MacKenna.

Polly Twhaites turned up in Sydney fresh and trim, at the beginning of September. He brought excellent news: Melbourne was operating in top gear, the Ballarat and Bendigo and Adelaide branches were open. The younger Fournacs were busy tackling Perth and Fremantle with formidable efficiency. The figures were rising everywhere. Another Fournac was newly arrived from France, sporting luxuriant moustaches and big, predatory teeth that trailed along the ground. Obviously Tasmania and New Zealand could not hold out for long. And apparently, further French emigrations were to be expected, which would strengthen the troops already deployed under the command of Jean-François.

'Hannah, you're going to have to bear the responsibility to future generations for having populated Australia with an incredible number of Fournacs. But you couldn't have found better partners. The Fournacs are even more stingy than you, which is no small achievement. And as long as you keep a close eye on them . . . But you aren't going to be satisfied with Australia, I hope?'

She was not. In this she needed no encouragement; the idea of returning to Europe was becoming more and more attractive to her. And she knew exactly what she would do in London, Paris, Berlin or Vienna. She would land with plenty of money, at least forty thousand pounds according to her most recent calculations. And she could have a great deal more, of course, if she chose to sell off all or part of her Australian operations, which she was not going to do for the time being but which she might well consider doing, if the need arose. With this money, she would get settled, not living too grandly, but spending enough to offer Lizzie a house worthy of the name and above all be ready in case she found Taddeuz sooner than expected.

And she would start studying as well. What she pompously called her beauty parlours here in Australia were nothing but shops. To conform to her vision they would need to be staffed with trained women, with an expert knowledge of beauty matters, capable of giving well-informed advice and tailor-made treatments. Such women perhaps already existed in Europe; if not, she would train some. And she would begin with herself; she was, after all, only nineteen, which was not *too* decrepit . . .

She would follow the best courses she could find, on skin and skin complaints and methods of treatment; on hair, nails, teeth and why people put on too much weight, or not enough; on how to make your eyes brighter, and whether there might one day be some kind of elixir of youth. These were things she was not going to be able to learn in Australia. At the School of Medicine in Melbourne she had found no one capable of answering her questions. She would become an expert, perhaps even a doctor of medicine. Dr Hannah – that would impress people!

She would set up factories everywhere, and these factories would produce vast quantities of face creams, toilet waters, and astringent lotions. She would create a whole market on her own, with a complete range of products, leaving no room for anyone else to move in.

And, too, she would master the social graces. She had felt terribly ill at ease at that dinner party at the Governor of Victoria's home in Melbourne, when she had found herself in front of that line-up of forks and glasses, among all those people talking of things about which she knew absolutely nothing, every one of whom had a different title and needed to be addressed formally. She felt as if she had come straight from her *shtetl*, and – what was more – that it showed.

She also knew – much though she hated tapestry and embroidery and all the other stupid things that women did and much though she preferred to avoid talk of children and flowers and servants – that she should know how to be a woman as well; it could be useful, especially given her line of work. She must learn how to arrange a table; how to affect airs and graces when with men since that appeared to be what they liked; how to faint at the slightest draught, even though she was sound as a bell. It would be silly of her not to make the most of her little body, which had more going for it than it appeared. When she wanted to she could really bowl men over with it . . .

At the same time she decided she should not appear too intelligent. She would learn to seem stupid now and again, and to listen open-mouthed and full of admiration when necessary. She would pretend to be delicate and fragile and she would melt hearts. There was no point in letting everyone know that she was strong as an ox. And while she was at it, it was time to clean up her language.

Hannah thought seriously about sleeping with Polly. He was not a handsome man, but he was a dear. His hands were not too bad, although they were chubby; they were always very clean, which was something. He had good teeth and a pleasant smile, and he was certainly very sweet. His eyes sparkled: she thought him ridiculously intelligent. She suspected he would not give her as much pleasure as Lothar Hutwill, but thought that he might be fun, all the same. He would be capable of making her explode with laughter just when the Earth Moved, if indeed the Earth did move . . .

It had been a long time since she had slept with a man. She did not exactly miss it, but thought that taking a lover was the thing to do; all those chic women in Melbourne had lovers.

In the end she decided against; sleeping with Polly would change everything between them. He was a friend, loyal and intelligent, a bloody good adviser and prepared to follow her to the ends of the earth. She had been lucky to have met him, and she did not want to spoil everything now. So far as experience went, she reasoned that there would probably not be anything in it for her anyway. Everything she did along such lines she did to prepare for Taddeuz after all. Why did she have to keep reminding herself of that?

The women who were to be her clients – and there were hundreds of millions of them all over the world – would want to be beautiful and chic, even if they entered her shops with mud on their shoes. She was going to have to be more sophisticated than the most sophisticated of them. Or she would have to make them think she was, which came to the same thing. She was already as flirtatious as a whore, but sophistication was something else, something you learned, like botany or dermatology, love or literature. And only when she was completely sophisticated, when she had bitten into all this knowledge as one would into so many apples, only then would she marry Taddeuz. She would be very happy with him, he would write his books while she kept her pots bubbling away . . .

She knew too that she would have to be very careful to respect his male pride. She thought it ridiculous, and wondered why people thought it normal for a woman to be kept by her husband and not the other way round, but she knew that was the way it was. Men had always been stupid, and she would not be able to change that. They had arranged it all so that their wives washed nappies all day while they larked about and travelled the world, discovering this and that.

She would have two children with Taddeuz, she decided on the spot. No, three.

And surely too it was about time she began to do something about Taddeuz? What if he were to marry some stupid little goose with plenty of money before she was ready for him? That would really beat everything! Of course there was such a thing as divorce, but all the same, she did not need such complications. There was plenty to be done; in the first place she had to find him. And he was getting to be ancient – he was now twenty-one, two months and thirteen days old, and she was not exactly getting younger herself.

It was the reappearance of Maryan Kaden, who came back into her life never to leave it again, that would serve as the perfect aide-mémoire.

She had not known where he was, either. But undeterred, she checked first of all whether the Carruthers were still posted to Warsaw. Polly had explained to her – another of his cousins was at the Foreign Office in London – how things worked regarding diplomatic staff, and for those working in consulates, as in this case: they stayed two or three years in a country and then were posted elsewhere. If that had happened, the Carruthers could be in China already, or wandering among the Bantu . . .

But they were not. Rather than making her enquiry by letter, which would have taken weeks, Hannah availed herself of a new invention that she would quickly learn to master: the telegraph. In 1872 the trans-Australian telegraph wire had been set up, linking Sydney, via Melbourne, with Darwin, in the north of the southern continent, on the Timor Sea, opposite Indonesia. And three years before a submarine cable had been laid on the ocean floor connecting Darwin with Singapore. With the help of this new development, a direct connection from the Sydney General Post Office to London, and via London to Warsaw was possible.

In just one week, she had re-established contact with the Carruthers and conveyed her simple request to them. Delighted to hear from the girl who had so enchanted them, they assured her they would do their utmost to comply.

The banks took care of the rest. Three hundred and fifty pounds were placed at the disposal of Maryan's uncle in Warsaw, he whose services had already been enlisted as the front man for Hannah's shop in Cracow Avenue. However, the money was sent with the stipulation that no one but Maryan could spend it. He was only seventeen but Hannah was sure he had more common sense than any other man, with the possible exception of Mendel.

She received a letter from Maryan early in November and she was delighted to see her friendship for him so thoroughly justified. He had completely understood what she expected of him. He had received the money, it was indeed more than enough to keep his family for at least a year, and he was eager to set out on the task she had in mind for him without a moment's delay. He was leaving immediately for Prague, would go from there to Vienna, and on to scour all of Germany if necessary.

If Taddeuz was still north of the Rhine, Maryan would find him.

His reply contained no superfluous words, only the essential. He did not even say thank you. Later, she would smilingly reproach him for this. He would shift his weight from one foot to the other, his pale eyes not daring to meet hers.

'With all those people reading my letter and repeating my words to each other?'

In November she wrote to Mendel for the sixth time. She told him the very satisfactory news about her business affairs and assured him she could now repay him all the money with which he had entrusted her, along with interest at the usual rate.

Of course she considered him her business partner, however, and so half of what she had made, and half of what she would make in future, belonged to him. On no account was he to start arguing about this. Had she not travelled on a ticket that he had bought for himself? Had not the idea of going to Australia been his in the first place? She owed it all to him, she wrote, and she was not far from thinking that she was robbing him a bit in allowing him only fifty per cent of the profits. She was ready to discuss the matter, but he had better watch out: she had become very talented at negotiating . . .

She told herself she was crazy; Mendel had never got her letters, not a single one. Of course he was not dead, but this did not mean he was receiving mail from Australia in the remote reaches on the tundra! And she was just as crazy to think about men and women the way she did, programming their lives in advance. What if Taddeuz wanted *four* children, hey?

Still she forced herself to write, telling Mendel in detail about a meeting with an Austro-German count that had taken place thanks to Clayton Pike's mediation. The count was making a world tour in the company of a young woman he had recently married.

I'm not just mentioning them at random, Mendel, you'll see that I have very sound reasons for doing so. His name is Rudolf de Sonnerdeck, hers is Anastasia. I'd never seen a count or countess before. These two seemed completely normal. They eat just like everyone else, they're very kind and very courteous – no, I'm not wasting my time with tittle-tattle, wait and see. The countess travelled in a carriage throughout central Australia. She complained of the dust and the heat, of the effect they'd had on her skin. Pike brought her to me – they have a superb yacht, she and this count of hers. I slapped a bit of cream on her face, feeling a bit anxious, but she was delighted. I told her my life story, with a few modifications, as usual. This time it was a mixture of Cosette's story, from Les Misérables, and The Two Orphan Girls, with a dash of David Copperfield. She cried and set her heart on the count hearing the story of my adventures as well. They invited me to dinner, a very simple affair, thanks no doubt to our being in Australia, where social distinctions are not very great. In any case, it was useful being able to speak German. And never being at a loss for words, I asked them quite a few questions. That's when it happened, Mendel, the most incredible, most wonderful thing you could imagine. Because the count, who's so kind, and about as cunning as a street sweeper, is related on his mother's side to the Emperor of Germany, the one they call William II, who's the grandson, on his mother's side, of the Queen-Empress of England, Victoria, whose initials appear on all the policemen's helmets, here in Australia . . .

Yes, I know, I'm chattering on! Well. The best is yet to come. This Anastasia, the countess, is the cousin of a Princess of Hesse, who – are you with me, Mendel? – is the daughter-in-law of Tsar Alexander III, since she married his son, a certain Nicholas, who could well become Emperor of All Russia one of these days. Which means that with a bit of luck, one day when I'm in Europe, even if I have to make the journey especially, I shall be in a position to go and see the wretched tsar ruling over our Poland, and ask him to free my friend Mendel Visoker, who's nothing but a Pole, a Jew, and a pimp for that matter, and has only ever killed three or four people (or more, who knows?) in tiny fits of mischievousness . . .

Oh Mendel, you may think I'm laughing as I write these things, but my eyes are full of tears. I have faith in this stroke of luck, and I'm going to see if anything will come of it. Please, Mendel, don't die . . . Wait for me. With all my love and kisses.

'Are you going to marry Polly?' asked Lizzie.

'No.'

'He's not rich enough, is that it?'

'He's richer than he looks, he's only pretending not to be, as he's pretending that he thinks it's of no importance. I don't want to share my bathtub with him for the next fifty years, that's all.'

'I didn't know marriage was a question of bathtubs. Do I really have to go to school?'

'Yep.'

A clip-clop of hoofs rang out on the paving stones. Hannah and Lizzie were seated in a buggy drawn by a charming little bay horse, which Hannah had bought to drive herself. She had had the carriage painted black and Turkey red, which caused some very obvious amazement among the ladies of Sydney.

'And what if I were ill?'

'You're no more ill than I am.'

'There's no more to be said, then,' said Lizzie, trying her best to look miserable. 'And when we're in Europe, will I have to go to school as well?'

'Just as you do here.'

'Then I don't see the point in going. And what if I were to marry Polly Twhaites?'

'He's twenty-five years older than you. And at the rate you're growing, you're going to be a head taller than he is today. You'd look like an ostrich walking about with a guinea-pig.'

'Perhaps I could marry Maryan Kaden? He's handsome, isn't he?'

Hannah did not answer, realizing she had never looked at him from that point of view . . .

'Not as handsome as Taddeuz, obviously,' Lizzie continued. 'Who could be? But if he was even half as handsome, that would be enough for me.'

'Lizzie, shut up!'

'A lady does not tell another lady to shut up. Your language is really dreadful, you know. You could come to school too, Hannah, it would do you good. Will you tell me again about the time Dobbe the Hayrick lent you the money to buy the dress with the thirty-nine buttons?'

'I've already told you that story at least one hundred and twenty-three times.'

'I want to hear it again. And then I want to hear the story of when you went to see the landlady in Praga and told her that Taddeuz was your brother. I like that one too. You're a terrible liar, when it comes right down to it. And to think you're the person bringing me up! If Rod knew all this . . .'

'You're still too young for blackmail, Lizzie. And anyway, telling people what they want to hear isn't lying, it's doing them a favour.'

'My eye. And the time when you and Taddeuz . . .'

Hannah shot her a look.

'All right, all right,' said Lizzie. 'I've got the message. I'm no fool. You want me to shut up.'

The buggy stopped in front of Lizzie's school, the green eyes reaching into the grey ones. Lizzie's eleven-year-old arms went round Hannah's eighteen-year-old neck, and the little girl's lips touched her cheek.

'You know I love you, Hannah. As much as I loved Mother.'

Hannah could not answer because of the lump in her throat. She simply nodded her head as Lizzie jumped to the ground, sending all her petticoats flying up in the air and revealing her stovepipe knickers which, in conformity with the school rules, were laceless.

She took three steps, then turned around:

'And what if I were to marry Mendel Visoker?'

*

Simon Clancy, now Hannah's chief supplier of herbs and plants, came to visit Hannah in mid-August, when his first delivery came through. He was a man of about thirty, born in Australia, short but sturdy, a country fellow with a slow, almost shy manner of speech. When he did not succumb to his extreme terseness, he expressed himself in a rather disconcerting slang. For him a penny was a *brown* or a *stever*, a threepenny bit a *tray*, a shilling a *deaner*, and a pound a *quid*. The only environment in which he felt truly comfortable was the most remote areas of the bush. Still, he knew more about plants than Quentin had ever known and took the news that he would immediately have to increase threefold all his consignments to Meggie MacGregor's laboratory calmly. (Since July Meggie had had nearly thirty girls working for her making face creams, toilet waters, and Hannah's new hair lotions.) Though he could barely read and write, Clancy was scrupulously honest. He refused the sixty pounds she tried to give him; his own salary, he felt, should not be more than thirty shillings, as his job took up only a few hours of his day. And he did not need much to keep the Aborigine men and women who supplied the plants along Quentin's fifteen-hundred-kilometre stretch, from Queensland to Victoria happy.

'To pay them, do as you did before, the way Quentin told you. No cash, they'd drink it, but send the money to Travers, he's a good man who gives them food and gets them all the bloody bits and pieces they really need, but no alcohol . . .'

He explained that he was completely happy with his work; he could spend all the time he wanted *humping the bluey*, being a *sundowner*, or a *swaggie*; or *Waltzing Matilda*, just like their friend Quentin was doing. ('He's waltzing Matilda, like no one else before him, on that crazy expedition of his'.)

No, he did not think that Man-Eater Quent would come out of it alive. Certainly he would die in the great central desert, with his head among the stars. But what of it?

'Every man lives his goddamned life the way he chooses, ma'am . . .'

The Austro-German count and countess visited Sydney in December, 1893. The aristocratic couple intended to stay on until the end of the antipodean summer, then they would set sail again in their yacht, which bore the emblem of a double-headed eagle. They would visit China and Japan before heading across the Pacific to the United States, and thus would not be back in Europe for several months, at the earliest. Hannah and the young countess, who were actually the same age, had struck up a close relationship. They vowed to meet up again in Vienna or in the Tyrol, after Hannah's return. It was Anastasia who one day brought to the beauty parlour the most renowned Australian woman of the day, the highly celebrated singer Nelly Melba, who was worried about the state of her complexion. She had been born in Melbourne some thirty years before; Rudolf de Sonnerdeck had been present at her debut at the Théâtre de la Monnaie, in Brussels, twenty-four years later.

It was a great moment indeed when the diva, as thanks for her treatment, began to sing the great aria from Gounod's *Romeo and Juliet* in Boadicea's Garden.

The publicity resulted in more business than Hannah's facilities could handle, and made the first few months of 1894 more successful than anyone had anticipated. As early as mid March Hannah realized she was more than well on the way to winning her bet with Pike, which was to be settled on May 2nd. Her credit limit at the Union Bank of Australasia was sixty thousand pounds. All the subsidiary branches set up under her partnership with the Fournacs were now in operation. In themselves the holidays – which she had again spent on her own, depriving herself even of Lizzie, whom the Watts had kindly taken with them to Melbourne – had brought her a personal profit of more than six thousand pounds, after all deductions had been made.

On April 30th Clayton Pike arrived in Sydney on his private train, travelling from Melbourne. He had with him a cheque for twenty-five thousand pounds. Hannah refused it with a laugh: the bet was simply a challenge she had presented to herself: she had only wanted to attract his attention, to gain his sympathy and obtain his help, and in this she had succeeded beyond all her hopes. She protested that she did not really want any of his money.

Pike insisted. In fact he went quite red in the face; a bet was a bet. In the end Polly Twhaites worked out a compromise: Hannah would indeed get the twenty-five thousand pounds, but she would consider the money an unofficial loan, carrying a derisory interest rate of half a per cent per year, and entitling Clayton Pike, or any of his successors appointed by name, to five per cent of the shares in any company set up by Hannah in her own name during the next ten years outside of Australia and New Zealand.

Polly reasoned with her: 'Hannah, I know how much you hate

loans. This is a loan, and yet not a loan. You'll need some capital funding in Europe and you'll never get it on better terms than these. Don't even mention the half per cent you'll have to pay, it'll be more than amply offset by the interest you'll get by investing the capital in the money market in London, for instance. As a matter of fact, I have a cousin there who . . .'

Aside from these negotiations, Hannah led a quiet, family-bound life. Lizzie was like a younger sister to her and she revelled in their time together, allowing herself to be carried along by Lizzie's high spirits. It was in fact because of Lizzie that she twice postponed her departure for Europe, the first time because Rod raised objections to it, saying that he would eventually get married and didn't see why his sister should not live with him, the second because – having fixed their departure for the beginning of January 1895 – Hannah·realized that the school year in Europe was the opposite of Australia's, which meant that Lizzie would arrive at the English college that had been chosen for her in the middle of the second term.

The departure was then put back to the middle of June, 1895.

For Hannah this delay had its advantages; she knew she was afraid of entering the fray on the other side of the world and she welcomed any excuse for more time. The later she left, after all, the richer she would be . . .

She took advantage of the school holidays in January and February to take Lizzie to New Zealand. Accompanied as well by Charlotte O'Malley, seventy kilos of practising Catholic dignity, she travelled all over the two islands, from Invercargill to Christchurch and Nelson, on the other side of the Cook Strait from Wellington to Auckland. It was in Auckland that Jean-François Fournac had set up a clothes factory and acquired a financial interest in the wool trade; she was pleased to find hugely successful Turkey-red and black shops with the distinctive double H sign in all the right locations.

When she returned to Sydney she found a letter from Maryan Kaden waiting for her, the third she had received since establishing contact with him. He wrote in a curious mixture of Yiddish, Polish, German and Russian, perhaps as a precaution; he saw spies everywhere. With his usual thoroughness Maryan had scoured Prague, Vienna and Berlin as well as other towns in the Austro-Hungarian Empire and in Germany, ticking them off on a map as he went along. He picked up not a single trace of Taddeuz. He had no news either of Mendel, even though his uncle and a great many other people prompted by him had questioned the tsarist administration about his fate. He enclosed in his letter a fanatically detailed account of all the expenses he had incurred; Hannah laughed to learn Maryan consumed 74 slices of bread in a month. He assured her he had ample funds to live on for another two years, despite the fact that he had given his mother and his brothers and sisters a lump sum to draw on while he was away. He gave an address in Berlin where she could write to him in the future.

She did, straightaway. She told him she would be arriving in Europe that summer, and that she would meet him on September 15th, 1895 at nine o'clock in the morning at an inn in Baden-Baden that one of the Countess Anastasia's maids had mentioned to her. *'If the inn doesn't exist any more when you arrive, wait for me where the door used to be. Otherwise I shall see you inside. And for heaven's sake, spend a bit more!'*

After a restful summer excursion to the Great Barrier Reef aboard Clayton Pike's schooner, Hannah began to prepare for the great departure, a kind of fever overtaking her as the date approached. She was leaving for a new life, on a different continent, in another hemisphere; she had never been to *this* Europe before. Most important – and most nerve-racking – she was finally going to begin the great offensive of which Taddeuz was the final objective. She felt a bit like Quentin, waltzing across the globe.

Before boarding ship and settling into her first-class cabin on the Orient Line steamer, Hannah went over her accounts one last time: sixty-four thousand, six hundred and twenty-seven pounds sterling awaited her in London. Hers were considerable funds, and she had raised them in thirty-five months.

She set sail with Lizzie and Charlotte O'Malley on June 11th, 1895. They had an unexpected guest: Polly Twhaites, who now worked exclusively for Hannah, travelled with them.

Lizzie cried a bit as she watched Australia disappear from view. But she was easily appeased; Hannah had bought her twelve new dresses.

18

ST JAMES'S PLACE

'You remind me very much of someone I used to know in Australia,' said Hannah in a perfectly audible voice to a fat woman dressed in purple, 'though he was perhaps a bit more distinguished-looking. Down under, where he was surrounded by his sheep, people used to call him Archibald. He had a moustache just like yours.'

'This is scandalous,' hissed the fat woman, her breath quite taken away, as she tried to hide behind her diamond-encrusted lorgnette.

'There is one small difference however,' continued Hannah. 'Archibald used to wash. Not every day perhaps, but at least once a month. You couldn't tell he was twenty yards away when your eyes were closed.'

Silence descended on the large drawing room; if the painted ceiling had suddenly fallen down, the effect would have been the same. The private mansion overlooked St James's Place. There were thirty-two rooms, and the rent was six thousand pounds a year. The whole of the ground floor was occupied by the beauty parlour; Hannah had spent thirty-two thousand pounds furnishing it. As she spoke now fifteen beauticians wearing red-and-black dresses, some with caps, others without, froze. As did the fifty or so clients present.

'Adieu, madam, I hope you never come back,' said Hannah.

The fat lady reeled unsteadily. The three strings of pearls resting on her horizontally projecting bosom, as though on a jeweller's tray, jumped up and down, jerking about convulsively. She finally managed to walk out, white-faced. All was so quiet that the sound of the liveried coachman clicking his tongue could be heard from the street.

'For the love of heaven . . .' Cecily Barton, the director of Hannah's London salon, began to say in a very quiet voice.

'Not here.'

Hannah's eyes sought Lizzie's. Her ward was seated on a padded chair, wearing her school uniform with black boots, black gloves, and a straw hat with long ribbons. Lizzie's green eyes sparkled, and she wore a grimace on her face, a sign that she was on the verge of laughter.

'Come along with me, please,' Hannah said to Cecily.

She headed towards the offices, which were on the first floor. Halfway up the marble staircase, she turned around to make sure that Lizzie was following her, which she indeed was. She entered her office, whose windows looked out over Green Park and, if one leaned a little to the left, over Buckingham Palace and its grounds.

'For the love of heaven, Hannah . . .' Cecily started again.

'Just a moment, Cecily, please . . .'

Hannah smiled at Lizzie.

'You seem to have grown taller. Let's see.'

She and the Australian girl stood shoulder to shoulder. There was eighteen to twenty centimetres' difference between their heights, the younger now being the taller of the two.

'A veritable ostrich,' pronounced Hannah, as she drew Lizzie towards her for a hug.

'I missed you, you beast.' She pulled away. 'Did you hear the whole thing, Lizzie?'

'I'd have had to be deaf not to. I walked in just as the purple whale was coming out of the Montespan Room, with that poor girl Aglaë in tears behind her.'

'Do you know what happened?'

'The whale slapped Aglaë – that sounds funny; it sounds like a coded message of the kind spies send to each other. "The Whale slapped Aglaë and I have the document . . ."'

'You can clown about later, Lizzie. Was I angry, do you think?'

Lizzie burst out laughing. 'No.'

'So why did I make a scene?'

'Because the whale never pays on time?'

'True, but that isn't the reason. You're not even close.'

'Because she's a hopeless case as regards beauty?'

'That's also true, but it's still not the reason.'

'Because she's the very ugly Lady' What's-her-name, and she's very well known in London.'

'You're getting warmer.'

'Because she's a lady, and very well known in London, and when people hear that you've thrown her out of your beauty salon they'll be talking of nothing else in every drawing room in town?'

'You're getting hot now.'

'They'll be talking of nothing else, which will make them fight even more to get into your salon. The more elevated people are, the more you have to insult them.'

Hannah smiled. Without even looking around, she said: 'Cecily?'

Cecily Barton emitted a sigh of resignation. She was thirty-eight. Before taking the job at the beauty salon in St James's Place she had worked for fifteen years as the assistant secretary to a club for distinguished ladies in Grosvenor Street and, after she was widowed (her husband was an officer with the Bengal Lancers, and apparently died a heroic death), as a full-time secretary for an even more distinguished ladies' club – if such a thing was possible – in Cavendish Square.

It was January 3rd, 1899. Hannah and Lizzie MacKenna had been in Europe for forty-one months, as had Charlotte O'Malley and Polly Twhaites. In other words, Hannah's London conquest had taken her just over three years. She was now twenty-four; Lizzie sixteen.

And she still had not found Taddeuz.

19

ENCOUNTER AT TSARSKOYE SELO

Hannah entered the port of London on August 16th 1895, exactly three years and one month after she had first set foot in Australia. Lizzie, Charlotte and Polly were of course with her. At the sight of Tilbury Castle, Polly Twhaites reminded the little group of Queen Elizabeth's famous speech, delivered three centuries earlier as the invincible Spanish Armada approached the troops at Tilbury: 'I know I have the body of a weak and feeble woman, but I have the heart and stomach of a king . . .'

As soon as he set foot on English soil, Polly began to surprise Hannah. She had formed a certain idea of him in Australia: a sweet little man, pink and chubby, certainly very intelligent and quite savvy about business matters, but nonetheless a man who displayed an amused nonchalance, if not a complete indifference, to money. In short, she thought him a glorious failure.

Once in England, she discovered that he was the youngest son of a baronet, that his father had a seat in the House of Lords and was a Knight of the Garter (this almost made her choke with laughter); that his family had a mansion house in the West End, a manor house in Bedfordshire and an estate in Ireland, as well as a staff of no fewer than eighty servants and several leased properties; that Polly had been a brilliant much-lauded student, and that he had had, to begin with, and without having worked a single day, enough money to live on for the next two hundred and fifty years.

What was more, and what was perhaps more to the point, he knew his way around London. Thanks to him, she was able to enrol Lizzie in one of the poshest boarding schools in the country, in the heart of Sussex. Because the fees were much higher than Dougal MacKenna could afford, Hannah paid the difference out of her own pocket; only Polly would know she had done so.

She left Lizzie at school on the brink of tears, rejected Polly's offer to introduce her straightaway to London society, and at the beginning of September took the Dover mail to France.

Paris filled her with wonder. She would never get over its beauty; it would remain her favourite town for years to come. But she was hardly there as a tourist, and without wasting time sightseeing she set to work making her first appointments. She counted on visiting a certain Dr Berruyer, who had established a worldwide reputation for his work in what was beginning to be called dermatology, the study of the skin and of what lay beneath it. She had drawn up as well a list of specialists from whom she was going to solicit advice: a botanist at the Pasteur Institute, which had opened a few years earlier; a chemist at the same establishment; a surgeon by the name of Lartigau who was involved in a new practice called plastic surgery. She added to her list the names of various schools and libraries from which she hoped to extract information she had not yet been able to locate in accounting, commercial and industrial law, and the ways of the Stock Exchange. Furthermore, acting on an idea she had had at sea, she recruited a group of students from the Ecole Pratique des Hautes Etudes in the rue des Ecoles. Once they had got over their initial amazement at hearing this tiny foreign woman expressing herself in eighteenth century French they were easily persuaded to make a comprehensive study of all the beauty creams, health lotions, youth preservatives and elixirs currently available in France. She also asked her students to compile an exhaustive file of all the publicity material advertising these products, however far-fetched their claims.

She achieved all this within ten days; by the evening of September 14th she was in Baden-Baden. The next morning Maryan Kaden was there too, turning up within a minute of the time she had arranged – from a distance of twenty thousand kilometres – to meet him.

*

He had grown at least twenty centimetres and put on quite a few kilos in the three years since Hannah had last seen him. But he was still the same Maryan, his head sunk between his shoulders, a slight lisp marking his speech in every language, his movements sturdy and serious. He was eighteen, and he was not at all surprised that she was now rich. Only the opposite would have amazed him.

Maryan blushed when she kissed him on both cheeks, and though he did reply to a few of her personal questions, he forged directly on to his report as though they had parted only the day before: Taddeuz was not in Vienna, under his own name or any other. For weeks, Maryan had kept careful watch on the universities, the libraries, the bookshops and the cafés where writers and artists gathered. Nor was Taddeuz in Prague: he most certainly had not been there at all.

'If you remember, Hannah, he had an aunt, who's still alive. And he hasn't been to see her since leaving Warsaw more than three years ago.'

He wasn't in Cracow, or in Salzburg, either.

Although it took Maryan two months to ascertain as much, it was clear now that Taddeuz was not in Berlin. Or in Heidelberg, or Munich.

'As far as the aunt in Prague is concerned, I've arranged for her to be kept under surveillance in case he does contact her. Which he might well do: she has a bit of money and he's going to inherit it. She also happens to be rather ill at this point. I spoke to one of her lawyer's clerks, as well as to the assistant in the grocery store where she does her shopping: if anything happens, they'll write me at the address in Berlin. I promised each of them twenty roubles. That's not too much, is it?'

'But of course not,' said Hannah with a smile. 'Have you any money left, Maryan?'

He immediately pulled out of his pocket a notebook in which he had entered each of his expenses. He had enough money left to live on for another seven months. He explained that – working from the Baltic down to German-speaking Switzerland – he had already searched thirty towns, including several in Holland. He was now returning from Zurich, where he had drawn a blank. Had he not arranged to meet her in Baden-Baden, he would have surveyed Lausanne and Geneva as well.

In recounting all of this he stamped his feet and shifted his weight from one leg to the other in embarrassment, lisping more than ever: he confessed that certain ideas had occurred to him of which he was a bit ashamed, and of which she might not approve, but which he had acted on all the same. Knowing Taddeuz's passion for books, he had posted lookouts in all the bookshops where he had been, promising them – here he hesitated – promising a kind of reward to anyone who notified him of the student's visit.

Hannah stared at him, completely dumbfounded. And then she laughed, thinking: 'Heavens alive! We've put a price on Taddeuz's head!'

She kissed him again; she was ecstatic.

'Oh Maryan, I adore you! And how big is the reward?'

He told her. He had offered approximately five English pounds.

'Not enough,' she said, 'make it twenty times that. And that's not all. I'm going to give you four hundred pounds, and you'll buy yourself a new suit. And another pair of shoes; yours are really unforgivable, Maryan. This money I'm giving you, you can divide it in two, as you see fit. One part is for your family, who are being deprived of you because of me. The rest is to cover your expenses and the reward, but it's mostly for you to spend as you like. You'll see, you're going to need more than you think. And on top of that, we'll have to decide on a salary; you will of course be working for me full-time from now on, right? You have no other plans, Maryan?'

He gave her a reproachful look.

She smiled; that was settled then. She would pay him ten . . . no, twelve pounds sterling a month, or the equivalent in any other currency, and she would pay him six months in advance.

'Here, take this. And on second thoughts, have three suits made, two for everyday and one for Sundays. Don't spend too little on them, you'll need to be dressed like a gentleman. And be careful, I've got an eye for these things, I know what's what, and I don't want any second-hand suits that have been revamped. They must be new, made of good wool. And the same goes for the shoes. You don't even have a suitcase, I'm sure. You'll need one, a leather one; we'll go and buy that together, I've seen a few shops in Baden-Baden that will have just the thing. We'll choose some shirts as well; you will need at least six. And then all the other things a man needs. You must know what's required, don't you? I'm going to make a gentleman out of you. From now on people will call you "sir" wherever you go, even in Vistula Station. Oh Maryan, there's really no need for that tear in your eye!'

She dragged him all over Baden-Baden, letting the sales assistants in the menswear shops and the tailors have the rough edge of her tongue, seeing to everything, even his underclothes. As far as these were concerned, she went so far as asking him to try them on in front of her.

'What is it you're trying to tell me now? Why on earth shouldn't I be allowed to see my little brother in the nude! And stop blocking the door like that or I'll buy your shop just for pleasure of throwing you out!

'Maryan,' she called over the dressing room door, 'We're going to do millions of exciting things together. Do you know any French? No? What about English? That's what I was afraid you were going to say. Well, you're going to have to learn them for me, and fast. You already know four or five languages, what difference will another two little ones make? Fast and well, all right? Your idea about bookshops is a very good one, probably we should carry it to the extreme. He may be in Sweden, or in Belgium. Unless he's in Paris or London. We're going to put a price on his head throughout the whole of Europe; he can't have gone to live among the Turks, after all.'

'Shut up, Maryan,' she said. He needed some ties as well, and some handkerchiefs, and two hats; he had looked marvellous in a hat. She thought that he must have a walking stick; all gentlemen carried walking sticks. 'Good God, you're unrecognizable, have a look at yourself in the mirror. A real English gentleman.'

'Oh Maryan, I've so many plans my head's bursting with them. I feel like dancing on top of the world. You're really going to work with me, you know, not just go chasing all over the place after Taddeuz. You're going to learn about finance and accounting, about foreign currencies, about transporting goods across frontiers, and above all about how banks operate. They're very important, banks; you can't do anything without them. I'll want you to know more about them than any banker. I'll want you to know when they're lying so that you can tell me: "Be careful, Hannah, they're trying to pull the wool over your eyes." You're going to get a job in a bank, let's say in four months' time, next January, when you've finished setting up your network of bookshop spies and headhunters. Which bank? A German bank to start with, since you know German very well. I'll find one for you, I know just how I'll do it.

You'll work there in every department, one after the other, and you'll learn everything. Another thing: from now on you're my cousin — "Hello, cousin Maryan, give your first cousin a kiss, our mothers were sisters" — in any case that's what you must tell everybody.'

They arranged to meet again, in Paris, at the apartment she had rented on the rue d'Anjou. She told him she would be there for at least the next two years; she too was going to be studying. Maryan made a note of the rue d'Anjou address even though he did not need to; as she knew, his memory was exceptional in any language. He was altogether calm and attentive and he was marvellously reliable. Hannah thought of the question Lizzie had asked her: Maryan Kaden was not actually handsome, but he was not bad-looking either. He had a smooth face; rather sad, pale eyes; a firm and determined-looking mouth. Hannah knew only she could get away with pushing him around as she was doing; she also thought that if he smiled more often he would be better looking.

But thus far in his life he had not had very much occasion to smile. Hannah felt an enormous sympathy for her young accomplice. And she felt determined — as much for herself as for him — to integrate Maryan into her European empire-building.

Four days later she was in the Tyrol; Anastasia von Sonnerdeck welcomed her with genuine enthusiasm — if with a slight hint of aristocratic condescension; they were no longer in Australia after all — to the couple's summer residence near Jenbach, on the Achensee. The couple were actually on the point of returning to Vienna, and although they were happy to welcome Hannah to the Tyrol, they wondered if she might not prefer to travel back to the capital with them.

Hannah declined the invitation. She spent six days in the Tyrolese Alps, long enough to mother Anastasia's two eldest children a bit (and long enough to decide she and Taddeuz might well want four children instead of three), long enough too to make all the necessary enquiries concerning a certain bank in Cologne, where the Sonnerdecks' financial adviser had every possible con-tact, and — most importantly — long enough to ask the question that had been on her mind for months and months, ever since she had learned in an Australian newspaper that Alexander III of Russia had died and that his son had succeeded him on the throne. Naturally she had not forgotten that Alexandra Feodorovna, the wife of the new Tsar, Nicholas II, had been originally Princess Alix of Hesse and was a cousin of Anastasia.

Her request was greeted with silence. The sound of cow bells in the alpine meadows could be heard tinkling in the background. And the air was fragrant with the autumn smell of harvested hay. She thought – on account of the silence and the cold gleam in the young countess's eye – that this time she had indeed gone too far.

'And you want a chance to speak to Her Majesty the Tsarina?'

'To go down on my knees and beg her, just as I'm begging you.'

She never told Anastasia that she was Jewish and had always passed herself off as a German-Polish girl of good family; this time it took all her might to curb her shame at her own lies. Hannah dished up the only story about Mendel likely to save him, telling Anastasia how Visoker was, or had been until his arrest, an itinerant trader from Poland. He was the slightest bit Jewish and had an honourable reputation, as the Baltic Bank could testify. One day in Warsaw, though he had never set eyes on her before, he had saved Hannah from the clutches of four Jewish thugs. They had already beaten her up – she still bore the scars and could show them – and were about to rape her. Visoker had come running to her rescue. In his heroic fight against her four assailants he had been wounded, though not fatally, unlike the thugs, who turned on each other as they subsequently fought among themselves over the money they had stolen from her. And poor Visoker, who had never been guilty of anything but courage, had been condemned to twenty years' hard labour and deportation for life . . .

'It's so unjust, madam. Without him, I would now be forever dishonoured, more likely dead, from my distress if not my wounds. I cannot live with the thought of this appalling injustice . . .'

She even managed a few genuine tears as she said these words, so great was her affection for Mendel.

Anastasia finally conceded that she thought Hannah's request rather extraordinary but that she would discuss it with the count and her mother. It would of course mean travelling to Russia. She and the count had been there for Nicholas's coronation ceremony the year before, but they had had no intention of returning, at least not in the near future. Still, Hannah's tears upset her; she could almost weep herself, so dramatic and sad was her tale.

In the end she promised to do her best.

Hannah felt a burst of rage inside her, furious that Mendel's life should depend on this colourless, anti-Semitic aristocrat. She managed to smile, however, with just the right touch of humility.

'Thank you, oh thank you!' she cried, as the tears fell.

Hannah returned to Paris via Cologne, where she had spoken to the director of the bank to whom the Sonnerdeck's steward had recommended her. She began her interview by announcing to the banker, with tremendous nonchalance, that she was going to place with him a very modest deposit, a pittance really, of twenty-five or thirty thousand pounds, she did not know exactly how much, money was of so little importance and she knew so little about it . . .

She also mentioned that she had a young cousin who dreamed of nothing but finance – he had no choice, for that matter, if he wanted to inherit from his uncle who owned half of Melbourne, including a bank and a shipping company, as well as some trains and a million sheep. Would it be possible for her cousin, who was still rather rough round the edges – 'You know what it's like, he belongs to the poorer branch of the family, he could use a bit of polish. But he's extremely intelligent, a person to be reckoned with, and he knows German, Russian and Polish' – to be initiated into the business in Cologne, to get an introduction to it at least?

'I've heard people speak so highly of the Bank of Cologne and of your expertise. Incidentally, could you let me know what the possibility might be of making an investment? No, not with that sum I've already deposited, I'm talking of a much larger capital investment, I have four hundred thousand pounds that I really don't know what to begin to do with. As for my cousin, an apprenticeship of six to eight months would be just perfect. He should be able to move from one department to another. You wouldn't have to pay him anything, of course; I shall give him a small allowance myself. Just enough, no more. At that age, it's easy to squander money . . . How many hectares of land do we own in Australia? I really couldn't say exactly: no more than six to eight million. It's mostly our gold mines in Ballarat and Bathurst that . . .'

In Paris she interviewed at length the decorators whom she expected to transform the apartment at 10 rue d'Anjou that she was to keep for such a long time.

'I think that you'll have the inside of your coffin painted black and Turkey red,' was Polly Twhaites only comment, when he crossed the Channel to see her. (His cousin's husband was Her Majesty's ambassador to France.)

'I shall never die, Polly. Unless I want to. But it may be a good idea.'

Within a month she had filled the eight rooms with books; she made inquiries as she visited bookshops, but it appeared that no one had seen a fair-haired young man, very tall and very good-looking, who could be Polish or Russian or German or even French, aged about twenty-three, and with a visible passion for literature. She acquired a frightening number of books: not as many novels as essays on all the subjects she had acquired an interest in. She read books the way other people drank water, for ten-hour stretches, all night long, with an application that nothing could slacken. And she did not stop at reading; she in the end did take up the studies she had talked of pursuing, fired by an excitement that even Polly found staggering, and he was used to her. For the next two years, she very methodically filled all the gaps in her knowledge. As she saw it hers was an intellectual deprivation that dated back to when she was seven or eight, when she had stopped going to school because she had realized that she was not going to learn anything more there. Her aim was clear: she wanted to be the world's greatest expert in matters of beauty care. And to that end she pecked about like a hen, choosing between what was useful and what would only clutter up her mind, very much a woman obsessed.

She did not forget about refinement; in addition to all the other disciplines in which she would systematically immerse herself for twenty-three months, she added art in all its forms.

'Polly, you can take me to the theatre this evening. And tomorrow, to the opera,' she announced.

'Very well, Hannah. Whatever you say, boss.'

She registered at the School of Fine Art. To her great regret, if not to her despair, she discovered that she had no talent for anything: neither drawing, nor painting, nor sculpture, nor even the decorative arts. This put her in a fury: she felt as if she was fit for nothing more than taking off her clothes and posing in front of these bearded, ill-washed men, who wore ties as big as winding sheets and cared only about their easels. She had been asked to pose, and she had been quite tempted to say yes.

The fact of the matter was that she felt more and more the desire to have a man in her bed; someone cuddly, preferably, but not too

cuddly, a man who was both gentle and rough, who knew when
to be which.

One November evening, Maryan waited for her in the rue d'Anjou,
not having dared ring the bell or even enter the building, despite
the rain. Though he was wet and his shoulders were hunched up
against the cold he looked very elegant. He said nothing in Polly's
presence when the two arrived, though he had good reason for
this: he and Polly did not yet have any common language between
them. But he was his usual informative self when they were
installed in the apartment.

After scouring the length and breadth of northern Germany,
Denmark and Belgium, he was still no further forward regarding
Taddeuz. Taking advantage of his stay in Brussels, he had bought a
French conversation book and practised his lessons on the natives.
He knew a whole host of idiomatic phrases and was not far from
being able to speak the language. The proof being that he was now
jabbering away intelligibly, if with a bit of a Flemish accent. She
stared at him in amazement, and with a certain degree of pride.

She gave him all the details about the Bank of Cologne, where
he was expected at the beginning of January. She explained that
this arrangement would allow him time to spend Christmas in
Warsaw with his family.

'Why don't you come with me, Hannah?'

She explained she would not for two reasons: she did not want
to see Poland again, and she wanted to be alone during the
festivities, as usual. Besides, she had already made arrangements:
she would be back in England from the 20th to the 31st of
December, and would of course see Lizzie, though Lizzie would be
spending a very merry Christmas with Polly and his family. She
had explained herself once and for all to Polly, and once again to
Lizzie as well, and they had both understood her perfectly.

Maryan left after three days.

She took a lover at the beginning of December.

This was partly because her bed was cold, and to a considerable
extent because he was handsome, with hands the way she liked
them, and also a painter. She was beginning to rather lose her
patience with being pursued from one gallery to another, from café

to café and studio to studio, by all those bearded men who wanted to sleep with her, who claimed that they could not stop staring into her eyes. Or looking at the rest of her. By selecting one of them, who was among the cleanest and most intelligent and best-looking – and among the least impecunious as well; this fellow had adequate funds – she finally established a firebreak. She would now be left in peace. And she might finally, too, make peace in some way with that painter in Botany Bay, to whom she owed so much, and whom she had never met.

Her lover's name was René Destouches. He was fairly good at making love – *'That's from my point of view, Lizzie. He thought he was wonderful. Driving a car and making love are the two activities at which men are always convinced they excel'* – but he fell quite a long way short of the erotic daring of Lothar Hutwill, which surprised Hannah. He was, after all, an artist. He was even jealous, which amused Hannah to the point of tears, and he turned red with anger when she started posing in the nude in his studio in front of a group of friends, because she considered the model on the floor then to be 'a white pudding', as she put it.

'After all, I'm saving you three francs a session. And if the famous Colette poses in the nude, why shouldn't I?'

He sulked.

She thought they would not be seeing each other much longer.

Living in the rue d'Anjou, she was within a few minutes' walk of the rue du Faubourg Saint-Honoré and the rue de Rivoli. Every day, or near enough, she would explore the shops in these streets. And she did not content herself with peering into them and comparing them, criticizing the shop fronts and the displays, noting what was sold, in what quantities, and in what form: she went into each of them as well, presenting herself as a customer or – speaking with an Australian-Polish accent – as a milliner from the southern hemisphere on a study trip. This sometimes worked, and would encourage shopkeepers to impart some of the secrets of their trade to her. She bought little, but was all the same able to appraise the sales assistants, their techniques, their faults and their qualities.

She did the same with the city's best couturiers, preparing for her big moment which had not yet arrived.

René had no inkling of her plans, nor did he have genius as a painter. He compensated for these lacks with a fairly remarkable critical sense and with a wide circle of acquaintances; in their months together he introduced Hannah to Guillaumin, Pissarro,

Signac, Renoir, Léon Bonnard and Mary Cassatt, as well as a young poet with an accent that made his voice sound as though it came tumbling over the vanes of a water-wheel whose name was Paul Claudel, and to Georges Clemenceau, a journalist politician with a savage sense of humour. She watched Degas finish his painting of the Naked Woman Wiping her Neck, and would certainly have posed for him had it not been for René's jealousy; Degas was fascinated by her grey eyes. In the spring of 1896 he took her to Provence to see Paul Cézanne, who was having difficulty coming to terms with the lamentable failure of his first solo show at Ambroise Vollard's gallery. 'You want to buy one of my paintings? You're the only person who does. Take what you like . . .'

From Aix, still with René, she went to Monte Carlo, where she won seventeen thousand francs in one evening in the Casino.

She thought there was at least one thing she was good at, but this money had come so easily it had no value for her. It did not really feel as if it was hers. She was eager to be rid of it and when she was told about a twelve-hectare plot of land in the hills above a town called Cannes, she bought it sight unseen. Apparently it had a view of the sea, and that seemed good enough reason to buy.

Back in Paris, she broke off her relationship with René. He threatened to commit suicide if she left him; she offered him a rope she claimed was poisoned with cyanide, around which she had tied a black ribbon. He was not humoured by this. She broke off with him not for someone else, although there were plenty of eager candidates, but because in six months she had been through everything he was able to offer her. He taught her nothing that she did not already know about love and its physical attributes, although he did teach her a great deal about painters and paintings.

She had just left René, the second week of June, when she received Anastasia's letter.

She left the same day for St Petersburg.

'Say that again?' said Lizzie.

'Tsarskoye Selo. The Imperial village in Russia. It's fifteen miles, about twenty-five kilometres, south of St Petersburg, which is the Popovs' capital. I arrive there early in the afternoon of June 29th . . .'

'With your heart in your mouth.'

'Shut up. It's true that I'm very scared at this point, Lizzie.

Certainly not because I'm going to meet the Tsarina, I don't give a
damn about her being a tsarina, I'm just as good as she is . . .'

'Better.'

'I'm better than she is. Especially from my point of view. And in
absolute terms as well, in fact. Shut up . . . But Mendel's fate lies
in that woman's hands, and that's what scares me. We pass in front
of Tolstoy's house, his dacha. Further ahead on the left is the
Alexander Palace. I don't know why, we turn right, and drive into
the Montparnasse Gardens. Straight in front of us is the Chinese
Theatre . . .'

'Chinese now!'

'Lizzie, I don't feel at all like laughing.'

'I know.'

'We enter the palace, which has a façade three hundred metres
long . . .'

'I didn't say a word.'

'. . . The façade is extraordinary, all white stone columns with
gilt mouldings. The weather's very fine, there's lots of sunshine on
all these buildings and on the gilded domes of the churches and
these huge gardens. I've so much anxiety inside me that I'm
incapable of speaking or of replying when anyone speaks to me.
Anastasia has drilled me and made me practise a hundred times
the curtsy I have to make. I'm panicking like a child – me, Hannah,
a person who's afraid of nothing: I tell myself that if I make a mess
of this curtsy, my blunder could cost Mendel his life; he could die
because clumsy me crossed her knees the wrong way . . .'

'Hannah?'

'Shut up.'

'I love you.'

Silence.

'It's him I'm concerned about. There are an incredible number
of servants, of men in white uniforms, in black suits . . . We are
shown into a large room which Anastasia tells me is the famous
Amber Room, much in it is made of amber, Persian amber in fact.
An hour at least goes by. All kinds of grand duchesses and I don't
know what else have come up to greet Anastasia and kiss her, but
none of them has paid the slightest attention to me. I feel very
small, I feel Polish, and I feel Jewish, a *shtetl* Jew, poor and
ignorant, lost in this sea of Russian ladies whose father, or brother,
or son was perhaps the Cossack officer that Mendel nearly slaugh-
tered with his wagon shaft, the officer who allowed my father and

Yasha to be killed, while he stood by and stroked his moustache. Every now and again I feel absolutely incensed, overcome with a hatred that makes me tremble. I would happily set fire to this goddamned palace . . . But someone comes to fetch Anastasia and me and we're on the move again, walking through endless rooms with silk-covered walls.

'We stop again. We're told that the wretched tsarina is finally going to receive us. But no; another hour goes by and then we're taken outside into the park. We're led to a little building which is the Cameron Gallery, where the rooms are lined with agate. Just as we're about to reach it, there's what seems like a huge wave, the earth almost trembles, and Anastasia practically pushes me down on all fours: it's Tsar Nicholas going past, with that evasive look in his eyes, like that of a dishonest accountant. He disappears and the wave settles. Immediately afterwards, we come upon the tsarina herself, Her Majesty, in an uninteresting white dress with a lace collar. Her lips are hard, her eyes too, her voice is dry. She speaks to Anastasia in an irritated tone and only then looks at me, with all the scorn in the world. I tell myself that if Mendel's life depends on this woman he's as good as dead, that he was probably dead from the moment she heard his name. I speak very fast, not only because every second counts, but because I'm in despair. I can't remember a word, not a single one of the words I've uttered. But suddenly the tsarina turns away and simply walks off, along a ramp, towards the gardens, surrounded by all her attendants. I remain alone with Anastasia and three or four young girls who I realize are all crying: they say that I was ever so moving, that I moved them to tears.

'I'm completely puzzled . . . I've told you, Lizzie, I don't remember what on earth I could possibly have said to that Mrs Nicholas the Second.

'We return to St Petersburg and for once in my life I'm tired. Anastasia and I go to one of her uncle's palaces. It's on the banks of the Griboyedov Canal, not far from the Nevski Prospect and the Church of the Resurrection of Christ, which is being built on the spot where Tsar Alexander II was assassinated. We stay for two weeks, during which nothing happens. I assume that ice-cold tsarina has probably ordered Mendel's execution because of me, just because I told her that he was alive. Then at the beginning of the third week Anastasia came into my room one morning. She was white with rage and distress; she was trembling. She made it clear that she never wanted to see me again and asked me to leave that very day, at once. She and the other ladies in the Tsarina's entourage had been so moved by what I'd said that they had interceded for all they were worth on behalf of that Jewish pimp from Warsaw, bringing nothing but disgrace upon themselves! A minister had agreed to give the order for Mendel to be freed, for the lousy pimp to be pardoned; the pardon had been ratified by the Tsar himself, and the order had gone to the far reaches of Siberia, to the salt mines or wherever. And the Far Reaches of Siberia had replied that they would be pleased to free Visoker if they could only lay their hands on him again. Because it was more than a year already since the said Visoker had escaped, after attacking three or four warders, and set off on foot, all alone, heading for the North Pole, or Lake Baikal, the land of the Mongols, or the Himalayas. And they sincerely hoped the madman was dead.'

Silence.

Little Lizzie, who was then thirteen, asked as her own eyes filled with tears: 'And are you weeping with joy or sorrow, Hannah?'

'I don't know.'

'I've never seen you cry before.'

'Well,' replied Hannah, 'now you have.'

20

———•———

4 JANUARY 1899

In July of 1896 she had taken Lizzie for a vacation on the French Riviera. It cost them nothing at all: Hannah spent a single evening at the casino in Monte Carlo and the same thing that had happened with René began happening all over again. She won enough to pay for their trip and their stay at the Hôtel de Paris, as well as two new dresses for Lizzie and two for herself, and the year's rent, including gas, on the flat at 10 rue d'Anjou. She was almost disheartened by her luck. If she spent a whole month playing, doubtless she would become as rich as all the Messrs Rothschild put together. If only she knew how to play well, if only her moves were invested with the least shred of intelligence, or thought, or memory! But no. She placed her bet on the 18 (Taddeuz's birthday), on the 2 (Lizzie's birthday), on the 23 (her own birthday); she placed it on any number at all, and every time she won back thirty-six times her stake.

'How sickening. What an idiotic game!'

She had left Lizzie at the hotel of course, with Charlotte, and she reappeared to report on her winnings. Lying stretched out on her back, her arms and legs in the air, Lizzie was now choking with laughter.

'It's nothing to laugh about,' said Hannah, gnashing her teeth with considerable bitterness. 'It makes me look really smart trying to run a business!'

She tried to work off her annoyance by going over her accounts again and again, with her usual meticulousness. Part of her capital was in London and part in Germany, in the Bank of Cologne, where Maryan Kaden was working like a slave; this money was bringing her a return of nine and a half per cent. This was not a great deal, but she wanted her money to remain as liquid as possible. On Pike's twenty-five thousand pounds, taking into account her regular payments of half a per cent, she was left with only nine per cent interest; still, this amounted to nearly six thousand pounds a year in revenue.

Furthermore, her capital was increasing. First of all because she was not spending all of her annual six thousand pounds, secondly because in June 1896 more than eleven thousand nine hundred pounds, representing Jean-François Fournac's first payment to her, came to her from Australia. These monies were her first from the antipodean businesses.

'And you'll be receiving as much again in six months' time,' explained Polly. 'Fournac has reinvested the initial profits, as planned, but now the investment programme is concluded. You ought to be receiving thirty thousand pounds next year.'

'I can both count and read, Polly.'

'I don't doubt it, Hannah, I don't doubt it. It's just that your calmness amazes me.'

Polly, for his part, was beginning to ask himself some questions. Her apparent calmness amazed him, but her relative inactivity shocked him. He had not known her to be capable of such patience, and he made a point of checking in on her in Paris as often as possible. When she took René for her lover he had sulked a bit, but he had got over it; he had very nearly made a religion of Hannah, and had begun to reconcile himself to a greater or lesser degree to the idea that she would never be his. He was not the kind of man to die of heartbreak; were he to do so, it would be with a smile.

His visits were those of a friend; she was involved in nothing on which he could advise her. She had even refused his advice on investing her capital more profitably, so eager was she to keep her money to hand, to be able to have it at her disposal within the hour.

'You're reasoning like an immigrant, my dear.'

'That's what I am still, for the time being. And don't tell me that I'm not doing anything: I'm pursuing my studies. That's what people my age do, after all.'

What she said was absolutely true: in a year, having studied with the dermatologist Berruyer and with others, and having devoured piles of books, she had learned a staggering amount. She worked sixteen to eighteen hours a day when she did not have Lizzie with her and when she was not attending a party in the evening, to which she was generally escorted by one or another writer or painter or musician.

By October 1896 she was worth more than seventy-eight thousand pounds. She needed only to reach her target figure of one hundred thousand pounds and then sit back and wait.

Polly had read her correctly, as usual; she was in fact beginning to burn with the desire to be active again. She had discovered that making a fortune was not and could not be an end in itself, and that she was driven by a much more powerful urge: the absolute, almost pathological need to set to work her tremendous creative talent, which nothing seemed to curb.

In the end she broke the promise she had made to herself to wait two or three years before starting a new project.

She leapt into action.

In the event that meant taking over a failing shop situated under the arcades in rue de Rivoli, opposite the Tuileries Gardens. The shop sold all sorts of baubles and knick-knacks, from whalebone corsets to religious medallions. The shop's owner had died, and Hannah was able to obtain from his widow, for two thousand six hundred francs, the right do to whatever she liked with the business. (She had to promise not to turn it into a brothel, the owner's widow being a religious woman.)

Polly had told her so over and over again: there was something inexorable about her success. Within three months the customers were coming back, or rather coming for the first time, the clientele having changed completely. Her customers were now a half-century younger on average, drawn into the shop without the help of any advertising or sales gimmicks; the window displays and the décor, a subtle difference in the articles on sale, then two new sales assistants – the atmosphere alone seemed to do the trick. Hannah herself could not say exactly what it was. She did things and they worked. She realized that she had no talent whatsoever for drawing, painting, sculpture, or literary creation. She had in fact tried to write fifteen or so pages about Mendel, about his trips to her *shtetl* with his *brouski*, about the great plains of Poland, but she knew the result was cold, soulless, nothing like her. She had not been able to give of herself and had drawn only on her intelligence, which was both too much and not enough. Neither did she have any natural aptitude for music; in fact she was downright hopeless. When Debussy had played his 'Prélude à l'Après-midi d'un Faune' one evening she had heard nothing but noise, and she was just as deaf at the opera and at the concerts Polly and others dragged her to.

On the other hand, she possessed a certain talent for business and commerce. Polly even spoke laughingly of her genius; she had that magic ability of knowing what people, especially women, wanted before they did.

In February 1897 the Paris shop expanded, annexing the store next door, which led to four more assistants being hired. In May she opened a second shop in the rue du Faubourg St-Honoré. The business underwent drastic expansion a month and a half later, when the first consignment of face creams, lotions and toilet waters arrived on its shelves from Sydney.

This was an outright experiment. Hannah was no longer content with producing her cosmetics unscientifically, on the corner of a wooden table with a pestle and mortar. With all the practical knowledge she had acquired, she felt sure she could do better. With some reluctance, aware of the kind of commitment she was making, she began to scour the outskirts of Paris for a location to set up her first factory. Naturally, Polly accompanied her; not for an empire would he have missed the launch of an offensive he had begun to despair of ever seeing.

'Are you going to have your herbs sent to you from Australia?'

'Of course not. Australia's Australia, Europe's Europe.'

She explained that she had made the rounds of herbalists and found a most enterprising one who had agreed to work for her.

'His name is Boschatel. His hands wander a bit, but he's very knowledgeable about the plants I need, and he likes travelling up and down the country. He's going to set up a supply network for me from Normandy to Germany.'

She found her factory site at Evreux. She could certainly have chosen a location nearer to Paris, but she was eager to base the plant in the country.

'A business in town is affected by the place and gets swamped by it. At Evreux, I shall find people to work for me locally. I want good sound, loyal girls who know the difference between apple blossoms and cherry blossoms.'

As far as her sales force was concerned, she knew exactly what she wanted: her girls should be pretty if possible, astute, elegant, with all the qualities she had found in Jean-François Fournac, for example. They should be able to combine authority and courtesy in dealing with clients; she wanted them to be almost haughty. And she knew there was only one place to find them: in *haute couture*.

As soon as she had gained the necessary self-confidence, Hannah began to pay regular visits to Worth, in the rue de la Paix. At the time Worth was pre-eminent in women's fashion throughout the world, even in the Americas; almost all the women at Tsarskoye Selo had worn gowns that carried the signatures of Charles Frédéric or his son Gaston. She also visited Doucet and Madame Paquin, who fascinated her; she was a successful woman, the first person to open a subsidiary branch abroad, in London, and she ran her business in a most rigorous way.

Hannah became friendly with the son of the founder of Worth, who was principally involved in the firm's administration. Jean-Philippe and Hannah went so far as to begin to discuss a few joint projects, though without pursuing them very far: the house of Worth certainly had no need of her and for her part Hannah really had no intention of joining forces with anyone. But Jean-Philippe was kind enough to give her a few names, and laughingly made her promise that she would not start competing with Worth. Among these names was that of Jeanne Fougaril, who had joined Paquin when the house opened in 1891, at 3 rue de la Paix.

Jeanne was in her thirties, spoke English and Spanish fluently, and undoubtedly possessed every quality Hannah admired: ambition, exceptional flair for organization and public relations . . .

'. . . and a pretty strong minded character, I warn you, Hannah.'

'You've met your match, don't worry. I'm not too bad an example of that myself,' Hannah assured the French woman.

'And you want me to leave Paquin to run a firm that doesn't yet exist? Unless you call those two shops a firm?'

The two women discussed the matter for weeks. At first Jeanne was sceptical about the beauty industry; the most she could envisage was a future for perfumes: 'And that market's already cornered. Are you thinking of taking on Guerlain or Roger et Gallet?'

'I'll take on anybody. But what I really want to do is to break new ground, where no one else has yet ventured . . .'

An agreement was finally reached, with Polly's expert arbitration. For three years Jeanne would receive one and a half times what she was earning at Paquin (she was already better paid than a government minister), and at the end of this first contract she could choose between taking two per cent of the business's total profits or being compensated five years' salary. What the two women could not have known then was that they would work together for thirty-eight years, until Jeanne's death, despite their countless stormy arguments in which they would both find some delight.

Hannah also needed experts, women who in each beauty parlour – none of which had yet been founded – would advise clients on the use of her beauty products.

'And which no honest woman would possibly want to lard her face with. We aren't among the savages of Australia here, Hannah. The ladies here don't wear bones through their noses, in case you hadn't noticed.'

'I hate you, Fougaril. I've told you a hundred times already . . .'

In the end Hannah decided to found her own school, to train what she called, at the suggestion of a writer friend, aestheticians.

Her last chore was to develop her products; she wanted to do better than the poisonous concoctions she had manufactured in Sydney. Hannah went to see a certain Marie Sklodowska, because she was Polish, a woman and a native of Warsaw; she was a real scientist, and her married name was Curie. With a laugh she turned down Hannah's offer of a job overseeing production, but she recommended an acquaintance named Juliette Mann, a chemist who she thought would suit Hannah perfectly.

Only when Marie Curie, together with her husband, won the Nobel Prize for her work on radium six years later, did Hannah realize what incredible cheek she'd had. 'And I asked her to make beauty creams for me! I really had no idea!' she confessed to Polly.

Juliette and Hannah met and got on well together; they became immediate friends. Juliette was charged with overseeing the kitchen, and also with the training of the aestheticians.

Hannah analysed as well the contents of the enormous file compiled for her by the students of the rue des Ecoles. And she concluded that everything, or near enough, remained to be done: cosmetics in the future sense of the word did not yet exist. At best people were selling creams that could be said to be inferior to hers before they even touched the skin.

She conscientiously read through the volumes of advertisements that had appeared recently in newspapers and magazines and was reassured. They were of universally poor quality and were filled with the most outrageous lies, especially about the supposed elixirs of youth. Juliette had examined the products and assured Hannah that they were at best totally ineffectual when they were not downright dangerous.

She asked these same students to prepare a Europe-wide survey: she wanted to know where to set up her beauty salons. This idea produced very little by way of results: the students simply suggested the major capitals and holiday resorts. This she could have worked out for herself, she grumbled.

Her Paris salon would be, she decided, in the rue Royale. She would have preferred the Place Vendôme, but could not find a suitable location there.

What she needed now was someone to supervise this whole enterprise, someone who could keep an eye on the delivery, and indeed the straightforward collecting, of herbs and plants; on the purchase of the basic products Juliette needed; someone to make sure everything ran smoothly. She would have to send this person out too as a scout to examine possible new sites, to look for the best addresses in each town where a new shop was to open. She needed someone trustworthy, of course, someone who could supervise everyone working for her if need be, someone with whom she could share all her secrets . . .

She did not have to look for this person. Maryan Kaden had finished his training course in Cologne and now spoke French, although he did so – and would always do so – with a hilarious accent. He was now learning English, which, fortunately, he found easier to master. With his tremendous capacity for work, his near fanatical devotion to her, Hannah knew she could do no better.

'If you have a moment, it wouldn't do you any harm to know a little Spanish. The same goes for me too, in fact. We'll start right away. Lots of our clients come from South America, or they will come from South America. I'm expecting them any year now. They're like Russian princesses, they have lots of money . . . Fortunately we know Russian. You don't, do you, Fougaril? You see, you don't know everything!'

For all her confidence in him, she did not, however, make Maryan a director. She gave him no title and no office. He was already – and he always would be, even after he'd made a fortune on his own account – her shadow. She did not want to confine him to any one job, even though this meant paying him more than she paid anyone else, herself included. The men and women who were to spend thirty and forty years working for her would not set eyes on Maryan as many as three times; they would hardly know his name, in fact. He, on the other hand, with that amazing memory of his, would always know everything about them, wherever they were employed, throughout the world.

The whole of 1897 was spent planning this offensive. And Hannah managed to do it all, including the opening in Brussels, which came four months after the Paris opening, without encroaching on her capital, which was constantly yielding profits thanks to the interest rates and her regular income from Australia. She also made sure that the profits from the shops in the rue de Rivoli and the rue du Faubourg St-Honoré were reinvested so that they could be used to set up new enterprises without obliging her to borrow money. She managed, just, to meet the cost of her employees' wages by deducting money from her own income, which had now risen to four thousand pounds a year; this was how she paid her two chief aides, Jeanne and Juliette. And she continued to subtract in order to pay her share of the cost of Lizzie's education and in order to pay Maryan's monthly salary; she could always do without things, going a whole month without buying a dress or a painting, her only extravagances. Apart from the two thousand six hundred francs that she paid for the lease of the shop in the rue de Rivoli, she could just as easily have launched her Paris enterprise without any money at all.

She took another lover, after some reflection, having chosen from among fifteen or twenty candidates. His name was André Labadie, and he was a banker-poet from Bordeaux, a young senior executive with the Société Générale destined to a most glorious future. He also happened to be extremely well off, thanks to the income from a family vineyard. He had Jean-François Fournac's Gascon eye and the same moustache, a lilting accent, and a goldsmith's delicacy where she and her pleasures were concerned. He knew England well and spoke English; in fact he had Anglo-Saxon forebears, in the days of the Black Prince, and Jewish too, oddly enough, through the mother of Michel de Montaigne, of whom he was a descendant. He even knew America, where he had lived for more than a year, travelling in the Wild West. He set Hannah dreaming fabulous dreams, not just because he would recite Walt Whitman to her along with Rostand's *Cyrano* (he had taken her to the opening of the play, and she had been captivated) but also because he made her aware of her transatlantic possibilities, introducing her to a frontier that had previously seemed so very far away.

Above all he made love wonderfully, without the fantasies of a man like Hutwill, but with calm and patient gentleness, with charm and tenderness, and with the right degree of madness.

In fact she had chosen so well that she almost panicked: what if he were to take her away from Taddeuz? She went so far as to desert him for a whole month; she was preparing the ground in London, she said, but in reality she was afraid of herself. When she came back to him, he was waiting for her, unperturbed.

'You're not the kind of woman who leaves without saying goodbye, Hannah.'

Of all her lovers, with the exception of Taddeuz, of course, he was the one she came closest to really falling in love with. She only renounced him when he finally asked her to marry him.

But before that they would live together for a year.

She opened her London shop in January, 1898, in a private mansion she had rented overlooking St James's Place. The building was practically an historic monument, and the work she had done on it set London's high society talking. She made sure of that by calling on another of Polly's countless cousins; this one had supervised the repairs of Windsor Castle, and was redecorating some rooms at the Duke of Clarence's residence. He was homosexual, and although his first name was Henry, he preferred to be called Beatrice; on two or three occasions he came to inspect the work being carried out in drag. He was very convincing, with a counter-tenor voice that fooled even Polly. Henry kissed him on the lips and said he was terribly sweet, and Polly entirely failed to recognize his aunt's son.

Henry-Beatrice was going to become one of Hannah's great friends, and would remain so until his death in 1915, when he would commit suicide for love of a handsome officer killed in an attack on the Ardennes front. He quickly fell into the habit, as soon as she had settled into her rooms, of visiting her in her bedroom in the evening, on the second floor of the house. They would chat, like two women – '*The difference between women's chatting and men's discussions, Lizzie, is that the men smoke cigars. Otherwise, the amount of nonsense exchanged is very much the same.'* He had the most comprehensive, most sordid knowledge of London, indeed of British, high society, and he was more of a gossip than any man and woman combined. He knew who was sleeping with whom, how, why and when, and what had transpired. He delighted Hannah, and above all helped her conquer London. A genuine complicity sprang up between them, if a slightly discordant complicity; probably because it presented the ultimate challenge, Hannah more or less took it into her head to convert Henry, and as the months went by she played at seducing him.

One night he turned up after two in the morning, minutes after she had returned with Polly from Covent Garden, and just as she was getting undressed. He sat down on the bed as usual. He paused for a few seconds when she took off the last of her clothes, stared at her, then resumed his chatting, hardly moving away at all when she lay flat on her back next to him on the bedspread.

'I always sleep in the nude,' she said, 'forgive me. Do go on, Beatrice . . .'

Then he began to speak normally, which is to say in a low, masculine voice. Hannah saw his hand move a little – it looked as though it was trembling. It was not that he had never seen her naked before, or at least in a state of undress; he had often enough been present while she was changing, getting ready to go out to dinner. She had bared her breasts in front of him on several occasions – *'the prettiest breasts in Europe, my dear. I don't have any statistics for any other continent'* – and even revealed a bit more than that. Meanwhile he – knowing who she was going to meet at the dinner table or in the theatre lobby – would reveal to her in advance each person's characteristics and, better still, their weak points, so that she could use them to her own advantage.

'Be careful, Lady What's-her-name and little Mrs Armstrong hate each other, you'll only be able to make friends with one of them. Go for the younger one, she'll bring along fifteen or twenty of her friends who know nothing better than how to squander their husbands' money . . .'

Or else: 'Don't be taken in by appearances, that Hungarian countess is now penniless . . .'

Or: 'You want to attract more Americans to your salon? Offer Suzy Armbruster a free treatment – she won't spend more than three pounds in any case, if that. But if she talks about you, all the women in the transatlantic colony will be knocking at your door the same afternoon . . .'

(When ten months later, in January 1899, she began looking for some new publicity, it was Henry who advised her to put on a spirited show of throwing out the fat lady in purple: 'She's a lady, but of recent origin: she started out in marmalade. She's hated just about everywhere, although people are afraid of her. She's extremely rich, but mean; you've nothing to lose. Throw her out into the street and the very next day you'll have fifteen hundred of her London childhood friends, all of them eager to congratulate the person who dared to do what they themselves have been dreaming of doing ever since their coming-out balls . . .')

Tonight he continued to talk, though in his low voice, his eyes fixed on hers. The fingers of his left hand brushed against her naked hip. He broke off again and blushed a little.

'Sweet Jesus!' he exclaimed.

But he did not move away.

Then he said, very quietly: 'I'm not really a man, Hannah . . .'

'I don't know, Henry.'

'And you'd like to know. You really will have tried everything between now and the end of your life . . .'

'It'll be too late after that.'

'Very true.'

His hand rose slowly and slipped over her rounded hip, caressing its smoothness. It continued over her belly, his index finger and middle finger first brushing past the coloured bush of hair, then gently playing with it, twirling the silky fuzz. His other hand slipped very lightly between her thighs, which she had opened just slightly. He stroked the inside of them, where the skin was so smooth.

'Feel good?'

'Mmmmmm.'

'This is the first time, and I'm all shy. I have a lover who's seventeen but he isn't as soft as you are.'

'I can finally claim a victory.'

'Don't speak too soon.'

His hand moved up and down without ever touching the lips of her vagina; finally he leaned over and lightly ran the tip of his tongue over her nipples.

'What an odd sensation. I'm progressing through unknown territory. Even the smells are different.'

He kissed her on the mouth. And he allowed himself to be

undressed, shaking his head in advance. Sure enough, naked now, he had no erection, despite her best efforts.

'I warned you, Hannah. Not even for you.'

'I'll get over it.'

He returned to her body, touching her only with his tongue, managing to give her a great deal more pleasure than she had expected. Then he stretched out on his back and started to cry. She took him in her arms and they lay there, both knowing that they would not resume their lovemaking.

'Have you already tried it with another woman, Hannah?'

'No.'

'Would you like to?'

'No.'

'A malicious gossip spoke to me about you and a woman writer whom I don't need to name.'

She laughed. 'We've met. I was at a party in Paris where she made her entrance hidden under a huge dish-cover; she was naked and caressing another woman. That's all. I don't travel that way.'

'Just men, is that right?'

'I adore them. I'm very normal.'

'What's abnormal is that you should proclaim it. How immodest. An honest woman doesn't get any pleasure from making love. This is the reign of Queen Victoria, after all, my dear . . .'

Immediately after London came Budapest; she opened there in the spring of 1898. And at almost the same time, thanks to Maryan's remarkable preparations, she opened in Prague and Berlin.

'Warsaw, Hannah?'

'No.'

'Dobbe Klotz is still alive.'

'What a pity!'

She finally decided to write to her mother, composing a short, unemotional letter only a few lines long. She received no reply, which surprised her: she would not have thought Shiffrah had enough character to sulk. The explanation for her mother's silence came a few months later, in the form of a letter from her brother Simon, who was now a rabbi. Simon wrote twenty-eight pages of vehement reproach: Hannah was a disgrace to the whole of Poland and to the rest of the world as well. He denied her as his sister, as a Polish compatriot, and as a woman. And he wanted one thousand roubles from her.

She wavered, then sent the money, tripling the sum. She knew that she was making a monumental mistake: it was clear he would never stop asking for more. But she had no remaining links with her family, and if this was what it would take . . .

That year, at the end of August, Rod MacKenna came to Europe to see Lizzie for the first time in three years. Naturally, he had written to her, once every two months, like clockwork. His letters were deadly dull, and hardly varied: 'Work hard', 'Be good', 'Do us credit' recurred like a refrain, as cheerful as a dirge. He was now married and his wife, a blonde New Zealander, was travelling with him – 'If they have any children, tell him to put one aside for me,' Hannah whispered to Lizzie, 'they'll probably be three metres tall!' They burst into giggles, and kindhearted Rod – because he was very kind, in fact, like Dougal, who had apparently aged a great deal – stared at them uncomprehendingly.

One thing was certain: Lizzie refused even to contemplate going back to Australia at any time during the next fifty years. She would go for a holiday if it was necessary, but even then she was not keen.

'We'll see. There's no hurry. If Daddy wants to see me, why doesn't he come to England? My marks at school? They're excellent, I'm the best pupil in the Empire.' (This was virtually true; Hannah saw to it, with the vigilance of a Sikh.)

Rod and his wife left after two months. Maryan turned up next, having come from Spain where he had been learning Spanish and looking in vain for Taddeuz, who was not in Spain or Portugal. Lizzie was then finally able to meet him, having heard so much about him for years. She did not think him handsome, or very intelligent either, although she had only been talking to him for about twenty minutes. This did not stop her from asking out of the blue whether he was still a virgin. Maryan turned every shade of colour from purple to poppy-red, shifting his weight from one foot to the other, unable to reply. He was twenty-two, or very nearly, and he was then earning just a little less than the Governor of the Bank of England, but he was not at ease with this little girl.

Lizzie kissed him. She already loved him; she assumed she would marry the great oaf in two or three years' time. After all, she had only to grow a little to be of his height exactly.

'I was made to be happy,' she said to Hannah one day. 'Are you absolutely certain I shouldn't take a lover?'

'Positive.'

'You've got one, even though you're going to marry Taddeuz.'

'It's not the same.'

'Ha, ha, ha.'

'If you take a lover, I shall send you home to Australia. And don't try to tell me that you're going to swim back!'

'Just a little one?'

'No.'

'It's not a question of size, I take it?'

'Exactly.'

'Poor Maryan. He's going to have to relieve me of my virginity! I hope he knows how.'

'Lizzie!'

'And who do you think taught me to say such things, eh?'

Her credit stood at ninety-three thousand pounds according to the balance sheet for December 1898, in spite of the large investments she had made in Paris, Brussels, Budapest, Prague, Berlin and London. And as the weeks went by, these branches began to contribute to her expanding fortune.

She thought of Zurich and Vienna as her next conquests, Zurich first off for no reason she could give, and despite Maryan's counsel to do things the other way around. She dug her heels in, however, backing a hunch that she could not begin to explain.

'Vienna will be second, Maryan, and don't ask me why, I don't know.'

The rest of her litany required no discussion: she would open in Milan and Rome simultaneously, then in Madrid and Lisbon. Stockholm, Copenhagen and Amsterdam would follow.

'Still not prepared to consider Warsaw?'

'No.'

'St Petersburg?'

She did not like the Russians, those simple-minded anti-Semites, and he of all people ought to know that. The tone of her reply was chillingly curt. Once she had opened in Amsterdam, the great leap would follow: she would try her luck in America. And perhaps she would travel to New York as the scout instead of sending him. One of Polly's Irish cousins had emigrated and settled among the Yankees; he was in New York and held a very important position there; either as a stockbroker or banker or as a gangland boss, Polly did not seem to care to remember which.

The end-of-year festivities were approaching, and Hannah made her usual arrangements to spend them alone. She knew it was pure superstition on her part, that she was waiting for Taddeuz – though at her present rate it did not look as if she would ever find him again – and that she was afraid celebrating the New Year with anyone else, even Lizzie, would bring her bad luck.

She made plans, however, for Lizzie to spend Christmas and the New Year in Scotland with a schoolfriend, and she herself went to Zurich. At least this way she could make some use of the time: she would choose the location for her new branch.

She reserved a room at the Baur au Lac, where she spent her days and sometimes her nights watching the snow fall on the black waters of the Lake. She thought about André – from whom she had separated two months earlier when he had mentioned the word marriage – and she tried damned hard not to cry. He had understood her, and made a dramatic exit, and the following day as a farewell present he had the staircase and lift at 10 rue d'Anjou carpeted with two thousand roses. She read, or tried to read, but the memory of the room in Praga kept coming back to her, oppressing her to the point where she wanted to scream.

On December 28th she saw someone she knew; from the far end of the hotel lounge where she sat huddled in a wing-backed armchair, she saw Lothar Hutwill pass through the foyer. He had not changed; he was slim and elegant, calm and attractive, his hair silvering at the temples. A bright-eyed young woman, small and very lively, clung to his arm.

She waited until the couple had disappeared before signalling to the concierge who was happy to tell her that Hutwill had been widowed at least two years before, when his wife died in a boating accident on Lake Geneva. Mr Hutwill had remarried: it seemed he was very rich.

She was back in London on January 2nd, and Lizzie from Scotland on January 3rd, just in time to witness the injunction to quit the premises being served on the fat lady in purple. The two talked nonstop for the next seven hours, resuming their Sydney habits of sharing the same bed, this time burrowing beneath a profusion of pillows and black and Turkey-red cushions.

'For the love of God, Lizzie, quiet now! It's two o'clock in the morning!'

'A lady shouldn't swear . . .'

The next day Hannah got up an hour later than usual — five o'clock. She reviewed her accounts and wrote a few letters. At about seven o'clock she welcomed the first of the sales assistants to arrive. Leading the vanguard was Cecily Barton, director of the English operation; no one was higher in the hierarchy apart from Jeanne Fougaril and, of course, Hannah herself.

About an hour later, confident that all was in order downstairs, Hannah managed to drag Lizzie out of the canopied bed. As she was unable to separate the girl from the black silk sheet and pillow that she clung to, she plunged the whole lot into the bath, this being the only way of waking her Australian ward at what was for her such an early hour.

At about ten o'clock they went out shopping together. In Bond Street Hannah bought Lizzie a charming gold bracelet set with topaz, the first piece of jewellery the young girl had received. She was deeply touched.

It was just past one thirty when Hannah returned to the salon, having sent Lizzie off again to Sussex, accompanied by the chauffeur. Every room was operating at capacity, the entire operation was humming away quietly, the squadron of nine aestheticians and eleven sales assistants raced back and forth . . .

And there he was, sitting in a grosgrain armchair, wearing a heavy suit made of untreated wool and a poacher's cap. Placed as he was in the salon he looked like a tourist who had wandered into a harem with his Baedeker. He was smiling, wearing that expression of merry impishness that men sport when they know they are bound to be forgiven for their escapades.

Hannah literally fell apart. Her eyesight clouded and she experienced that feeling of weightlessness that great joy brings.

'Oh Mendel! My God, Mendel!'

21

MENDEL, YOU POOR FOOL

It had been very simple, he said: once he got to Lake Baikal, he turned left.

It was either that or go through Irkutsk, where a garrison was stationed. And he was not Michel Strogoff after all. He had walked for two or three, at the very most four, months. He had passed through Mongolia somehow, and then he had seen millions of Chinese; more than he could believe existed, after he had crossed the Great Wall of China. Ultimately he had made his way to Shanghai. That must have been ten or twelve months before, after he had got involved in a bit of a scrap with some chaps called Boxers, who tried to bar his way. Had it not been for several Chinese women, who were just as friendly as women anywhere else in the world, he would have had a few problems.

'You never received my letters from Australia, did you, Mendel?'

He had. And he still carried them with him, as he had over the thirty or thirty-five thousand kilometres he had crossed, and as a matter of fact he knew them by heart. For the third time he took hold of her by the waist and lifted her up in the air.

'Hannah, that would have been the last straw if they hadn't bothered to give me my mail. It wouldn't have been only three or four of them – including the prison governor, I'm sorry to report – that I knocked out when I left! And I wouldn't have left them with only a little tap on the head.'

He thought he was perhaps overdoing it, but he could not

disguise the powerful emotion he felt. It had been more than seven years since he had seen her, and throughout those seven years hardly a day had passed when he had not thought of her. The last time he had seen her was when he had left the prison in Warsaw and had cried out 'Happy Birthday, Hannah', waving his hands with all those damned chains round his wrists. They had put them back on for good after the sixth of his nineteen attempts to escape. He owed his survival to the certainty that if he allowed himself to die he would be letting her down terribly. He would never say as much to her, but the truth was that he had been to hell and back. The Siberian warders did not much care for his insolence, his refusal to resign himself to his fate, his laughter during the most excruciating whipping sessions, his proud affirmation that he was Jewish. (He cared as little as ever about religion but since it annoyed them that he was Jewish he was happy to make the most of it.) He was sent from one camp to another, ending up in the most isolated in the taiga, where the temperature sometimes fell to seventy degrees below zero, and where the mortality rate was about nine out of ten.

Getting to Lake Baikal had in itself taken him five months of travelling sixty kilometres a day. It was tiring, especially with all the zigzagging he had had to do to escape his pursuers. And the cold was followed by the drought and heat of the Gobi Desert, which he had crossed on foot, surviving on snakes, lizards and the decaying remains of the odd camel left behind by a caravan, often drinking his own urine. The Boxers in China also made life difficult for him: he was recuperating in a German Protestant mission – in bed with the wife of one of the missionaries, in fact – when the sect of the Great Knife came bursting in. He survived that pogrom as he had others, but not without having been slashed rather seriously around the shoulders and on his buttocks. He managed to cover several thousand kilometres more with the assistance of several Chinese women, who were, it seemed, more accommodating than their restricted life might have led one to believe. In Shanghai he became a sailor, despite his fear of the sea. Somehow or other he ended up in Japan, and from there sailed to San Francisco because there was no way of travelling directly from Japan to Australia . . .

'How many of my letters reached you?'

'Six. In the last, written in December '94, you said you were in

Sydney, you were well and that you had met those Austro-German aristocrat friends of yours.'

'There was a seventh, in which I told you I was leaving for Europe. With details of where to find me.'

'Didn't get it. One of two things is possible: either the postman came after I'd left, or else they were slightly annoyed with me. I was beginning to irritate them a bit towards the end. I left in the spring of '95, during the best Siberian walking season. There couldn't have been more than two metres of snow on the ground.'

From San Francisco, which had pleased Mendel considerably, he had booked a passage to the Philippines, where he had worked for a while on a plantation in order to earn himself a bit of money. Then he reached Java. He spent some time in prison there, as the result of some vague story involving a Dutch woman, who preferred Mendel to her cheesehead of a husband, who was now quite dead. After the time it took to arrange an escape, he had had no choice but to sail around all those blasted islands – God, how he hated the sea! – until the day he finally stepped on to Australian soil in Darwin.

'When was that?'

'Last year. April, May, thereabouts.'

He had roamed a while, happy to be on dry land again and surrounded by wide open spaces. A month and a half later, in the Darling Mountains in Queensland, a funny thing had happened:

'Does the name Simon Clancy mean anything to you?'

'Yes.'

'We met under a eucalyptus tree, skirting a kangaroo. We spoke of one thing and another, and when I told him that I'd come to find a kid no bigger than a sack of wheat with eyes one metre in diameter, he told me that, bloody hell and goddamnit, he knew you . . .'

'That's sounds just like him,' said Hannah, delighted.

'. . . That he not only knew you but that he worked for you, cutting grass for rabbits, as you might say. And that you'd gone to Europe.'

'Did you go to Sydney?'

'What for? You weren't there any more.'

'What about Melbourne and Brisbane?'

'No, I didn't go there either. For the same reason. I liked that Simon Clancy, and he and I . . .'

'Mendel! I'd left messages all over the place, in Sydney, Melbourne and Brisbane, for when you arrived. I left money for you in each place as well!'

And where in God's name had she picked up the idea that he was worried about money? He very nearly lifted her off the ground for the fourth time but preferred to take refuge in a corner of the fabulous library on the second floor of the mansion, which was lined with elm wainscotting and contained no fewer than five thousand books. Henry-Beatrice had insisted on retaining the original décor, replacing only the brocade panelling with Turkey red.

Mendel kept his distance from Hannah for the most part, afraid of what would happen inside him if he were crazy enough to hold her close. He would not be able to resist; he would completely dissolve; he would let himself go; they would end up in bed together. And how could he come to terms with that? He would never forgive himself, it would make him suffer more, until his dying day. He knew she was still stuck on that Polish fellow, if not on some other chap as well. But he could clearly see that – her joy and affection aside – she was not in love with him. He pretended to examine the books.

'And Quentin MacKenna – is that a name that means anything to you?' he asked.

'Yes,' said Hannah again, this time in a much more subdued tone.

'Love him?' he asked, deliberately using as few words as possible in phrasing his question so as to avoid having to use the past tense, which would have tipped the kid off.

'No,' said Hannah. 'Not really.'

'He's dead,' said Mendel. 'Probably dead. You know that he tried to walk across Australia, from Brisbane to the other side, something no one has ever done before?'

'Yes.'

'I'd be amazed if anyone ever succeeds. Even I wouldn't try, not even if I'd eaten the whole crew of a boat, the passengers and sails as well. But it was a bloody fine act of lunacy, it was like spitting into the face of the stars. He told Simon Clancy that if he succeeded in crossing the continent he would leave this thing – a pile of stones, a cairn – at a specified place. He was going to lay these stones out in the shape of a five-pointed star. We went there, Simon Clancy and I, on our way north via Fremantle. The stones were there, or at least most of them were. The star was missing one point, and next to it lay a skeleton which the vultures had beaten us to. A stone sat in the bones of the right hand.'

Afterwards, Mendel had earned his way to Perth, shovelling coal on a boat. He had suffered a few mishaps in the Indies, met with a typhoon or two in Bombay, and had had to spend a month looking for another ship at the foot of Table Mountain, in Cape Town. But after that it was plain sailing, and he had arrived in London as fresh as a daisy the previous day. He had been in town only long enough to wash off the layers of coal dust and find out where she was, and here he was.

Still, she should not get any ideas into her head, he reported. He was not stopping here, he had only come by to say hello. He could happily have stayed in Australia; it was a country he liked, with all that space there, but he had wanted to see her again. And he preferred to return to America, which he had liked even more, and where the women were exactly to his liking.

His heart turned over when he asked: 'Did you sleep with this Quentin MacKenna, Hannah?'

'Yes,' she said, wondering what the devil it had got to do with Mendel.

'And with others?'

'There haven't been three hundred and fifty,' she said, laughing. 'Three or four, in all.'

'One in particular?'

She contented herself with staring at him, a peculiar gleam in her eyes. Suddenly he understood the impossible thing she was trying to communicate:

'The Polish student, Hannah?'

'Yes.'

'Is he here?'

'I don't know.'

'You haven't found him yet?'

'Not yet.'

She said this in a very calm, clear voice, as she might have reported that she had not yet sewn on a button that was missing. It was insane, so much so that he felt he must sit down, if only to master his anger at seeing her waste away on account of some moronic Pole who might well be handsome but probably had about as much intelligence as a coal shovel.

'You haven't seen him again since little Klotz died and I was arrested?'

'No.'

'Have you had any news at all?'

'None.'

'You have absolutely no idea where he is?'

'None.'

'But of course you've looked for him.'

'In one way or another,' she said. 'I've quite simply put a price on his head; it was one hundred pounds to start with, it's five hundred today. It won't take me long to go as high as one thousand. Or even ten thousand. I'm rich now.'

Speaking of which, he did not want any of her money, and he would like it very much indeed if she would stop going on about wanting to share the goddamned stuff between them. As if he was going to take the slightest interest in those blasted creams she slapped on those poor women's faces! If it would really make her happy, she could simply give him back the twenty-two thousand roubles he had handed over to her . . .

'What interest, for God's sake?'

'Seven years and eleven days at nine and a half per cent per year, that makes . . .'

'Hannah, stop playing shop with me, will you? Or else I'll put you over my knee and pull your knickers down and . . .'

'Like hell you would!' she said.

That calmed him suddenly.

'Bitch.'

'Yep,' she agreed, enjoying herself wildly (and to tell the truth, she was wild with happiness; there he was in front of her).

'Are you sure, in any event, it was twenty-two thousand roubles?'

'I'd stake my life on it,' she replied imperturbably. 'Twenty-two thousand nine hundred and nine roubles.'

'That's a bloody lie. I've never had so much money in my life.'

'You must have forgotten while you were in Siberia. At seventy below zero, a person's memories can be lost to the frost. So I owe you twenty-one thousand four hundred and fifty-three pounds eleven shillings.'

'I'd be very surprised,' he grumbled, 'if the rouble was worth as much as that. Don't try to put one over on me, Hannah; I was stealing apples — as well as what's under women's skirts — long before you were born. Twenty-two thousand roubles, that can only come to three or four thousand pounds at most. Shut up, kid.'

They dined together, facing each other at either end of a table so long that they needed a French maid – who eyed Mendel with obvious lust; his black hair and glittering smile were more attractive to women than ever – to carry things from one end to the other. They spoke Yiddish, as was their habit, although between the two of them they must have been able to speak fourteen or fifteen languages; travelling around as much as he had, Mendel had learned – in addition to English and the Hebrew, Polish, Russian, German and French he already knew – Spanish and Tagalog in the Philippines, Dutch and Javanese in Java, several Siberian dialects and a fair bit of Chinese.

Towards the middle of the meal he fell silent, admiring her in the warm light shed by the gilt candlesticks, well aware – as was she – of the current of feeling that had passed between them when she'd said: 'Like hell you would.' He already knew that he was going to sleep elsewhere tonight, and every night. Furthermore, he knew he had better set sail for America, or anywhere, as soon as possible. If he stayed near her, he would certainly go mad . . .

Once dinner was over, they moved to the drawing room. She offered him a cigar and some French brandy. He emptied the bottle on his own, without getting the slightest bit drunk, so he would always know that the alcohol had nothing to do with what he was about to offer.

'And Maryan hasn't been able to find him?'

'Not a trace.'

'I'd like to see Maryan again.'

'He's in Berlin; he leaves tomorrow for Prague. Then for Vienna, to prepare the ground for the salon I'll be opening there in the spring. I have his itinerary and dates. I can send him a telegram and ask him to come to London.'

'I'll go and see him. We can travel a bit together.'

'As you wish.'

Silence.

'Hannah? You know what I'm going to say, don't you?'

'You're going to find Taddeuz for me. And you will find him.'

He closed his eyes, overwhelmed with grief. *The worst of it was that he was going to do it, he was going to collar that bastard who fascinated her when she was seven and had become a myth to her since. He would do it even though he thought he was no good for her, that he loved no one but himself and he would only condescend to being loved by the kid, who was worth a thousand million of him. He would not flatten him as much as he might like to. He would take him by the scruff of the neck and drop him at the kid's feet, like a dog reporting home with his game. You poor fool Mendel, you're a bloody idiot . . .*

22

SHE COULD ALMOST WRITE
THE KAMA SUTRA

In all, he stayed a week in London. He did not sleep at her apartment; he was not much taken with the ducal bedroom with the coffered ceiling in which she would have put him, despite the French maid, who was indeed most alluring, and would have been only too pleased to offer herself to him. It was all a bit too easy for him. Besides he wanted to try an Englishwoman.

She took him to Sussex to meet Lizzie.

'She'd tear my eyes out if I didn't introduce you to her. I've told her everything about you and, in her mind, you're just a little smaller than the Himalayas.'

He would not hear of getting rid of his cap or the twelve-shilling suit which, she told him, made him look as hairy as a Carpathian bear, except that he was bigger. He made rather a striking entrance into the parlour of the stuffy private school, reducing the other visitors to silence. For her part Lizzie remained open-mouthed in front of him, frozen with awe. She could not manage a single word all the time he was there. Hannah was shocked by Lizzie's uncharacteristic silence, but as well quite delighted and proud of Mendel's effect on the girl.

Three days later he left for Vienna, where he was going to meet up with Maryan.

As he said goodbye he asked plainly: 'And what do I do when I lay hands on this student of yours?'

'Keep your hands off him, please.'

'And what do I say to him?'

'Tell him . . . No, don't say anything. He must not know that I'm looking for him.'

'Don't I bring him back to you?'

'I simply want to know where he is. You can speak to him if you like, but not about me. And be careful, Mendel, he's extra-ordinarily intelligent.'

Now he was sure she was mad.

'And if he's married?'

'There is such a thing as divorce,' she spat back.

In Paris, two months later, she received a letter from him, from Warsaw, dated February 6th: *Went by your shtetl. Saw your mother. She's fine, thank Heaven. Told her you sent your love.*

Nothing else.

She had already been in Paris, on the rue d'Anjou, for three weeks. Her Kitchen was located on the left bank, at 6 rue Vercingétorix, on the third floor. She had chosen this address for the sole reason that Juliette Mann, the chemist Marie Curie had found for her, lived just around the corner, in the Avenue de Maine, and she was eager to make things as convenient as possible for Juliette. It was only after she had signed the lease that Hannah discovered who lived upstairs, above the laboratory: it was the French painter Gauguin, who, five years earlier, had returned from the South Seas for the first time, accompanied by a Javanese woman. They became friends, and she bought four of Gauguin's paintings, which joined the Manets, Monets, Degas and Cézannes that now hung in the rue d'Anjou and in London. At parties in Gauguin's studio, she met the Norwegian painter Edvard Munch, and she made particularly close friends with the Swedish writer August Strindberg, whose play *Miss Julie* she adored.

As for herself, she worked as furiously as ever. It seemed to her that Mendel was bound to find Taddeuz sooner or later; she must get as far ahead as possible with her business affairs so that she could be free when the time came. And there was no longer any question of taking a lover, despite the many offers that came her way; that would be the last straw if Taddeuz were to arrive and find her in bed with someone else! She reconciled herself to the fact that . . . in that sense at least . . . her studies were now over.

With the help of several actresses – Ellen Terry and Sarah Bernhardt among them – she completed her survey of the known

world of cosmetics. These were the only women at the time who
had any experience of make-up, because their profession required
it. Even so, their knowledge was limited. Off stage, they hardly
dared use more than the traditional rice powder made in China –
and they had only to use a little too much to be transformed into
white-faced pierrots. Hannah noted all this and wrote up a report.
With Juliette's invaluable help, she produced five new creams
designed to protect the skin and make it more radiant. These
creams would replace those she had sold in Australia; they were
the product of some dogged scientific experiments and much
thought. They were totally innocuous: Hannah hired a number of
guinea pigs, and later relied on volunteers, to try them out. The
creams had to be used in the proper quantities and applied with a
specific technique so that they would dissolve properly into the
skin and allow the desired radiance. But this was exactly what her
aestheticians were there for, and the results of their professional
applications were impressive.

'It is absolutely imperative that any woman who passes through
your hands ends up looking more beautiful, but without it being
exactly clear why. The creams must remain invisible. Even a
woman's husband or lover should not be able to understand why
she looks more beautiful. It must all remain mysterious. I want
magic.'

Foundation cream: this was her name for her magic. And it very
quickly became clear to her that she would need as many varieties
as there were types of skin, and types of women: she would need
creams for each hair colour, and each eye colour, for night and
day, for changes of clothing.

'Women won't be able to put on the same kind of make-up to
go to Longchamp or the Epsom Derby, in the open air, as they will
for the impressionistic lighting of a restaurant in the Bois, or for an
evening at the Opera . . . Or for bed. Don't snigger, please, ladies.
The door remains open for anyone who finds me boring.'

She was not content, moreover, with a wealthy, and therefore
limited, clientele. She felt very nearly as if she had a sacred mission
to fulfil. She and Lizzie invented an imaginary character, a Mrs
Sophronia MacDuschmoulski, whose name was a fanciful distor-
tion of that of a chambermaid they had employed when they had
first come to London. Sophronia MacDuschmoulski could not have
been more common. She spoke English with a Cockney accent so
thick you could cut through it with a knife; French with a terrible

provincial accent; German with the guttural intonations of North Germany. (Mrs MacDuschmoulski was all nationalities at once; she was also Polish, Spanish or American; in this last case she came from Nebraska, as Polly had told them it was a very out-of-the-way place.) She was Presbyterian, Muslim, Jewish, Roman Catholic, Confucian or Buddhist; their frenzied imaginations balked at nothing. She had a husband who drank, and who sometimes beat her. She worked eighteen hours a day and had to count every sou, every penny, every groschen of what she earned and her husband spent. She lived the life of a slave, all the more so for working in a factory. And yet she dreamed. She dreamed not of being as beautiful as the ladies of Belgravia or Mayfair, but of dolling herself up a bit now and then. And if these dreams had not yet come to her, then they would; Hannah would see to that. She was rather fond, after all, of Mrs Sophronia MacDuschmoulski, who was rather like her, or who at least resembled her as she had looked the day she had seen her reflection in the shop window in Cracow Avenue, wearing her grey velvet dress, and those boots that were too big for her. You did not forget things like that; they were fixed in your stomach and your heart all your life; they made you cry with rage whenever you thought of them, even if you lived to be a hundred.

And she would not listen to those bloody fools who thought she was crazy: she could clearly see the day when all the Sophronias in the world would use her products, as long as she made sure they could afford them. Which she would do, come what might.

'That would be a revolution,' said Juliette Mann, stunned by her ambition.

'You're the one who said it,' replied Hannah, herself a bit unnerved by her own dreams.

Cosmeticology: the word had a lovely, scientific ring to it. And this science went far beyond foundation creams; its study included such disciplines as colouring the lips, for example, which became necessary once one started covering the rest of one's face with a scented foundation cream. Hannah conducted a considerable amount of research in this particular area as well. For at least two hundred years women had been using resin, a kind of ointment that had the texture of mastic and was generally scented with rose water or jasmin and dyed with alkanet or ordinary grape juice to strengthen the colour of their mouths to make them more attractive. Later they had tried cerates, pastes with a wax and oil base.

These they moulded into little sticks that could be carried around in a small bag, although this practice was limited almost entirely to actresses and tarts. For a society woman, for an ordinary bourgeois soul, the idea smacked of heresy and of prostitution. Hannah knew that she would have to tend to some social conventions that did not die easily, with her clients' timorousness in the face of all her innovations. But she was determined to do so, to make the most of the curiosity her clients evinced. She was a little more concerned with ensuring that these rouge sticks, if produced on an industrial scale, would be perfectly safe and would not turn the fairer sex into victims of scurvy.

'That's a matter of chemistry, Juliette. Over to you.'

She fully realized that she could not accomplish this kind of thing in three or four weeks; research of this sort could take five or ten years if not decades, and Juliette could not do the job on her own. She would need more chemists and more laboratories, not necessarily in France. Hannah would have to invest some money, take on more staff. She was ready to launch a full scale offensive; it was to this end that she had been amassing her fortune.

She went to Vienna in April and was angry that she had not done so earlier. It was a lovely city, and she wished that – coming from Poland – she had started out here.

Maryan Kaden was at his post; he had taken care of all the ground work and reconnaissance, with his usual efficiency. According to him, there were two acceptable sites for the beauty parlour, as well as four other sites for the shops she expected to open. He saw the salon located either in the old town, where it would be very near the ancient and aristocratic Herrengasse, which ran from the Kinsky Palace to the Hofburg, and where the Emperor Francis Joseph and the Empress Sissi whiled away their days . . .

'Or else?'

'The Ringstrasse – the chain of wide avenues circling the historical part of the city. It's newer, and there would be room for your clients' vehicles.'

Unlike other large European cities, Vienna had preserved almost all its early fortifications. Only about forty years earlier, from about 1850, had the city begun building its walls on the sloping wasteland that had served to keep the popular quarters at a distance. Maryan believed that his new district had a future. He even thought he had located its centre.

'Moving away from Schwarzenberg Square, where all the nobility live, you enter, as you travel west and north-west, following a curve, the upper middle-class area. Like everywhere else, it's the middle-class that has the money, much more so than the nobility. But you mustn't go too far north; once you go past Parliament, there's nothing of any significance, apart from the university.'

'And you think the Ringstrasse is better than the old town?'

'Yes.'

'And where on the Ringstrasse, Maryan?'

'Either in Beethoven Square, in the east, or in Reichsratstrasse. Reichsratstrasse would be better.'

They went together to the second street, that ran right behind the *Reichsrat*; the parliament building. It was wide – eighty-one feet according to Maryan, who had measured it – and led to the City Hall gardens on the left. The building Maryan had found was number seven; it had been built in 1883 but looked practically new. The entrance was magnificent, as was all the ornate ground floor. Upstairs, on the other hand, the architect had been more parsimonious. The *Herrschaftssiege*, the main staircase, ended abruptly at the foot of an ordinary staircase leading to the rooms above.

'I certainly won't allow my clients upstairs.'

He could well imagine that she would not. He had been told that the rent for one of the grander floors was the equivalent of two thousand eight hundred pounds a year, which became two thousand five hundred after a lot of bargaining. The owner was an archduke who loved poetry.

'Hannah, didn't you talk to me once about a French poet called Rimbaud?'

'He's my greatest friend. We were at school together,' replied Hannah, who had actually never set eyes on Arthur Rimbaud in her life. As he had been dead for about eight years, however, he was unlikely to contradict her. She had, however, read his work, knowing that Taddeuz was bound to love him and wanting to prepare herself. And she knew several artists who claimed to have spent a good deal of time with the absinthe drinker.

'If you talk to the archduke about Rimbaud he'll drop the price,' said Maryan.

What a memory the fellow had, thought Hannah. He had been able to remember a name that she herself couldn't recall even having uttered in front of him! She studied him. Lizzie wasn't wrong, when all was said and done. Maryan might not be very handsome, or very intelligent on the face of it – but in fact he was not bad at all. He was solid, and his presence was comforting. You could understand how some women might find him attractive indeed. His eyes looked calm and peaceful, sometimes even dreamy; they completely belied the methodical brain that lay behind them. He was strong and healthy, and since his meeting with Hannah in Baden-Baden four years earlier, he had learned how to dress. He was now well off, and well educated; he told her about investments he had been making on the stock exchange. To reassure herself that he was not being naïve in his financial speculations, she had taken him to see a cousin of Polly Twhaites who was an important figure in the City of London. And to her surprise, the young man from Warsaw and the Oxford man in the stiff collar and striped tie had got on like a house on fire, so much so that she got the impression – and she was no fool in such matters – that they did not really need her around.

'Are you having an affair with anyone, Maryan?'

They were retracing their steps across the Ring, heading back to the Hofburgtheater. The afternoon air was soft and hazy; some very pretty carriages drove past; a gypsy played a violin on a nearby corner. Hannah realized that she was thoroughly enamoured of Vienna.

Maryan did not answer her question.

'It's none of my business, I know, Maryan. But imagine what would happen if tomorrow, or in a month, or a year, you fell under a woman's spell? And you became wholly enchanted, to the point that you put on a top hat and satin cape and went squandering all your money with her all over Europe, singing dirty songs.'

He stared at her in amazement.

'And left me,' she added.

She knew she was overstating the case; she was not exactly afraid he would leave her, probably because she could not imagine his ever really doing so. But in the event that that crazy girl Lizzie really wanted to marry him – and he probably would have little say in the matter, the poor boy, she would have him at the altar in a flash – it would be better if he were experienced. Lizzie had no experience herself; ideas, certainly, but no practical experience. And then there was all Hannah had told her, with which she could practically write the Kama Sutra. But these things were important in marriage after all, Hannah reminded herself, thinking of the room in Praga and the terrible disappointment she had felt with Taddeuz . . .

'I'll never leave you Hannah,' said Maryan, staring at the ground in dismay. 'Never.'

'All the same, you ought to have a mistress. Three or four would be even better. It's like food. You have to taste everything to know what you like.'

He gulped, visibly panic-stricken. She found it both very comical and very touching to see this determined and loyal young man, so capable in so many spheres of activity, looking so intimidated at the mention of women.

They sat down at the table she had reserved in the garden of the Grillparzer restaurant. He sat to her right, still reeling from shock; without consulting him, Hannah ordered *Backhendel*, fried chicken in breadcrumbs, and *Sachertorte* for two. She assumed she knew what was good for him, in more ways than one. She would have to see to this mistress question of Maryan's.

As well as to a thousand other things. She had decided to put her plan into effect in Vienna; it would be even better than Paris, which had until then seemed the only suitable place.

And at the same time she would set up her new beauty parlour, there being no connection whatsoever between the two.

Johann Strauss smiled at her.

He was not actually Johann Strauss, although at the same time he was. He was not the composer of *An der schönen blauen Donau*, nor of the Emperor's Waltz, nor of the *G'schichten aus dem Wiener-wald*, though he too shared her admiration for these works.

'I'm Johann III, son of Edward, who was the brother of Johann II and Joseph, who were all sons of Johann I. I'm touched by your compliments, all the same, even though they're really those for my uncle.'

He was very amused by Hannah's mistake. She need not worry, he reassured her, she was not the first, and certainly would not be the last, to confuse the two Johann Strausses.

'Especially as, in addition to we Strauss musicians from Vienna, there's another Strauss musician from Germany, whose first name's Richard, and who recently produced a wonderful work called *Thus Spake Zarathustra*. But he's no relation of ours. So you know Claude Debussy, do you?'

She had obtained a letter of introduction from the French

composer. Strauss had hardly read it. In his view it would have said very little for Viennese gallantry if she had imagined for one moment that a pretty woman would need any introduction before she was received by Johann Strauss . . .

'Well, I have a rather unusual favour to ask,' Hannah said, tilting her head to one side and opening her eyes slightly wider. The effect these motions had on men could generally be relied upon. And they worked again now. Johann Strauss listened attentively while she told him what she was planning to do in Vienna, the city of her dreams. It was the logical place to choose for the most important event in your life, if you were a Pole, was it not? She told him everything – or nearly everything – about this forthcoming event, which she had planned down to the minutest detail. She omitted a few small points, for fear that he would call the men in white coats.

No, there was no connection between this enterprise and the beauty parlour in Reichsratstrasse that she was preparing to open, which was similar to those she had already opened in nearly all the major European cities. Unless Madame Johann Strauss or any of her dearest friends would like to visit her salon as clients, of course; they would be treated free of charge, that went without saying. But that was just an incidental connection . . .

'I hate talking about money,' she said, 'but it goes without saying that I . . .

He laughed, examining her face with great curiosity. 'You're a very unusual young woman, my dear.'

He turned out not to be, however, director of balls for the Imperial Court, as she had been told; it was his father Edward who occupied this important position, previously held by his uncle and his grandfather. He himself, Johann III, was a concert performer and conductor, and he had travelled the world in these two capacities. In any event the evening of December 31st was out of the question; their Imperial Majesties were to give a grand ball that night in the Hofburg ballroom, which would be particularly splendid as it was to mark not only the beginning of the new year but also of the new century.

'However, if it was to be on the evening of 30th December, why not? I can make sure I'm free and I think I'll be able to persuade my father. Your idea is so . . .' He hesitated.

'Crazy?' suggested Hannah.

'Romantic,' said Johann Strauss. 'It's so romantic. And so Vien-nese . . .'

In no time at all, after a recitation *concertante* of Rimbaud's *Bateau Ivre*, which she had learned by heart for the purpose, she came to an agreement with the archduke over 7 Reichsratstrasse, settling on the equivalent of near enough two thousand and thirty-two pounds sterling a year. When she told the archduke she had been with Arthur Rimbaud in his last hour, at a hospital in Marseilles, her landlord was so deeply moved he burst into tears. He was a very sensitive archduke.

'But you could have got him to knock off a bit more,' said Maryan. 'Especially the thirty-two pounds . . .'

'The *Bateau Ivre* saved me five hundred, more than poor Arthur ever got for it, I'm sure, which is a real disgrace. But just think, Maryan, our archduke has loads of daughters, you'd think he collected them, and they all have girlfriends, who have other girlfriends, aunts, cousins. That's about one hundred and fifty to two hundred clients in one fell swoop. And one day they're going to more than make up for the thirty-two pounds, they're going to bring all the women in Vienna to me. Do you want to bet on that?'

He did not, really. Maryan never bet; money was a serious thing, he was not one to leave it lying about on a casino table. All of which brought up a subject very much on his mind: he had as always, the greatest of respect for Hannah, but in his opinion she was spending far too much money. What was she up to? On her arrival in Vienna she had been content with a modest accommo-dation, then she had moved to the Hotel Sacher, the best hotel of its kind in Vienna. And now look at her! She was definitely wasting money, a bit more every day. She had rented a vast apartment and had it redecorated to suit her, with no regard for the expense, when she already had homes in London and Paris. Furthermore, she had hired servants and bought a horseless carriage, which involved the additional expense of a chauffeur. Maryan was worried. Was the light Viennese air making her extravagant?

He wondered all the more since the work on the salon was progressing satisfactorily, as was to be expected, considering how experienced their team was. It was scheduled to open in June, but this was not a very good time: Vienna became noticeably empty in the summer, as did every other capital. Accordingly, Hannah con-sented to put off the opening until September, when everyone would start returning from the spas and their summer homes. Still her presence in Vienna was hardly required between now and then.

She reassured her young friend not at all, telling him nothing of the other preparations she was making, of her idea that was 'romantic and Viennese'. Instead, she made it clear that for the time being he would stay in Vienna and forsake his tour of inspection. He would just have to make more use of his brothers so far as tracking down Taddeuz was concerned. And she did not want to hear another word about money. Just after the opening, she wanted him to go to America, to New York, where he was to undertake a preliminary study for a new salon. This prospect pleased her greatly: she could see all kinds of symbolic significance in tackling America in the first weeks of the new century.

'I'm sure you'll get on very well with the Americans, Maryan. You've got everything it takes.'

Except a mistress, she thought. His obstinate refusal to acquire one was really very annoying! She had brought up the subject in the course of the week twenty times, but every time he had seized up, scarlet-faced and horribly embarrassed, and begun staring at his feet as though he were hypnotized by them.

Fortunately, she thought, to every problem there are always plenty of solutions.

She called on Gustav Klimt. Everyone was beginning to say he was the greatest living painter in Vienna, which would have been reason itself to visit him. It was all the same not her only one.

She bought two paintings from Klimt. At first he was rather reluctant to sell, but he finally allowed himself to be persuaded when she revealed the extent of her private collection. He was quite flattered to be asked to appear in the company of Claude Monet, and Degas, even if he pretended not to be, but he looked at her with greater interest still when she mentioned her affection for Gauguin and Bonnard, as well as for the Scotsman Charles Rennie Mackintosh, from whom she had purchased several watercolours. And reading, as she did, *La Revue Blanche*, and *Jugend*, and *Ver Sacrum*, she knew the names of Voysey, Lalique, Tiffany . . .

'And do you like them?'

'I would not have bought their works if I didn't. I only buy paintings that I like.'

He said that he had met Mackintosh at the Exhibition in Brussels in 1897. And that he had known Van Gogh well.

'No doubt you're too young to have met him?'

'No, I never met him. But a friend took me to Auvers-sur-Oise, to the house where he committed suicide. It was very moving.'

(It was true that René had taken her on a pilgrimage to Auvers, and true too that she had been very moved. So much so that she set out to acquire more Van Goghs in addition to the two she already owned, one of which took her eleven months to buy from a dealer who didn't want to part with it.)

'Would you sit for me?' asked Klimt.

'I'm not beautiful enough,' she said automatically.

He began to laugh, no doubt thinking she was being flirtatious, although she was in fact absolutely serious. He explained that he would like to capture and reproduce a certain attitude she wore, which he had not seen in any other woman, a kind of high tension that his painter's eye had noticed.

'I warn you, I shan't sleep with you,' she said. 'I've someone else in mind.'

He assured her that he was devastated, and would be until his dying day, but what he most wanted was to paint that movement in her head and shoulders, her bust and chin. He made her half-sit on a very high stool, her feet just touching the ground: when she unfastened her dress and lowered it to her waist, removing her chemises, he began drawing in charcoal, making fifteen or twenty attempts, amassing a pile of sketches . . .

'I can't get it right. Would you like to get dressed again . . .'

She bent down to look at the sketches strewn across the floor of the studio. The way he had depicted her was very strange.

'I'm not as tall as that.'

'I see you as tall.'

'And why are my eyes almost closed in all of them?'

'Because if I were to reproduce the look you have in your eyes, that's all one would see . . .'

Many years later she stopped in her tracks, in a museum in Venice, in front of a work by Gustav Klimt. It was all there this time: the very straight, very long line of the eyebrow, the equally straight nose, that sensual crease in her red mouth, the sharp angles of the face, the small, high breasts, the mass of hair tumbling on to the nape of the neck, above all the heavy eyelids that allowed only a glimpse of the clear pupils beneath. Klimt had painted the canvas in 1909; she had become Salome. Her likeness gripped the hair on the head of a martyred John the Baptist, with very white hands. And this almost premonitory vision of the Viennese artist made her sick for weeks.

Having thus established a relationship with Klimt in the spring of 1899, it was quite easy to get him to agree to the small favour she had come to ask him.

In fact, Klimt found her approach extremely comic.

She agreed that she sometimes had strange ideas, although in this case it was simply a matter of helping her cousin . . .

'And has he any preferences?' asked Klimt.

'I don't think so,' said Hannah. 'I should be very surprised if he had settled on anything specific yet.'

'Blonde, brunette or redhead?'

'Blonde,' Hannah replied firmly, thinking that would at least prepare him for Lizzie.

'Big breasts or small? A Renoiresque derrière? Or wasp-waisted. I have the full range.'

They both giggled; it was as if he was selling her a saucepan. But she really did not know what to say.

'What do you think?'

Klimt said that his own preference was for long thin women, but that in the present circumstances he would suggest a fairly plump blonde, smooth-skinned and soft to the touch, very feminine — comfortable, in a word. Here he was overcome with another fit of laughter, but he continued: about twenty-five years old, who would therefore have all the amorous experience necessary but on the other hand would not have had too much. And he knew just the woman . . .

'If I may make so bold, Hannah . . .'

The woman he was thinking of was not only one of his models, but was as smart as could be; it should be easy to persuade her to — how should he put it? — assist in the initiation of . . .

'His name is Maryan Kaden,' Hannah told him. 'And he isn't at all ugly, really he isn't. As far as I can tell, his constitution is normal, with no major defects. A person could fall in love with him. I know a young girl who has.'

'Not you, I hope?'

'No.'

'Thank God for that,' said Klimt. 'That would have complicated things further, and they're complicated enough as it is. So Grissi is to fall in love with Maryan. All right. Do you know where, when and how?'

Yes! She had already planned every detail of the events that were to lead Maryan straight into the arms and bed of . . .

'Griselda Wagner.'

It was all to take place in the apartment she had rented near the Bohemian Chancellery. Maryan had a room there. She would hire Griselda Wagner on some pretext or other, and would make sure that she and the young man were left alone together. Griselda would have to take the initiative, gently, and with infinite subtlety, as Maryan was very astute. She would have all the time she needed; it was no use pouncing on the boy at their first meeting.

'There's no risk that she might . . . that he might get attached to her and not want to leave her? I need him badly.'

'Grissi has a heart of stone. In fact, that's the only thing about her that isn't soft.'

'Maryan is very shy with women, it's his only fault. All his life, ever since he could walk, he's worked like a slave. He's never had time to think of women. I'll arrange things so that he has some free time and for one reason or another spends it with Griselda. I don't yet know why, but I've enough imagination to be able to think of something. And once they're alone, if she's no fool . . .'

'Hey presto!' said Klimt, doubled up with laughter.

'Hey presto!' repeated Hannah.

She laughed as well, then asked if the model would prefer money or jewellery. Klimt replied that he would rather not be involved in the negotiation of such clauses. But he did have a suggestion to make: he could ask Grissi to come around the next day and pose in every conceivable position. That way, Hannah could see if she was suitable, from a physical point of view.

'Then you won't be buying a pig in a poke.'

Another gale of laughter . . .

'And as for the matter of payment, you women can sort it out between yourselves . . .'

More hysterics.

He would not ask for a percentage.

The idea of being able to examine the merchandise appealed to Hannah, so the next morning she examined, from every angle, with almost unnerving thoroughness, the model's naked body. It would do very nicely, she decided.

And events would unfold as she had anticipated, in the heady

sweetness of the Viennese spring. Maryan fell for Griselda; he even
went so far as to take his conquest dancing in Grinzing. And almost
overnight his complexion – which had always been problematic –
cleared up. That's better for business, thought Hannah.

It was May again, and she was begining to grow anxious. Since his
first message in February, Mendel had written only once, and this
letter was hardly any less laconic than the first: *Have met a certain
Rebecca Singer here. The one from Dobbe's. Very beautiful. She's married
to a very rich American. Will give you her address.*

The letter had been posted in Nice. What the devil was he doing
there? she wondered. She maintained a tremendous confidence in
him, and did not for a second doubt that he would find Taddeuz,
but he was taking longer than she had expected.

It was all beginning to test her nerves, especially after all the
preparations she had made, all the detailed plans she had put into
operation, and all the dreams she had fostered. She was doing all
she could to turn them into reality after so many years; it would
be a shame if Mendel failed her! Or even if he simply failed to meet
her deadline.

So it came almost as a relief when, on May 10th, Maryan passed
on to her some secret information.

It had nothing to do with either Taddeuz or Mendel; it concerned
her business affairs.

There had been a kind of invincible, delightful magic in the way
her affairs had progressed for the last five years, in the way her
salons had established themselves, and expanded, one after the
other. They had enjoyed a constant and inexorable success month
after month, year after year.

But now things were changing. The first real, very sizeable
danger had appeared on the horizon many months earlier, confrontation was coming about only now.

And if it had to happen, this first battle could not have come at
a better time than in this spring of 1899, when she was already in
an exasperated state of waiting. At a less tense time, she would
have reacted only with her usual determination and combative-
ness. Now she was in a burning and irascible fever, however, and
the clinching of the Van Eyckem affair came as a release, a welcome
liberation.

She threw herself headlong into it, a 42-kilo ball of fire.

23

TO BE A WOMAN IN 1900

'Lizzie, I didn't belong to that century in which I lived the first twenty-five years of my life. Now that we're both two old birds I can say with no mistake, that I didn't actually belong to the fifty or sixty years that followed either. You'd think I was some extraterrestrial creature who'd stepped out of a flying saucer. You must remember what it was like to have been a woman in 1900, and even for a long time after that. It wasn't just all those bloody – sorry – those awful dresses, petticoats, veils, wasp-waisters and corsets, hats and gloves, all those frills and flounces we had to tolerate. To choose a lover and admit as much, to sleep with a man simply for the pleasure of it, these were offences worse than murder . . .

And as for making a fortune, that was worse still. When I began to open my shops and salons, there was no problem; I was just some little lady selling little knickknacks to other little ladies. It raised a smile and that was the end of it. But afterwards! Afterwards, when I set up my factories and laboratories, and founded my companies, when I began to earn real money and had real financial questions, then there was a problem. As though it were necessary to wear trousers and have something inside them – don't pretend to blush, Lizzie, you're almost as brazen as I am, and anyway, at your age, it's unbecoming to blush – before you could take an interest in the movements of the Wall Street Stock Exchange . . .

The Van Eyckem affair was the first of my great battles. Perhaps not the hardest, but certainly the most dangerous. I almost lost everything. I was frightened. And Lord knows, I was a frightened woman.

*

It all began in 1898 with several discreet visits, in various cities, from mysterious emissaries. They were always men, dressed in black with gimlet eyes. They scrutinized what went on in the salons and shops; they asked questions; they were seen taking notes.

It was fleeting contact of a kind, in the darkness, with an enemy that was still unidentified.

But which was soon known: acting on the orders they had received, Hannah's local directors – such as Jeanne Fougaril in Paris – referred a number of enquiries to Polly Twhaites' office in London, giving his name as the companies' accredited representative. In April, Polly gave her the news: a group of financiers had just contacted him, and had made some specific and generous offers. What should he do? Keep them hanging for a while, or tell them to go to hell straightaway?

I want to meet them. Rendezvous at the Ritz in three weeks, Hannah cabled him by return. (She was travelling from Budapest to Prague at the time.) She had first thought she should refuse to see them at all, but in the end caution and curiosity had advised her to agree to a meeting. She chose the Ritz for their rendezvous for no other reason than the fact that she did not have an office in France.

Three nondescript men sat in front of her and Polly, who had rushed to Paris from his country seat in Surrey. They began by telling Hannah that they would rather deal directly with her 'employer'. She very nearly began to foam at the mouth, but managed to control herself and reply that as far as she knew she had no employer. This was the first time, but not the last, that she would find it necessary to make this kind of statement. What annoyed her most of all was that these industrialists, two of whom were British, and the third Dutch, began talking directly to Polly, despite her statement, almost as though she were not in the room and had gone back to Australia. 'The next thing I know they'll be asking me to give the floor a wipe, or to dust the place, or serve them tea!' she thought.

In the end, her sense of humour prevailed. Instinct told her that she would learn more if she kept out of the discussions, and in fact she learned a great deal about the scale of her enterprises, for example. Until that moment she had simply established her salons and shops one by one in the cities that seemed to favour them, thinking of each as a separate operation. They were islands in her mind; if they formed an archipelago this was because the décor was always the same and because she was the sole proprietor, without anyone's financial support, without any loan. Certainly, on Polly's insistence, she had registered her trademarks and formulae, and her signature, but she had officially registered nothing more. Apart from Maryan, Polly and herself, no one knew exactly how many business concerns she operated. She had spread her bank accounts around, largely because of her distrust of bankers. She now had accounts in London and Cologne, in Paris and Zurich, in Vienna, Berlin, Brussels and Rome. She never dealt with two branches of the same bank, and insisted on numbered accounts whenever possible. Even Polly and Maryan would be incapable of calculating her holdings.

Each salon, and each shop, was totally independent of the others, even within a given town, save at the outset. In the early days, before and immediately after an opening, she would use the profits of one shop – that on the rue du Faubourg St-Honoré, for example – to finance the fitting-out of another. (In this case the Viennese shop on the Herrengasse.) As soon as the newly created shop was afloat, however, she cut all ties between the two. That was the end of it: once the loan advanced by its Parisian counterpart had been repaid, the shop in the Herrengasse had to stand on its own two feet. Generally she allowed it a year to do so.

As long as a business was in debt, all the figures relating to it would be written down in red in Hannah's little notebooks. She had a system of accounting that drove Polly almost to the brink of madness: she used sheep.

'In memory of Australia, Polly dearest.'

There were blue sheep for the beauty salons, purple sheep for the shops, green for the factory in Evreux, orange for the school for aestheticians, red for the training school for shop assistants, yellow for the collection and supply of plants and other base products, red-dotted sheep for the distribution network, and sheep with black and white squares for her bank accounts. 'Sheep with squares, sweet Jesus, Hannah,' Polly had exclaimed.

Naturally there was no question of referring to any one of her establishments other than by the number each sheep bore. To make things even less straightforward, she had not numbered her sheep from one to ten any more than she had put down a number that indicated how many beauty salons, or how many shops there were. Anyone at all could have spied on her that way. Instead she turned again to her beloved Choderlos de Laclos, to the 1841 edition of *Les Liaisons Dangereuses*. Accordingly, the shop in the rue

de Rivoli bore the number 186/4, because the fourth line on page
186 began with the letter R for Rivoli.

('Do you understand, Lizzie?'

'No!'

'But it seems childishly simple to me . . .'

*'Hannah, do you mean to say that you kept your accounts like that for
years on end?'*

*'Until the twenties, yes. It worked very well. No one else could
understand them.'*

'You surprise me!')

Hers were frizzy little sheep, to each of which she added a tail,
no less tightly curled, when the business each represented ceased
to be in debt and became profitable; she added one leg every time
this same business exceeded the one-thousand-pounds-a-year
profit line. (The sheep for the rue de Rivoli already balanced on
seven legs: those representing the beauty salon in St James's Place
held the record with eleven.)

'It's the most absurd accounting system anyone's ever likely to
see!' Polly had sniggered sarcastically. 'And what will you do when
you have to put seventy-five legs on each sheep? Let me tell you,
they look as much like sheep as I look like the Emperor of China.
On top of it all you draw terribly!'

'Your criticisms as regards pictorial art don't bother me in the
least,' Hannah replied. 'If it will make you any happier, I'll change
my sheep into porcupines. Which I'll call pollies, after you: one
polly, two pollies, three pollies. And I'll add needles as I go along.'

The industrialists who were so pointedly ignoring her at the Ritz
– and who knew nothing about her, or her sheep – suggested
forming an association. They were prepared to invest a tremendous
amount of capital. They had great plans, they were thinking of a
vast network, covering every town in Europe and marketing the
products created by Hannah's 'employer'. To these products they
would add perfumes. 'As if I hadn't thought of that, you fools!'
Hannah sneered under her breath . . .

With his usual quick-wittedness, Polly recognized her fury and
ran the meeting accordingly. He did his best to get the three men
to talk, in order to learn as much as possible about their plans. He
then assured them that their interesting proposition would be
referred to the proper quarters and that they would have a response
with the minimum delay.

The industrialists made a dignified exit.

'Hannah?'

'I shall never form a partnership with anybody.'

'You're going to run into them again sooner or later, I fear.'

'I'll give them a pasting. Too bad for them. No partners. On the other hand . . .'

She stood and began to walk around.

'Please don't get up Polly. Polly, I want to set up some new companies.'

'Like the ones in Australia?'

'Exactly. One for the salons, one for the shops, and so on.'

'Watertight compartments, like they now have in the Navy; I read about it in *The Times*. I understand.'

'I'm sure you do. Limited companies, if that's possible.'

'Certainly.'

'But of which I shall have sole control.'

'All right.'

'To which I shall sell my signature, in completely separate deals.'

He nodded.

'Could I see a detailed plan in June? On the fifteenth?'

'Earlier.'

'Do I pay you enough, Polly?'

'I think so. I'm intending to buy Buckingham Palace from Mrs Victoria one of these days. After that I shall acquire the Tower of London, where I could happily house my snuffbox collection. Hannah, when should I tell our friends the answer's no?'

'Keep them waiting as long as possible.'

'Raising their hopes of a positive reply?'

'Exactly.'

'Do you want me to check them out?'

'I've already checked them out. The two Scotsmen are of little importance. They have money but no ideas; they're simply bankers. I have a file on them.'

'And the third man?'

'Peter Van Eyckem, forty-six, born in Batavia, married with three children, the eldest a girl, aged eighteen – she looks like a cabbage painted pink. He has a mistress who's a dancer at the Théâtre de la Monnaie in Brussels. Name of the dancer: Mathilde Beylens. She's nineteen years seven months old, and five months pregnant, through the good offices of the aforementioned Van Eyckem – or so she claims, at least. The Van Eyckem family has considerable wealth, some of it in Indonesia, some in South Africa, most of it in gold mines and spices. Our man believes himself to be a business genius.'

'Is he?'

'More so than I would like, less so than he believes.'

'Could he cause you problems?'

She was not convinced he – or anyone else for that matter – could, however. And with good reason: she already had a ten year start on anyone else in the cosmeticology world.

The files on Ramsay and Ross, and the one on Van Eyckem, had been compiled, of course, by Maryan Kaden. By 1898 Maryan's full capabilities were very much in evidence: he had an extraordinarily analytical clear-thinking brain. He never said anything that he hadn't personally verified. He was free from any form of partiality. And he had an alarming memory. He asked Hannah for permission to employ three of his brothers on a permanent basis; he had already been using them as emissaries and agents. She readily agreed; she did not want Maryan himself to get bogged down in inferior tasks. He had ultimately dismissed one of his younger brothers, who was not capable enough, in his view; as for the other two, he had put one in charge of consignments going into and coming out of the factory in Evreux, the second he sent to London, at his own expense, to work as a messenger boy in the City, and to learn English and finance. Hannah suggested that she finance this training but Maryan calmly refused. He showed her his personal accounts ('I shall never hide anything from you, Hannah, never. And I shall look after my own affairs only in the free time that my work for you allows me . . .') which revealed he was in the process of making his fortune too, largely on the stock market.

At Hannah's request Maryan had organized a surveillance and intelligence-gathering group. With all the humour he possessed, he called these people the Ferrets. Originally, they were to keep an eye on the salons and shops, but as the months went by, their activities expanded. It was the Ferrets who compiled the dossiers on Ross, Ramsey and Van Eyckem in April 1898. And it was the Ferrets again who sounded the alarm in June. While Polly was doing his best to prevaricate, keeping the three men waiting for a reply from Hannah's supposed 'employer', the Ferrets revealed that Van Eyckem had gone to attack without waiting for their reply.

In secret.

*

In secret, but with considerable funding. He wasn't a man to be content with hiring or leasing; he bought. And he bought the best, such as premises in the Place Vendôme in Paris, where the prices had kept Hannah out. With the greatest discretion, he was in the process of establishing a foothold in all the commercial centres in Europe. When Maryan suggested a counterattack, she replied that for the time being the only solution was to sit back and keep a very close eye on Van Eyckem.

'Hannah, they're going to ruin you if you let them.'

'I know.'

She knew it only too well; but she did not immediately know how to fight against men who could draw on two or three hundred thousand pounds (at Polly's latest estimation) to tip the scales, not to mention the bank loans they might raise.

Maryan searched her face. And because he knew her so well, he asked: 'Have you got something in mind, Hannah?'

'No.'

This was almost true.

At the beginning of July, having hummed and hawed for as long as he possibly could, Polly Twhaites gave the supposed employer's reply, in the negative. He also allowed himself to make some revelations – to Ross and Ramsay alone – about the identity of the real owner of the chain's salons and shops: he was a certain prince whom he was not at liberty to name but who was directly descended from the late George III, and was therefore a first cousin of Her Majesty Queen Victoria.

Polly was of course only spreading lies Hannah had invented. She hoped this might be enough to drive the Scotsmen from the battlefield, and leave her to confront the Dutchman head on.

She never said this outright, and it was not really her chief preoccupation. She was simply advancing her first pawn, nothing more.

'And if our Dutch friend is as dishonest as I hope he is, Polly . . . Let's keep our fingers crossed, and pray.'

He replied that he had been praying since the day he met her in Melbourne. Praying furiously.

The summer and autumn of 1898 passed uneventfully. Maryan's reports and the reports of his Ferrets confirmed that Van Eyckem was pursuing his silent expansion. The most irritating thing was the strategy that he employed: the Dutchman was content to do nothing more than copy her success in every respect. Maryan was sulking; the Henry-Beatrice affair had done more than anything else to put him out of sorts. Why the devil had Hannah not tried to do anything to stop that bloody decorator from working for Van Eyckem? For it was Henry-Beatrice who was supervising the décor of the rival network throughout Europe.

'Hannah, he's betraying you, there's no other word for it! I thought he was supposed to be a friend!'

'He is my friend but he's a professional who needs money to survive. And with the crazy fees he's got out of Van Eyckem . . .'

As Hannah spoke these words a fierce gleam came into her eyes. Between Maryan and herself there would always be a great degree of understanding. He shifted his weight from one foot to the other, lowered his head, raised it, nodded.

'I think I understand what all this is leading up to,' he said finally.

Not another word was exchanged, but she knew he had indeed understood.

It was agreed: he was going to ask his Ferrets to increase their surveillance in a few key areas.

'As long as he does what you expect him to do, Hannah.'

Her grey eyes widened.

'He's going to, Maryan.'

She was quite sure of it now.

'My reasoning was very simple, Lizzie. At that point in my career the way to ruin me was to steal my ideas. I was bloody afraid that was what he was going to do. With the Scotsmen's backing, Van Eyckem had enough money to do just about anything. But he wanted everything, and he wanted it straightaway, and he did not want to take any risks. If he'd taken his time, not only to recruit chemists but also to let them work for two, three or four years, if he'd tried something new, I would have been finished. I would have been ruined, or at best forced to sell . . .

But thank God, he was dishonest and greedy, and impatient . . .

And by December 1898 I knew I had him.'

'Eleven girls in all,' reported Maryan on December 6th 1898. 'Two in Paris, three in London, the others in Berlin, Anvers, Prague and Zurich. Five are what you call aestheticians, six are sales assistants. He lured them all away in the same way: by offering a contract guaranteeing them double the salary you've been paying them. They've assembled in Lausanne, all expenses paid, and are working as instructors to another fifty girls.'

'Is Van Eyckem running this operation himself?'

'He's using his business agent, Wilfrid Meeus. I have a file on him.'

'What do they teach in Lausanne?'

'Everything. Everything you devised, word for word. I've copies of the texts they're using in class.'

'And how did you get hold of them?'

The ever-resourceful Maryan had arranged for one of his sisters to enrol as a student aesthetician.

'Oh, Maryan!'

He did not laugh; Van Eyckem's shameless plagiarism was in his eyes outright theft.

'He could of course choose a man to run the whole show, but until now he's copied you down to the last detail. So its logical to think that he'll want a woman. And women with experience don't come a dime a dozen. He'd have to . . .'

He broke off and stared at Hannah. Then he smiled.

'I understand,' he said. 'Unless we help him, is that it?'

'Precisely,' said Hannah.

They agreed on a name.

The scene took place several days later: Hannah had a messy argument with Jeanne Fougaril, director of operations in France. It was a violent scene – their arguments were already renowned, but this one went beyond the pale – and above all it was public: a number of employees and even a few clients were witnesses to it, in the rue de Rivoli. The reason for their quarrel: the Frenchwoman had opened a shop in Monte Carlo without consulting Hannah. Both women quickly reached a state of cold fury, and came close to physical violence, particularly after Jeanne threatened to take the matter to the 'real bosses' in London, and ask them to arbitrate.

Jeanne then travelled to the British capital, returning three days later with an impenetrable sulky expression on her face: obviously the 'real bosses' had decided in Hannah's favour.

And Jeanne refused to talk to her after that.

On January 7th 1899 she was discreetly approached by Wilfrid Meeus. (Hannah was in London at the time; her joyous reunion with Mendel had taken place three days before.)

Jeanne refused Meeus's initial offers. She admitted that she didn't get on at all with the 'little Polish bitch'. But she wasn't going to leave a job that brought in sixty-five thousand francs a month, not to mention her share of the profits. *Sixty-five thousand francs?* Meeus was horrified by the figure.

'What do you think, Mr Meeus? Without me, that business wouldn't last two months. It's simply recognition by London of how valuable I am . . .' She showed him the contracts she had made with Polly Twhaites, outlining the terms she had reported.

Meeus went away impressed. And he contacted her again on the 16th of the same month, the same day Mendel Visoker had left London and begun his search for Taddeuz.

Meeus came up with a new offer: sixty-five thousand francs a year, with a three-year contract, and two per cent of the profits. Jeanne refused again. She was not interested.

But if she were offered one hundred thousand a year, with a five-year contract, plus an additional payment of one hundred thousand francs by way of a transfer bonus, as it were . . .

She settled for eighty thousand francs a year for five years, plus the ex gratia payment, of which there was to be no record.

All on the condition that before making up her mind she could see for herself how serious the organization she was being asked to head was. The Dutchman agreed.

At the end of January she made a European tour of all the establishments Van Eyckem had been setting up with a view to a general opening in September 1899. She declared herself impressed by the overall sumptuousness of the enterprise (there was good reason for her to be impressed: Henry-Beatrice had involved the Dutchman in the most staggering expense) but she nevertheless pinpointed the weakness in the system.

'Congratulations on the salons and the shops, congratulations on the school in Lausanne, but what do you propose to sell?'

Van Eyckem's men finally told her what even Maryan Kaden's Ferrets had failed to find out: one factory was ready to start production at Breda in Holland, another was being built on the outskirts of Berne in Switzerland, and a dozen chemists were gathered in a laboratory in Strasbourg. They had already been at work for several months, and had managed to reproduce some creams that were in every respect identical to those . . .

Jeanne sneered. Was that all they were going to do: copy the original? They could, they must, do better. And she knew exactly how. Her mind was made up: she was going to change camps, and would hand in her notice to her present employer on 1 September. She would very much like to work with Mr Van Eyckem as director-general for Europe. And for only fifty thousand francs straightaway, she would tell him how to outclass all the beauty products currently on the market. If he considered her information as important as she thought he would, she would be paid another one hundred thousand francs.

'You'll pay me only if you are satisfied. That's an honest deal, don't you agree?'

The Dutchman agreed after some initial reservations. Fifty thousand francs discreetly changed hands on February 7th, the day after Hannah received Mendel's short letter from Warsaw.

Having pocketed the money, Jeanne talked. She revealed that the whole organization – supposedly run by the little Polish bitch, who, by the way, owed her position entirely to the fact that she was the mistress of one of the largest English shareholders – rested on the work of a laboratory headed by one Juliette Mann.

'I know that you know that, Mr Van Eyckem and Mr Meeus. Just as you know that it's impossible to buy Mrs Mann. But what you don't know, on the other hand, is that Juliette Mann herself is – how shall I put it? – nothing but a front. All the products have in fact been developed by a Russian chemist who's a real genius. She remains in hiding because she was an anarchist three or four years ago; the poor young woman lives in dread of being arrested. As a matter of fact that is how the little Polish bitch and Juliette Mann maintain their hold on her: through shameful blackmail. With the Russian woman, it wouldn't even be a question of money. You would simply need to win her trust – which might be difficult; she's been living for so long as an outlaw that she is a nervous wreck – and above all, help her to make a new life for herself. I know her a bit. I can put you in touch with her. If she answers your prayers, and I think she will, you'll pay me the balance . . .'

The name of the ex-anarchist: Tatiana Popinski.

She looked like a bulging tobacco jar. On her head she wore a thick woollen *babouchka* from which escaped some not very clean strands of hair. She had a greasy, fairly repulsive-looking face that seemed to be covered in pustules. She wore enormous glasses, with wooden frames she had apparently fabricated herself. She expressed herself in a dreadful pidgin mixture of Russian, German and French, constantly rolling her eyes in panic as though the Tsarist police might at any moment come bursting in. She arrived in Strasbourg for a visit to the laboratory, taking the kind of elaborate travel precautions a hunted spy would resort to. The Dutchmen's first impression of Tatiana Popinski was not enthusiastic. But beneath her outward appearance as a fanatical bomb-manufacturer, her dexterity in wielding the tools of cosmeticology was seen to be quite exceptional, out of the ordinary. Before the very eyes of Van Eyckem's dumbfounded chemists, she sniffed at each of the creams they had manufactured and correctly identified the most minute trace of each ingredient, amending their mistakes.

'This needs comfrey and fenugreek . . . This one has too much hawthorn and not enough horsetail . . . Do you think you can cure acne with this muck? What do you know about acne, you miserable *dourak?* Do you know how many different types of acne there are? *You don't know?* You don't know that acne can be hepatic, intestinal, gastric or nervous, and yet you think you can cure it? But what kind of moron are you?'

Within a few hours she had established herself as an unbalanced cosmeticologist, irascible and obsessed with the idea of her imminent arrest, to the point that any strange face terrorized her . . .

She was indisputably a genius, however. She locked herself in a room in the laboratory in Strasbourg and after forty hours' uninterrupted work, produced a new beauty cream that the chemists in Alsace agreed was truly remarkable. Van Eyckem insisted on seeing her in person. He entered the laboratory, all smiles. He was thrown out to the accompaniment of an explosive torrent of shrill abuse, uttered in an almost unintelligible gibberish. He was delighted by it. This was indeed the genius Jeanne had heralded.

He felt even more triumphant by mid-April of 1899, at which time Maryan Kaden was on site in Vienna, preparing for the opening of the salon in Reichsratstrasse; Hannah had just joined him there, having received no further news from Mendel on his quest for Taddeuz other than the short letter the drayman had posted in Nice, in which he mentioned his meeting with 'the Rebecca from Dobbe's'.

At the end of the month Van Eyckem learned that the crazy but inspired Russian cosmeticologist had perfected five completely new creams, different from anything else on the market, two beauty lotions, and most important of all, something quite extraordinary.

'You could call them "beauty masks",' explained Wilfrid Meeus.

'Any woman who kept one on her face long enough would shed ten or fifteen years off her real age. Mr Van Eyckem, this lunatic is worth her weight in gold. We could revolutionize the world, and make thousands of millions . . .'

Van Eyckem welcomed the news all the more enthusiastically since he had just suffered a major setback in London, where he learned that his Scottish partners were pulling out on him. With some coldness they explained they had found a better investment for their capital: they were putting money into another very interesting enterprise that was solid and already well established. Their new partner was a fine fellow from Melbourne. He was of French origin and his name was Jean-François Fournac.

'The two things happened simultaneously, Lizzie. Though not by chance, of course. I wanted to prevent Van Eyckem looking for other partners, over whom I would have no control, when the Scotsmen defected. He had to carry on alone. Hence, the simultaneous announcement of Tatiana Popinski's inventions: Van Eyckem saw in them the possibility of a fantastic success. Why should he share his guaranteed millions?

That's how I snared him.'

In the dreadful non-language that she spoke, Tatiana told Meeus her terms; before giving them the formula for her inventions, she wanted a German passport that would pass as genuine, and that would allow her to change her identity once and for all. And she did not want anyone trying to fool her; as a former anarchist, she could judge the quality of false papers! She also wanted ten thousand pounds in a London bank, as well as a passage booked to New York, where she would at last go and pay a visit to her ailing mother whom she had not seen since she was seven years old. Then she would return to Europe and create all the products they wanted.

The ten thousand pounds (this seemed rather a modest sum to them) and the boat ticket presented little difficulty to the Dutchman, although Van Eyckem was beginning to reach his limit, financially speaking, as the Scotsmen's withdrawal had halved his resources. The passport, on the other hand, presented more of a problem. This passport was to be used by someone who was destined to work for them for many years to come. A poorly documented assumed identity could put them in a very delicate position indeed.

But they would do their best.

On May 4th one of Maryan Kaden's Ferrets – a younger brother and the only one with a sense of humour – sent word: '*A German passport in the name of Augusta Schlegel, born 16 February 1869, has just been issued in Königsberg with the connivance of a man named Anton Gerber, employee of the registry office in this town. Gerber received three thousand marks. The money was paid to him by Wilfrid Meeus. Attached is the list of witnesses who can be called upon to give evidence. The real Augusta Schlegel died of smallpox on 3 March 1876. Attached is her death certificate, made out before the fire – intentionally started by Meeus – at the registry office. Also attached is a list of those who can be called upon as having witnessed this intentional fire.*'

The false passport was handed over to Tatiana Popinski by Meeus six days later. In exchange he was given the complete formulae, authenticated by a chemist from Strasbourg, of her 'inventions'. Their last meeting took place in the porchway of a building in Clos Fauquière, in Paris's 15th Arrondissement, then the haunt of Russian émigrés. It was a very short meeting; the former anarchist seemed more terrified than ever, and her jargon was almost incomprehensible.

On May 17th, one week later, a singularly nervous Jeanne Fougaril announced to Wilfrid Meeus that she had given up the idea of becoming the future director-general of the Van Eyckem organization, although it was now only four months before their launch.

'There are rumours circulating about Tatiana Popinski that worry me terribly . . .'

'Rumours? What rumours?'

She refused to say more, but returned one hundred of the one hundred and fifty thousand francs that she had been paid under the table, and swore that she would return the rest. She then literally ran off.

Meeus hardly had time to inform his employer of this development. For the same day, Paul Twhaites turned up in Van Eyckem's office in The Hague and closeted himself with Meeus's boss.

Polly was speechless with indignation and anger. But for his natural inclination to favour compromise, he would have already acted on the instructions of his principals, who wanted to cry vengeance in the courts. The facts were clear: a burglary had taken place a few months earlier at 6 rue Vercingétorix, and had been reported at the time to the police; some secret formulae for products created by Mrs Mann's laboratory had been stolen.

'We don't know yet the identity of a certain chemist taken on by a laboratory in Strasbourg, but this honest fellow was horrified to discover that he was party to a misappropriation. He has made a formal declaration to the effect that the products you were planning to manufacture in your factory in Breda entirely owe their existence to the theft committed on the rue Vercingétorix.

'And that's not all. A certain Tatiana Popinski formerly worked with Mrs Mann. She's disappeared, and certain other formulae have disappeared along with her. Add to this the fact that an anonymous letter has been sent to us, alleging that your principal colleague Wilfrid Meeus sent the said Tatiana Popinski to the United States with ten thousand pounds in sterling – a payment, the letter claims, for the robbery she was asked to commit. Even more damning, your friend Meeus arranged for the wretched girl to travel under a false identity, that of one Augusta Schlegel, born in Königsberg, in Eastern Prussia. I've checked this out: the real Augusta Schlegel died more than twenty years ago. A death certificate was enclosed with the anonymous letter. Here is a certified copy of the original. Would you like other facts, Mr Van Eyckem? Three French citizens of Russian origin are prepared to swear that they witnessed Wilfrid Meeus handing over a false passport and a boat ticket to the so-called Augusta Schlegel. Furthermore, we have tracked her down in New York; she has made a deposition before a judge, and I present you with a copy. She states that she had no understanding of what you and Meeus were up to. It would be reasonable to suppose that you and your accomplice used this unfortunate girl to cover up the thefts you'd committed . . .'

At this point in the prosecution's summing-up, Van Eyckem attempted to defend himself. Supposing – only supposing, mind you – that he had paid any money at all to Tatiana Popinski, it would have been because she was a chemist and a brilliant cosmeticologist and he had bought from her some rather useful . . .

Polly Twhaites raised an eyebrow.

'What kind of distasteful joke is this, Van Eyckem? Tatiana Popinski, the girl who worked in Mrs Mann's laboratory, was employed as a cleaning lady. And with good reason: she is completely illiterate and would not be able to distinguish a chemical formula from a gas bill!'

Robbery, conspiracy to rob, several offences against the laws of
industrial property, issuing a false passport, forgery and use of
forgeries – the list of Van Eyckem's offences was long. Particularly
as in addition to all the witnesses already cited there were two
more who carried considerable weight: the Scotsmen Ramsay and
Ross. These men of unimpeachable honour – there was some talk
of Ross being knighted by Her Majesty – had revealed to Polly that
if they had terminated their association with the Dutchman it was
largely because of their doubts about his moral principles, following
a number of very distasteful rumours that had come their way.

'And there's also this letter that you sent to Mrs Jeanne Fougaril,
promising to employ her from next September onward for a salary
three, indeed four, times as high as we're paying her now. Mrs
Fougaril, thank God, is probity itself: she informed me of your
ignominious offer. Mr Van Eyckem, you risk going to prison. The
clients I represent have contacts in almost every government in
Europe. Should you doubt this, you can ask Ramsay and Ross. At
best, you would be professionally and socially ruined. But as I've
already said: I'm a man who favours compromise . . .'

In short, Polly could pacify his clients if Van Eyckem agreed to
give them a ten-year lease on his two factories and on most of his
buildings . . .

And if he returned to Batavia in the Dutch East Indies, which he
should never have left, in Polly's humble opinion.

'And did he go away, Hannah?'

*'Yes. When darling Polly gave him proof that he wasn't bluffing. And
when he learned from Ramsay and Ross the supposed identities of the
"real bosses". The prospect of taking on all the noble and royal houses of
Europe made him lose heart; it would have made me lose heart too.'*

'Hannah?'

'Yes, Lizzie?'

'Do Tatiana Popinski for me again.'

*'The hell I will! I've just done it for you. We're not going to spend all
day . . .'*

'It's surprising that Van Eyckem didn't recognize you.'

*'He hardly looked at me, at the Ritz. And he hardly saw me in
Strasbourg. Anyway, I was wearing one eiderdown down my front and
another down my back. And then there was the hair, the glasses and the
grease on my face. It was mixed with blackberry pips – I looked disgusting.'*

'And what became of the real Tatiana Popinski?'

'She'd always dreamed of emigrating to America. I paid her husband's passage and her children's. She didn't have any idea what it was all about but she did everything I told her to. The last time I heard from her was in 1949. One of her grandsons had just received his diploma from the naval school in Annapolis. She was wild with joy. She still had not learned how to write but was still living off Van Eyckem's ten thousand pounds, which Polly had judiciously invested on her behalf.'

Silence.

'Hannah?'

'Yes, Lizzie?'

'If you think about it, you pulled off one hell of a swindle really.'

'Thank you. The worse thing about it, as far as Van Eyckem was concerned, was that he should have been swindled by women. In the nineteenth century no less!'

Silence. The setting sun was reflected in the still waters that stretched out before the two old ladies.

'How long did your battle with Van Eyckem go on?'

'Thirteen months. From April 1898 to May 1899.'

'And you still had no news from Mendel, and so no news of Taddeuz?'

'Not a word. It was nearly the end of May and after that letter he sent from Nice, Mendel hadn't shown any further sign of life.'

'A worry, eh?'

'A worry, Lizzie. A dreadful worry. I would have given my right hand to know where Mendel was . . .'

24

I WOULDN'T HAVE LOVED
JUST ANYBODY

A little Italian with the heavy moustaches of the Carbonari stood before Mendel. He was waving his short arms and chattering away energetically, obviously proposing the sale of some service in exchange for money.

'I don't understand a single word you're saying,' lied Mendel with great amiability in French.

He was behaving quite agreeably as a matter of fact. Taking hold of the Italian under the armpits he raised him almost a metre off the ground, then put him down behind him and continued on his way. The black eyes that attracted interested looks from women wherever he went were fixed on a group of four people walking about eighty metres ahead of him, along an old street in Rome, near the Piazza Navone. The group consisted of two young men and two charming young girls in light summer frocks and straw hats trimmed with long ribbons. Mendel did not know who the young ladies were; judging by their feet he would have said they were English. He had heard them speaking English with a fairly nasal accent, however, and he had had a glimpse of their wide smiles, so he was beginning to think they must be American. One thing was certain: they were rich. The palazzo they had emerged from two hours before, with its clear view over the Pincio Gardens, was not the kind of place where you lived if you were poor. Mendel had seen two of those damned horseless carriages there, all made of metal, and very smelly – he would prefer a good *brouski* any day. He had been afraid the young ladies might climb in and make their escorts jump in as well, in which case he would have looked pretty foolish chasing after the vehicle on foot . . .

As for the two young men, he knew exactly who they were. He had been following them now for twenty-three days without once letting himself be seen. And without ever being able to take a break from following them: those bastards were constantly on the move, they had not once stayed more than two days in the same place. He began to wonder if they were not doing so deliberately, just to annoy him.

He had picked up their trail at the beginning of May, when he had found out – from a maître d'hôtel in Monte Carlo who had overheard a conversation in German – that they were going to Genoa. As they had only one day's start on him, he had managed to catch up with them fairly easily. From that moment on, he had not let them out of his sight: he had travelled all over Italy on their heels. They had dragged him down to Naples, to Capri and other sunny places (it was hellishly hot and all things considered, Mendel would have almost preferred the coolness of Siberia); they stopped in God knows how many little inns. They obviously did not have much money, although this was not impeding their nomadism. With perfect nonchalance, they had now returned to Rome, where they had been for three days.

And they had already warned their hotel-keeper in Trastevere that they would not be staying more than a week.

One of the two young men was of course Taddeuz Nenski, who scarcely looked his age, which was twenty-seven. In fact he looked younger than his companion, who, according to enquiries Mendel had made, was just twenty-four.

Mendel knew little about this companion of Nenski's: he was German, knew French, and regularly gave a Paris address in the inns in which they stayed. His name meant nothing to Visoker.

Who the devil had ever heard of Rainer Maria Rilke?

He could not kid himself; part of him really hoped that those two snuggled up in bed together. It would have been damned mortifying for Hannah, but it would have suited him perfectly had Taddeuz turned out to be a homosexual. He felt ashamed of hoping that might be the case, but in any event he was soon disappointed: there was no doubt the two liked women, especially the Polish fellow. Worst of all, he had quite a way with the ladies. In Sorrento, in no time at all, he had had that very beautiful young woman who lived in that no less beautiful villa ripe for the plucking. If it hadn't been for Rilke, who was beginning to fret, he would probably still be in the lady's bed. In Genoa and Florence it was the same. The Pole paid for a hotel room for nothing; two brunettes kept him from ever seeing it. Mendel had to admit, much as it annoyed him, that the boy had almost the same aptitude for womanizing as he did. And he was bloody good-looking on top of it all.

It was this admission – which came to Mendel in Genoa, when he set eyes upon Taddeuz for the first time – that galled him the most. He had hoped that Hannah had overrated her student, idealized him, because she had been looking at him through the eyes of a childhood love. And even that was a matter for debate, he told himself. She was completely infatuated with him, and had been ever since she was seven. She had never got over the wonder she felt then, and she had made up her mind to have him, with that incredible determination she put into everything she did. All of which went to show, as far as he was concerned, that you can be the most intelligent woman in the world and at the same time be as stupid as a chair . . .

The boy was bloody good looking. For twenty-three days these words had been preying on Mendel's mind, he had been muttering them to himself in fury. Taddeuz was not only good-looking, he was elegant. Watching him for three weeks, Mendel had had plenty of time to examine the boy closely. He had even observed the student naked, as he bathed with his German friend and two rather pretty girls in no less a state of undress in Anacapri, below the Castello di Barbarossa. And there was nothing at all objectionable about his looks.

Mendel had other doubts about the Pole, however. Anyone as handsome as that fellow must be stupid, self-important, extremely pleased with himself, a hopeless moron. And then there was the matter of the book, which had led him to Taddeuz in the first place.

He had begun his search in January, with a visit to Maryan Kaden in Prague. The boy had changed dramatically, but the friendship that the two men had felt for each other during that long ride through Warsaw on the night of Pinchos Klotz's death revived the moment they set eyes on each other. Mendel and Maryan picked up where they had left off, perhaps because of their mutual affection for Hannah, perhaps because they realized there was a great deal of similarity between them, as though they were father and son in a way. Maryan had given Mendel a rundown on his investigations to date and Mendel had taken over from there. He had gone to Warsaw, where he picked up a lead that dated back to the time of his own arrest, but which was too old to be of any use. He found nothing in Hannah's *shtetl* and nothing in the neighbouring Catholic village either. But Maryan's idea of scouring bookshops gave Mendel another; Hannah had said that Taddeuz was going to become a writer and even though he had decided as much when he was seven years old it seemed within the realm of possibility . . .

So he visited the publishers, one by one, a complicated enterprise since Taddeuz could have had himself published in Polish, Russian, German, or French. Who could tell which language he might write in, or what name he might decide to publish under? It seemed likely that he would have changed his name, if only to avoid the repercussions of the Dobbe Klotz affair.

Three months later, in Munich, Mendel found a small publisher who had brought out a thin volume by an unusually handsome, fair-haired young man who had said his name was Terence Newman. Had the author given the address of a bank to which his royalties could be paid?

The publisher laughed derisively. Terence Newman's poems, written in German, had sold even fewer copies than those of the other dreamers whose work he had been crazy enough to publish.

'I printed three hundred copies of his book and to this day, three years later, I've sold nine.'

'I'll take ten,' replied Mendel. 'Your sales have doubled in one fell swoop. Now, did this Terence Newman, who signs himself Thomas Nemo, say much about himself?'

Terence-Thomas-Taddeuz Newman-Nemo-Nenski had given his publisher only to understand that he lived in America and visited Europe occasionally . . .

'Where in America?'

'New York, I believe.'

The young man had been quite elegantly dressed; he seemed well off financially and had stayed at one of the best hotels in Munich . . .

'When was he here?'

'August '96.'

'Did he look as though he was married?'

'How could anyone tell?'

'Are his poems any good?'

Taddeuz's publisher gave Mendel a deeply offended look. He only published books of distinction, which explained why he was on the verge of bankruptcy, and Newman's volume happened to be among those he was most proud of having published.

'The boy has talent and personality. I'd swear to his having a future as a writer . . .'

'As usual, the kid was right,' thought Mendel, despondently. 'Shit!'

The Bank of Nice had never received any money other than the first ten francs with which the account was opened. However, Mendel was directed to the Hôtel de Paris in Monte Carlo. 'Mr Newman has spoken of it,' he was told.

Mendel went to the hotel: no Terence Newman had ever stayed there.

Nor had anyone called Nemo or Nenski.

It was April by then, about the 15th. Mendel began to make the rounds of all the hotels in Monte Carlo, ultimately along the entire Côte d'Azur; most of them were closed. He knocked at the door of every house that had been bought or rented by Americans. For the most part he had little response; they were empty at that time of year. Several weeks later, in Cannes, he passed in the street a strikingly beautiful young woman, radiant in her furs, and at the moment deep in conversation with her uniformed chauffeur. Her face reminded him of someone. It took him three days to put a name to it: Rebecca Anielowicz, the Rebecca who used to work at Dobbe Klotz's. He eventually tracked down her magnificent property, situated on the heights above Cap Ferrat, but Mrs Singer, of New York's Park Avenue, had just sailed for Greece on her husband's yacht with some friends. And there was no tall, fair-haired young man among the party . . .

For want of anything better to do, Mendel returned to the Hôtel de Paris. After all, the clerk at the Bank of Nice had sworn that 'Mr Newman' often stayed there when he was in Europe. Mendel again checked with all the hotel staff, one by one. This took him two days, because of the hotel's shift system. Finally he met with success: one of the waiters was a young Swiss from Lugano, who knew a Newman who answered to Mendel's description.

'But his first name isn't Terence . . .'

'Thomas? Taddeuz?'

Yes, that was it, Taddeuz. He was not a guest at the hotel, but he would often enough come to drink at the bar. In fact he stopped in whenever he was in Monte Carlo, usually with a woman or two but rarely – here the Swiss smiled politely – with the same one.

It seemed 'Newman' visited Monte Carlo whenever his employer came to stay at his villa, the Beausoleil. His employer? An American by the name of John D. Markham, a very wealthy man who evidently had been the United States Ambassador in St Petersburg. Newman had been his secretary for some time.

'And is Taddeuz Newman here at the moment?'

'You're out of luck, sir. As a matter of fact he left yesterday, on a trip to Italy. I heard him say he and his friend Mr Rilke, secretary to Rodin, you know, were going to visit some musician or other . . .'

In Rome the four young friends had just entered an antiques shop in the Via dei Coronari. Mendel leaned against the façade of Santa Maria della Pace. For the last time he took out of his pocket the little volume of poems published in Munich under the name of Thomas Nemo. He had read and reread these thirty-two pages, always with the same consternation. The boy had a strange, irregular way of writing verses; quite simply, they did not rhyme.

'It's free verse,' Taddeuz's publisher had explained impatiently, as if he were offering a recipe to cannibals. 'Are you familiar with Jules Laforgue? With Wedekind? You do know how to read, don't you? Of course it's not like Dumas or Paul Féval. But it is literature and literature of the best kind; literature of our day. The boy belongs, if you like, to the Expressionist school of writing. The primal scream, the *Urschrei*, you understand? No, obviously you don't understand . . .'

Mendel almost laid him out cold.

Taddeuz and his friends emerged from the antiques shop. For the next two hours they walked all over Rome, stopping here and there, then moving on, stopping again to go into raptures over some shop window or another. Mendel followed after them, kicking his heels. He hated walking around towns. They finally returned to the Pincio Gardens from which they did not emerge for the rest of the night; evidently the two birds had invited

Taddeuz and Rainer in. Fine morals they had. That should please his Hannah!

Mendel spent the night in the bed of a Roman woman he met late in the night, then spent the next day walking the length and breadth of the Eternal City again, trailing the foursome. On two or three occasions, he noticed Taddeuz's demonstrations of affection for the prettier of the young girls. Her name was Mary-Jane Gallagher and he had discovered her to be the daughter of a moneyed industrialist from Chicago. There was quite obviously some prospect of a marriage between them as the two were behaving like a formally engaged couple.

Three days later, however, the couples split up. Taddeuz and his German friend caught the train back to France, their vacation over. And in Nice the two young men took leave of each other. Mendel followed the Pole to Monte Carlo, where he himself met a lady who had shared her bed with him on his previous visit, and where he completed his enquiries about John D. Markham and his future itinerary. The ambassador, now retired, was apparently writing his memoirs about the Russian Imperial Court. He would not be arriving in Europe for several days; Taddeuz was to wait for him in Monte Carlo.

At that point, Mendel could easily have returned to Vienna. But he wanted to be very, very sure. He stayed on for nearly another week, waiting for the right moment. His chance came when Taddeuz went to Nice, in a horseless carriage that he drove himself; there seemed to be nothing this boy could not do. Fortunately, Taddeuz had told the chambermaids at the Villa Beausoleil of his intentions, and one of them happened to find Mendel very much to her taste.

In Nice the Pole spent a full day in the library, slept at a little hotel in the port, and the next morning wandered as nonchalantly as ever around the city's flower market.

It was there that Mendel accosted him, planting himself in front of the boy and pretending that he wanted to buy a bunch of carnations but could express himself only in Russian.

They spoke together.

Five days later, Mendel was back in Vienna.

'I don't understand what's going on at all,' Maryan said to him. 'She's become . . .'

'Crazy. But she's always been crazy, so what's new?'

'. . . become strange. For a start, she's always on my back. Usually she lets me get on with my work in peace, she trusts me. But now, ever since we've been in Vienna, not only will she not let me leave to get on with things but she won't leave herself. If she does go away, as she has had to, it's only for two or three days at a time, and she comes straight back. And every time she returns, she's like an eagle diving on its prey. On me, that is.'

Mendel laughed.

'I wouldn't mention it to anyone but you, of course,' Maryan went on. 'But the truth is that it worries me. I wonder what's got into her. She's been having problems with a Dutchman, but that's not the real reason. That problem's almost completely settled, in any event. No, it's something else that's making her behave oddly. She's put back the date of the opening again, even though everything is ready. A team of aestheticians has arrived from Paris and trained the girls here; we've never been so well prepared, and I don't understand why: Vienna is no more important than Berlin. But in Berlin she let me have a free hand, she hardly even bothered to come and take a look around.'

Mendel studied the young man's face. And it suddenly dawned on him.

'What's she called, Maryan?' he asked.

'Hannah?'

'Don't act stupid.'

He shifted his weight from one foot to the other, then said: 'Griselda.'

And Maryan began to recount how, without really intending to, he had seduced Hannah's Austrian secretary, a sweet, shy blonde girl. In fact, he was a bit worried he had got her into a bad way . . .

'I don't believe it!' thought Mendel. 'She's even managed to make a man of him! What an infernal brat she is!'

Maryan talked and talked and talked, about Grinzing and its dance halls, about dancing, and speaking of which . . .

Mendel gave a start.

'Hannah's what?'

'She's learning to dance. Thanks to a very famous Viennese musician called Johann Strauss, she's taking lessons from the Master of Ceremonies at the Hofburg – the Hofburg is the Emperor's palace, you know.'

*

There were three bankers and as many businessmen in Hannah's office in her apartment near the Bohemian Chancellery. As would always be her practice, she asked the men to sit down while she remained standing, walking about and sometimes even planting herself behind them, her pale eyes studying the backs of their necks. She smiled at Mendel and asked him to sit down, to stay for the meeting. He did so and for the next two hours listened while, sometimes in English, sometimes in French or German, she gave orders, asked for clarifications, corrected a mistake or even – as she did on one occasion that day – smiled with a frosty look in her eyes and said: 'I think you ought to give that more thought . . .' Roughly translated this meant: 'Go on refusing to give me what I'm asking for, I'll sink my teeth into your throat and suck every last drop of blood out of you . . .'

She was already worth between one hundred and twenty and one hundred and thirty thousand pounds, and at the rate things were going she would be worth three or four times that within five years.

The men left.

Her grey eyes plumbed Mendel's. Suddenly she turned away and as if in a trance clutched hold of one of the braided curtain loops.

'Where is he, Mendel?'

'Monte Carlo. He'll be there until the end of August.'

'Is he well?'

'Yes.'

'Married?'

'No.'

She noticed, of course, the very slight hesitation in his voice.

'He's getting married?'

'If you let him. To an American by the name of Mary-Jane Gallagher.'

'Rich?'

'Very rich.'

He began to give her a nearly complete report. She resumed her place behind her desk and did not once interrupt him, remaining still and impassive, her delicate white hands resting calmly on the desk top. Mendel told her that he had managed to piece together Taddeuz's whole itinerary since the day Dobbe Klotz ran him out of Warsaw and he went to Paris. In the French capital the Polish student had found work in a restaurant near the Opera, as a washer-up at first and then fairly soon afterwards, because of his appearance, as a waiter. He worked there for several months before earning enough money to return to Poland . . .

'To Warsaw?'

'Yes.'

'That was foolish. The police were looking for him.'

'Apparently that didn't worry him.'

'When was that?'

'June. You weren't there any more. You'd already set sail from Danzig.'

'Why did he go back?'

'No idea.'

'*Mendel.*'

But Mendel said again: 'No idea, Hannah.'

With a toss of her head, she said: 'Go on, please.'

Taddeuz had not stayed long in Warsaw, perhaps on account of the police. He had returned to Paris and to his job, until the day when he heard a man at a table he was serving say that he was looking for a secretary who spoke Russian and French and was capable of writing in both languages. Taddeuz, who was not usually so forward, took his courage in both hands . . .

'How do you know all this?'

'No suspiciousness, please, Hannah. I went to the restaurant. And I went there because when Taddeuz returned to Warsaw in June of 1892, he mentioned it to one of his university friends.'

'That sounds plausible.'

'You can say that again. May I continue, you little brat?'

'You may, my dearest Mendel.'

. . . and introduced himself. He was hired a few days later by John D. Markham, millionaire and personal friend of President Cleveland, who had twice been elected to the White House. Markham had just been appointed Ambassador to St Petersburg. The Polish student travelled with him first to the United States, where he became a naturalized American citizen under the name of Newman; probably, Mendel speculated, because of the Russian police . . .

'He's now an American, Hannah.'

'I don't give a damn,' she said.

He then spent three years at the Russian court and returned to America in March 1896.

At that point Cleveland left the White House to be replaced by MacKinley, and old Markham, who was over seventy, decided to

retire and write his memoirs. Taddeuz had remained with him,
living most of the time in New York and Virginia and travelling
about Europe. He had met Rainer Maria Rilke at Auguste Rodin's
house, when Markham had stopped in to buy a sculpture . . .

'After that came the trip to Italy. Now you know everything . . .
Hannah, Maryan told me about a Dutchman you were apparently
having some trouble with?'

'Those problems are settled now, we can forget them. Do you
have Taddeuz's poems?'

'I took ten copies.'

'You might have bought them all.'

'You can do that yourself. Hannah, the Markham family and the
Gallaghers are very close. Mary-Jane stayed at Villa Beausoleil last
summer.'

'Pretty?'

'Not bad, yes.'

'A brunette?'

'Blonde. A kind of ash blond, hazel eyes.'

'Tall.'

'Fairly.'

He anticipated the next question, which he read in Hannah's
eyes.

'Hannah, she's as different from you as anyone could be. She's
nearly twenty centimetres taller than you, she goes into raptures
and squeals over furs and flowers, she has to be helped out of a
carriage or up a staircase. She can't have any idea whether a loaf
of bread costs a penny or five pounds.'

'Does she play a musical instrument?'

'The piano.'

'I tried,' said Hannah calmly. 'Debussy showed me. Then I had a
teacher. I got nowhere. Absolutely nowhere. Can she drive a
horseless carriage, like Taddeuz?'

'Yes.'

Hannah finally stirred.

'I'm going to buy myself one and learn. What else can she do
that I can't?'

'There are a thousand million things you can do that she doesn't
know the first thing about. And . . .'

Suddenly Mendel began to worry about just that; the alarming
number of things she could do that other women could not, her
awesome personality, the way she dominated people. She had

even managed to make sure that poor devil Maryan lost his virginity! Mary-Jane Gallagher was just an ordinary rich girl, the kind a man could marry without worrying, without too much fear of being eaten alive . . .

'Well, Hannah,' said Mendel sadly, 'are you going to have him come to Vienna or pretend to meet him by chance at the Hôtel de Paris in Monte Carlo, with a full moon to order?'

'Vienna.'

'You've damned well prepared everything, haven't you?'

'Everything.'

'And what if I hadn't found him?'

She smiled. And the drayman recognized the expression he had seen on her face fifteen years earlier, when he had asked the seven-year-old kid a question that was really too naïve for words. That look reminded him that she had always been old and wise, always well informed about life.

'And what story did you tell him about yourself, Mendel?' she asked suddenly.

'Where did you get the idea that I spoke to him?'

She shook her head, eyeing him disapprovingly for having told such an obvious lie.

'You must have spoken to him, Mendel. You followed him for more than a month. In the end, you had to have spoken to him; if nothing else, you would have wanted to know what was going on in his mind.'

Silence.

'I think I'll leave for America tomorrow,' said Mendel coldly. 'I've delayed long enough.'

'I'm sorry, Mendel.'

'Go to hell.'

'I'm going to marry him on December 30th of this year. Here in Vienna. We'll dance together on the first day of the new year and the new century. Then we'll go away on our honeymoon together. To Italy. I've rented a house there, while I was supposed to be in Switzerland. Everything's arranged.'

'Congratulations,' said Mendel. She made him feel like weeping, which was something even the Siberians had never managed to do.

'Mendel, I owe you more than any other man or woman I shall ever know. Don't leave feeling angry with me, please . . .'

She did not simper, she did not act the little girl. She spoke to him calmly, almost man to man. Eventually he decided to look her in the face. She was sitting upright behind her desk, looking tiny with her big owl-like eyes. It was too much for him, far too much. Even if he had wanted to he would not have been able to wipe from his memory the thousands of images he had of her, beginning with that first time when he had come upon her dancing her waltz of death in the midst of the blaze, when she had emerged from the smoke and the flames. Then there were those regular visits to her *shtetl*, as he watched her gain in intelligence and maturity, and beauty. And taking her on his *brouski* to Warsaw, always looking after her, marvelling at her progress even while he expected it, because he had always known that she was exceptional. Even after that, when he had more than risked his life for her and been sent to hell for it, when she was on the other side of the world, the understanding between them had never been lost. Without those bloody wonderful letters she had sent him from Australia, he would probably have given up and died. Then there were her crazy ploys to get him out of Siberia. When she met him again, she had wanted to give him half her fortune and she actually thought he would accept it; what man, be he father or brother, would have demonstrated loyalty such as the kid had shown him?

He knew he adored her, that she was the only woman he had ever known who had got through his loneliness, the loneliness of a wanderer. And he knew no acrimony or rage, or jealousy on his part was going to weaken for one minute her obsession with that Pole. Certainly he was worried about what she would do to Taddeuz: he sensed it was bound to end in disaster between them, especially because after all the hours the two had spent talking together in the flower market in Nice, he had a very good idea of what was going on in Taddeuz's mind. He could be wrong however, and whether he was or not he did know he could not leave feeling angry with her . . .

He walked over to her and took her in his arms. She kissed him, full on the lips, with her mouth open. He returned her kiss, put her down and said:

'He's quite amazing, Hannah. Really. More than that. I would never have been able to find you anyone like him, even if I'd scoured the world for a hundred years. He's damned intelligent. Perhaps even more than you are, in a way.'

She closed her eyes and smiled triumphantly.

'I know, Mendel. I wouldn't have loved just anybody.'

25

---◆---

AUTUMN IN THE PRATER

When Lizzie came to join her in Vienna towards the middle of July, 1899, she reported only that Mendel had gone to America, and she shared with her the results of the drayman's enquiries. But she said nothing, or very little, about her own preparations. Nor did she mention the Van Eyckem affair at the time, although it came to a conclusive end in August when the Dutchman set sail from Rotterdam for the distant Dutch East Indies. She would never really speak of the whole business, of the calculations she had made and of her anxiety during that period, until many years later, when they were both very old, and the difference in their ages had long since become negligible.

The Lizzie who stepped off the Orient Express in Vienna, arriving from London for the last summer of the nineteenth century, was gaiety itself. She had fulfilled all her promises to Hannah. Now aged seventeen, she had brilliantly completed her studies; she was staggering under the weight of her diplomas, of which she had a whole suitcase full. She had acquired an exhaustive knowledge of everything a well-bred young girl was supposed to know: she knew seventy-eight different ways of opening a letter, a bit of spelling, Latin and Greek, a minimum of arithmetic, and a fair bit of history; she could embroider, she could play the piano, draw up a menu, and curtsy in seven different ways, depending on the formality of the situation. She also knew a bit of poetry, though not too much, and nine ways of serving tea; she had been taught enough geography to know exactly how far the boundaries of the Empire-on-which-the-sun-never-sets extended as well as how to treat a foreigner, which was to say anyone alien to the British Empire; she knew enough French to be able to give orders to nannies and to the maîtres d'hôtel in restaurants; she could ride a horse to hounds, and she knew what kind of Oxford, Cambridge, Sandhurst man she was supposed to marry.

'Oh Hannah, I've missed you so! I feel that at last my life's beginning! And in Vienna too! I'm choking with happiness. You didn't tell me you'd bought an automobile. What make is it?'

'Don't try and change the subject, please. Answer my question.'

'No.'

'What do you mean, no?'

'I kept my word. There was nothing, not the tiniest, weeniest lover, not even the shadow of one. There were just three or four boys I allowed to kiss me.'

'It depends where,' said Hannah suspiciously.

'Hannah, you ought to be ashamed of yourself, with the seventy-two lovers you've had. Not to mention the painters you've taken your clothes off for. They only touched my lips. I kept a careful watch on their hands, just as you told me. In any event I needn't have bothered, they behaved as if they might just as well have been amputees. There was only the little lieutenant in the Cold-stream Guards who nearly fell down the front of my dress, he peered into it so closely. He had eyes like kitchen scissors. Anyway, when I asked him if he knew the Missionary of Yunnan's Position they practically had to take him out on a stretcher.'

'For Heaven's sake!' said Hannah.

'Oh Hannah Hosannah! You're the one who taught me all these things, remember?'

'You dreadful child, I've never spoken of any missionary to you. Nor of any position, either.'

'Are you sure? I must have dreamed it. Do you know how to drive this machine? Gosh, it's fantastic! Will you teach me? What's the matter with my suitcases? I only have nineteen. As well as the trunks, of course. I left all my winter clothes in London. Polly drove me to the station and told me I ought to have enough to wear with what I have here. By the way, did you know that Polly is getting married?'

'Yes.'

'It's about time, he's nearly forty. Can a man who's so old still

give a woman children? Oh, while I'm thinking of it: I got a
postcard from Mendel Visoker, from New York. He writes in
telegraphese. He said that he was sorry not to have seen me again
and that he adored ostriches. Don't you think that was sweet of
him? He also added something rather odd: "Look after her". "Her"
is obviously you. What's been happening? Why did Mendel ask
me . . .'

She broke off just as Hannah parked the Daimler in front of the
Bohemian Chancellery. They knew each other too well . . .

'My God, Hannah, you've found him, haven't you?'

Hannah grinned, but remained uncharacteristically silent.

'Oh Hannah, I'm so happy for you, so happy . . .' To herself
Lizzie thought: 'At last I'm going to meet him.'

Hannah had considered several extraordinary plans to entice Taddeuz to Vienna ranging from straightforward abduction to the
bribing of a Viennese publisher whom she would pay to go into
ecstasies over Taddeuz's poems. He would say he could not rest
until he had added such an admirable writer to his stable; he would
offer Taddeuz all the time he needed to write, books, plays or
poems, paying him generous allowances while he did so.

Like Mendel, Hannah had read and reread Taddeuz's Munich
volume. If anything she had been left even more disconcerted than
Mendel: she was uncomfortable discovering the strange things that
went on inside Taddeuz's head, which even she had not been able
to detect before. Among other poets, Hannah had read the works
of Baudelaire, Verlaine and Rimbaud: she had a great fondness for
Heine and Wedekind, Donne and Yeats. She was infinitely more
widely read than the drayman, and she was infinitely more
impressed than he had been. She was hugely impressed by Taddeuz's gift, by the intensity of his expression; to tell the truth, she
was even a little intimidated by his work. As she was by one
particular quality of his poetry: a sensuality whose existence had
not at all shown itself in the room in Praga.

Either he had changed a great deal, she told herself, or I wasn't
able to see him for what he was. He is a real writer, capable of
creating his own universe, whereas I am only a reader; he is an
artist and I am not. All I can do is make money, she thought with
a bit of regret.

She and Lizzie regaled themselves with discussions of Taddeuz's
abduction, both of them devising all kinds of improbable schemes:

their favourite was that of Taddeuz being captured by Calabrian bandits and freed by Hannah riding a black and Turkey-red charger, heading up a squadron of mercenaries recruited from the French Zouaves. They would laugh uncontrollably, but there would always come a moment when the other Hannah, the one who remained coldly clear-sighted, would put an end to this fooling around. She did not underestimate the danger Mendel had so clearly seen; she knew that this was no game, that she and Taddeuz were now too old for games. She tried to be simple and spontaneous, for once; it would not be easy for either of them to live together, and she did not want to spoil things from the start . . .

She decided to write him; during the last days of July she wrote and rewrote her letter daily.

She finally posted it, sixty or so drafts later. And she let a silent Lizzie push the envelope into the letterbox.

She wrote: *I have never stopped thinking of you. I want to see you again, I need to see you again. Neither of us is married. I would rather you didn't reply if, should we meet, we were only to talk of the past.*

She signed it simply 'Hannah' and gave him her three addresses, one in Vienna, one in Paris and one in London.

It was a torture to her to be so terse, and to appear unarmed (despite the three addresses, that is, which gave a clear indication that she was rich) and to leave the choice so much to Taddeuz.

Her only transgression in this respect was to ask Maryan to have someone keep a watch on Taddeuz, at the Villa Beausoleil or wherever else he might go; she said she wanted to be sure he actually received her letter. She could not bear the idea of waiting around with her heart in her mouth for a reply to a letter that never reached its destination.

This pretext was as good as any other. When Maryan assured her that her letter had been safely delivered, however, she said that she would settle her account with their detective herself; she then asked the man to carry on with his surveillance until further notice, without Maryan's knowledge, or even Lizzie's.

Certainly, she felt ashamed of herself, but she could not help it.

She was in Paris throughout August and into September, when she met Clayton Pike and his Australian horde at the Ritz. His laugh was as booming as ever, but he had aged considerably. As often happens to corpulent men as death approaches, he had shrunk; it

was as if his skin was now too big for him. But he was not yet so
senile that he was going to suffer any nonsense from ninety pounds
of pink perfumed flesh:

'What's all this rubbish – and I'm minding my language . . .'

'Don't mind your language: you aren't about to frighten me, you
giant kangaroo!'

'. . . this bullshit that your lawyers have been telling mine . . .'

'Seduce me – it's just possible you might succeed. I'm wary of
you, Pike, and your lovely blue eyes. I've always liked real men.'

'For Christ's sake, will you let me finish my sentence? I don't
want any goddamned five per cent of your business. A bet's a bet.'

'You make me laugh, Pike. You'll get the money whether you
like it or not. Inexorably, as Polly would say.'

'Hannah?'

'Pike, you're my partner. Thank God, you're always on the other
side of the globe, and I can cheat you as much as I might like . . .'

'*Hannah!*'

'Yes, my dear Pike?'

'I'm going to die, Hannah, I've done my time.'

Silence.

She reached up and kissed him.

'Don't talk such nonsense. Pioneer Pike can't die.'

'Hannah, if I'd known you when I was young, God knows what
I might have done . . .'

' You wouldn't have had to rape me, in any event. I would have
jumped inside your pants, feet together, you old charmer.'

He smiled and stroked her cheek. It was true that she felt a great
fondness for this large man, who shared her vigour and spirit of
adventure, and who was at the same time vulnerable enough to be
close to – and strong enough to protect – a woman. He belonged to
a race of great pioneers which Hannah thought of as her own.

Pike said: 'Hannah, according to the contract that wretched
Englishman Twhaites drew up for us in Sydney, you are, I admit,
to give me my five per cent. I can't get around that. But there's no
question of my passing it on to my heirs; I'm leaving enough for
them all to be rich. If they want more, that's up to them, they can
make it themselves. I've reread that goddamned contract, and I
know how to get my revenge for this villainy of yours. It says that
if the case arises your five per cent will go to my "successors
appointed by name". I'm going to appoint one right now: your
second son.'

'I haven't any children.'

'You're going to have children, aren't you?'

'Yes, three.'

'Perfect. So the money will go to the second, assuming it's a boy.'

'It'll be a boy. That's the plan. What shall we bet on it?'

'God damn it, I'm certainly not betting with you any more! Hannah, do you already know who the father of these three children will be?'

'Yes.'

'He must be an extraordinary fellow if you've chosen him.'

'He is extraordinary, Pike.'

She had made the trip to Paris for business reasons; her figures were continuing to rise everywhere with a steadiness that was indeed inexorable. And she was receiving offers on all sides . . .

She also made the trip because she could not bear the waiting any longer. The reports she was getting from Monte Carlo offered descriptions of a disappointingly stationary Taddeuz. John D. Markham had arrived in France, and was spending his time at various parties, to which Taddeuz generally accompanied him. Otherwise, apart from two hours at the end of the morning when he worked with Markham on the former ambassador's memoirs, he spent most of his time shut away in his room, writing. If the chambermaid bribed by Hannah's detective was to be believed, he was at work on a play.

'So the young gentleman hasn't time to send me a reply, not even to tell me to go to hell!' thought Hannah. 'Why did I ever send that blasted letter?'

She had made arrangements to be alerted instantly by telegraph should a reply arrive either in London or Vienna during her absence. After all, she had not told him exactly where she would be.

She and Lizzie bought an astounding number of dresses; and invested as well in all the accessories that went with them. The two of them invented a game that consisted of sending Lizzie to one of the four shops that Hannah had opened in Paris, where she would pretend to be a client, and where she would be as exasperating as possible. Once Lizzie had come out, Hannah would go in. The young Australian girl was initially enchanted with her role as secret agent, until she realized how cruel it was.

Hannah bought eight paintings, for twenty francs apiece, from a strange character whom Gauguin swore to her had some sort of talent. The man was a little under sixty, with a toothbrush moustache, raised eyebrows, a proud chin, and a great air of self-satisfaction. He wore a student's beret flat on his head. When she first met him, Hannah took him for a fool; later she decided that he was a moron. A former employee of the municipal customs service at the gate at Vanves, his name was Henri Rousseau. She bought his paintings less because of Gauguin's recommendation than because Lizzie very much liked his work.

'When I've given birth to twelve children by Maryan Kaden I'll have something to decorate their rooms with. Why is he called "le Douanier"?'

Lizzie had seen Maryan on several occasions and announced her delight at his having taken a mistress.

'He may as well sow his wild oats now, because afterwards I shan't let him out of my sight!'

She still seemed determined to marry him, though of course Maryan knew nothing of his impending nuptials. This calm stubbornness in the young MacKenna girl was one cause of surprise to Hannah, but there was a second: the loyal Maryan did not seem particularly attached to Griselda. His liaison with her had completely liberated him, and after three or four weeks he had found some other lady friends on his own. He spent only the necessary amount of time with them, neither more nor less than it took to get himself fed or have his hair cut. The third surprise for Hannah was also sprung upon her by Maryan: one of the five young women he had recently taken on as Ferrets was Griselda Wagner.

'You hired her as a secretary, Hannah, so you must have seen something in her, apart from her being very pretty. I looked for those qualities and found them: Grissi has a great talent for wearing clothes and behaving badly with the junior staff in the shops and salons. That was already something, but better still, she has an innate penchant for espionage, and a liking for acting different parts . . .'

Hannah thought Maryan might be making fun of her, but she saw nothing on the young man's face but extreme calmness.

'. . . and a natural inclination to travel,' Maryan went on with all the placidness in the world. 'She has a fairly good memory and she's honest enough, as long as you keep an eye on her. And I shall of course have someone keep an eye on her. She needed only to be taught to be exact with numbers. She has been. Already she's very nearly one of my best Ferrets. Do you still want me to go to America?'

'Yes.'

'I'm sailing on September 30th on the *Majestic*, with the White Star line. I shall be in New York in less than a week. I've made some enquiries; according to Mr Twhaites and some other people I've consulted, Fifth Avenue is very elegant. It sounds as if that is where you will want to open your salon. I'll see.'

'All right.'

Now she was sure that he had been making fun of her a bit when talking about Griselda. So much the better: by discovering her ploy to initiate him into adulthood, he had demonstrated all the intelligence she credited him with. How lucky she was to have met him!

Maryan asked impassively: 'Do you want me to come back for your wedding?'

She held his gaze.

'You'll have a lot of work to do,' she said finally. 'And in any case it'll be a rather unusual ceremony.'

After all, it was not yet clear that the bridegroom would be there. Not only had Taddeuz not given any sign of life, but a report from her detective, dated September 6th, informed Hannah that John D. Markham was soon going to be returning to his native Virginia. He was due to leave shortly, in a few weeks' time. And all the signs indicated that he was going to take his secretary with him. However steely Hannah's nerves, however strong her confidence, she lived through those weeks in a state of increasing anxiety that even the orgy of work she threw herself into could not quell. She stayed on in Paris longer than she had planned, busying herself with concerns she would normally have left to others and ignored her instinct that she should be in Vienna.

She asked her conclave of students, the composition of which changed at the beginning of each academic year, to compile a report on perfumes for her. The market was already very crowded, with more than five hundred different scents in existence, more than one-third of which were made by Guerlain. But she had asked her chemists to create something that would change everything: synthetic products that would replace natural fragrances, bringing down production costs and, above all, resulting in the launch of perfumes for which there was no natural equivalent. The future obviously lay in this direction.

Hannah recruited two more chemists, former colleagues of Juliette's from the laboratory at the Ecole Polytechnique, and installed them in new premises near Les Gobelins. She entrusted them with a mission: to make 'Hannah', which in all modesty she hoped would be the most expensive and most luxurious perfume in the world. (It would not appear on the market until 1905, the same year Coty would launch Origan.) They were also to develop some less expensive products, which would be more generally accessible. She wanted these as soon as possible; she could not bear the idea of her shops selling products that were not of her own manufacture. What were they to be called? She drew up a whole list of names, with the aid of her atlas and her memories: the South Pacific islands provided some wonderful names.

She devoted whole days to sniffing preparations and talking about coumarin, piperonal, vanillin, ionone, artificial musks, aldehyde, astonishing her own specialists with her knowledge. But her frenetic activity did not necessarily distract her. Every day that passed, indeed every hour, was a torture to her, to the point that Lizzie avoided making any allusion at all to what might happen in December, acting out of an affectionate kindness that Hannah found all the more excruciating. She was practically unable to sleep, obsessed with an idea she fought against daily: that of boarding a Paris-Lyons-Mediterranean train and travelling to the South, to the Côte d'Azur, and planting herself defiantly in front of him.

She berated herself for not having plagued Mendel with questions; certainly he had hidden something from her. The two must have spent hours, perhaps even days, talking to each other. How could she be in love like this after seven years? To pass the time when she could not sleep she tried to read. Laclos was no more successful than Melville in raising her spirits; worse still, on an impulse one night she opened her Oscar Wilde to reread 'The Ballad of Reading Gaol', which had been published the year before, and which now seemed terribly ominous:

> Yet each man kills the thing he loves,
>   By each let this be heard,
> Some do it with a bitter look,
>   Some with a flattering word.

told him that she felt she had her head sufficiently well screwed on not to have need of any doctor messing around with it. It was no doubt this simple confidence in herself, her firm conviction that as long as you really wanted something it would come to you sooner or later, that fascinated him about her. He seemed to think there was a trace of madness in such level-headedness. He did not say as much, but he was obviously intrigued. He let her talk, and she easily opened up with him. One evening when they were alone together in his consulting room on the ground floor of 19 Berggasse, she suddenly found herself talking about her *shtetl*, her meetings with Taddeuz by the stream, about how they had rashly ventured into the wheatfields, about the death of her father and of Yasha, and about the pogrom . . .

She broke off, feeling more embarrassed than she might have had she taken all her clothes off.

Freud smiled, but not with his eyes. She was sitting cross-legged on the famous sofa.

'Nothing is more pernicious than childhood memories,' he said finally, and he said nothing more.

She left him with the same unease that one might feel if, after having studied one's palm for a long time, a gypsy were suddenly to fall silent and move away.

Autumn came to Vienna. The trees in the Prater turned every shade imaginable, but the town's gaiety did not suffer as a result. Though Hannah remained as determined as ever not to dance, the same could not be said for Lizzie. At the time she was being courted by a horde of charming young officers who dreamed only of fighting duels over her. When the two of them went out together that fall they were generally followed by an entire squadron of plumed cavalrymen; a fact that did not bother Lizzie in the least.

On this particular Sunday afternoon they had lunch in the open air, in the garden of the Sacher Hotel. Five officers in their shako headdress went off with Lizzie, who wanted to ride on the big wheel, said to be sixty-five metres high. Hannah was left on her own at the round table below, beneath a charming little canopy that could be closed if one wanted to isolate oneself from the other tables under the trees. She drew down the curtains; she was more than sad, she had begun to feel crushed, defeated. Three days earlier, in two telegrams, one sent from Monte Carlo, the other from Paris, her detective had informed her that John D. Markham had taken the Blue Train to the French capital, accompanied by his secretary and a number of other people. From there they had gone on to Le Havre, and from Le Havre they had sailed to New York.

If she had not had Lizzie with her, who knows what she might have done?

She drew out of her bag two notebooks bound in black and Turkey-red leather and engraved in gold lettering with the double H. She had just begun to check the figures in the first of them when she felt a large shadow fall over her. Hannah looked up expecting to find Charlotte O'Malley before her.

A large hand closed over her notebooks.

She began to tremble, her eyes as wide as they could be: she did not have the strength to look around. With an extraordinary gentleness he took away her pencil and her notebooks and lifted her from her black cane chair. Pulling her to her feet he held her face between his palms, then bent down and kissed her eyelids, forcing her to close her eyes.

'Don't say anything.'

'There's nothing more to say.'

'Be quiet, Hannah.'

In a panic she thought: 'If I were to open my eyes, he might disappear.'

But he was there all right.

26

FOR THE BENEFIT OF
POSTERITY

Lizzie came back from her ride on the wheel with Charlotte and all her admirers in tow; so many young men trailed behind her it looked as though she were leading a column. She froze instantly when she came within sight of the canopied table. Although she had never seen Taddeuz before she knew immediately who he was. The introductions were made, but even Lizzie MacKenna, with whom it was normally so difficult to get a word in edgeways, found herself at a loss for words. She stammered, practically squealed, and quickly said that she was going to drink a chocolate with her officers at the Heinrich Hof Café opposite the Opera House. Of course she would take O'Malley along as her chaperone.

They were left on their own.

'I'd like to walk a bit,' said Hannah.

She still had not recovered from the shock. Even the part of her brain that could generally be relied upon to remain detached and analytical had gone numb. She had scarcely dared look at Taddeuz, and had not really taken in what she had seen.

She did not know why she had asked if they could walk; she had said this without being conscious of forming the words. Not only was she in a state of complete turmoil, she was not even trying to get a grip on herself. She'd succumbed completely to her vertigo, aware only of the very light touch of Taddeuz's fingers on her left elbow.

They strolled about the Prater, walking past the puppet theatres on the Wurstel. She did not notice a thing however; she might just as well have been walking on the moon. It was only much later that the memory of that day would return to her with photographic precision: the crowds of children with their nannies; the young men in their boaters; the Montenegrin lemon-sellers; the Siberian knife-grinders; the Slovak pedlars; the hodgepodge of nationalities which was Imperial Vienna all out in their Sunday best, all of it blissfully unaware that it had only fourteen more years to run before that dark day when a starchy old emperor would sign the ultimatum that was to trigger off the Great War.

The day was sunny and mild; the fragrance of spring was very nearly in the air. Hannah and Taddeuz walked along without having exchanged a single word since the moment they had been left alone together. At last they began to talk, not about her, or about their past, or about the eight years since they had last seen each other, but about Taddeuz's play. He had almost finished it; he thought he would have it completed in two or three weeks' time. He told her what it was about, and in doing so, marked out some neutral conversational territory where they could proceed without too much risk. Did she know of a Swede called Strindberg, who also wrote for the theatre – a real genius of a man?

'I met him in Paris at Gauguin's,' she said.

He did not ask her how she had been able to meet the playwright and the artist, both of them famous, but went on very calmly to talk about *Miss Julie*. Not only had he seen the play three times but he had bought a copy of the script, which he now knew by heart, having read it so many times. From Strindberg, he went on to Melville; he thought as highly of *Moby Dick* as did she, perhaps even more so. But she ought to read Henry James he told her, and, in a different vein, Mark Twain as well. He said that he knew the author of *Tom Sawyer* and *Huckleberry Finn* personally. His real name was Sam Clemens and he had a great sense of humour.

'If Sam's to be believed, he had a twin brother when he was born, to whom he bore an amazing resemblance. Alas, one day when their mother was bathing the twins, she accidentally drowned one. And sixty years later, Sam is still tortured with doubt, wondering whether it was he or his brother who died that day . . .'

Hannah laughed. And as she did so, her head cleared. She grew bold enough to take a good look at Taddeuz: she was struck by the fact that he had not changed at all. He was a little thinner in the face, perhaps, but that was all. You could easily take him for a twenty-year-old. She, on the other hand, felt ancient.

'It's well known that women age faster than men,' she told herself. 'Especially in your case, after spending all that time among the kangaroos, and working your way through all those lovers, when you weren't that much of a beauty to start with. That's enough, Hannah, stop it! This is the biggest moment in your life, so don't start feeling sorry for yourself. He's come back to you, that's something. Now you have to make sure he doesn't leave you again.'

She definitely was her old self again.

'Has any director taken on your play yet?'

It was his turn to laugh. He had not yet reached that stage. But one of his French friends, Jacques Copeau, had read the first two acts.

'Jacques's only twenty, or twenty-two, but he already knows more about the theatre than I'll ever know. He has some fascinating ideas about *mise-en-scène* . . .'

She was not listening, although she reproached herself for it; she was remembering. In Warsaw as well, when they had met again, they had resorted to literature as a way of getting close to each other.

'I'm going to turn into a walking encyclopaedia,' she told herself, 'if we keep meeting every seven years! There, you see now, you're starting to laugh – at yourself, of course. You're not at all dazed any more. What a strange creature you are, Hannah.'

That was the only point of similarity between this meeting and their encounter in Warsaw. She had told him in her letter that it would be better if he did not come back if it was only to talk about things that were past; an intelligent fellow like Taddeuz must have considered those words very carefully . . .

Because it was obvious, was it not? It seemed as though he was just about to get on that wretched steamer and sail to America, when he had decided to take a detour instead. Was that not proof that he was here to finish off some outstanding business?

Well, what was he waiting for, for Christ's sake? she wondered. His reserve was understandable while they were strolling around the Prater, in the midst of all those people. But now that they were in a cab – Taddeuz had told the coachman simply to drive on – he could, at least, have made his intentions clearer. Darkness was falling, the streetlamps had come on, Taddeuz's profile was beginning to catch the lamplight, making her heart beat faster. Further-more, she groaned inwardly, that absolute moron of a cabby seemed to derive a perverse pleasure from driving them along the best-lit avenues. Did he not know a dark street in all of Vienna?

Her eyes were fixed on Taddeuz's lower lip, which she would have so much liked to bite. She gazed at his large hands, and down at his thighs; why the devil does he not want to kiss me, she asked herself again and again. God damn it. There were times when it was thoroughly dreadful being a woman after all!

'Rainer Maria Rilke . . .' Taddeuz was saying in a voice so calm it sounded as though it was coming from a distance, 'is my best friend, and I'd be happy if I could write half as well as he . . .'

'I don't give a damn about your blasted Rilke,' she cried sud-denly, incapable of containing herself any longer. 'I don't give a damn!'

The horse clip-clopped along; inside the cab was a silence loud enough to make the ears ring. Taddeuz slowly turned to look at her. He smiled.

'I was wondering how long you'd hold out, and when you were going to explode.'

'Well, now you know!'

'Do ladies say "blasted" and "I don't give a damn"?'

'I'm not a lady and I never will be.'

The farce is over, she realized. Probably he had been making fun of her all along, probably that was all he came to Vienna for: to tell her it was time to put an end to her little Jewish girl fantasies, to all this chasing after him and persecuting him. Perhaps he had come to take his revenge for what happened to him in Warsaw and . . .

'Hannah?'

. . . what happened to him in Warsaw and perhaps most of all for the humiliation he must still feel whenever he remembers his headlong flight from the Temerl barn . . .

She was at the same time full of despair and rage.

'*Hannah*! I've never had any pretentions to being an exceptional speaker,' said Taddeuz very calmly, almost laughingly, 'but the least I could expect is that my future wife listen to me when I ask her to marry me.'

Her hand was already on the doorhandle.

'Did you hear me this time, Hannah?'

'You're making fun of me,' she said, finally managing to get the words out.

He did not bat an eyelid.

'It must be perfectly clear that I'm marrying you solely for your money,' he said. 'The money you have now and the money that you're going to have, in even greater quantities, I'm told.'

'Don't make fun of me, Taddeuz, I beg you.'

'I've never made fun of anyone. Except myself.'

She removed her hand from the doorhandle and bent all the way forward, her arms circling her handbag and notebooks, her upper body almost folded over horizontally.

'You're so passionate, Hannah, you have such a thirst for life, it's incredible . . .'

She closed her eyes and thought: 'Why doesn't he come right out with it and say that I frighten him?'

He asked: 'You've made all the preparations for our marriage, haven't you? Right down to the smallest detail?'

'Yes.'

'The date?'

'December 30th, next.'

'Why not the 31st?'

'I wanted Johann Strauss to play at our wedding. But on the 31st he was to play for that wretched fool of an emperor, who's also giving a ball. Johann couldn't get out of it, and anyway . . .'

This was not the only reason for her choice of date, but she did not see that there was any great hurry to explain further. Taddeuz's undauntedness was beginning to worry her.

'Didn't Johann Strauss die recently?'

'In May. Nothing has turned out the way I wanted it.'

'I'm here, though.'

'That's true.'

'And where is it to take place?'

'I've rented an archduke's palace on Beethoven Platz.'

'Is it to be a church wedding? Or simply a civil ceremony?'

'Both. It's not difficult to become a Catholic.'

Silence.

She saw him, or sensed him, close his eyes; obviously, I appal him, she thought.

'I've learned to dance,' she continued. 'And I've learned typography, so that I can reread your manuscripts. And how to drive a car. And a bit of cooking. And how to knot a tie.'

A pause.

'Among other things.'

Another pause.

'My cooking isn't up to much.'

She had added the untruthful bits about ties and cooking in the hope of making him laugh. It was a futile attempt; Taddeuz did not so much as smile.

'I know I'm a bit crazy,' she said.

'That's not the word I would use.'

Silence. She almost wished he would hit her.

'Hannah? Are we supposed to live together until our wedding?'

'No,' she breathed in immediate response, surprising herself by blushing.

'I see.'

With the knob on his cane he carefully tapped the back of the cabby's seat; the vehicle stopped.

'All right then,' said Taddeuz.

'What's all right?'

'We can say for the benefit of posterity that I asked you to marry me and you did me the honour of saying yes in Vienna, one October dusk in a cab. We'll be married here on December 30th, 1899, in a civil ceremony as well as a religious one. That's all very clear.'

He opened the door and began to get out.

In a very small voice she said: 'You might kiss me . . .'

He looked at her impassively.

Slowly his hand reached out and lifted her chin; their lips barely touched. When she opened her eyes again, he had already stepped down. She could see him walking past the Opera House along the Ringstrasse. He was so tall, he towered nearly a head above everyone else.

And he did not look back.

He wrote to her first from New York, where he went immediately on leaving Vienna in order to resign from his job with John D. Markham, and also to collect his personal belongings.

He wrote next from Monte Carlo, where, he explained, he was living alone in an empty villa, taking advantage of the friendly hospitality of his former employer. He was trying to finish his play, which was apparently not going well.

In both letters he confirmed that he would be in Vienna, as

agreed, on December 29th, in the early afternoon, in order to sign the marriage contract. He and Hannah, together with their witnesses, were to meet at the notary's office on the Graben, the long square in the heart of the Inner City.

The day after they met in the Prater, he sent her an enormous bouquet of red roses, accompanied by a rather lukewarm note: *To my fiancée.*

Intrigued, she had counted the roses, as he had no doubt anticipated she would; she found there were seventy-four. It took Hannah some time to realize its significance: seventy-four days separated their reunion date from the one fixed for their wedding.

The next day an identical bouquet arrived, containing only seventy-three roses. And the day after, a bouquet of seventy-two.

Then thirty-seven, twenty-three, nineteen, eleven, five, three, two.

Taddeuz brought the last one himself.

27

A STRANGE FEELING FOR
A MAN . . .

'No archducal palace?'

'I'd rather not,' he said with deadly casualness.

'And no Johann Strauss either?'

'He's dead.'

'*The* Johann Strauss, yes. But not his nephew. His nephew is alive, and he's also called Johann Strauss, Johann III.'

'Only if you really insist. I certainly wouldn't want to spoil your wedding.'

'I think I can do without Johann Strauss III,' she conceded, making a very painful effort to at least keep a light tone to their discussion.

Since his arrival the day before Taddeuz had not shown her the least sign of affection, let alone love. She had met him at the notary's office on the Graben, immensely relieved that he had actually turned up as agreed. He was waiting for her with Rilke, and he had handed her the last rose. Aside from that gesture he had remained frosty, hiding behind that slightly mocking, almost sad, half-smile of his. He had no more than brushed her gloved fingers with his lips when she arrived, and he signed the contract with complete indifference, not even having read a word of it. That evening they all dined together, she and Taddeuz, Lizzie and Charlotte, Estelle and Polly Twhaites, as well as Rilke, Hofmannsthal, Alfred Adler and Gustav Klimt.

Taddeuz accompanied Hannah and her friends back to the

apartment near the Bohemian Chancellery, then left them, with Hofmannsthal and Rainer Maria Rilke to bury his bachelorhood, as he put it.

The same witnesses were present on the morning of December 30th at the civil marriage and the two religious ceremonies: one Catholic – not in the wonderful Church of St Charles, where she had dreamed it would be, but in the Dominican chapel, where it was perishingly cold – the other Jewish, in the Synagogue on Sterngasse. Taddeuz made all the arrangements for these two blessings. He had kissed her on both occasions, though he had done so less kindly than either Rainer or Klimt, to say nothing of Polly, who was in tears.

She said her goodbyes to Lizzie, who was going back to London with the Twhaites, and to everyone else, hoping against hope Lizzie would say nothing about the strangeness of the ceremonies.

Then she boarded the train with him; he sat opposite her in the Pullman carriage.

'And what do you have planned next?' he asked her.

'Switzerland.'

'Why not? And where in Switzerland?'

'On absolutely no account are you to let a single teardrop appear in your eye, Hannah!' she told herself. 'If he can remain as calm as this, so can you. You'll eventually find out why he married you, or allowed you to marry him . . .'

'In the south of Switzerland, practically in Italy. Lake Lugano,' she explained.

'I see.'

'Have you fixed up a house for us there, Hannah?'

'Mmmmm.'

'Have you bought one?'

'In a way.'

In fact, she had not actually bought the house, which was in any event a castle. She had rented it at a very high price, but the terms of the lease negotiated by Polly included an option to buy, and stipulated that her rent payments would go towards a deposit on the purchase price.

It was snowing; snowflakes blurred the woods of Vienna. This ought to have been perfectly wonderful; for years she had hoped it would snow on their wedding day.

She had dreamed all of this, in fact, a thousand times. After this train, they would make two connections, and finally a carriage would be waiting for them. They would be at the house by the lake well before the twelve strokes marking the change of the century. And she and Taddeuz would listen to those twelve strokes sounding together, having dined in front of the fire in the hearth, having perhaps already made love, or better still, just preparing to make love. At the birth of the twentieth century she would be lying naked in his arms, with him inside her, and no doubt feeling slightly tipsy from the champagne they would have drunk . . .

'I suppose your programme is that we should spend the first night of our honeymoon in that house and nowhere but that house?'

'Yes.'

'And how many times am I to make love to you?'

She held his gaze.

They changed trains in Munich, and again in Zurich. She finally fell asleep, while he read, still sitting opposite her. He had been so good as to converse with her for a while, if with the quiet playfulness of a friendly travelling companion. She was still very sleepy, almost lethargic, when they arrived at Lugano station and took their seats in the red-and-black landau harnessed with four grey horses. It was no longer snowing; the lake was completely black. Their twelve-kilometre journey was shrouded in silence, broken now and again only by the tinkling of the little bells on the two front horses. They entered Morcote down the picturesque main street, its arches decorated on this New Year's Eve with multicoloured Venetian paper-lanterns. The landau turned into a steep, narrow street, and drove directly up it; the château was at the end, towering above everything. And just as Hannah had ordered, all its torches were lit as the carriage approached, casting a red glow on to the snow.

'May I smoke?'

She nodded. They had arrived just after seven, and explored the château's two floors together, missing nothing. When they came to the huge bedroom with its enormous four-poster bed and its windows that looked out over the lake Taddeuz had made no comment. He did, however, stop for a moment in surprise when he saw the office she had had set aside for him on the top floor, with a generously furnished library next door. He noticed that a few shelves had been left empty.

'For my books, Hannah?'

'Yes.'

'I don't have that many.'

'You might buy some. Or write some.'

'There's no answer to that.'

He ran his hand across several volumes. There were books in German, French, English, Russian and Polish. She had had all Rilke's published works specially bound in leather, from *Life and Songs* to his most recent book, *The White Princess*.

'Thank you, Hannah. It was a very nice thought,' he said with his usual inscrutable smile.

She went to dress for dinner; the change began to come over her then. She did not care what was in his mind, she would meet him head on and to hell with the consequences! She put on the dress she had had made in Paris for precisely this occasion. It was white, set off with a black and Turkey-red trim; it had a high neckline and thirty-nine tiny buttons down the back. If nothing else, she deserved credit for being stubborn.

And for much more than that. Throughout dinner, it was she who did the talking. She told him the whole story, from the time she left the *shtetl* on Visoker's *brouski* to her ambitions for North America; she left out nothing. She made plain to him how rich she was, and how rich she was going to be. She also told him about her four lovers.

'That's including you, of course. The best was André, but Lothar wasn't bad either. I saw Lothar again in Zurich – it's more than likely he murdered his wife . . .'

They'd finished their meal and moved into the large drawing room where the fire was blazing. They had been served coffee, the servants had disappeared.

He lit his cigar.

'Who decorated the house?'

'Someone called Henry-Beatrice.'

He raised an eyebrow. 'Male or female?'

'Both. The Stendhalian atmosphere was his idea. What time is it?'

'Nearly eleven. A little over two years ago, I went into a bookshop in the rue de Rennes where I was told that someone had been asking questions about me.'

She froze. She was sitting on the sofa with her dress very carefully spread around her.

'Hannah, what's the name of the boy who was looking for me?'

'Maryan Kaden. He's the one I sent to New York.'

'It was an ingenious idea. But I was only reading in English at the time. And after that, I was careful.'

'Because you knew that he was working for me?'

'Who else would he have been working for?' He smiled at her. 'Hannah, I knew where you were. Several of my friends, really Markham's friends, are among your most faithful clients. Eighteen months ago I was in London. I saw you there.'

She closed her eyes. He nodded in reply to the question she had not asked.

'Yes, I could have spoken to you. All I had to do was cross the street.'

'But you didn't.'

'Evidently.'

She sat up straight, and opened her eyes.

'Then there was that superb fellow Visoker,' he said. 'I wouldn't like to have him as an enemy. But he loves you, more than his own life. Maybe you should have married him instead of me. We had a long talk.'

'Man to man.'

'Man to man. I'd never once caught sight of him even though he'd been following me for an entire month. On the other hand, I spotted your English detective immediately in Monte Carlo.'

'What did Mendel say to you, and what did you say to him?'

'Later, Hannah, please. It's a strange feeling for a man, to be pursued like that.'

'You're right, women are more accustomed to it.'

'That's true. Thank God you never sent me flowers or jewellery. And don't tell me that I had only to come and see you and you would have stopped. You'd never have given up. Not even if I'd been married.'

'You weren't.'

'I very nearly was.'

'Mary-Jane Gallagher.'

'I've come much closer to marriage than that.'

'I wrote to you.'

'That's the most intelligent thing you ever did, as far as I'm concerned. And I didn't reply because I didn't know what to say. I already felt grotesque, but I reached new heights then.'

'I love you.'

'I know. I even think you love me as a woman and not just as a little girl with an infatuation for her childhood friend. Did Mendel Visoker tell you that I returned to Warsaw in June '92?'

'He didn't tell me why.'

'He knew though. I looked for you all over Warsaw . . . Be quiet, Hannah, don't say anything . . . No one could tell me where you'd gone. I even went to your *shtetl* at night, but no one there had any idea either. Hannah, if only you hadn't lied to me so much in Warsaw! Why do you always make the most simple things complicated? Why did you have to tell me those absurd stories about your alleged inheritance? I almost believed you at the time. You had that wonderful dress – it was a bit too old for you, but very pretty. Just like the one you're wearing this evening, if I'm not mistaken . . . I didn't believe you for long. You seemed so exhausted, more and more so as the weeks went by. And I didn't know how to tell you there was no need to put on that act for me, you seemed so set on it. That night, the only night we spent together in Praga, on New Year's Eve . . .'

'I've never spent another New Year's Eve with anyone else.'

'Let me finish. I should have spoken to you that night. I didn't and after that you disappeared. I now know why. Visoker told me all about it, that business with Pelte Mazur, in more detail than you've just given me. But at the time I had no idea what was going on. And years later I found you, already well aware that you'd had people searching for me all over Europe, already more than aware that you were beginning to make a fortune. People talked of little else but you and the success you'd had in Australia. It isn't the fact that you have so much money that bothers me – even though it does bother me a bit – it's the fanatical passion with which you seek success, and what I know of your character that does . . .'

'What about the Temerl barn when you were ten years old,' she asked with a quiet fierceness.

He nodded, and paused for a moment. 'Yes, there's that too. Your brother wouldn't be dead if it weren't for me.'

'I've never held it against you. Mendel could tell you that.'

'He did tell me that. It would be difficult to find a better advocate than him; I think that you reckoned on his talking to me and pleading your cause. There's no calculation you're not capable of making. Hannah, in October I came within an ace of going back to America and getting married, to Mary-Jane or some other woman.

Because I thought it would be madness to live with you. Suicide, really.'

She stared at him in bewilderment. 'And you don't think that any more?'

'I don't know.'

'But you did come back to Vienna.'

'You know very well why I came back.'

She shook her head incredulously. 'It's not true. You don't love me. You've never even given me a proper kiss.'

'Was I supposed to make love to you in a cab? When you had everything planned, including this house? I'll bet even the sheets are special, Hannah.'

'I love you.'

'You wanted to wait until you were married. Until you'd become a virgin again, in a way. I love you too, more than you'll ever believe. So one of two things is possible, as your friend Visoker would say: either we make love here right away . . .'

'In bed,' she said, having recovered all her mischievousness. 'The bed upstairs. The sheets are very special.'

'. . . or else we wait until the first stroke of midnight. Because, God damn it, I'm beginning to have had much more than enough of waiting!'

Upstairs he said: 'If I'd been as calculating as a certain woman I know, and anticipated everything with extraordinary meticulousness, I would have spent weeks practising unfastening buttons.'

'Tear them apart.'

'Certainly not. There's no hurry. We still have nineteen minutes before the turn of the century. Hannah, the Taddeuz you knew in Praga was lacking in experience, to say the least, we both know that . . .'

'But there was something else,' she interrupted.

'Sit still. There was another reason.'

She sat up straight, with her back to him, while he knelt behind her and undid the thirty-nine buttons one by one.

'The other reason, Hannah, was that that same Taddeuz was almost paralysed with the love he already felt for you. Do you understand?'

'I understand.'

A few minutes earlier he had gathered her up in his arms and carried her from the drawing room to the bedroom. He had put her down in front of one of the two fireplaces that faced each other at either end of the room. She sat less than a metre away from the flames; despite the bronze fireguard she could feel the heat of the fire all over her body. He was unbuttoning her dress without the slightest hurry but without wasting time either. And beneath the white silk she was naked to the waist.

In compliance with her instructions, the servants had added some eucalyptus and vine stocks to the pine logs, in mathematically precise quantities. The resulting fragrance was exactly what she wanted.

'It can't be possible to be any happier than I am at this moment . . .' she thought.

Taddeuz's fingers scarcely touched her, and yet she felt her dress loosening with every button unfastened.

'Hannah wasn't very clever then, either,' she said. 'Let's not talk about that any more.'

'All right. You're a completely new person.'

'Don't make fun of me.'

She heard him laugh quietly.

'That isn't exactly what I have in mind.'

'And don't make fun of yourself either, if you please.'

'It's a promise.'

At that moment the buttons at the small of her back ceased to offer any resistance; the body of her dress came free. But she had forgotten all about the seven buttons that secured the material at each wrist!

She began to panic.

'There's no hurry,' said Taddeuz, gently. 'No, don't turn around. Just give me your hands.'

She held them out, having to arch her back in order to do so. Her nipples rubbed against the silk, almost making her moan.

'Three, four and five,' said Taddeuz very calmly, as though he were humming a nursery rhyme. 'If I'd had anything more than the most fleeting contact with you in that cab in October, my resistance would have given way completely and I would have pounced on you like a wolf. It was better that I kept my distance . . . Seven, eight, nine, we're getting there.'

'Sadist.'

'You're the one who chose this dress. Not to mention the Pullman carriage. I must have read the same page fifteen times. The worst of it was when you fell asleep. There was an incredible gentleness in your face. I'd never seen you sleep before; not even in Praga, you left before dawn. If ever a woman came close to being raped, it was surely you tonight, between Zurich and Lugano . . . Ten, eleven, twelve. Only two more.'

'*Please* . . .'

'There's no hurry. Everyone has their share of waiting. Besides, a lady ought never to feel desire for a man, it goes against all the rules. An honest woman doesn't know what pleasure is as the French song says. Thirteen, fourteen, that's the lot. Fifty-three buttons in all. Now don't move, and that's an order.'

He finally slipped the dress off her, peeling it from her body very slowly, first one shoulder, then the other. With the tip of his tongue he traced the ridge of her naked shoulders, then the small of her back. He pulled the dress to just below her waist, half-way down her rounded hips.

'Loosen your hair yourself, Hannah. It's not that I don't know how to do it, but I like the curve of your breasts when you raise your arms . . . that's it. Lovely.'

'Don't hurry, please, we still have fourteen minutes. I saw the drawings Klimt made of you, you must have posed for them half-naked at least.'

'He only saw my breasts.'

'That was more than enough. Don't do it again.'

He was using his hands as well now. His long fingers finally moved below the middle of her hips, and reached around her. He made her turn around, and said in a husky voice:

'My wife has the most wonderful body in the world. But what a lot of petticoats!'

With infinite dexterity and feigned clumsiness, he untied the last ribbons and lowered the multiple layers of her dress, the five chiffon silk petticoats, and the lace knickers, down to her bush of hair, but not a millimetre more. He pressed his cheek to her belly, then his lips and tongue. Meanwhile, she did as he asked, holding up her loosened hair behind her, breathless now, her face thrown back.

'Now, Taddeuz . . .'

'There's no hurry.'

He picked her up and carried her just as she was to the bed, from which he removed the bedwarmers and warming pans. He laid her down and only then removed her clothes completely, taking off the dress, the petticoats, the lace knickers, the garters, and the stockings, which he rolled down slowly, punctuating his movements with kisses applied to the white, white flesh of her thighs.

'You're driving me crazy.'

'I hope so. But we were already crazy about each other.'

She wanted to help him undress, but he forced her to lie down and wait. At last he climbed into bed. She immediately moved her body against his, his erect penis pressed between their bellies.

'Take me.'

'It isn't yet midnight. The way you planned it . . .'

'Take me.'

He raised himself on to one elbow and looked at her in the flickering glow of the candles. He nodded his head.

'Your proposal is being seriously considered.'

'I hate you.'

'Me too. Very gently now. At least to start with . . .'

'I'm afraid we've changed centuries without noticing,' he said.

'What time is it?'

She was kissing him all over his body.

'As you may have noticed, Hannah, I'm not wearing a watch.'

'Get it.'

He stretched a bit further, but could not reach the edge of the bed.

'This bed is as big as the Prater, Hannah. Where the devil did you find it?'

'It was made specially. When your husband is three metres tall, it's wise to take precautions.'

He moved along on his back, and she pursued him, nibbling at whatever she could get hold of. He nevertheless managed to get to the edge of the bed, and rummaged among his clothes. Miraculously he located his watch.

'Nearly four o'clock. How time flies . . . Hannah, stop it!'

She laughed. 'You're panting a bit, aren't you?'

'I'm asking for a truce, madam.'

She pulled herself up the length of his body, from his feet to his head, as though climbing a ladder. When she finally reached his mouth she spread her hair around their faces like a tent.

'And since when have you loved me?'

'I don't know exactly. Perhaps since Warsaw. In that bookshop in Holy Cross Street, when you were asking for the Lermontov in your loudest voice.'

Her grey eyes widened. She was lying on top of him, and he was stroking the long, deep furrow down her back.

'Hannah, you didn't deceive me that day.'

'You don't think it was a chance meeting?'

'Knowing you the way I do? Not for one second.'

'Liar.'

'No.'

'I didn't realize. I didn't have the slightest inkling.'

'And that can't have happened to you often.'

She closed her eyes, and snuggled up to him, nestling her head in the curve of his neck.

'Taddeuz, what would have happened if I hadn't lied to you in Warsaw? If I hadn't, as you put it, complicated things?'

'I don't know.'

'You must know.'

'All right. We would have got married when I finished my studies, because that way I would have finished them. Or perhaps even before. You would not have gone to Australia, you would not have started to make your fortune, you would not have had any other lover but me, we would have settled down in Warsaw, I would have set up practice as a lawyer, and in between cases, when I had some free time, I would have written. We would have had children. And we wouldn't have wasted all those years.'

She wept very quietly; he was right.

He held her very tenderly and drew a sheet – a black silk sheet, with Turkey-red and white trim – over them both.

Silence.

'I love you, Hannah. And I always will.'

'We're going to have some.'

'Children?'

'Three at least.'

'And you already know on what day they'll be born and what sex they'll be, right?'

"I have to plan everything, that's the way I am.'

'I know,' he said. 'No one in the world knows that better than I do.'

He made love to her again, despite the tears she could not hold back. Or because of them.

*

The snow began again the next day, and through the windows in their bedroom where they were to remain for four days, they could see that the lake below had frozen over. Though she searched her memory, Hannah could not think of another time since she had left her *shtetl* and gone to Warsaw – in other words, in nearly ten years – that she had spent a day not working like this, forgetting about her notebooks and her future plans. It was a feeling that was very new to her, almost shameful, but she could not have been happier . . .

'How long, Hannah?'

She was at that moment about to raise a cup to her lips, a cup from Ginori's, in Doccia, near Florence, a cup that like all the other pieces in the china service was more than a hundred years old.

'How long what?'

'You aren't going to stop working.'

She put down her cup.

'If I were a man, Taddeuz, would I be expected to stop working?'

'I'm not asking you to, and I never will.'

'I have to be in New York by about February 15th. And before that, I want to visit Rome and Milan, where we'll be opening soon, and then I'll need to go to Madrid and Lisbon, for the same reason. Then Berlin, Paris and London. And immediately after that, America.'

'I've no vocation to be a prince consort.'

'You're a writer.'

'I try to be one. Rightly or wrongly.' He smiled. 'And this isn't our first marital row, Hannah. I knew and you knew that we were going to have this conversation.'

'It could have waited.'

'That's just what I was asking: how long? I don't want to trail along after you, from one train to another, from one hotel to the next. If I want to write, supposing I'm capable of it, I'll need to have some peace and quiet to work in, I'll need to have my books around me.'

'This house is yours as much as mine.'

His words of their first evening together – '. . . it would be madness to live with you, almost suicide' – were on both their minds just then. He might repeat them, and she knew this. She could reply with a million vows and promises, but they both knew there would be no point. The most she could say for now was:

'We must try, Taddeuz. At all costs.'

'All right.'

'That's why you hesitated so long before joining me, isn't it?'

'Yes.'

'Is that the only reason?'

'Absolutely.'

'And if I hadn't written to you?' She thought of the trap she had considered laying for him with a generous publisher and withdrew her question.

'Don't answer that,' she said. 'I didn't ask you that question, all right?'

'All right.'

'Have you finished your play?'

He smiled. 'If the directors I've sent it to are to be believed, no.'

Then the smile faded. 'Hannah, don't interfere, please. Don't ever interfere. Under any circumstances. Whatever happens.'

'I love you. Are you going to rewrite your play?'

'No, I have another idea.'

He told her about it. And again she had the feeling, which she had already experienced on reading his poems, that they belonged to different worlds. In the next hour, however, and during the days that were to follow, a genuine, very sweet peace was established between them. He was marvellously good at outlining his ideas for plays, books, short stories. Part of his head was inhabited by another world, by a cast of characters unlike any she had met. He would relate their tales so well he could make her double over with laughter, or cry, or sit on the edge of her seat biting her nails, within minutes. She was bewitched as she rediscovered in him, some eighteen years later, the Taddeuz she had known in her childhood.

All in all, she had not been mistaken about him, whatever Mendel and other people might have thought. (She knew Mendel's distaste for Taddeuz was due to jealousy, and was ready to forgive him this.) Taddeuz was, in many ways, more intelligent than she was. He was more subtle, and he understood her better than anyone else did. The difference between us, she thought, is that I know things before he says them, and he knows them before I think them. It had nothing to do with the fact that he was a man and she a woman.

Nonetheless, that was, she knew, the whole problem. If the roles were reversed, if he were to devote himself to business and making money, and she were to devote herself to books, everyone would consider things normal. No one would mind if she stayed at home, tended the fire like a vestal virgin, cooked the food, produced children, brought them up, waited for her lord and master to come home, and allowed him to hitch up her nightdress whenever he wanted to. And if she were to feel like writing in her free time, not many people would find that particularly astonishing. But it was the other way around after all, and it was, as Mendel would say, damned dangerous. . . . She thought that probably money would be a problem as well. Taddeuz could not have very much; how much could an ambassador's secretary earn? And as time went on, the difference would become greater still, since her assets would only increase. She wondered whether a writer could become rich, thought it was perhaps more likely – and more desirable – that he would become very famous. The ideal thing would be if people were to start saying not that he was Hannah's husband, but the opposite: 'Hannah Who? Ah yes, the wife of the writer!'

She had planned to spend a whole month on honeymoon; she had had high expectations for it and her expectations had actually been surpassed. This was not only because of the extraordinary physical pleasure they enjoyed together; she was also discovering the simple joys of daily companionship, of shared silences; of the private language that can develop between a couple without their knowing it; the pleasure of a glance exchanged over the breakfast cups, of a presence in the darkness of the bedroom, of an intimacy that increases day by day. She had never looked to the future with anyone else, not even with André. Often as she had slept with him, theirs was just an affair, not much more than a convenient arrangement. And on top of all these satisfactions was her delight at having triumphed: she had her Taddeuz. What else mattered?

After the first four days they started going out a bit. She had asked the chauffeur to drive the Daimler down from Vienna. Warmly wrapped up in her white sable coat, she slipped, without thinking, behind the wheel, into the driver's seat. Her eyes met Taddeuz's.

'As you wish,' he said evenly.

She changed places and let him drive. And very quickly she had to admit that he was the better driver, which did annoy her a little.

'It's just because I haven't had the experience. I've only driven four or five times round the Prater, that's all!'

'All right.'

'Don't say all right and look as though you don't believe a word of it! I could drive very well if I wanted to!'

'All right.'

And he laughed, the monster!

On their first outing, they drove across the border into Stresa, circling round Lake Maggiore. They could not wait until they got back to Morcote and booked a room at the first inn they came to, paying for the day but staying only for about two hours, leaving under the extremely disapproving gaze of the Italian onlookers.

They also spent six days in Florence, during the third week of January.

He told her about the Etruscans, the Farinata, the Uberti, about Savonarola and Machiavelli, about the Medicis. Hand in hand, or with his arm around her waist, they visited all the sights of his favourite town, from mornings in the Boboli Gardens, when the light was milky, to evenings on the banks of the Arno, when a heavenly light bathed the hills of Sant'Ansano or Fiesole. He found them a large room overlooking the Ponte Vecchio, and he began to sketch out a rough outline of the historical novel he wanted to write – and that he would write – about the *condottieri*, and in particular about Giovanni of the Black Bands.

At the same time, enamoured though she was of her Taddeuz and the town, Hannah automatically made a mental note of possible sites for one or two shops, and for a salon as well. She was amazed it had taken her so long to expand into Italy . . .

There were letters waiting for them both when they got back to Morcote. Though they tried not to notice the difference in volume of the two piles it was terribly symbolic – and a bit awkward. Everyone had written to her in her maiden name, the news of her marriage not yet having reached her companies or even most of her acquaintances. She opened only the most important envelopes: three letters from Maryan in New York; two business letters from Polly; one from Rebecca, who signed herself Becky Singer; twelve from her chief deputies, as well as letters from Juliette Mann, and Boschatel, the herb and plant collector, and Jean-François Fournac, who sent his accounts from Melbourne, and the Wittaker lawyers in the same town, and the director of the factory at Evreux and . . .

She decided to leave the rest. It would take her hours to sort through, and collate her weekly statements, and to add a few tails and legs to all those curly, coloured sheep in her notebooks.

'Why don't you get on with it, Hannah? I'll find something to do.'

'Only if you really want to be rid of me.'

'Not really,' he said with a mocking smile. 'Not really . . .'

He had not until then asked her any questions about her business activities, continuing to show the same indifference as he had when they had signed their marriage contract. He asked now, out of politeness. As of the first month of 1900 she had twenty-seven salons and shops, and though she realized he was not really interested, she allowed herself the luxury of telling him in detail, and not without some pride, about the other establishments she had set up in addition to the retail shops: the factory at Evreux, the chain of warehouses, the two schools – one for aestheticians, the other for sales assistants – and the two laboratories. She had more than four hundred people working for her, not counting her part-timers.

'It's impressive, Hannah.'

'You don't give a damn about it all, do you?'

'It's not that. I simply don't believe I could be useful to you in any way whatsoever.'

'No more than I could help you to write. Taddeuz, come with me to New York. You're an American, after all.'

He laughed. 'So are you now.'

She was flabbergasted. It had not occurred to her! She had changed her nationality without even noticing!

'Even more reason why you should come with me. Just for a few weeks. Please . . .'

She put on her kittenish act, as she thought: 'Apart from the fact that I can't really see how I'd manage without him – or he without me, I hope – he must know heaps of people in America. His famous John D. Markham, for starters, is bound to have loads of contacts who would be very useful to me in getting my American salons off the ground . . .'

Truly, she told herself, you can be dreadful, Hannah.

28

_____

THE LITTLE MECHANISM
INSIDE HER HEAD . . .

They disembarked in New York on the morning of February 26th, having sailed on the *Campania*, a Cunard ship. She had cancelled her trip to Berlin, but had made it to all the other cities she had planned to visit, including Paris and London, the last because of Lizzie. There Hannah was treated to an additional dose of happiness, for an immediate affection sprang up between Taddeuz and the young Australian girl.

'Hannah, I adore him.'

'Me too, would you believe it?'

'I've always thought that you were being a bit fanciful, but no, the real thing is even better than what you dreamed up: he's wonderful . . .'

It was agreed that Lizzie would come to America later in the spring.

In New York, where he had now been for five months, Maryan had done a good deal of work. Everything was ready. As he had written in one of his letters, he had found the ideal location, not on Fifth Avenue, but on Park Avenue, opposite the Waldorf Astoria.

'That's for the beauty salon. And I have three other sites where we could open shops, one of which is certainly perfect, in my view: on Fifth Avenue, very near to Tiffany's.'

Hannah was impressed by the height of the Waldorf – one hundred and ninety metres – but what she really wanted was to see Wall Street. For a day, she and Taddeuz explored downtown Manhattan, from Clinton Castle to the Brooklyn Bridge, accompanied on their tour by a young brother-in-law of Becky Singer's. His family had emigrated from Germany at the end of the 1860s, and within the space of one generation had built up a considerable fortune. The young man was the same age as Hannah, nearly twenty-five; he had been born in New York and was currently studying at the School of Law. His name was Zeke, short for Zachariah, and he had worked as a broker with the very large firm of Kuhn & Loeb.

Hannah was a little disappointed by the New York Stock Exchange. It was a modest building, and there were plans afoot to build on to it. There was much talk as well of plans to erect huge buildings in all the streets running parallel or at right angles to Wall Street. That day Hannah discovered that Wall Street was more an area than a thoroughfare, and a very young, very lively area at that . . .

'Taddeuz? I'd like to live here.'

She said these words before she was even aware of having thought them. The mechanism inside her head – the one that guided her before she knew where she wanted to go – must have been operating again.

Of course she did not mean that she wanted to live on Wall Street itself. But she was seduced by the United States. Until that moment, she had had no other aim than to 'open up' in New York, just as she had opened up in Berlin or Vienna, Rome or Madrid, Paris or London. Once that task was accomplished, in two or three months' time, she had intended to return to Europe, either to 10 rue d'Anjou, or to St James's Place, where her headquarters were. Now all of that had changed. In Europe, she had the feeling she had gone as far as she could and that all that remained were the finishing touches, which was not very exciting. Here, on the other hand . . .

'Taddeuz, this really is the New World . . .'

Zeke Singer took them to the southernmost tip of Battery Park to see the fifteen-year-old Statue of Liberty. He then took them up through Lower Manhattan, pointing out the port installations on the East River, the pubs on Fulton Street, Hanover Square and the pretty Bowling Green, whose residential buildings were beginning to be abandoned in favour of addresses further north; then Walsh and Nassau and Cedar Streets, Broadway and Trinity Church, and

City Hall. Singer finally drove their car on to the monumental ramp of Brooklyn Bridge.

'You could, you ought to, write in English, Taddeuz . . . You're capable of doing just as well as that fellow Josef Korzeniovski. I'm not saying we should leave Europe forever, we both like it too much to do that. But it's strange that I should be telling you these things: after all, it's because of you that I've become an American citizen . . .'

She was convinced that what she had done in Australia, and then in the old European cities, she could do even more successfully in this huge country, all of whose inhabitants were immigrants like them. Even this magnificent bridge they were driving along had been designed and built by Germans from Thuringia. Otto Singer, Becky's very successful husband, had been born in Berlin. Simon Baruch, whose son Bernard was so intelligent, came from Posen in Prussia, and now he was one of the top American surgeons, the first surgeon in the world, apparently, to perform an appendectomy. And the Isidore brothers, and Nathan Strauss, who had in Macy's the largest department store in the world – and who was evidently extremely interested in her products.

They must find themselves a house, or have one built, in addition to the apartment she was going to rent. A house in the country, on Long Island, perhaps, that he could choose, and fill with his books, and decorate to his taste since he would be working in it. Except of course when he wanted to go to Europe, to Italy or France, which he could do whenever he liked, although they would do their best to make these trips together. It must be made clear that he would be completely free; she realized that it was her duty to make sure that he was. She would not in any way hinder his career as a writer, even as she knew she was talking to him as a husband talks to a wife.

'I won't interfere, Taddeuz, I swear. Anyway, why should I? I'm sure that you'll become very famous, much more so than I am, with my shops and damned pots of cream . . . Don't laugh! . . . All right, I shouldn't have said "damned". Particularly as I don't regard them as that. I adore what I do, it's exciting.

. . . And heavens alive ('I can at least say "Heavens alive", can't I? Don't laugh!') . . . it must be possible for them, with the great love they had for one another, to have a life together, as well as their own separate lives, whatever any damned fool – any *wretched* fool – thought. People were bound to sneer and laugh for all they were worth, but they could go to hell. It would probably take him a while to make his name, a writer wasn't born in a day. Although it would be rather annoying to become famous only after one's death, would it not? Better to synchronize oneself with public tastes.

'Is yours working . . . Don't be so silly, I meant is your watch working.'

The car was stopped in the middle of the bridge, forty metres above the river.

'Taddeuz, this house in the country that we're going to find, it'll have to be suitable for children, as well. We both want children so we should be able to work something out . . . from a horizontal position, preferably. I want you. We haven't made love since this morning . . . Yes, I know. I've no shame. I'm doing my best to blush, but nothing doing . . . Of course Zeke Singer can't hear. He's obviously deaf!'

She would rather wait a bit – if possible – before having the first of their three children. Unless he wanted four or five – there was always room for negotiation. You never knew what was going to happen, of course. The ideal thing would be to wait until she had done the bulk of the work that setting up in America would require. She was interested in New York but in other towns as well: in Boston, Philadelphia, Chicago, and in San Francisco, which she was eager to visit.

'Oh Taddeuz, Becky loved it, I'm going to send Maryan there as soon as possible. And talking of Maryan, we'll have to marry him off to Lizzie. She's adamant. She'll soon be eighteen and she's getting tired of being a virgin. Will you talk to Maryan and tell him that he's engaged, or shall I do it? It would perhaps be better if he got the news from a man. In case he's sensitive . . .'

She thought she could make her American conquest fairly quickly. She was going to take on Zeke Singer. And also someone called Josuah Wynn, recommended by John D. Markham. Particularly as Josuah had an intelligent wife who was good with figures and 'almost as much of a shark as me, she ought to be ashamed of herself'. In short, she was going to get organized. It was great fun building things up. And talking of building, she was already considering a very tall building, all of her own, with the word Hannah in large letters on the top. Not straightaway, of course, but in five or six years' time. She had already chosen the site, however, and the architect: she would want Louis H. Sullivan to build her headquarters across from the Waldorf.

'Talking of Becky, don't get too close to her, if you don't mind. She may well be my childhood friend and the most beautiful woman in New York . . . Yes, I know you've noticed that too, you villain. Anyway, it's a good thing she is so pretty. That's what enabled her to make such a good marriage, otherwise, being the widow of a little Polish rabbi and as thick as three planks . . . No, I'm not jealous, not at all, whatever gave you that idea?'

She was perhaps a bit jealous. But she was really very fond of Becky, and she owed her a great deal: it was Becky who had put her in touch with the Strauss brothers from Macy's.

'Oh my darling, my love, we're going to be so successful together, and lead an extraordinary life! Do you want to bet that our first child will be a boy and that he'll look just like you? I hope so, my love, I want two Taddeuzes, as alike as two peas in a pod . . . What do you say to going back to the Waldorf to make love?'

Taddeuz was about to give Zeke directions to move on when Hannah stopped him. Four horses drawing a splendidly decorated carriage were making their way towards them from the Brooklyn side of the river. The carriage was fit for a prince: a chorus of little bells rang through the air as it moved.

'Mendel!' cried Hannah, even before Taddeuz recognized him, jumping out and running towards the drayman, who was only about ten metres away.

Taddeuz followed Hannah out of the car and indicated with a glance that Zeke Singer could drive off now. Then he turned his back on Hannah and Mendel to look out over New York, which was bathed in an afternoon glow.

Mendel caught Hannah in his arms and twirled her around until her head was spinning and she had to beg for mercy.

'Are you still as rich as ever, little one?'

'Even richer. And there's no end in sight.'

'Is your Taddeuz good at making love to you?'

'As a matter of fact we were . . . Yes, Mendel, it's better than any dream.'

'And what about those children?'

'I think it would be reasonable to think of having the first on June 21st. It will be a boy. And I shouldn't be surprised if the second – another boy, I'm afraid – were to be born on September 18th 1906. After that, we'll have to see about having a girl . . .'

The four horses stood perfectly still, their manes occasionally combed by the breeze.

'Good,' said Mendel. 'You don't need me any more now.'

He looked over to where Taddeuz stood a few metres away, leaning over the bridge.

'I'll always need you, Mendel . . .'

'That's enough. Let's not talk about it any more. And stop looking at me with those big owl eyes of yours. God damn it, you've done it. And what you haven't done yet — because you haven't put your mind to it, I imagine — you'll make a success of too. So . . .'

He looked into Hannah's eyes.

It was true that he had always been able to read into women's eyes, Hannah's better than anyone else's. But then who else's eyes had haunted him over those tens of thousands of kilometres he had travelled in Europe, Asia, Australia, and now America? What memory had sustained him throughout his adult life if not that of this strange and fantastical little girl in the heart of Poland, who had suddenly appeared before him on a wheat-covered plain? He had devoted his entire life to her and the crazy part was that he knew that, if given the choice, he would do it all again.

Taddeuz now turned towards them. His golden hair caught the light; his sculpted face seemed to look at them questioningly.

Mendel felt his heart lurch. He could not tell her this now, he might never be able to say as much. He should never have lent her all those novels . . .

While Taddeuz slowly walked towards them, Mendel went on: whatever she might want, she must leave Taddeuz free, she must not try to drag him into the whirl of her new life; she must accept his mistakes, and not give way to any mad desire to make — or buy — a better life for him.

'Don't ever do that to him, kid.'

'I know. I'm going to make that work too, Mendel.'

Mendel did not reply.

He helped Hannah, then Taddeuz, into the carriage. With a laugh, he assured them that now they were well and truly married according to all the rites, because he, Mendel, had held their hands, joined them as man and wife, and was about to send them on their honeymoon from Brooklyn to New York.

They drove off to the regular jingling of the horses' bells. Mendel heard it, but did not see. He was imagining the thousand faces of that woman – as she sat up straight beside him in terror, as she laughed and threw herself into his arms, as she asked him to make love with her, as she coolly commanded him with her eyes to find Taddeuz. And now she was driving off in a carriage that in a moment of madness he had prepared for her. The sun made his eyes mist over; it was already midday. Suddenly Mendel realized that the splash of colour on the horizon was about to disappear over the bridge into Manhattan. Before that could happen, he turned around and started walking back to Brooklyn.